# Carrie Gray

## Rex Mangin

First Published – 2023
Revised - 2026

Contact the author at: **rex.mangin@xtra.co.nz**

Also available as an e-book

Cover Design: Alexandra Taylor

ISBN 978-0-473-70046-1

## Books by Rex Mangin

### Available as paperback and e-book

Infidelity Gun Running & Other Tales

Cold War Warrior

Flying The Pacific

Mercenary

Albert McConachie's Bad Day

Carrie Gray

Travel Bites

# *Foreword*

A young girl leaves New Zealand for Europe on the big OE and disappears. Her boyfriend goes after her determined to find out what's happened, he disappears. His father Frank, a retired detective, goes searching for both of them. He soon finds himself involved in a world of crime and drug dealing. Powerful families who control the meth business in Europe have recruited these two kids from New Zealand into their ranks.

A wide ranging action filled story set in Paris, Athens, and Istanbul, and spills out to New Zealand and Tonga.

# Contents

# Introduction

The body was hanging by its heels from a meat hook in an abandoned abattoir, terribly mutilated, blood and gore spilling over the concrete floor, entrails hanging from a slashed abdomen. The man was not quite dead, a flicker of life, the eyelids. He has been tortured to the point of death, his life ebbing away.

'Come on you murderous bastard, we know you killed Nikias and what about Ariana's man? did you drown him as well?'

'Fuck you.'

His tormentor has an electric drill with a big auger bit, he places it in front of his right eye.

'Last chance.'

'Fuck you.'

He plunges the drill into the eye, the scream is sickening. Blood and brain tissue sprays around the room, his suspended body convulses, shudders then goes still, he's dead, the auger deep inside his brain.

# The Beginning

Something's not right, Carrie has been in Europe for quite some time, her letters home have become infrequent. There's a man involved, has to be. She's very attractive, vivacious, bit of a risk taker.

Out of the blue, a wedding invitation, all the way from Athens. Carrie is going to marry a Greek fellow, *a Greek fellow*! Carrie what are you doing?

She went to Europe on the big OE. The plan was to get a job on a cruise yacht, one of those luxury boats the mega rich like to show off. Carrie Gray, small-town girl, grew up on a farm south of Auckland, her folks are; 'country.' She was an experienced boatie, did a lot of sailing during her teenage years and developed into a competent yachtie involved in the Auckland sailing scene. The idea was to capitalise on these abilities in Europe. It appears this has not happened. Carrie had gone by herself. Communication has not been good. The letters home had tapered off. Apparently she's working as a nanny for a wealthy Greek family who travel a lot, homes in Athens, Istanbul and Paris. Carrie goes with them, looking after their two young children.

There's a boyfriend, Michael, nice lad, keen on Carrie. He was not impressed when she took off to Europe. Wanted to go by herself, experience the big wide world. The deal was to be away no more than eighteen months. This has not happened either, it's now into year three. Michael had gone to Europe determined to find her, bring her home. He was certain all was not well, that Carrie had become involved in something shady. *Michael disappeared*. His father, a retired detective, was very concerned, he made inquiries with

Interpol. Nothing, not even a suggestion, and when he pushed it, wanted them to investigate the Greek family who Carrie was working for, Interpol cut him short, would not proceed with his inquiry. Alarm bells, something's not right. Frank, Michael's father, decides to go to Athens, do his own investigation, find out what is going on, find his son.

# *Athens*

Athens, August, hot. A long flight from Auckland in economy, not the greatest. Frank's on a mission. A couple of things, where's his son and what's with this wedding. He has a contact, Christos Galani a former detective with Athens CIB. Frank met him a couple of years ago. He'd been in Auckland on an Interpol investigation, they 'clicked,' had kept in contact. Suddenly Frank is very dependant on his Greek friend. He had e-mailed Christos, told him all he knew, which was not much, and asked for his help. Christos said he would make inquiries and suggested that Frank come over and stay with him in Athens, the two of them could do some detective work. This was a real break, without Christos Frank would be uphill. Making inquiries in a foreign city knowing that Interpol were not favourably disposed would be difficult.

'Frank, good to see you.'

'Glad you're here Christos, bit out of my comfort zone.'

'Relax my friend; come back to my place, you'll need to get rid of that jet lag. I've been making inquiries, discovered a few things. Good to get back into it, retirement does not sit well with me, how do you cope?'

'Not the greatest, I miss poking my nose into mysterious goings on, the challenges, the extraordinary things people do. This time it's a bit close to home, family, it's got me worried.'

'Well Frank I won't fill you in with the details just yet, rest a little then we can get into it.'

A lovely green leafy quarter of Athens, swimming pool, big garage, couple of late model cars, large garden, a nice home. Then there's Karisa, his lady, a stunning blue-eyed brunette. Hard to pick her age,

I would guess mid-forties, not sure if she's actually Christos's wife, I guess I'll find out in due course.

'Nice to meet someone from the other side of the world. Christos tells me he enjoyed your company when he was in New Zealand. He's mentioned several times that we should visit now that he's retired, nothing to occupy his time, isn't that right Christos?'

'Yes, she's right, we've done very little traveling, it's something Greek people don't seem to do, no reason, we just don't get around much.'

Now that you've come all this way Frank you have to stay, you're more than welcome, stay as long as it takes to sort out whatever's going on.'

'Thank you both, you're very kind.'

'Frank have a nap then we'll go around the corner to our local, you on for that?'

Their local taverna, all locals. Frank gets a few inquiring looks and Christos sort of introduces him with a fairly loud 'my friend from New Zealand' to anyone who's listening. They seat themselves at a long trestle table and get a couple of carafes of wine. The idea is to drink up and enjoy whatever the chef's cooking this evening, no menu, just whatever's placed on your table, different.

'Frank, let's talk. I've made inquiries with some contacts I have and yes you have cause for concern. I've traced the family Carrie is working for, the news is not great. Leonidos and Zoe Stathos, very wealthy. They dominate the spice business, have interests in Istanbul and Paris. The word is their wealth far exceeds any earnings from the spice business. What else they are into is a bit vague. I also picked up on a certain wariness from my contacts, a reluctance to say too much. I suspect the Stathos family have some influence in our local CIB, perhaps the local Interpol branch as well, we will need to tread warily. There are two young children and somehow Carrie has managed to secure the nanny position. She travels with them on their frequent visits to Istanbul and Paris. The family seem to like her, have taken her 'on board.' Whether this has drawn her into any shady dealings is an unknown. Leonidos has an eighteen year old daughter, Dioni, from an earlier marriage.'

Christos's briefing is interrupted, plates of food, the chef's offerings. 'This evening you will enjoy what I decide.' No idea what it is but it looks good. The arrangement is popular with the locals. There's an endless supply of dishes, all delicious.

'Frank, the idea is eat whatever you fancy, if something appeals just ask for more. It's a fixed price meal, very popular, the Greek way.'

'Christos do you think we can contact Carrie? I would like to talk, see if she knows anything about Michael? and what's with this getting married?'

'I'll look into it, might be difficult. The Stathos family are very private people, don't want outsiders getting too close, probably have secrets. Could be Carrie is aware of these things, that's why she's not communicating.'

'Michael, any news about him?'

'Afraid not, he did come to Athens looking for Carrie, right?'

'As far as I know; he just took off. I think he went to Paris; he did mention Athens. I doubt if he had any contacts, any starting point.'

'Hmm, not good, a stranger asking questions connected to the Stathos family could land him in trouble, that's if Michael had made the connection, I'll inquire further Frank.'

We stay for some time in the taverna. The locals are a friendly lot, language not a problem, great atmosphere, how the Greeks live.

Next morning. 'Frank, after breakfast come with me, we'll tackle the local Interpol office about Michael, if he did arrive in Athens they'll be able to trace him. From what you've said there's good reason to worry. They should cooperate, there's no reason to make any connection between Michael and the Stathos family so there's no reason for them not to be forthcoming.'

'Michael Conchie, and you are his father Frank Conchie, you both come from New Zealand, is that correct?'

'That's right, we think he came to Athens some time ago looking for a New Zealand girl, Carrie Gray, his girlfriend, she's been in Europe for a while. As far as we know she's employed as a nanny for a family here. She's stopped communicating with her family back in New Zealand and we are understandably worried.'

'I see sir, what has your son found out so far?'

'We've not heard from him since he left New Zealand, that was four months ago, we're worried.'

'Do you know the name of the family here in Athens that Carrie Gray is working for?'

Careful Frank, you have not been in contact with either of them and you don't know who the family are, well you are not supposed to know. If you admit to knowing it's the Stathos family that will indicate that you have been doing your own detective work and this Interpol Officer may become a bit wary, remember Christos suspects that the Stathos family may hold some sway over the law here in Athens.

'No, I don't know the family's name. Is it possible to trace my son's movements, there will be a record of his entry into Greece and perhaps his movements after that.'

'Possible sir, give me a couple of days, I will make inquiries. We should be able to locate Carrie Gray. If she's working for a Greek family there will be a record.'

'That sounds great, shall I get back to you in a couple of days?'

'Yes do that, I'm sure I will be able to find something for you.'

'Well Christos what did you make of that?'

'We'll know in a couple of days. At this stage it's just a normal inquiry, the sort of thing they probably get all the time. If the Stathos family name comes up their attitude could change, that would be an indication that all may not be above board.'

'Bit of a worry, what can we do in the meantime.'

'I've got an idea. I know some crims from my time as an active detective. Inquiries amongst the criminal element might turn up something on the Stathos family, perhaps we can get some idea of what we're dealing with.'

'Sounds good, bit different to what I've been used to in New Zealand.'

'No it won't, crims are crims wherever they are, they just speak different languages.'

'Well ok, but I'm sure the Greek variety will be different, a little more interesting, what do you propose Christos?'

'There's a bar down town, popular place with the underbelly of Athens' society. You've probably got places like it in Auckland that you used to use.'

'Yes we do, not frequented any recently, retirement takes you away from all that, can't say I miss it.'

'Me neither however let's take a step back in time and play detective, you on for it?'

'Yep.'

It's a real dump in an unsavoury part of the city.

'Detective Galani, been a while, a long while, don't you like my establishment anymore?'

'Never liked it in the first place Nico, still watering the drinks?'

'Detective, what a thing to say, my clientele are so discerning they would not notice if I pissed in their drinks.'

'Always thought you sold piss, now you admit it.'

'You are a case Detective Galani but it pleases me that you've returned to my establishment, and you've brought a friend, that's nice.'

'Nico meet Frank Conchie, a retired detective from New Zealand.'

'Nice to meet you Frank. New Zealand eh! it's on my wish list, doubt if I'll get to tick that box, never know though. Now then Detective Galani what are you really here for, what bit of information are you seeking and what would you like to drink, on the house, old times sake.'

'Couple of Mythos beers Nico, in the bottle!'

'Nico, you may not be able to help, we are inquiring about the Stathos family, just how kosher are they with their spice business?'

'Careful Detective, you are into dangerous territory. I don't really know however rumour has it they are into drug smuggling in a big way and you did not hear it from me. Why are you interested?'

'A couple of youngsters from New Zealand have gone missing here in Athens, we think there could be a connection with the Stathos family. Frank's son Michael is one of them.'

'Detective Galani I don't like what you have just told me, how much do you know?'

'There's a girl, a New Zealand girl, Carrie Gray, she's a nanny for the Stathos's two children. Her family have lost contact, they are worried. Michael is her boyfriend. He came over here to find her and he's vanished. I've been onto Interpol, they are looking into it. An initial inquiry by my friend here, in New Zealand, turned up nothing.

'Detective Galani you are very definitely in dangerous territory. From what I've heard the Stathos family are not to be messed with. I do have a couple of customers who might know something about the Stathos's family business. Give me a few days, I'll see what I can find out after all I think I owe you some favours for your assistance over the years.'

'Thank you Nico. Frank and I want to get to the bottom of this, we want these kids back.'

'Come back in three days, I'm sure I can find out something. Would not want to disappoint someone who has come all the way from New Zealand and besides I would like you to patronise my fine establishment again, just like old times eh!'

# The Investigation

Next morning, what do we do? We've put out feelers, we now have to wait for some feedback, in the meantime, what? Last night we walked around the corner to the taverna again, myself, Christos and Karisa. A few carafes and the chef's dinner, it was good. The citizens of Athens certainly enjoy a great life style. I was worried though, what we learnt yesterday was cause for concern.

'Frank, been to Athens before?'

'No, it's been on the want to do list, but that's a long list.'

'Well we have a couple of days before anything's likely to develop. I suggest Karisa and I show you the sights, do the tourist thing. We could do with an update as well. We live in the place and it's too easy to get a bit blasé about it. Today we'll do the Acropolis, the Parthenon, then the Acropolis museum, tomorrow we will take a drive out to Delphi, it's not far, well worth a visit.'

The Acropolis and the Parthenon, what can I say. We spend most of the day marvelling at these places. To think an ancient civilisation could create these structures, hard to comprehend. I managed to attract the whistle blowers attention a couple of times. If you get off the marked route, even a little bit, an officious guide will blow a very loud whistle to get your attention. There was quite a lot of whistle blowing at the Acropolis. The museum? put it on your bucket list, very impressive.

That evening we went along to a park in the city, there was entertainment, buskers, musicians, mimers, it was great, then an upstairs taverna. Sat out on a big balcony. Again the food was whatever the chef happened to be cooking. Seems to be a common practise in Athens and something I liked. Karisa and Christos are good company, she's a sexy lady, still not sure if they are actually married. No mention of children, if there are they would have flown the nest by now.

Next morning. 'Delphi, been a while since we've been there, need to catch up.' Christos's briefing for the day. How do you catch up with something that's existed for over three thousand years, longer according to some historians.

We drive north west, it's hot, the landscape is dry and featureless, very different to a drive in the New Zealand countryside. No sign of any serious agriculture, just barren hillsides. A few scrawny cattle and some sad looking sheep. Something I did notice, the 'bridges to nowhere.' A lot of bridges but no roads connected them to anything. Apparently a major road building program had been initiated throughout Greece a few years earlier and the first thing you build when a new highway is planned are the bridges. Not long after the program started Greece got into financial difficulty and the program was halted leaving all these beautifully constructed bridges with no connecting roads; 'the bridges to nowhere.'

Delphi, a small village on a hillside, very touristy. Just beyond the village is this incredible archaeological site, probably the most significant one in the world. It stretches up a steep hillside. A vast number of structures all incredibly ancient, very impressive. A huge amphitheatre, numerous temples, banks, yes the ancients had banks, and right up at the top, a long way up the steep hillside, a stadium. The Pythian Games were held here, second only to the Olympics and would you believe, way up high on this steep hillside, a whistle blower just in case you went where you were not supposed to go. Delphi's an impressive place.

Back in Athens and another session in the local taverna. Not much eating at home in Athens, why would you with a place like this around the corner, and cheap, probably cheaper than eating at home.

Tomorrow perhaps we will find out something about Carrie and Michael, it's got me worried, I've got bad vibes on this one.

'Christos, tell me, what's your gut feeling?'

'Not good Frank, I suspect it's drug related and there are some real bad dudes in the drug business.'

'Yes, I've got the same bad feeling, be interesting what the Interpol fellow comes up with. I just hope the kids have not got in with a bad crowd, not looking good though.'

'I think we're going to find the family Carrie's working for, the family that's taken her into their lives, are not model citizens. It's more than likely their spice business is a cover for something more profitable, a lot more profitable, and probably illegal, that means drugs. I've been out of the business for a while now, enjoying retirement, not wanting to hear about societies underbelly, not giving any thought to what used to occupy my every waking moment, however, here we have a situation that needs to be resolved. Kids don't cut themselves off without good reason. We need to make contact with Carrie and we need to find Michael.'

'You don't paint a very good picture Christos. Could be Carrie's aware of what she's become party to, that's why she's cut herself off from family, lost, does not know what to do, and this wedding thing? a real red herring.'

'Let's get back to our Interpol man, see what he's got.'

We front the Interpol building and seek out our contact. There's quite a delay before he shows, his body language is not reassuring.

'Don't have much for you I'm afraid. Carrie Gray arrived in Athens twelve months ago and found employment with a family as a nanny for their two young children. She travels quite a bit with the family. At the moment they are in Istanbul and that's all we know.'

'The family's name?' I ask.

'Stathos.'

'What can you tell us about them.'

'Nothing really, they are in the spice trading business and that's all we know.'

This fellow's stonewalling, not going to divulge anything about the Stathos family. Alarm bells, better not push it, don't want to get offside with the local Interpol people, pretty obvious they are in the Stathoses's pocket.

'About Michael Conchie?'

'He arrived in Athens five weeks ago, stayed in a hostel for a week then moved to Istanbul, that's all we know.'

'Well thanks for that, does not help us much. I don't suppose you can give us an Istanbul address for the Stathos family or perhaps for Michael Conchie?'

'Afraid not and if you will excuse me, I have other business to attend to.'

'Well that was enlightening, about all we learnt was there's no help forthcoming from the local Interpol people in fact I got the impression that if we push it things could turn sour.'

'You've got it Frank, Interpol has been compromised, that's a worry. It does confirm what I suspect, the Stathos crowd are definitely into something illegal, how big or how bad, we can only guess but the fact that they have the local Interpol in their pocket is a worry.'

'What now, perhaps your underworld buddy Nico might be more enlightening, we need someone on our side.'

'He'll turn up something. If the Stathoses are involved with the criminal world Nico will hear about it, he's been a big help in the past. We've looked after him for years and he's favourably disposed towards us. Good man to have on our side, looks like we're going to need some help.'

'Hello Nico, couple of Mythos beers; in the bottle.'
It's mid afternoon. Christos and I have enjoyed another taverna meal in downtown Athens, chef's choice again. There are menus at these places but not many diners seem to use them. I feel a bit out of sorts. Finding out what we have has not been reassuring, now having to be wary of the law for no good reason is a worry. Christos is not happy that the local Interpol appear to have been compromised, this was not the case when he was active in the police force, well he was not aware of anything untoward. The concern now, have the local police been compromised as well? If they have then we really are on our own. Suddenly I'm totally reliant on Christos, what chance would I have by myself?

We are seated at a small table in Nico's bar, it's a warm day, the Mythos beer hits the spot.

'Detective Galani, back so soon and you bring your friend from the far side of the world as well.' Nico seats himself at our table. 'I have news, not good I'm afraid.'

Nico has been busy. He's obviously well connected in the Athens underworld which is just as well because right now he's all we've got. Nico gives us a full rundown on the Stathos family.

'Leonidos and Zoe Stathos head up a criminal ring that moves large quantities of methamphetamine between Istanbul, Athens, and Paris. They are the biggest operators in the business and protect their empire ruthlessly. They have compromised law enforcement agencies in all three cities and enjoy considerable protection as a result. There's competition, another criminal gang, big and well organised. At the moment there's an uneasy truce between the two. In the past there have been turf wars and numerous murders. The Stathos family source their meth in Istanbul and spend a lot of time in that city. In the past, turf wars have mainly been in Istanbul.'

'Perhaps another couple of beers while you absorb what I have just told you.' Nico goes back to his bar to do the honours.

I'm a bit shellshocked, this is way outside what I've experienced in New Zealand. What now, what can we do? We need to get the kids away from this. Carrie has to be taken away from the Stathos family and where is Michael, is he involved, why the lack of contact?

'Christos, I think it's important I make contact with Carrie, let her know we are unhappy with what she's probably tied up in, we want her back in New Zealand; now! Perhaps she can give us a lead on Michael as well. I'll need to go to Istanbul and I'll need an address. The Interpol man will know the address where the Stathos family are, perhaps we could confront him with the request.'

'Hmm, you're probably right Frank. About confronting Interpol, not a good idea, they've already said they cannot help with an address, let's see if Nico can help. If you decide to go to Istanbul I'm coming too.'

'That's not necessary Christos, I can't impose like that.'

'Rubbish Frank, you're not imposing this is good old detective work. You've got me interested now, like old times, besides, you will be way out of your comfort zone in Istanbul. A mysterious middle eastern city will be a formidable obstacle for a fellow from the South Seas. Karisa can come along, turn it into a bit of a holiday for her, she's good company, a fun person to have along, could help with the Carrie problem as well, a female input.'

'Christos what can I say, yes I would like you along, your own back yard, well almost. Me, I would be floundering not knowing where to start. Perhaps we can have a word with Nico about it.'

Nico arrives with another couple of beers.

'What do you make of it, not a good scene, eh?'

'Nico do you think you could find out whereabouts in Istanbul the Stathos family are. They have a home there, must be possible to get a lead on it. The girl we are trying to find will be with them, we must get to her, pull her out.'

'Possible, yes I'm sure it's possible. The opposition will know where they are, probably got the place staked out. I could try for a lead on your Michael as well, never know what information turns up in my fine drinking establishment.'

'That would be great Nico, we are relying on you quite a bit, you're the only source of information we've got, we owe you.'

'No you don't, you don't owe me anything. Christos here has done me many favours over the years. I could be in jail, *would* be in jail, if it were not for him, it's me that owes you. Besides it pisses me off that a couple of kids from far off New Zealand appear to have become caught up in the Athens underworld. Give me another couple of days and I will have something for you, I'm interested now, it's become a challenge, find the kids from New Zealand.'

We drink up and take our leave from Nico and his 'interesting' bar. Our new found source of information.

A couple of days, nothing much we can do to progress things, we need more information, then we can formulate a plan. Christos suggests a bit of sightseeing. We take Karisa with us and head south for Olympia. Christos has a big Mercedes, makes travelling a pleasant experience.

The Corinth canal and the very high bridge that crosses it, incredible, a marvel of nineteenth century engineering. The canal is a bit narrow unfortunately which has restricted its use in recent years, however, the bridge is a mecca for bungee jumpers.

'Karisa, Christos, did you know bungee jumping is a New Zealand thing, dreamt up by a Kiwi fellow years ago, made him a lot of money, spread all over the world now.'

'No we did not know that, what else have you Kiwi fellows given to the world?'

'Well, a lot of things but I don't want to bore you. Right now the thing we have saddled you with is a couple of missing kids.'

'Try not to worry Frank, we'll find them. It's a challenge and I love a challenge. I've got a couple of contacts in Istanbul, we'll not be flying blind. A retired detective and a retired crook, well I think he's retired, never know with people like that. We will have somewhere to start.'

We drive across the Peloponnese peninsular to Olympia on the west coast, just a village, no indication of the incredible archaeological treasure in the valley behind. It's vast, goes on and on, huge stone structures, temples, immense stone columns everywhere. Most of the structures have collapsed over the centuries, earthquakes and the passage of time have not been kind to Olympia. We wander around, Karisa and Christos are just as fascinated as I am.

'Not been here since I was a child, typical; tourists see more of Greece than the people who live here; thank you Frank.'

'Same at home, can be embarrassing at times when we have overseas visitors, that will be you two in the not too distant future, once we've got this mess sorted, right Christos.'

'Right Frank.'

We attach ourselves to a guided tour group, English, no language problem. The tour guide is a flamboyant Greek girl who appears to know her stuff, well we think she knows, how can we tell, certainly entertaining. She tells us about what used to happen at this temple we are at, now just a pile of collapsed pillars.

'The ancients carried out human sacrifice to the gods at this temple. Strangled people while beautiful virgins sang.' Well that's what she said, who knows?

We wandered around for hours it was fascinating, the imagination roamed. The ancients certainly enjoyed an incredibly civilised way of life, well that's if being strangled while beautiful virgins sang can be called civilised, but it was a good story well told by the Greek girl. It's very warm, a beer is called for. Unfortunately there was nothing available at the archaeological site. There was a horse drawn carriage by the main entrance that took people up the hill to the village, 'that's for us.' We enjoyed an interesting ride up the hill to Olympia, a real tourist village with plenty of kerbside bars, we picked one and ordered some beer, straight down, another, it was a hot day.

'I think we should drive down the coast a little, Kyparissia, it's a fishing village that features a well known seafood restaurant, there's good accommodation available as well. We'll spend the night there, go back to Athens in the morning, that ok with you two?' Christos's take on the situation.

'Sounds good to me, you ok with that Karisa?'

'Yes indeed, get to spend a night with two handsome men.'

What am I hearing, this could be interesting.

It's a small restaurant with an unpronounceable name right on the beach, quite a romantic spot, seafood is what they do. This will be different, coming from New Zealand expectations are high.

We had found a small boutique hotel further along the beach and checked in. There had been a hitch, only one big double room available, a moment of awkwardness until Karisa came out with, 'we'll take it, I can get to sleep with two handsome men.'

What to make of that statement, bit embarrassing. What's Christos's take on it? he did not appear to be fussed. When we get to the room it was indeed a big double, and one very big bed, whoops! There's a big settee as well, I can use that.

'Frank you are going to share the bed with us, forget the settee, it will be nice bedding two men at once.'

What is this woman saying where in hell is this leading. She's a sexy lady but hell, how far does this go, whatever will Christos be thinking. The die is cast, go with the flow.

There's a swimming pool, it's a hot day and we are rather travel soiled, a swim. Karisa turns out in a little bikini, she has a stunning figure, I feel a stirring in my loins, bugger this could be awkward. A French couple are in the pool as well, we get talking. They come to this place every year, love it, and the seafood restaurant along the beach, their favourite, sounds good. The idea is to walk along the beach to the restaurant in the late afternoon and enjoy the sunset with a wine or two. We get cleaned up, Karisa is not the most modest of people when it comes to the shower, she's not exactly running around naked but it's not far off, deliberate perhaps? Along to the restaurant.

I peruse the menu, nothing I recognise and all in Greek, I do see what looks like yellowfin, would that be what we have in New Zealand, a big juicy fillet of yellowfin tuna, I turn to Christos for guidance.

'No Frank it's not, it's a little fish very popular in this part of the world, served whole, you pick the flesh off the bones.'

Hmm, perhaps I'll pass on the yellowfin, in fact the meal is a huge disappointment. People in New Zealand are spoilt for choice when it comes to seafood, we don't realise how lucky we are with our big fillets of 'real fish.' The rest of the world does not have big fillets of real fish, particularly around the Mediterranean. I eventually settle for something that Christos recommends but it's a disappointment, my expectations are far too high. Back to the hotel, how will this play out?

'Let's have a drink before we turn in.' I need some time before we get to the bedding bit.

'Good idea, let's do that,' from Karisa.

It's a well appointed cocktail bar. We enjoy several drinks and the atmosphere becomes quite intimate. It's the wine we enjoyed with dinner. I had not enjoyed the food, but the wine was good plus these few drinks. We get to talking about personal things. Christos and Karisa are not married, been living together for several years. Karisa is quite a bit younger than Christos. They've both been married, there are children on Christos' side. They are now living together in a fairly loose arrangement, both free to do their own thing. I sensed there were others involved in their relationship, could be other sexual partners, interesting.

'Bedtime,' Karisa says this with a provocative tone to her voice. What's going to happen I wonder, just go with the flow, see where it leads.

We're all in the big bed. Karisa has on a skimpy see-through nightie that's causing me real problems. She's planted herself in the middle of the bed between the two of us and she's not being very modest about anything. Does not seem to worry Christos but it's sure causing me a problem, a huge erection, which must be pretty obvious. So what happens now, go to sleep, yeah right, with Karisa pressed up against me, fat chance. What to do, is she expecting me to make a pass. They had both indicated in the cocktail bar that their relationship was a fairly loose affair, did that mean they were sexually active outside their relationship? Best if I just control myself and try to get to sleep, don't want complications in my relationship with Christos, I'm reliant on him, totally reliant, but Karisa in her see-through!

'Morning, Frank,' it's Karisa, she's got a hand on my thigh, it triggers an instant erection, her hand slides up my thigh.

'My my Frank, what have we here.'

'Cut it out Karisa, I'm not sure I can restrain myself.'

'You're right Frank, I'm being naughty, another time perhaps.'

There it is, out in the open, Karisa is on for a sexual relationship. Wonder how that will sit with Christos, perhaps I should sound him out, I definitely need to clear the air before I even suggest anything to Karisa. Bit of a revelation really, I would never have guessed this. We enjoy breakfast out on the hotel's restaurant balcony, it's another warm day.

'A swim perhaps, then we can drive back to Athens.'

'Good idea.'

Karisa turns out in the tiny bikini again, she's got a beautiful body and she knows it. Does not make it easy for me, my erection is clearly visible, a huge bulge in my swimming costume. She's pushing up against me in the pool, her hand brushes against the bulge in my costume.

'My my Frank, are you like this all the time.'

We're back in Athens, it's the following day and Christos suggests we visit Nico, see what he's found out, perhaps he's got a lead on Istanbul.

'Detective Galani hello, and Frank from New Zealand, you are obviously a very discerning person, only the finest bars, a beer perhaps.'

'Thanks Nico, but not just yet, bit early in the day for me, need a clear head, serious matters to deal with.'

'I have news. The Stathos family home in Istanbul is in the Yesilkoy area out by the airport, 22 Papalya Street. They are there at the moment, have been for the past three weeks. Apparently they spend a lot of time in Istanbul. It's methamphetamine, they are the major players and the word is don't cross them, they are ruthless.'

'Bugger, looks like we could be up against it, might not be easy extracting Carrie. I need to talk to her face to face, definitely have to go to Istanbul.'

'Frank, I've got a lead on your son Michael, it's not good. Soon after he arrived in Athens he came to the attention of the Düzgün family, they are the Stathos family's opposition in the meth business. Michael's become involved with Dione Stathos, Leonidos's daughter. It appears he's been recruited into the Düzgün ranks the idea being to use his connection with Dione, where this has got to I haven't been able to find out. As far as I know Michael is in Istanbul at the moment.'

'Nico I'm in your debt, thank you.'

'Frank, what are you going to do?' Nico asks.

'Looks like a trip to Istanbul.'

'I'll come along, I've got connections, you'll need some help, a lot of help, these are nasty people and besides I've not been to Istanbul for a long time. I think I've made my peace with the law there. Got thrown out of the place last time but things have changed, I think it's safe for me to go back, hope so.'

Christos cuts in. 'Nico you sure? we had decided a trip to Istanbul would probably be required. We are going to take Karisa along, make it a holiday. If you really want to come there could be advantages, seek out information from both sides of the law. What about your bar here, can't just walk out?'

'You've not met my business partner, Zinovia, she'll run the place, she's good at it, people don't argue with Zinovia.'

'Well four for Istanbul, quite sure Nico?'

'Yep quite sure.'

We are in yet another taverna in the city, lunch, use the menu this time. I let Christos do the ordering, not quite up with the play yet.

'Nico in Istanbul, what do you think Christos?'

'There could be advantages, he will have the inside running and he's on our side. We have to get to Carrie and Michael, have to pull them out of there.'

'And Karisa, will there be time for a bit of holidaying and will it be safe?'

'An unknown, I'm sure we can handle things. I've already mentioned it, she definitely wants to come along, she's set her sights on you Frank.'

'Excuse me?'

'She wants to bed you, haven't you noticed.'

'What are you saying?'

'She wants you to fuck her Frank, don't be embarrassed, we have an open relationship. We both have occasional partners outside our relationship and it works, been like that for sometime.'

'I'm lost for words, sure about this Christos?'

'Yes very sure, it happens. Karisa gets the hots for some man and goes after him. I do the same thing from time to time. We both enjoy the freedom, it works for us.'

'Well this is a revelation, what am I supposed to do, this changes my relationship with your lady?'

'Don't have to do anything, Karisa will let you know, don't worry about me.'

'Now let's put this sex business to rest and plan our rescue mission in Istanbul.'

# *Istanbul*

A Greek couple, a fellow from far off New Zealand, and a shady character from the Athens underworld, an odd assortment of characters. We check into a small boutique hotel, the Arena, on a side street in the old part of Istanbul close to the Blue Mosque, that extraordinary Ottoman structure from the Middle Ages. Easy walking distance to all the things you want to see. The Hippodrome, Grand Bazaar, Spice Market, Hagia Sophia, Topkapi Palace, Golden Horn, there's a lot to take in.

'How long will you be staying with us sir?'

'Not sure, a week perhaps.'

'We'll leave it open, not heavily booked at the moment, enjoy your stay. Here, discount vouchers for some of the attractions.'

'Right, let's formulate a plan,' I offer. 'We need to contact Carrie. I suggest we hire a car and stake out the Stathos house at 22 Papalya Street, catch her if she leaves the house, goes for a walk perhaps, what do you think?'

'Yep, that's a first step, I'll visit a couple of contacts, see if we can get word to her that we are here and want to talk.' Nico's input.

'Karisa, I guess you'll want to visit the Grand Bazzar, the ultimate girls shopping heaven.'

'No, not right away, prefer to come along with you two on a stake out.'

'Ok, that's settled, let's do it.'

Looks pretty luxurious, 22 Papalya. We're parked down the road, don't want to be obvious. Gives us a good view of the place, able to observe any comings and goings. Four hours on, nothing. Nico's gone to look up his contacts, if he can he will get word to Carrie that we are here and want to talk. Movement, a car has stopped outside the house, high gates bar the entrance, it's a couple of minutes before they open. Half an hour later they open again, the car comes out and turns in our direction, as it drives past I get a good look at the driver, *Michael*.

'Quick, follow that car, don't let it out of our sight.'

Christos is driving. he's done this before. We keep a discreet distance back but stay in contact, the traffic gets heavy. Christos is no slug he's practised in the skills required. We follow for a while then the car pulls into a gas station, Michael gets out, seems he's going to get petrol. We pull up and I hop out.

'Michael.'

'Dad,' he looks petrified.

'Dad, I don't understand, what are you doing here, are you following me?'

'No Michael, I'm not following you, I'm trying to find you, you've got us worried sick. I'm here to find out what's going on, now why don't you get in our car and we will talk.'

'I can't Dad, I can't stop, I have to go.'

'No you don't Michael, you have to get into our car right now.'

Shit this is not looking good, Michael appears to be frightened, he might make a break for it. He *is* going to make a break. Suddenly Christos is right there, grabs Michael and forcefully drags him over to our car. The poor kid is terrified, shaking uncontrollably.

'Settle down Michael, I'm not some thug I'm your father and I want you to tell me what's going on. This man here, Christos, is a detective, you're in safe hands.'

'You don't understand Dad, I can't stay with you, it will put me in danger, things you will never understand.'

'Try me Michael, we've got you now, not the Düzgüns.' A startled look, 'what do you know about them?'

'A lot, and the Stathos family, and the methamphetamine business now you are coming with us. I'm not letting you out of my sight, there are people back home worried sick about your disappearance.'

'The car, I can't leave it here, I have to return it.'

'Return it where Michael, to whom, what were you doing just now?'

Michael cracks up completely and starts to cry.

'You'll never understand Dad I'm in too deep.'

'Too deep into what Michael, the smuggling business, we know you've been recruited by the Düzgün family and Carrie is in with the Stathoses. I am here to get you away from all that, get you back to New Zealand before you go right off the rails.'

'Shit Dad, I've got it all stuffed up. I could be in big trouble if I don't do as I'm told.'

'That's right and I am telling you now that you're coming with me. Now where has this car got to be returned to?'

'I've got to do it. I was sent to make a drop to the Stathos family then return the car to the Düzgüns. I've got to do it Dad, no one else can.'

'I'll do it, you stay here with Christos.'

'That won't work Dad, it's got to be me, you've no idea how suspicious these people are.'

'Ok, you do it, we will be right behind you. If you don't come out straight away and get in our car then we will come in with guns blazing.'

'You're joking Dad, you can't be serious.'

'Try me Michael, remember I used to be a detective. I can sense when extreme measures are necessary, this is an extreme situation, ok, got it. You drive and come straight out when you've dropped the car.'

'Shit, this is dangerous Dad, I don't think you realize how dangerous.'

'Don't you worry about it, it's not a first time. I've brought down a lot of crims, this is family, you don't know how nasty I can get.'

'Ok, it's a garage down town. I can probably just drop it there and walk out, they won't have any reason to think I'm about to abscond.'

'Right get the petrol you want then do it, we'll be right behind you. If you don't come out we will be coming in.'

We follow Michael into the city, the poor kid is terrified, what the hell has he got himself into, I wonder if he knows himself?

Ten minutes, Michael does not appear, shit, another five and Christos and myself decide to have a look. We wander into the garage, a big maintenance facility for Citroen, nothing untoward. We ask a fellow working on a car if he can tell us where we can find Michael Conchie, the New Zealand lad, no joy.

'That car there, a chap just dropped it off, where is he now?'

The fellow shrugs his shoulders.

Better back off don't want to arouse suspicions. We walk out of the garage and get back into our car with Karisa.

'What now, Christos, what do you suggest?'

'I'll give Nico a call, see if he's turned up anything.'

'Yes I have, meet me at the Gar Bar, it's in the Eminönu district near the waterfront.'

'We're on our way, could do with some help right now.'

Christos has an Istanbul roadmap app on his cellphone, not hard to find the Gar Bar, pretty scungy place.

'Meet my friends Kenzo and Lambani, I know these fellows from way back, they can help us.' Glad they are his friends, would not want them on the other side. Two of the hardest looking characters I have ever seen. Both understand English, can speak it a bit as well. Kenzo and Lambani know about the Istanbul underworld, they can tell us about the Stathos and Düzgün families. Nico helps with the language. We are given a run down on what's currently going on. Both families are into the methamphetamine business in a big way, both operate in the same market, there's competition. In the past there have been murderous turf wars, right now there's an uneasy truce. Attempts to combine forces have been made but big egos are the problem. They are using the younger members of both families to try and forge marriage links, lower the risk of falling out, present a united front to potential rivals. There are three sons in the Düzgün family. Leonidos Stathos has a daughter from an earlier marriage and two young children with his current wife. The Stathos family have taken on a nanny who appears to have been well received, she's been seen around town with the elder Düzgün lad, Oziris, there are rumours about a wedding.

This is not good, looks like Carrie has been completely taken in, I need to talk to her. What is Michael's position, he must know about these things, marriage to a Düzgün, how will he react to that?

'Tell me Kenzo and Lambani, how can I get to talk to the girl the Stathos family have taken on board, she's from New Zealand, a relative, we've lost contact, I'm here to get her back. There is a young lad, Michael, also from New Zealand, we understand he's in the pay of the Düzgüns. He is, or was, Carrie's boyfriend.'

Nicos's two mates from Istanbul's underworld tell us, yes they are aware of the recent arrival, Michael, he is indeed in the pay of the Düzgüns. They are using him as a go between, his friendship with Carrie being the point of contact. He has also been seen out with Dioni, Leonidos's daughter.

'Is it possible to get a message to Carrie, ask her to phone Christos's cellphone. Tell her that Michael's father is here and wants to talk to her face to face.'

'I think that can be done,' from Kenzo.

'One more thing, I want to talk to Michael, my son, can this be arranged?'

'All things are possible.'

A huge feeling of relief, there's progress, I think we have people on our side. How can I ever thank Nico, without his help where would we be? The police? Interpol? not an option, the criminal world is a lot more helpful.

'Some beer, you fellows have taken a load of my shoulders, how can I ever thank you?'

'A beer would be nice but we're in a Muslim city, nothing during the day however there is a way that would please us enormously,' it's Lambani talking. 'When we've got these kids safely out of this predicament then in a perfect world we would like to see a turf war, a really nasty one between these two shit families, get them to wipe each other out, that would make us very happy. They are crowding us right now, hogging all the business, they're too big.'

'Well that's a thought Lambani, how is that achieved?'

'Just joking, no not joking. I'd love to see something like that happen, perhaps opportunity will present itself during the course of this problem, who knows. Give us a couple of days. We'll get a message to Carrie, and we'll find your Michael and bring him to you.'

'How can I thank you fellows.'

'You don't have to thank us, we owe Nico, he's saved our asses on numerous occasions and you are Nico's friends.'

We come away from the Gar Bar somewhat relieved, things are going our way. We now have a couple of days for the situation to gel, see what develops.

'Bit of sightseeing, never been to Istanbul. I've heard about the Grand Bazaar and the Blue Mosque and that's about the extent of my knowledge.'

Nico has stayed behind with his Istanbul 'friends,' he'll meet us later. Karisa is looking a little out of sorts, I guess it's been a bit boring for her, there is one way to cheer a girl up.

'What about the Grand Bazaar, bit of window gazing, ok with you Karisa.'

'Yes please, all that gold; got your wallet Christos?'

*Ding ding*, 'look out,' there's a train coming along the road, *a train*? It's an Istanbul tram, they're different, they run along the centre of the street, big long affairs with two or three carriages in tow. Tucked in behind are several little yellow taxis. There are a lot of little yellow taxis in Istanbul. They use the part of the road that's protected for trams, different. We take our car back to the hotel and put it in the car park, don't need a car in Istanbul, it can be a hinderance, we'll walk to the Bazaar.

It's huge, a high roofed rambling structure, several entry points each crowded with humanity, every nationality imaginable. The place is a major tourist attraction. The shops inside are incredible, everything you could possibly think of is for sale. There are material shops, rug shops, metalware shops, furniture shops, there's a shop for everything, and the gold shops, they are fabulous and there are a lot of them. We wander around trying not to get lost, the place is a labyrinth of alleyways, hundreds of shops. Some of the displays are extraordinary. Karisa is showing a lot of interest in the jewellery shops, particularly the ones with lots of gold on display. Christos is trying to appear indifferent. I sense a case of 'yes dear it's lovely, now can we just move right along.' After a while the novelty of the place fades a bit, not a boy place.

'How about the spice market, it's just down the hill, not far.'

Another extraordinary sight, the Istanbul spice market, I've never seen anything that even approaches it. The displays, the variety, the aromas. The steep street we walk down to get there from the Grand Bazaar is another extraordinary experience. The street life, the fellows doing döner kebabs, big meat assemblies on a vertical rotating grill. Slice off as much as you want and serve it on a bun, delicious. There are delivery boys scampering about with trays of food and drink held high, kerbside coffee shops with a noticeable number of women customers, burkas and all, enjoying coffee; skinny fellows getting around with ridiculously big loads on their bikes, it's a fascinating scene. Occasionally a car trying to navigate its way through the throng.

Getting late in the afternoon, a beer would be nice, Istanbul, Muslim city, alcohol, forget it. How about our hotel, let's go back there, we're guests, must be able to get a beer.

'Try the rooftop bar sir, it opens at six.'

Up we go, spectacular setting, no beer, 'come on, almost six.'

'Here you are sir, my watch is a little fast today, three cold beers.'

Nico arrives, he has news. It appears the meth trade in both Istanbul and Athens is open slather, several gangs trying to control it, there's *'bad blood.'* The Stathos and Düzgün families are the major players, however, others want in, the Maniot gang in particular. Nico's mates, Kenzo and Lambani, have ties with the Maniots. Nico believes hostilities could break out at any time. Getting our two New Zealand kids away from it all is a good idea, sooner rather than later, but it will be difficult. Once you are tied to a gang there's no leaving. Both Carrie and Michael appear to be in with the two major players, how this has happened, who knows, more to the point, how do they get away. Nico tells us Kenzo has an in with the Stathos family, he will get word to Carrie to phone us, he has Christos's number.

'Thanks Nico, guess we wait for a phone call, any luck with Michael?'

'Nothing yet, Lambani is the man for that one, he's got contacts inside the Düzgün lot, he will get word to Michael that Dad wants to talk and won't take no for an answer. The Düzgüns spend most of their time here in Istanbul. Right now both the kids are here, Michael will probably stay here, Carrie could well be going back to Athens, there's to be a wedding apparently, Carrie and the older Düzgün boy,

Oziris.' I'm wondering, what's happened to the relationship between Michael and Carrie? and Michael apparently working for the Düzgüns. It's their eldest son who's going to marry Carrie, how is Michael handling that?

We order some more beers. It's quite spectacular up here in the rooftop bar, a view out across the eastern part of the city running down to the Bosphorus and the three huge bridges that span it. Below us across the narrow street on an abandoned weed covered piece of land there's a tower, a very ancient tower, all alone and crumbling. How long has it been standing there defying time and man, what has happened around it during the time it's been there? Hard to comprehend the passage of time in a place like this. We enjoy several more drinks in this incredible setting then we get to thinking about dinner.

We're in a restaurant with an unpronounceable name in Istiklal Street, restaurant alley, a fascinating area. The dish to have, Testi Kebab, a mixture of beef and a lot of other stuff cooked inside a sealed pottery container. When it's time to eat the container is broken open at the table, quite a performance. The food inside is something else. Plenty of local red to wash it all down. The eating experience in Istanbul is proving to be really good, I think I like Turkish food. There's 'lavash,' Turkish balloon bread, a great big puffball of delicious dough. The four of us enjoy a really good meal. Background music permeates the whole street, different, very middle eastern, creates a real atmosphere. Turkish music is quite haunting, quite unusual.

AAAaaaHHHaaaEEEeeeaaahhhAAAaaa, right in my ear, suddenly I'm wide-awake. What the devil's the racket? It's six in the morning. The racket is the Islamic call to prayer, we're in a Muslim country, remember. There's a mosque across the cobbled street right outside the bedroom window, the window's down at street level. What's making it worse, we had opened the window after the traffic noise had died down last night. I'm sharing a room with Nico, a basement room, well not quite. The small window is at the same level as the narrow sloping street that runs past just a meter away, when you look out you can see feet walking by. As the traffic, all small cars, accelerates up the steep street the tyres make a slapping noise on the cobbles, 'keep the window shut.' The call to prayer, it goes on for some time, a haunting sound. We are to hear this frequently during our stay.

Up and out. Breakfast, different, no bacon and eggs here. I elect to go for a walk after breakfast, across the narrow road to the mosque that had caused me to start the day early. The grounds are covered with headstones, every size and shape imaginable, most of them quite tall and close together. The Turks do a lot of vertical burials, the body facing Mecca, better utilization of space. I look inside the mosque, deserted, I do not go in, not sure of the protocols involved. I walk on down the hill towards the waterfront, the Bosphorus. Wooden houses, lots of old two and three story wooden houses painted in bright colours, reds, yellows, blues, different. The streets in this part of the city are all steep narrow cobbled one-way affairs and the traffic, mainly small cars, moves very quickly. I walk back to the hotel. My three companions, the investigating team from Athens, are up and about. We decide to do a bit of sightseeing, fill in the time until something develops. Nico tells us he's going off to make inquiries, see what he can turn up, we have to decide what we want to do, there's a lot on offer. Blue Mosque, Hagia Sophia, Taksim Square, Topkapi Palace, a boat trip on the Bosphorus, there's so much to see.

Topkapi Palace, let's have a look. The Topkapi diamond, the 86 carat 'Spoonmaker's Diamond'. Remember that 1965 film, Melina Mercouri, Peter Ustinov. We can take in most of the other 'must see' places as well, they're on the way.'

First attraction, the Blue Mosque. There's a long line of people, every possible nationality, every imaginable language, this could take a while, but it doesn't, the line moves along quite quickly. We are soon inside 'shoes in hand.' What a sight, quite overpowering, the sheer size, the splendour, and yes there's a blue tinge to everything. It's the glasswork, the tiling, way up in the towering domes, the incredibly ornate ceiling, there's a lot of blue hence the blue tint. We move on through, heads turned up the whole time, the high ceiling, the domes, just incredible.

'Frank,' it's Christos, 'Nico is on the phone, he's spoken to Carrie, she's able to meet us in a couple of hours, the Gar Bar, Kenzo will be with her.'

'Great, we're going in that direction now, couple of hours, we can wander along through Sultanahmet Square, take in more of the sights.'

'Carrie.'

'Mr Conchie.'

She looks scared, Kenzo is right there, her protector, glad he's around.

'Hello Carrie, is it good to see you, relax, we are not going to do anything precipitate, just want you to tell us what you've been up to, we're worried about the lack of contact. As you know Michael is here trying to find something out but he's dropped off the radar as well.'

'It's a long storey Mr Conchie, one that I'm not very proud of and now I'm tied to the Stathos family, there's no way I can escape.'

'About this wedding?'

'Oziris, he's a nice boy, I'm quite fond of him. The wedding is being forced on us, I'm too scared to refuse. If I don't go along with it things could go badly for me.'

'Carrie, we can take you right now and put you on a plane to New Zealand, there's nothing these people can do about it.'

'If it were only that easy. I would never make it past the check in, these people own the place, their influence is frightening.'

'How has it come to this, what is it that's binding you to them?'

'I don't like to admit it however a combination of my foolishness, my naivety, and a bit of blackmail, has put me in considerable danger.'

'What is it Carrie, you can tell me, I want to know what we are up against. We do have friends. Kenzo here is no stranger to these things and he's no friend of either the Stathos or Düzgün families.'

'Come on Carrie, tell me, it won't go beyond these walls if that's what you want.'

'Can you promise me Mr Conchie? if Michael ever found out it would kill him.'

'Promise.'

'Alright then, you will be shocked.'

Carrie settles, takes a deep breath and proceeds to tell us her shocking story.

'As you know I came to Europe by myself, I wanted to be free, able to do whatever I wanted, no restraints, to experience everything, kinky sex, perversions, I wanted to get it all out there, really experience life. In Paris I took to going to night clubs, casual sex, drugs, it was very easy. I took up with this fellow, this very wealthy fellow who had a big boat on the Riviera. I went and crewed on his boat. There were wild sex parties, drugs, perversions of every kind, I became his sex toy. Much of the time I was drugged out and didn't know what went on, what they were doing with my body. It went on for several months then one morning in Paris I woke up and my man was lying there next to me with his throat cut, blood everywhere, all over me. The French Police were convinced I had done it. What could I do, I had no idea what had happened the evening before, total blank. I finished up in a cell, handcuffed, not a friend in the world.'

'Carrie, stop there, this is upsetting you I can tell, perhaps we can hear the rest of the story another time.'

'No, I want to get it off my chest now, I've not told this story to anyone. A couple of days later this fellow, a Greek, comes along, takes me out of jail, onto his private jet, and flies me to Athens, it was Leonidos Stathos. I was now his private property, he owned me. There was nothing sexual involved, however I would have to do whatever he asked. What choices did I have? He made it quite clear that if I did not go along with what he wanted he would return me to the French Police. That was a year ago. Since then I have been doing various jobs for him mostly involved with his smuggling business. I'm also the nanny for his two children. The nanny thing is a cover. I'm the pretty face who charms people, softens them up so Leonidos can rip them off. I've got no choice, I have to do it. I've been too ashamed to write home, I would have to tell lies if I did.'

'Carrie, we can still get you out of this.'

'Stop right there Mr Conchie, if I flee Interpol will come looking, murder is a serious crime. What I was involved in before the murder would not look too good either, I'm caught, there's no escape.'

'Shit; sorry Carrie I should watch my language.'

'No, shit is far too mild, fucking great mess would be more appropriate.'

'Carrie!'

'I'm beyond caring what people think Mr Conchie.'

'About this wedding?'

'Oh that, the least of my worries. Oziris is a nice fellow, I could get to like him if the circumstances were different, it's just a wedding of convenience. Leonidos wants to have a closer relationship with the Düzgüns. I don't think Oziris knows about my past.'

'Michael, what are your feelings for him?'

'I think he's found out a few things, it will be destroying him, I feel bad about that, he's a nice lad, I still feel for him. There's no way I can take up with Michael again, all my bridges have gone up in flames. He's working for the Düzgüns. He's the go between for the two families. I get to see him occasionally.'

'Carrie, this is an unacceptable situation, we can't let you go on like this, something has to give, we have to get you back to New Zealand, I've no idea how we can achieve that.'

'You can't get me out Mr Conchie. If I disappear the French Police will be notified and Interpol will come looking. I'm a murder suspect and I've no idea if in fact I have committed a murder.'

'Murder, no way Carrie, you've probably been set up and it would be a good bet that Leonidos Stathos is involved, what do you remember about it?'

'Nothing, absolutely nothing, total blackout. My sugar daddy was into the drug business, there was always plenty of everything in that line readily available, meth, cocaine, heroin. I'm afraid naïve little me could not cope, I went right off the rails. I can see that now, bit late to get out. Leonidos is using me to forge closer ties with the Düzgüns. He wants a united front against the opposition, the Maniot family, they are becoming a problem, they want in on the meth business.'

'Carrie, here's what I suggest. You are trapped, well trapped until we can figure something out. Find out as much as you can about what's going on, everything about the families involved, what they are doing, how much influence they have with the law enforcement agencies, anything that's relevant. Information like that will be invaluable when we try to clear your name at some future date. There will be a day of reckoning and you will need everything going for you. If you can find out who murdered your benefactor, that would be a huge plus but probably impossible to find out, keep it in mind though, you never know what you might hear.'

'If you can Mr Conchie could you let Michael know I would like to have a meeting. I do see him from time to time but it's always in controlled circumstances, he's perceived as a Düzgün, not to be trusted, we cannot talk freely. I've let him down in the worst possible way, that's cruel, Michael's a nice boy, I want to try and re-establish a relationship.'

'I'll do that Carrie, how can we contact you.'

'Kenzo can do it, I think he's got a mate in the Stathos family, that right Kenzo?'

'No, there's no mate,' from Kenzo but I suspect he speaks with forked tongue. 'I can get messages to Carrie though.'

'Ok we'll do that, I want to talk with Michael as well, he appears to be in deep.'

'I must go now, if I'm away too long people will get suspicious and the little freedom I do enjoy could disappear. Find Michael and arrange a meeting; please Mr Conchie!'

What a mess, how in hell are we going to resolve this? I've lost interest in Istanbul's tourist attractions, I just want to crawl into a corner and cry. Carrie goes off with Kenzo, he's keeping an eye on her, I'm grateful someone's helping. Now, find Michael. A call on Nico's cellphone, it's Lambani, Nicos's other mate, the one with the in on the Düzgüns. He's spoken to Michael, he will come around to the Arena at six this evening, rooftop bar. A surge of relief, Nico's underworld contacts are paying off. We've got a few hours to kill till six, can't settle ourselves into a bar, there aren't any, Muslim country. How about we take a trip on the Bosphorus, real tourist stuff, I've heard it's good.

'That ok with you Karisa?' she's been the silent observer of all that's been going on, wonder what she's thinking? Perhaps I should give Karisa some attention after all she has indicated she wants to bed me. The tension of the past few days has driven any sexual thoughts right out the window.

It's big, bit like a retired ferry, long open deck covered with seating. We're heading up to the northern end of the Bosphorus, the Black Sea end, and Russia. We pass under one of those huge bridges to Asia. The Fatih Sultan Mehmet Bridge, an incredible sight. We had seen it from the Arena's rooftop bar, now we're up close and personal. The sheer size of the thing, it towers way up above us. I've never seen anything like it before. The tourist boat hugs the west side of the waterway, the European side. All along the waterfront are these magnificent houses, huge ornate affairs, small palaces really. Most are Russian owned. There's a huge Russian presence along the Bosphorus, after all it's in their interest to be here, the only warm water link Russia has to the oceans of the world. There are old fortresses, castles, towers, mosques, the whole waterfront is covered with buildings, old and interesting buildings. The boat goes quite a way up the Bosphorus then turns and comes down the Asian side, what a difference. Stone is replaced by wood, all the buildings are made of wood and there are some big ones. The boat trip uses up most of the afternoon. We dock back where we started and walk up the steep street to the Arena.

The rooftop bar, almost six, have to wait this time. Michael walks in.

'Dad,' he gives me a big hug, he's not far from tears.

'Michael, relax, you're amongst friends, sit down, have a beer, take your time. When you feel like it tell us whatever you want to tell us. These people are my friends from Athens; Christos, Karisa, and Nico. Christos, like myself, is a retired detective, Nico is a practising underworld intelligence gatherer and he's very good, it's his contacts who have found you Michael. Karisa is Christos's lovely lady.'

'Dad, I've messed up big time, now I'm stuck, obligated to a Greek family, it's a long story.'

Michael does not look happy, does not look well either, far removed from the fellow he was back in New Zealand, what's gone wrong?

'Take your time, let it all out, we are listening, we'll understand. We're not judging you Michael we are here to help, get you back to New Zealand.'

'Ok, where to start. Well as you know I became concerned about Carrie, the way she just disappeared, stopped writing home, she's not like that. Going off to Europe by herself, why would she do that? I wanted to go with her, but no, she wanted to go alone, did not want anyone along with her, wanted to be a free agent. I heard she was in Paris. I took myself off to Europe, Paris, hoping to find her, find out what had happened, why the big silence. It took a while. I made inquiries around the night spots. I thought she might be known after all she is a very attractive girl, someone might recall something. A girl, Dioni, knew about her. She's Greek, attractive, she told me she had met Carrie. Dioni was a Stathos. She let me know in a nice way that Carrie was a wild party girl and had been involved in an underworld murder. The word was she had been the bait to set the victim up. The Stathos family had whisked her out of Paris to Athens. She's now deeply involved with them. Dioni and myself 'clicked,' I saw quite a bit of her in Paris. Then she moved back to Athens to be with her family, she suggested I come along. I jumped at the opportunity, after all Carrie was in Athens. I finally caught up with Carrie, she was not good, looked terrible, drugs, addicted to methamphetamine. When I tackled Dioni about it she was noncommittal, I think she was aware her father was responsible for Carrie's addiction. Leonidos wanted her kept that way, compliant, useful. I suspect Leonidos was behind the murder and he was using Carrie's belief that she was responsible to keep her in line. Soon after I arrived in Athens I was approached by a couple of hard looking dudes, foot soldiers for the Düzgüns. They were interested in my friendship with Dioni Stathos and the suggestion was that perhaps I should keep in with Dioni, find out what her family were up to. Why should I, all I wanted was to get Carrie out of this mess. I was way out of my depth, did not know how to deal with it. They pointed out a few things, shocking things. Carrie was a meth addict, totally unreliable. She was convinced she had committed a murder. If she got out of line she would be handed back to the Paris police. She had also taken up with the eldest Düzgün boy, Oziris. Both the Stathos and Düzgün families were in favour of this, a combining of forces. Oziris was giving Carrie a lot of attention, really going for her and she seemed to be responsive. The suggestion was that the Düzgüns would like me to get really close to Dioni, keep them advised about the Stathos family's activities, in return they would take me under their wing, look after me. My long term goal was to get Carrie away from the Stathos family. In the meantime I would be working for the Düzgüns, furthering their interests. Bloody risky, these people are ruthless and I'm an outsider. My being close to Dioni does not bring the two families any closer, neither does Carrie's relationship with the Düzgün boy Oziris, there's no blood relationships. That's it dad, that's where things are at the moment.'

'Can of worms Michael, need to think about this for a bit, all things are possible, don't despair, Dad's here,' yeah right!

'What about dinner, why don't we go back to the place in Istiklal Street with the unpronounceable name, it was good, no need to look further.'

It really is a can of worms, these two kids are donkey deep in a very nasty world, there's no obvious way out. Getting offside with any of the players could be fatal. I wonder if a direct approach to Leonidos would work, someone from the other side of the world with no vested interest, try and get him to just let Carrie go. Who runs the Düzgün crowd? would a similar approach work with them, get

Michael off the hook? No, I'm dreaming, that's not the way it works. People who become a nuisance end up dead. The youngsters, what are their relationships? are there any strong ties? does Carrie care for Oziris? has she lost her affection for Michael? or is she so messed up she does not know what she's doing? Michael, does he really care for Dioni? I got the impression that yes, he does. A meeting, Carrie and Michael need to meet, unencumbered, sort out their relationship, I put it to Michael.

'Yes Dad, I'd like that. I do get to see her occasionally but it's always in the presence of others, the Stathoses are very suspicious. I suspect she's fallen for Oziris Düzgün but I'm not sure it's for real, well not as far as the Düzgün boy is concerned, it's just a conduit into the Stathos family for them. Carrie's so mixed up I'm not sure she can make informed judgments anymore.'

Nico joins the conversation.

'I've got a number here, it's Carrie's, well I think it is, Kenzo gave it to me, why don't you give it a try Michael, invite Carrie out to dinner right now, nothing to lose.'

We're in the restaurant with the unpronounceable name in Istiklal Street, Carrie is with us, the number was good. We seat ourselves apart from Michael and Carrie, give them space, there are tears. An hour later they join us, the tears are gone, they both look much better.

'So, what's the scene?' I ask.

Carrie speaks first.

'We let things roll for the time being, doing anything precipitate could court disaster, these are not nice people. I still feel for Michael and he for me. We are both pretty much soiled goods now. Michael has been doing things with Dioni that I would never have thought him capable of and me, well I'm disgusted with myself, however that's the way it is. We both accept that our lives have been corrupted but life goes on. We will go along with what is being asked from us for now. Our eyes are open and right now there's no other way. This wedding thing? disregard it, means nothing to me, opportunity will present itself, these two families will have a falling out, it's inevitable, the resulting chaos could well open escape opportunities.'

'That's the way it is Dad, we need to go with the flow for the time being, play our roles in the power game these two families are involved in and keep our eyes open for an escape opportunity. I think I have an in with the Stathoses, they know I'm in with the Düzgüns and they see me as a spy in that camp, the reality is quite the opposite. Dioni has an insatiable sexual appetite and the Stathoses think I'm hooked, that my allegiance is with them.'
So, where to from here? There's nothing obvious we can do right now, this wedding is in two weeks. Stamna, a hilltop village near Missolonghi.

'I'll have to go now, they don't like me going out, don't completely trust me. They think I'm meeting Oziris when I do go out, seducing him, extracting Düzgün family secrets, sorry Michael, that's the way it is, bit like your relationship with Dioni.'

A bad night's sleep, whatever happened to the two innocent kids from New Zealand. Sleeping with the enemy, anything goes, innocence lost. I'm sharing a room with Nico.

'Nico you awake?'

'Yep, I'm troubled by tonight's revelations as much as you.'

'What can we do, have to do something, make something happen.'

'Perhaps we should see if the Maniots can help. Kenzo and Lambani are with them and the Maniots are no friends of the Stathos or Düzgün families. We really need them to start scrapping amongst themselves, that would open up all sorts of opportunities, high risk but what the hell, couldn't be much worse than what we have now.'

'Reckon we should Nico?'

'Well it could help our case, it's not as if we are horning in on their business, we are not the enemy, we just want two kids back. I'll talk to Kenzo and Lambani in the morning, get their thoughts, they are scrappers from way back, a gang war would be right up their ally.'

I wake with a start, the call to prayer from across the narrow cobbled street, hell of a racket. If I were to express my thoughts right now there would be death fatwas left right and centre. A new day, what to do? how can we progress things? make something happen? It's early, that bloody mosque, did not mention that when we booked in. No sleeping in at the Arena. We gather for breakfast in the dining room, not quite my style but ok, an experience. What to do? Nico wants to do his own thing, check the local underworld scene, see what can be arranged, see if some mayhem can be organised. Nothing more we can do here, the next thing of interest will be this wedding. I guess we need to think about going back to Athens, then the wedding in Stamna. I broach the subject with Christos and Karisa.

'We have no great calls on our time, is there anything you would like to see or do Frank before we leave Istanbul.'

'Yes there is, Gallipoli. People from New Zealand want to visit Gallipoli sometime during their lives, it's a hangover from the First World War.'

'Yes Frank, I'm familiar with it, down south from Istanbul, about a four hour drive, would you like to go there?'

'Yes I would, it's on the bucket list, a rite of passage for people from New Zealand.'

'Tell you what, I should really get back to Athens but you could stay, hire a car and go down to Gallipoli, Karisa might be interested as well.'

What am I hearing, is Christos clearing the way, giving Karisa an opportunity to satisfy her desire to bed me, giving me an opportunity to fuck her without any embarrassment.

It's a lovely drive down the Gallipoli peninsular. Karisa is right there in the seat beside me.

'Frank you know I want to bed you, Christos has given his consent, it's the way it is between us. I suspect he has someone back in Athens he will be visiting in my absence, but that's ok. I have you all to myself right now, no restrictions, no embarrassing moments, we can do anything we want with each other, anything.'

This conversation has got me into a real state. Karisa has her hand on my thigh and it's sure causing me a problem, she knows it too. She unzips the front of my pants and my mighty erection springs forth, christ I can't drive like this.

'Pull over Frank, I can't wait any longer.'

As she says this her head goes down and she takes my erection into her mouth, it's too much I pull over, she straddles me immediately, thrusts my erection deep inside her and starts moving her whole body up and down, it's the most magnificent sensation, we work ourselves into a frenzy. Karisa is moaning loudly and thrashing about on my lap, we climax together and collapse in a heap.

'God, that was so nice, what now? bit of a rest then carry on down to Eceabat. The vehicular ferry across the Dardanelles Strait to Çanakkale, find a hotel with a big bed and take it from there.'

'Yes please Frank, we could fuck each other all night.'

'Yes Karisa we could, you'd like that?

'Yes, I would Frank.'

The following morning, breakfast on the hotel dining room balcony in Çanakkale, feeling a little tired from the night's love making.

Karisa was insatiable, she wanted me to take her every which way, it was magnificent.

'Right, back across the Dardanelles Strait to Eceabat then drive across the peninsular to Anzac Cove, we can look around the old battlefields. Back here for the night, the big bed again, ok with you?'

The car ferry does not take long. We're soon on our way across the Gallipoli peninsular to Anzac Cove the place that's special to people from New Zealand. There's a small museum on the roadside. A local farmer has gathered together all the detritus of war and created it. He tells us he's constantly ploughing up these things, guns, bayonets, boots, clothing, helmets, smashed up gun carriages, every sort of thing an army takes into battle. It's all broken and showing its age. There's a big collection of unexploded shells and shell casings. He tells us it just goes on and on, every time he ploughs his fields more remnants of what happened around here turn up. The farmer grows tomatoes, it's a great place to grow tomatoes.

Koyu Beach, Anzac Cove, it has a powerful effect on me. The sight of all those graves in the small beachfront cemetery. Kids from a previous generation, teenagers, kids in their early twenties, a whole generation from far off New Zealand, wiped out at this place. The formidable hinterland behind the beach they were required to take. Vertical cliffs towering way up with the enemy firmly entrenched, an impossible situation. The death toll was horrendous, but somehow they made progress up those cliffs, all the way to the top, well not quite, they were stopped at Chunuk Bair, never quite made it over the top, never got to see the Dardanelles. Three days of hand to hand fighting and there were no more Kiwis left to continue. Over seven hundred killed at this place, terrible. We wandered around the remains of the trenches, the statues, memorial plaques, long lists of names, youngsters from New Zealand who perished, it got to me, I was all weepy eyed, a lump in my chest, the sheer waste of life. We move on to Lone Pine where the Australians suffered a similar disaster. There's a pine tree there, a big cemetery, hundreds of graves, a big stone memorial, more long lists of names, Australian and New Zealand kids. The lone pine? it comes from Melbourne. There's a big Turkish cemetery nearby. They suffered more casualties than the Anzacs at Gallipoli.

Back to Çanakkale, it's been an emotional day. I was surprised how it affected me. We are at a small waterfront café enjoying a wine in the late afternoon sunshine, I was very subdued. I had in my hand three small pieces of marble from the beach at ANZAC Cove. These very same pebbles would have been witness to the terrible events that unfolded there all those years ago. I will treasure them, take them back to New Zealand, a piece of history from that time, that terrible time. Karisa was very understanding, comforting, Christos you're a lucky man.

'Frank, tell me about yourself, you're a nice man, I like you a lot, it's not just the bedroom thing either, I really do like you, is there a lady back in New Zealand?'

'No, cancer, lost her three years ago, married twenty-eight years, two children, boy and a girl. Rebecca's a fashion model back in Auckland, then there's Michael, my wayward son; no there's no lady. Not sure I'm over losing Ginetta. I retired from the Police Force recently, a couple of private outfits are chasing me, will probably go with one of them, might start my own detective business, don't know at this stage but I will get into something, how about you?'

Karisa looks reflective, not eager to answer my query.

There's a scruffy three-legged cat hanging around the waterfront, two little kittens in tow. A few fishermen are tying up their boats, the cat is right there, begging. It works, a sardine is tossed in its direction, the cat grabs the sardine and scampers away, the kittens follow.

'Survival on three legs, that cat has it figured,' Karisa's

observation; 'me? it's not a nice story. My man Nikias was a lawyer, no kids which is sad, I would have liked children. Nikias got tied up with the gangs running the methamphetamine business. He was murdered four years ago, never solved, but I have my suspicions. A considerable sum of money came my way, I think it was meant to shut me up, not to make waves, not to try and find the killers. It still hurts, I loved Nikias. I've not let it go; one day!'

We enjoy several wines, it's a lovely spot this waterfront café in Çanakkale.

'Christos and me got together a couple of years ago, he lost his wife to cancer as well, nasty thing the big C. I'm pretty independent, so is Christos, but we like each other a lot. We get on just fine with our rather loose partnership arrangement. I suspect leaving me here with you was a ploy, allows him to bed one of his girlfriends in Athens without embarrassing me, we try to be discreet, not flaunt it in front of each other, and it works. I can have you here for as long as I want, as long as you want me Frank, right now? or shall be wait a while, dinner perhaps.'

She's got me aroused, I'm in trouble again, Karisa is a real sex bomb, can I wait? It's washed away the melancholy from the Anzac thing. Dinner at the waterside café, no need to move, this little café is good, a couple of bottles of red, an excellent meal, back to the hotel room, the big bed.

'Stay there Frank, you don't have to do anything, it's been an emotional day for you, let me get you aroused, get you to want to rape me, I'd like that.'

She certainly gets me aroused, off come the cloths and we fall onto the big bed. It's an arousing sight, Karisa has magnificent full breasts and she has them right in my face as she mounts me.

Breakfast on the balcony again.

'Perhaps we should drive back to Istanbul, spend a couple of days there then back to Athens. This wedding has me worried, it's going to happen, can't see us stopping it. We could go to Missolonghi beforehand, that's if you want to be involved Karisa? Stamna, where the wedding is supposed to happen, is near Missolonghi.'

'Yes Frank, I do want to be involved, want to be around you, you've lit my fire. The wedding, are there parents? does Carrie have a mum and dad?'

'Not sure about them, they're small town folk, probably can't afford to come over here. The invitation was quite unexpected, first they had heard from Carrie for over a year. I've not been in contact, don't know them really, probably quite shocked by events. No I don't think they will be at this wedding, if it is a real wedding.'

'Ok, back to Athens, check in to the Arena, wonder what they will think? I checked in with Christos last time.'

'There's Troy, could have a look, it's not far from here but I believe it's not worth it, nothing there, just a pile of really old rocks; pass on Troy.'

It's a lovely drive back up the Gallipoli peninsula, Karisa is a little more circumspect with her behaviour during the drive. I think her desire for sex has been sated for a while. The receptionist at the Arena is quite nonplussed when we check in, same girl who checked us all in when we first arrived. This time it's a second floor room, one big bed, perhaps the receptionist is a bit of a mischief maker. Rooftop bar, late afternoon, quite a romantic setting. Karisa is seated next to me her head lying on my shoulder. I feel a little odd, not felt this way for a long time, am I falling for Karisa. I feel very at ease in her company, where is this leading? Along to Istiklal Street, different restaurant this time, just as good, better perhaps. It's very romantic, the food, the wine and Karisa giving me dreamy looks, I think she's happy. Back to the Arena, another night of love making. Do we have to go back to Athens, there's no rush, once we're back we can't just fuck each other when we feel like it, different rules.

Morning, we decide on another two days, take in some more of the sights, another two nights of uninhibited sex then back to Athens with a view to going to Missolonghi, a few days there, then the wedding. There are a couple of tourist things, Topkapi Palace and the Hagia Sophia. We were going to see these places originally but our 'problem' intervened, this time we should be ok. Don't know where Nico is, probably still here in Istanbul, I'll check, yes he's still checked in here at the Arena, I'll leave a message, he might have more news.

Topkapi Palace, impressive, better than the tourist brochures. Incredibly ornate the only detraction, hordes of sightseers, seem to be thousands of them, spoils it a bit. The diamond, the Topkapi, there it is in a glass cabinet, a big fellow with a very big gun right beside it. He tells us it's the real diamond; 'really, surely a fake,' 'no it's real,' well it's nice to believe him. Then the Hagia Sophia, fifteen hundred years old, a Christian cathedral turned mosque, turned museum. A huge dome sitting on a square of four huge stone walls, an extraordinary architectural feat. It's enormous, full of ancient freezes, murals, icons, paintings, a mixture of Christianity and Islam. We wander around marvelling at it all. Back outside, sunshine, rather gloomy in there.

'Let's walk down to the Golden Horn, it's not far and walking in this place is fascinating.'

Karisa is enjoying it all, hanging on my arm, that's nice but I hope she's not getting too close, could create problems.

We walk down the hill to the waterfront on the Golden Horn and its low bridges, some are being rebuilt to allow boat traffic, all of them sport dozens of fishermen hanging their rods over the side. Did not see any fish but I guess they must catch something, or is it just the relaxation of fishing, all the bridges are crowded.

It's now late afternoon, back to the rooftop bar, it's such a delightful spot, why would we go anywhere else. Nico is there.

'Hello you two, no Christos, been behaving? don't answer that.'

What does Nico know about Karisa and Christos's relationship, pretty perceptive fellow Nico.

'Anything for us Nico, any developments?'

'Yes, nothing definite, however, something's up, it's the Maniots. As you know, well I think you know, Kenzo and Lambani are Maniot soldiers, they are going to Missolonghi for the wedding, why would that be?'

'Why indeed, I doubt they received invitations, what interest would the Maniots have Nico?'

'Good question, the possibilities are boundless. Kenzo and Lambani are not talking, I've had a few drinks with them but they are not saying anything about the wedding, I found out accidentally. I was in a toilet having a shit, they both came in for a pee, they mentioned about going to Missolonghi for a wedding, interesting.'

We have a couple of drinks with Nico, then he excuses himself.

'I'll leave you two to do whatever it is you are doing. I'm going back to Athens tomorrow. I think the Düzgüns are moving back as well, probably take Michael with them. They could leave him here, keep him close to Dioni, a spy in the oppositions camp.'

'What shall we do Karisa, want to go home, nothing more we can do here. We'll leave Michael in the tender care of the Düzgüns. Need to think about a move to Missolonghi, the wedding. Stamna's up in the hills behind Missolonghi.'

'Yes, back to Athens, will not be able to play around in bed. I'll be back with Christos; be able to handle that Frank?'

Athens, it's hot, we're in the pool at Christos and Karisa's place recapping. This wedding, a coming together of the Stathos and Düzgün families. I wonder what Carrie really thinks, is she willing or is she so compromised there's not much she can do about it. Just what is her role in the Stathos family business apart from the nanny thing? Michael, he's got himself tied up with the Düzgüns, they are using him as a conduit into the Stathos empire, his affair with Dioni. Wonder what the Stathoses think about that? a lot of balls in play. If the two families are able to bury their differences, form a united front, then what? what will the other players in the drug business do? It's a moving target, nothing is certain in the criminal underworld. It will be interesting to see who turns up at this wedding. Stamna, unusual place to have it. The Maniots, from what Nico found out, are going to be there, why would that be? what interest could they have?

'Christos, this wedding, I want to be there, someone on Carrie's side, you interested?'

'Yes, very, an insight into the affiliations of the various parties, bit like old times, sort out the bad people. The more we know the better placed we are to rescue the kids. Once a detective always a detective.'

'What about you Karisa? you did mention you would like to be there.'

'Yes Frank I did, I still do,' she gives me a mischievous wink.

'How about we drive to Missolonghi in a couple of days, spend some time there, it's a nice place, right on the coast. We can check out Stamna up in the hills as well.' Christos' suggestion.

'Hi Dad,' there's a girl in a bikini, a very attractive girl, at the side of the pool, early twenties would be my guess.

'So hot, thought I would make use of your pool.'

'Frank, my daughter Dimitra, Dimitra this is Frank from New Zealand.'

'New Zealand, really, but that's on the other side of the world.'

'Yep, just a couple of hours in a big jet; I wish.'

'I want to go to New Zealand and all those Pacific Islands, it's on my wish list, I will do it.'

'Not seen you for a couple of weeks Dimitra, what gives?'

'Been away with Felipe, few days on Santorini, he wants to marry me, now, I'm not sure, he's very nice but I don't want to get married, well not right now.'

'Where have you been Dad? Karisa's not been here either.'

'Istanbul, finding Frank's wayward son from New Zealand.'

'Wayward, tell me more, I would like to meet a handsome man from New Zealand, wayward you say?'

'It's a long story Dimitra, I'll get around to telling you sometime, by the way we are thinking about going to Missolonghi for a few days.'

'Missolonghi, what's the attraction?'

'A wedding.'

'I love weddings, well as long as I'm not the bride, am I invited?'

'No, not sure it would be your thing, some shady underworld characters are involved.'

'But Dad you're retired, you don't chase crims these days, you said so yourself. Old habits die hard, can't help yourself Dad?'

'Something like that, Frank's the interested party in this one, I'm the interpreter and professional advisor, how does that sound.'

'Rubbish Dad, I bet you're right into it, now a swim, it's so hot.'

She's a vivacious girl, very attractive. I notice Karisa giving me a curious look as I stare at Dimitra, and I am staring. There's something about these Greek females, they all have good figures. I sense a certain degree of personal pride, an awareness about their appearance, they certainly look after themselves. Different to New Zealand, there it's a disaster, very little personal pride, don't seem to care about their figures; more McDonalds please!

'Dad, I've got a few days off owing, how about I come along to Missolonghi with you, don't have to be involved with the wedding. Missolonghi's lovely, bit of a holiday, be nice to have some time out away from Filipe, he's getting very possessive, not sure I like it.'

'Yes, alright, might get to meet Frank's son, well it's a possibility. Not sure he'll be there, Michael is his name, from New Zealand in the exotic South Seas.'

'Thanks Dad, Missolonghi let's go, Michael, be there.'

# Missolonghi

An afternoon in the pool then around to the taverna, chef's selection, excellent. Missolonghi, we'll make the trip interesting, take the scenic route. Cross the Corinth Canal then along the south coast of the Gulf of Corinth to the spectacular Rio-Autirrio Bridge just before Patras, an engineering marvel. That will bring us back to the north side. Then along the coast to Missolonghi.

The wedding? The invitation that arrived in New Zealand gave a date six days out from today. The suggestion is we set out the day after tomorrow, Dimitra will come with us, we'll take our time. Might be an idea to speak to Nico, see if he's interested, his knowledge about the characters likely to be at the wedding could be helpful. The following morning Christos gives Nico a call and suggests a meeting.

Mid morning, we're in Nico's bar, his good lady, Zinovia is there.

'You fellows want to take my Nico away again so soon, can't trust him, he's mine, I think. Don't want him chasing the ladies, he's been allowed out a bit too much recently.'

I glance at Christos, 'talk about a ball and chain.'

'I heard that, I'll knock his block off if I catch him playing around.'

'Ok, ok Zinovia, Nico has been invaluable to us so far, we think he could help us in Missolonghi.'

She's a strong woman Zinovia, would not want to cross her.

'Be wanting me to look after things Nico while you holiday in Missolonghi, is that the deal, have to stare down your underworld mates for a couple of days will I?'

'Yes my darling, you do it so well. I hear the place is very popular when you're running it, all the old boyfriends come out of the woodwork, and you wonder about me?'

'Piss off Nico.'

We seat ourselves in a corner, Zinovia tends the bar.

'She's a feisty lady Nico.'

'You're right, and I love her.'

'Anything to report Nico, any straws in the wind?'

'Yes, and I don't like what I've heard. It's possible the Maniots are going to do something at the wedding. Apparently Kenzo and Lambani will be there, they don't know that I know that. They are pretty unsavoury characters. I get along with them and they know who you are, but I would not like to be a Stathos or a Düzgün. The question is why are they going to be there, what are the Maniots up to? I will be in Missolonghi in a couple of days and I will be in Stamna. The wedding's in five days right?'

'Yep, right Nico. We'll be staying in Missolonghi, what are you planning?'

'I've got a friend in Missolonghi, I'll be staying with her.'

'Her?'

'Don't even mention it if Zinovia's around, ok?'

What are the Maniots planning? they are up to something, whatever it is it won't be in the best interests of the Stathoses or the Düzgüns, sounds like trouble.

It's a stunning sight, the Rio-Autirrio Bridge, the longest fully suspended cable stayed bridge in the world, three huge spans and four towers, it's got a space age look about it. We drive across from the Patras end to the north side of the Gulf of Corinth, what an experience. It's more than spectacular, it's out of this world. The road west from the bridge, on the north side, is equally spectacular. Clinging to the side of a cliff initially then inland through spectacular valleys and more of those bridges to nowhere. There's a huge park full of rusting road building machinery, looks like it's been there a while, Greece's road building program really has stalled.

Missolonghi, a place with a long and bloody history. The place where major battles between the Ottoman Turks and the Greeks took place in the early eighteen hundreds, thousands were slaughtered around Missolonghi. Today it's a lovely laid back coastal town, a pleasure to visit. We check in to the Hotel Theoxenia on the edge of the Klisova Lagoon, it's very hot again.

A taverna in the centre of town has been recommended, we go along in the early evening and would you believe Carrie and Oziris are there.

'Mr Conchie, what are you doing here?'

'A wedding Carrie, we got here a little before the event, want to have a look around, never been to this part of the world before. This must be your man Oziris?'

'Yes this is him, the man I'm going to marry in a few days.'

Carrie says this with no great conviction in her voice. 'He's a nice lad, aren't you dear.' Oziris looks decidedly uncomfortable and mumbles something, his English is not good. I'm getting bad vibes, time to change the subject.

'Let's eat, wonder what the deal is? how does this chef run his taverna?'

Similar deal, 'you'll eat what I cook but you can make your own additions.' Christos takes control and we enjoy another excellent meal. A couple of carafes then quite unexpectedly Oziris makes his apologies and leaves.

'What happened there Carrie?'

'He's a mess, this wedding is a real shotgun affair. I want no part of it. Oziris is being forced into it. Leonidos is determined to forge links with the Düzgüns and he's using me as a pawn in his power play. The Düzgüns have offered up Oziris, I have no say. If I don't go along with it I could find myself back in a French prison. Oziris? I don't know what hold his family have on him. We quite like each other, but marriage? not by choice.'

'What about Dioni, Leonidos's daughter, why is she not the bride?'

'The Stathos family hate the Düzgüns, no way is a Stathos girl going to be sacrificed in the cause of unity, use a surrogate, me.'

'I'm lost for words Carrie, how in hell can this be sorted, how do we extract you from this mess? The problem as I see it, if we whisk you away, get you on a plane to New Zealand, then Interpol could come looking, murder is an extraditable offense. I'm sure you did not do it, but how can we prove it?'

'From what I've picked up during my time in the Stathos household Leonidos ordered the murder of my benefactor, Pierre Gorbet, he was becoming a threat to the family meth business. The hit was contracted out. My being incriminated was not intentional, well I don't think it was but you never know with Leonidos, he's not a nice person, he's certainly capitalised on it. I'm just his slave now, too scared to make a move. The only out I can see is to find the hit man and get something on paper, impossible I know, who's going to confess to murder.'

Who indeed? We do have an 'in' to the underworld, Nico and his two mates, it could be possible to find out who carried out the hit on Pierre Gorbet, or perhaps get some evidence that it was Leonidos who ordered it. Anything to show it was not you Carrie, I'll get Nico onto it, must be something we can do. Nico will be here in Missolonghi, I'll get Christos to give him a call now.

'Detective Galani, keeping tabs on me, has Zinovia got you on the case?'

'Nico, how about coming along to the Taverna Ziro right now, we have a proposition for you. Taverna Ziro, in the main square.'

'Evening, the detective team from Athens I see, let me introduce my friend Katarina, she's the other woman I love.'

Katarina is a fading beauty, has been a good looker but the ravages of time, and probably a hard life, are starting to show.

'Nico, this is Carrie, the young lady from New Zealand who's got herself caught up with the Stathos family, she's about to become a Düzgün bride. You've spoken to her on the phone. The Paris murder thing has got her terrified, unable to make a break, we want you to find out what there is to find out about the murder of Pierre Gorbet?'

'I'm ahead of you detective, I figured you might be asking that question and I've had Kenzo and Lambani on the job. Pierre Gorbet was the boss of a French crime syndicate that had a stake in the methamphetamine business in Paris, he fell out with the Stathos family who are also active in Paris. The word is that Leonidos Stathos sanctioned his killing. It was contracted out to the local underworld. The Stathoses did not want to be implicated. A couple of local crims did the deed, there is a witness. The killers had a falling out and one of them turned up in Istanbul, the Düzgüns took him on, Lambani has spoken to him. He did not do the deed himself, he was the lookout man and now he's worried that the murder might be laid on him. He's prepared to talk to save his own arse but terrified that his mate might get to him first. There is a nasty twist to this. Leonidos wanted to stick it to the Gorbet crowd so the deal was to cut Pierre Gorbet's throat while he was having sex with his girlfriend, he would then recruit the girlfriend who would be totally compliant with his every wish believing she was the murderer, they did a good job. The victim was on top of the girl, right into her, when this fellow pulls his head back from behind and slashes his throat, apparently it was real bad. The girl was covered in blood and quite oblivious to it all, high as a kite.'

'Nico that's really good stuff, you've been busy, how can we ever thank you. The girl was Carrie here. The witness thing, it's important for Carrie, vital, it's the only hope she has of escaping from this murder charge the French have apparently laid on her. It's the thing that's binding her to the Stathoses. If we can discredit that we will be in a better position to get her out of this. Do you think it's possible to get this witness to put pen to paper in some sort of legal manner. He's got a vested interest, does not want to be accused of murder. In a worst case scenario these two killers could start making counter accusations. That would work in Carrie's favour; she did not do it, they did, but then should they realize they could both be charged they could plead innocence, the girl did it, but then again what were they doing at the scene. There are a lot of variables, a lot of possibilities. Something on paper, suitably witnessed, would tilt things in our favour, what do you reckon Nico?'

'This witness, he's a Düzgün man now and the Düzgüns would not be averse to anything that sticks it to the Stathos lot. If he can state that Leonidos ordered the hit, but then he probably doesn't know for sure. It would be a hit for cash, who ordered it would not be known to the hit men, but something on paper implicating his buddy would let Carrie off the hook. We need to get to him, see if he will help us.'

'Carrie, what's your take on what Nico has told us.'

'Doesn't say much for the way I've been behaving however it could free me from this murder thing. I'm keeping my eyes and ears open but not much is said in the Stathos household when I'm around. All they involve me in is making drops to their distributors and looking after their kids. If I'm caught, tough luck, who am I? expendable.'

'Carrie how do you feel towards Michael, he's taken up with Dioni, what's she like, you must see a bit of her?'

'Yes I do, I don't think it's anything much, not sure Michael has any real feelings for her, I think he's being forced into it. Dioni's a nice girl, she does not involve herself in the family business as far as I can tell and I'm not sure she's that crazy about Michael either, there's a lot of sex apparently. I don't know what Michael's feelings are for me at the moment, pity, we used to be really keen on each other, then I went off the rails. I think Michael's got himself in deep with the Düzgüns; where to from here?'

During this conversation Karisa and Dimitra say nothing, the looks of incredulity on their faces says it all, *what are you talking about*.

Back at the hotel, Christos and me are sharing a room, Karisa and Dimitra another. Couple of drinks in the cocktail bar, off to bed. Christos and I get talking.

'This wedding Christos, what's your take on it.'

'Well it's a wedding of convenience, neither of them seem keen, driven by family interests. It's big business the methamphetamine trade, the Stathoses source their meth in Turkey smuggle it into Athens, and apparently Paris. The Düzgüns also source their product in Turkey and distribute in Athens, I think they are trying to establish in Paris as well. How their Paris ambitions sit with the Stathoses, who can tell but I would hazard a guess that the Stathoses don't want them there. Why the wedding? there are many reasons, depends which way you look at it. Perhaps they have concluded a united front is better than a turf war and a close association could allow an insight into each other's operation. The wild card is the Maniot family, why are they here?'

Why indeed, do they intend to disrupt the wedding, they must be here for something.

'Change of subject Frank, how did you get on down in Çanakkale?'

Shit, loaded question, how do I respond, what do you say to a fellow whose partner you have been screwing?

'Ah, alright, we took in the sights, did the Gallipoli thing, Karisa's a lot of fun to be with.'

'She's certainly that, she confided in me that you are a great fuck, she wants more.'

'Christ Christos, how to embarrass a fellow.'

'Don't worry Frank, we have an arrangment, I was doing the same with a lady I know in Athens.'

'Ah, ok then, that's cleared the air, it's just that I find it embarrassing.'

'You're a worrier Frank, get some sleep, tomorrow might throw up a whole new scenario for us to deal with.'

Breakfast in the hotel dining room, very Greek, different, not quite my thing. The four of us, Christos, Karisa, myself, and Dimitra.

'How about we drive up to Stamna, lunch in a village in the hills.' Christos' suggestion.

It's a pleasant drive. Christos's big Mercedes is air conditioned, just as well, it's even hotter today. The road gradually deteriorates. We pass under a couple of bridges to nowhere, how many are there in Greece? and another big parking lot full of rusting roadbuilding machines, the economy must be in a mess. The road gets really narrow and quite steep. I'm wondering, what's with this Stamna, we seem to be getting out into the wop wops when suddenly we round a corner and there are houses lining both sides of the road, we are entering a village, Stamna. The road is very narrow, houses crowded together right on the edge of it, then an opening, some space, the village square. All around are groups of men sitting on benches in the shade, nothing seems to be moving, no activity, a real sleepy hollow. Our car gets curious looks, outsiders, what are they doing here? We park and find an empty table outside what appears to be a café. A couple of locals are seated nearby, elderly men, leaning on walking sticks while seated, the whole place has an atmosphere of neglect and inactivity. An old fellow says something, all Greek, no English here, it's only me who can't understand, I'll have to rely on my friends. There's a bit of conversation, basically why are we here in their village. A wedding, that brings a response, the Stathos wedding in a few days. Apparently the Stathos family own the village, well they are the major landowners around these parts, that will be why the wedding is here in Stamna. It's olives, the land around Stamna is a major olive growing area, the Stathos family control it. That's why the wedding is going to be up here in the hills, Stathos country, safe. There's a church at the side of the square, presumably this will be the wedding venue. It's Greek Orthodox, how will that sit with Carrie, she's not Greek Orthodox.

There's a menu on the table and amongst the offerings I think I see a burger, something I can relate to.

'What about a burger,' I suggest.

'Good idea, Greek burgers are great,' from Karisa.

'Four burgers please.' We let Christos do the ordering, all very Greek.

They are seriously good, quite a surprise.

It's very pleasant sitting in the sunshine, well in the shade, too hot to be in direct sunlight, in this village square on top of a hill, spectacular views in all direction, olive groves as far as the eye can see, presumably all Stathos territory. There's a view back down the valley toward Missolonghi where we've come from, it's very picturesque. A bottle of wine, we linger over the burgers and wine, it's so lovely here, perhaps a look inside the church.

It's incredibly ornate, Greek Orthodox, icons everywhere, a lot of gold, very impressive, a wedding here will be an experience.

The following morning, another hotel breakfast back in Missolonghi.

'I suggest we go into the town centre and have a look around, be interesting to see the fish market, I'm interested in fishing, do a bit in New Zealand.'

'Done,' from Christos. My real motive, I want to get something to eat that agrees with me, bit hungry. A Greek breakfast does not quite cut the mustard, it's ok, but I want something a bit more substantial and a look at the local fish market could be interesting.

'Where are your real fish?'

We're in an open-air fish shop, plenty of fish on display, all little fellows, baitfish.

'These are real fish, as you put it, where are you from?' The shop owner speaks English.

'New Zealand, I'm interested in fishing.'

'These are a delicacy, yellowfin.' He shows me some little fellows, baitfish, a far cry from a 60kg yellowfin tuna ripping line off a 24kg gamefish rig off the Northland coast. Ah well, different country, different fish. I've got my New Zealand cellphone with me, not been using it here in Europe, not done what's necessary to get it to work here but the camera works and there are some fish pictures on it, some good sized snapper. I show the fish shop fellow a picture of a snapper, a big one being held out in front of the angler, makes it look even bigger.

'That's a fish, yours are just bait.'

The poor fellow looks incredulous. I show him another couple of pictures, he's blown away. But it's the Mediterranean, there are no big fish. I had noticed broadbill on a menu somewhere, I asked this fellow if he had any, yes he did and he produces another little fellow.

'Very tasty, very popular,' a far cry from the hundred kilogram monsters back home.

We wander around the centre of town soaking up the atmosphere. It's a lovely morning, not too hot yet, but it will be. We find an outside café and take a seat, coffees. I spot an omelette on the menu, that's for me. It's a monster, a real omelette, everything's in it, delicious.

Christos asks, 'worms? bit peckish? Greek breakfasts not your thing? we had noticed. Those fish you showed that fellow, was that for real?'

'Yes Christos they were for real. I'll show you when you come to New Zealand, bring Karisa, and Dimitra, hopefully not too far into the future.'

'Really,' it's Dimitra, 'I'd love to go to New Zealand. Dad get organised, stop mucking around, get onto it.'

'Yes dear, problem or two to resolve here first. Now then it's going to be hot, every day is hot, there's a swimming beach, Tourlida, I hear it's good, why don't we have a look, enjoy a bit of swimming.'

It is a good beach, some distance out of town at the end of a long causeway across the Klisova Lagoon on the shores of the Gulf of Patras. We stake out a patch of beach, a couple of umbrellas and some sun loungers, then we do what you do at a beach, lie in the sun, the very hot sun.

'Into the water, need to cool down.'
I do need to cool down. Karisa and Dimitra are sporting brief bikinis, they are both good lookers and they know how to show off their bodies, it must be a Greek thing.

'Ouch, what the hell,' there's blood, I've been bitten by something. There are these very small fish and they have nipped my nipples, there's blood on my chest. It's more surprise than shock. I don't think I've been mortally wounded, 'bloody Greek Piranhas!' I'm not alone, I notice other people 'ouching,' different.

Christos and myself get to talking. The girls are out of earshot in the water, the nipping fish seem to target men only.

'Christos, what do you think our next move should be, probably the wedding in a couple of days. The invitation that found its way to New Zealand was a bit vague, invited the Gray family, that's Carrie's family name, and her friends to this wedding in Stamna, that's all we know, I think we should be there. You know Carrie so you're included. It'll be different, well for me it will, Greek Orthodox, don't see that in New Zealand. I wonder if there's going to be drama? Why are the Maniots here? well we think they are, from what Nico told us Kenzo and Lambani will be here, why? I would like to talk with Carrie some more, we know she's here but I've not got a contact, could give Nico a call, he might have a number for Carrie, yes he will have her number, he will have got it from Kenzo, worth a try.'

'I'll give him a call right now, by the way Frank, your phone, give it to me, I'll get the local telecom outfit to set it up so you can use it here, will make life a little easier. Can impress them with those fish pictures as well.'

'You're kidding me, you're at the beach,' it's Nico, 'I'm along at the south end with Katirina, we'll come along to where you are.'

'Nico, what's going to happen at this wedding?'

'You tell me, I can only guess, something, but what? I suspect the Maniots are going to cause trouble, why?'

'We could give Carrie a call, you've got her number Nico?'

'Yep, I've got all the numbers.'

'Carrie, it's Frank Conchie, I would like to have another talk. Almost wedding day now, how are you fixed?'

'Not that well, we're at the beach, Oziris and myself, I doubt if I can get away, Oziris is reluctant to let me out of his sight. The idea was for us to come down here to Missolonghi for a few days before the wedding, get to know each other a little better, perhaps get to like each other, doubt that's going to happen. I'm scared, getting bad vibes, where are you?'

'Tourlida beach.'

'That's where we are, whereabouts are you?'

'North end.'

'We're there too, hang on I'll stand up; can you see me?'

They are all of twenty meters away, small world, bit of a crowd on the beach, could say all these beach goers look the same.

'Carrie, can we talk, is Oziris party to all that's going on?'

'I doubt it and he hardly understands English, not the brightest lad, we can talk freely.'

'Carrie we suspect the Maniot lot are going to disrupt the wedding in some way, a few straws in the wind, you heard anything?'

'No, nothing, why would they do that?'

'Don't know but starting a turf war is a possibility, by the way do you know if Michael will be at the wedding?'

'I don't know, we seldom get to talk, the Düzgüns keep him away from me, don't know why. They let him see Dioni, in fact they encourage it. Look I can't talk too long, Oziris will get suspicious and give me a hard time, best if I just say good to see you and goodbye for now.'

'Before you go Carrie here's our long term plan. We will try and get something on paper that lets you off the hook with the French Police for this murder business, then we will whisk you back to New Zealand, how's that sit with you?'

'Bloody high risk, but what the hell, my life's stuffed anyhow.'

'Come on Carrie, don't be so despondent, it's not all bad, there's always hope, cheer up, and Michael, it appears the only hold the Düzgüns have on him is the threat of violence, get out of line and you're dead. If we can get him out of here, back to New Zealand, he should be ok, nobody will come looking.'

'There is one thing, tomorrow I'm going to be baptised into the Greek Orthodox Church, I have to be otherwise there can be no wedding, it's really just a procedural thing. Perhaps you can be there, bit of moral support. Church of Agia Paraskevi, eleven tomorrow morning.'

Carrie and Oziris disappear, we spend the rest of the afternoon with Nico and his lady friend Katarina. She's a bit of a character, a worldly lady, been there, done that, done everything would be my guess. She lives in Missolonghi, wonder what she knows about the local underworld, how do I ask? perhaps I'll ask Nico.

'My guess is one of the parties is going to stir things, try and generate bad blood, who will profit from it, depends whose side you're on, which way you look at it, how much bad blood?' Nico's take on it.

'What do you think Katarina, a woman's perspective, how do things work in Missolonghi's underworld?'

'They kill each other, little mercy around here, the local gangs are a murderous lot but what you've got here is not local, it's a far flung international operation. Stamna is a Stathos stronghold, I would be surprised if anyone took them on in their own backyard, but who knows.'

Saint Paraskevi Church, an imposing stone structure. Inside, very Greek Orthodox. Icons, pictures of Saints, a lot of gold, high ceiling, quite an imposing place. The baptism, different. My recollection of a baptism was a priest holding the little one and sprinkling holy water on the forehead, this was different. Carrie was dressed in a thin white gown affair that did little for her modesty, even less when it got wet. She had to get into a barrel of water while the Priest, in full regalia, sounded off in what I think was Latin. After a bit she was pushed down into the water, all the way down, under the surface, complete immersion. She came up spluttering while the Priest kept up the deluge of Latin. There was a girl standing near me, don't know what her connection was, I whispered to her.

'Do you speak any English?'

'Yes I do.'

'What's the Priest saying.'

She rolled her eyes.

'No idea,' a broad smile on her face.

Eventually Carrie climbs out of the barrel, bit embarrassing, all white see through, shivering and cold, different.

We're in a coffee shop not far from Saint Paraskevi Church, Christos, Karisa, Dimitra, myself, Carrie, and the girl I had spoken to in the church, Myrine, she's a friend of Carrie's who lives in Athens. They had met in Paris, had kept up the friendship, one of the few friends Carrie has in this place. Myrine is going to be at the wedding, Carrie has arranged it, demanded it, bit of support, no sign of Oziris.

'Carrie, allowed out by yourself?'

'Yes, Oziris couldn't come, didn't ask why, don't really care, the whole wedding business is not of my choosing, just a bloody pawn in some power game. Quite frankly I wish I could just drop dead, should of drowned myself in their bloody barrel of water.'

'Come on Carrie, put it out of your head, we are your friends, cheer up.' It's Myrine, her English is excellent, she's a lovely girl, very attractive, another Greek girl with considerable self-esteem. I find this attitude the Greek girls have very refreshing.

'You're right Myrine, you are a ray of sunshine in my shit world; care to take my place, marry someone you don't much care for?'

'Come on, things will get better, we're on your side, your luck will turn, life's like that.'

Bit of a worry, Carrie's in a bad place, life has taken her a long way in the wrong direction, she's lost, doesn't know what to do, we need to get onto it, get something in writing that gets her off the hook, get her out of here sooner rather than later before she cracks up completely. She's in a pretty fragile state right now. Carrie's cellphone rings.

'No I won't come right now I'm with friends, if you want you can come along to this café, it's by the church.'

It's all in Greek, Oziris speaks very little English, Myrine is giving us a blow by blow translation.

'He's not a nice fellow Carrie's Oziris,' Myrine's take on the conversation, 'he's liable to cause trouble if he shows up.'
This might be difficult, don't want a scene, poor Carrie's in no state to be burdened with something like that, perhaps we should all just move on, find another café.

'No bugger him, I'm not moving, if Oziris makes a scene I'll tell him to stick his wedding, I've had a guts full.'
Shit this is spinning out of control. Christos and myself might have to lean on this fellow if he turns up and makes trouble. The girls are all looking a bit apprehensive, the situation needs a bit of levity; change the atmosphere.

'Now then girls, settle, nothing unpleasant is going to happen. Christos and myself have been here before, there are quite a few bad people in this world who have been the recipient of our favours in the past, this is nothing new to us, right Christos?'

'Indeed, there are a couple of fellows in the local graveyard who thought they could muck me around, how wrong they were.'

'Dad, what are you saying?' Dimitra looks a bit shocked.

'I'm saying that nothing we can't resolve quietly is going to happen, now cheer up, it's a lovely day.'

Oziris turns up, he's in a bad mood and starts in on Carrie. Christos puts a hammerlock on him and marches him around the corner out of sight of the girls, I stay with them, some calming down is required. Not sure what Christos is doing, whatever it is it works. Five minutes and they both reappear, Oziris looking a bit sheepish. Christos has a hard look on his face, he's a big fellow Christos, not someone to be crossed.

'Now then Oziris, a coffee perhaps and we can get to know you a little after all we are going to be at your wedding tomorrow.'
Christos is doing the talking, all in Greek, it's only me who's not party to the conversation but I get the drift. The situation mellows,

don't know what Christos did around the corner, whatever it was it's changed Oziris's mood. We have a coffee then Carrie and Oziris take their leave from us.

'See you at the wedding.' Carrie's parting remark.

'Well that was all a bit unsatisfactory, this wedding tomorrow will be interesting. Myrine how are you fixed for transport to Stamna, would you like to come with us?'

'Yes, that's kind of you; are you people friends of Carrie's?'

'I'm Michael's father from New Zealand, you know Michael?'

'Carrie has mentioned him but no, I've not met Michael.'

'The other three are my friends from Athens, we are driving up to Stamna in the morning.'

It's quite late in the evening when Christos gets the call from Nico. We are in yet another taverna, Myrine is with us. She's a lovely girl and has struck up a friendship with Dimitra. Nico's worried, somethings going to happen at the wedding, something unpleasant. He had run across Kenzo in the street, he was nervous, unhappy that Nico had spotted him. He did not say anything about why he was here in Missolonghi and that's aroused Nico's suspicion. Nico suggests that we keep to ourselves at the wedding, away from the two families, and be prepared for trouble. What? what could happen? what scenario will we be faced with tomorrow? I do not sleep well.

# The Wedding

Great day for a wedding, clear sky, fine and warm; what will unfold today?

The narrow winding road to Stamna, under the bridges to nowhere, up the hill, around the corner, suddenly the village, five of us, myself, Christos, Karisa, Dimitra, and Myrine. The village square is crowded, we find a spot down the road and park. Seems the whole village has turned out for this wedding. It's a Stathos stronghold so I guess the locals feel obliged to be there. I wonder if they really want to, or is it fear. There are two distinct camps, a big crowd of Stathos people and a noticeably smaller group, presumably Düzgüns, no sign of Michael. I guess he's not going to be here, does not want to be at the wedding of the girl he loved, perhaps still loves. Will Dioni be here I wonder. There's some mingling amongst the guests, our little group are a bit out of it, strangers. All these people have an allegiance to one of the families this wedding will bring together, well not really, Carrie is not a Stathos but the word is that she's now an honorary member of the family.

The church, we've already had a look inside. We're holding back, letting it fill up before we enter. Somewhere at the back for us, might be a better place to be if something unpleasant happens, but what? It's quite a while before the ceremony gets under way. Very colourful inside, all the gold, the icons, religious paintings, saints, and the church clergy, their colourful robes, and the head gear. Greek Orthodox, quite different to anything I've experienced. It's a very long service, the Priest goes on and on in what I think is Latin, I ask Myrine, she rolls her eyes again.

'I don't know and I'm not sure anyone else does either. These priests do a lot of grandstanding, they think they are very important.'

The ceremony drones on and on and on. There are some elderly men in seats to one side behind the Priest, church elders I think. They are in various stages of what appears to be sleep, bored out of their trees. There's some laying on of hands on a big book and some swinging of small metal gourds dispensing smoke, all very different to what I've ever seen, certainly colourful. I notice Myrine is a bit weepy eyed, why? She seems to be a bit down that Carrie is getting married, perhaps she's closer to Carrie than we realize, could it be something more than close? Eventually it's over and there's a move outside. Nothing untoward has happened and I'm wondering if our fears are unfounded. Outside there's a big crowd milling around. The reception is back down the valley, a big place in a garden setting, another Stathos possession.

There's a crowd out on a spacious lawn, it's now late afternoon. The reception will go on into the wee hours, Greek weddings are like that; there's a lot of dancing to come. The Greeks like to dance, especially at weddings. There's music, haunting Greek music, very different, quite emotional, there's a bit of a lump in my throat. It's quite a while before the bridal couple arrive, been away at a scenic spot for the photographs, the pictures that I wonder if Carrie will treasure. The crowd applaud as the bridal couple move across the lawn, there's a move indoors into a big reception venue. Bit of segregation, well I think there is, bit hard for an outsider to tell but the Stathoses appear to occupy one side of the venue and the smaller group, presumably Düzgüns, the other. The top table is quite long, Stathoses on the right, Düzgüns on the left, there does not appear to be any intermingling. No one has said anything to us so we take a table towards the back that has no place names on it. I run my eye along the top table, Carrie and Oziris take the centre spot and it looks like the Stathos family lined up on their right. Leonidos, Zoe, Dioni, then some elderly people, uncles, aunts; grandparents perhaps.

Several younger ones who I guess are relatives then the two young Stathos children, Carrie's charges. On the left the Düzgüns. It's the first time we've seen the Düzgüns, a hard looking lot. The head man, Andreas, and his equally hard looking wife Hestia. Then there are two young fellows in their twenties, presumably sons, and two girls, also in their twenties, daughters? girlfriends? Some more older people, aunts, uncles; it appears the sharp end of both families are present.

The master of ceremonies is a big fellow, a real thug. He takes control with a loud and forceful welcome, he's a good public speaker. All Greek of course, 'Myrine, translate the good bits.' There are introductions, congratulations, everything you expect at a wedding. It goes on for a long while then there are the speeches, all the men have a say, nothing from the women, certainly nothing from Carrie. Eventually we get to eating, it's good and it keeps on coming.

We are well into eating when it happens. Two masked men appear at either end of the top table, they've got guns, machine guns, they open up on the top table. The loud noise of gunfire, pandemonium, people diving for cover, shit, we're out of here. We make a run for the door at the back of the reception lounge, out on the grass, away from the chaos inside. Suddenly there's no more gunfire the sound replaced by screaming and shouting, people are tumbling out of the building onto the big lawn. There's the sound of a motor vehicle, screaming tires, what do we do, what can we do? We gather our group together and decide the best thing is to get away from here, what about Carrie? she was at the top table. There's no more shooting. We have to go back in, we have to get Carrie. Christos agrees, we need to know what's happened to Carrie. We both enter the lounge cautiously, total chaos, the place is a shambles, furniture scattered everywhere, nobody left inside. The top table is a horror scene, bodies piled up in disarray, shit, Carrie, we have to find her. She's not amongst the tangled bodies littering the top table, well not that we can see, there are sounds, moaning, they're not all dead.

'Mr Conchie.' It was a quiet little voice coming from behind an upturned table over in a corner, Carrie!

She was crouched behind the table, there's blood. Silence has engulfed the lounge, the only sound, some moaning from the pile of bodies.

'Mr Conchie, help me.'

'Carrie, thank god, let's have a look, have to get you out of here, are you hurt?'

'It's my leg, it hurts and it's bleeding.'

Carrie's leg has a gunshot wound just below the knee, there's quite a lot of blood.

'Can you stand on it Carrie? try.'

She tries and fails, the leg appears to be broken. I tear off my shirt and make a tourniquet just above her knee, it works, the blood stops flowing. Christos and myself pick her up and carry her out onto the lawn. Total bedlam, people are screaming and crying, some quite hysterical. The best thing we can do is get away from here, *right now*! We've got Carrie, nothing else matters.

It's not far from the reception lounge to the main highway back to Missolonghi and Christos makes short work of it in his big Mercedes. Several Police cars pass us going the other way, sirens screaming, lights flashing, we don't want to get caught up in the aftermath of this, we do need a hospital though, Carrie's leg needs attention. Fortunately Christos knows where the main hospital is, even better he's known there, 'the detective from Athens,' he's a good guy, not a local thug. His story will be believed, a gunshot wound, questions will be asked.

It's a clean break of the fibula in Carrie's right leg, been struck by a bullet. An operation will be necessary to repair the damage, it will be a moon boot and crutches for several weeks. Christos knows the doctor, there will be no problems as far as he's concerned however the law will be asking questions, a mass shooting at a gangland wedding? Carrie tells us what happened, well what she saw happen, why? she has no idea.

Carrie had taken a little meth before the wedding, she needed something to carry her through the ordeal, and it was an ordeal. A forced marriage to someone she did not care for, the alternative, a murder charge in Paris. Nothing untoward during the wedding then at the reception just after the speeches a waiter passed her a note telling her to go to the ladies' room right away and stay there. That rang alarm bells. She left her seat at the top table and almost made it to the ladies' room when the shooting started. Another few seconds and she would have been out of the firing line. It was a stray bullet that struck her leg, she dropped down behind a table and froze. What had happened? the possibilities are boundless.

'Well Christos where to from here,' I ask.

'Good question. I suggest we do nothing for a day or so, the authorities will come asking questions for sure. We could give Nico a call, he might have an idea on what's happened, in the meantime I think we need to stay close to Carrie, don't want the Stathos lot to come calling. They might want to take her into their care, probably don't know we have her. That's if they are organised, looked to me like there may not be too many of the Stathos family left alive.'

'I'll stay with Carrie,' it's Myrine. 'Carrie is my friend, my good friend, I will see that no further harm comes to her, believe me I really will.'

Myrine is quite emotional, perhaps her association with Carrie is closer than we thought, a bit more than just friendship.

'I'll stay here at the hospital with Carrie tonight, Mr Conchie, can I call you Frank? Your phone works in Greece now, right? and I've got your number. If anything untoward happens I'll call you, there could be more trouble from these underworld people. The hospital may want to operate on Carrie's leg tonight, certainly in the morning, I'll look after things here. You people go and sort out the mess, there will be a big mess to sort, a lot of questions.'

It was good to see Myrine taking control of Carrie's wellbeing, letting us deal with other things, she's quite a girl, glad she's around.

We get to bed well after midnight, quite a wedding, different, horrifying! No sleep for me, the mind's in overdrive, the possibilities are limitless. The more I think about the past twelve hours the more scenarios I conjure up. We need to get back to Athens and get onto locating the hit man who can help us clear Carrie's name, get something in writing, then get the girl on her way to New Zealand. We need to snatch Michael as well, get him heading home.

'Christos, you awake?'

'Wide awake, forget sleep, it's not going to happen.'

'What now?'

'The police will be around in the morning, won't take them long. Hospital reporting a gunshot wound, probably more than one case, they'll soon make the connection and want to talk to Carrie, could even be at the hospital already, Myrine will let us know I'm sure.'

Myrine calls at eight in the morning, the police are at the hospital. Christos and myself are out of bed and on our way. Fortunately it's a situation that Christos is experienced in, just as well, the police are quite aggressive with their questioning. A gangland shooting, everyone involved must be a criminal, it's obvious in their attitude. Christos is uphill for a while, if he was not a retired detective then things could have been difficult. What had happened? the police either did not know or they were not letting on, the other worry, are the police impartial, have they been compromised by one of the criminal families. Their line of questioning was more orientated to what had happened and who did it. I guess the deeper motives for the massacre will involve more detailed questioning at some future time.

It was a couple of hours before the police finish their questioning, however, they require us to remain in Missolonghi for the next two days, no going back to Athens just yet. That's ok with us, Carrie's going to be operated on later in the morning, her leg's not too bad, a straight forward fracture, no splintering of the bone, she's been lucky, if you can call being shot in the leg lucky, so there's no rush to move Carrie anywhere, just keep her out of reach of the Stathos lot. Myrine wants to stay at the hospital for the operation, that's nice, she really feels for Carrie. What will we do? pick up the girls from the hotel, some breakfast in Missolonghi, might give Nico a call, see how his day was yesterday, what does he know?

The morning papers are on the newsstands complete with graphic pictures, *eleven people murdered at wedding massacre,* the headlines scream it out. Eleven, that's a lot of people, wonder who they were, Stathoses, Düzgüns?

'Nico, what do you know, what can of worms has been opened up?'

We're at Taverna Ziro again having breakfast with Karisa and Dimitra, they are lost for words about what happened yesterday, finding it hard to comprehend. Nico and Katarina have joined us. Katarina could be a source of information, she's a Missolonghi local, will probably know the local underworld.

'Nothing yet, however, give Katarina and myself twenty-four hours, I'm sure we can turn up something.'

I tell Nico about Carrie being warned just before the shooting, what does that indicate? Christos advises he will look up a couple of contacts he has in the local police, see what he can find out. It's decided that Nico, Katarina, and Christos will spend the day seeing what information, what straws in the wind, they can turn up, the rest of us will try and enjoy what Missolonghi has to offer the visitor, see if we can get our minds off the horrendous events of yesterday, if that's possible. We agree to meet for breakfast again the following morning, see what we have found out, plan our next move.

Taverna Ziro the following morning. Christos has come up with something that could be significant. He's found a detective in the local police force who he had worked with some years ago, this fellow filled him in on yesterday's developments. A car had been found in a ditch just outside Missolonghi on the Stamna road, inside were two bodies and two machine guns. Forensics had established that the guns were the ones used at the wedding reception. Both men had been shot in the head, an execution. It appeared at this stage that the massacre was not the work of either the Stathoses or the Düzgüns, it had to be a third party. The two dead men in the car were known to the local police, small time criminals. The assumption is they had been contracted to carry out the shooting then silenced. Who would benefit from having the Stathoses and Düzgüns taken out? Nico's view, it had to be the Maniots, the presence of Kenzo in Missolonghi reinforced this view, Kenzo was a Maniot man. The other clue, who had warned Carrie that things were about to go bad? Again Nico was of the view that it must have come from Kenzo. If it was him, and his mate Lambani, who had organised the hit then they would be aware that Carrie was not involved in the nasty things that the Stathos and Düzgün families did. Carrie was the unfortunate girl from New Zealand who had become involved, who wanted out, 'make sure she is not in the firing line.' Nico's reasoning added up and it was probably Kenzo and Lambani who had silenced the two hit men. The question now, would the Stathos and Düzgün families make the same connection and if they did what would they do about it? Who was left to run things. Were there survivors? yes there were. Zoe and Dioni Stathos were dead, Leonidos was critically wounded, shot in the head, the two younger Stathos children, Carrie's charges, had survived unscathed. The Düzgüns had been hit hard, both Andreas & Hestia were dead and the bridegroom, Oziris, was badly wounded, his two brothers were dead. There were five more dead, grandparents and uncles from both families. It did not appear that either of the two families had been specifically targeted, the heads of both had been taken out which gave credence to it being a third party, who? had to be the Maniots. Did it matter, our only concern was to get Carrie out of this mess, family gang wars were not our worry. What did concern us was the apparent murder charge hanging over Carrie, we needed to pursue this. From what we had been able to gather it was Leonidos who had managed to get Carrie away from the French police, and out of France. We did not know if in fact there was a murder charge, we would need to find out for certain. It could be an empty threat that Leonidos was using to keep her in line in fact the more I thought about it that seemed to be the most likely scenario. Leonidos would need to have powerful connections inside the French police to be able to get her out of France if she had been charged with murder. If a murder charge does exist, or is a possibility, then we would need to investigate getting one of the two hit men who had carried out the murder in Paris, onto our side. He was now in the Düzgün camp and our thinking is that if we can get him to lay the actual murder on his estranged mate then it will exonerate Carrie, how can this be achieved? We need to get back to Athens and get Christos on the job, he can possibility find out if there is, or might be, a murder charge involving Carrie. Nico can possibly get onto Lambani about tracking down the hit man.

The local police in Missolonghi require us to stay for another couple of days, they want to talk some more with Carrie, her absence from the top table when the shooting happened will have been noticed. That will raise a few questions. Perhaps her absence was not noticed? We can't move her yet anyway, the leg. The plan now is to get back to Athens as soon as possible. We'll take Carrie with us, she can stay at Christos and Katrina's place, keep her away from the

Stathoses. If they come looking? well we'll deal with that if it happens, right now the Stathos family are headless. Leonidos is probably the only person who can impose his will on Carrie and he's in a bad way.

The Missolonghi police do find out Carrie was missing from the top table, they're suspicious. She strenuously maintains she went to the ladies' room out of necessity. The police will not accept that Carrie is not a Stathos family member, perhaps she's an insider for whoever did this terrible thing. We have a hard time getting them to believe that Carrie is simply an innocent girl from far off New Zealand who has become involved because she took on a nanny job with the Stathos family. In the back of my mind is the fear that the local police might get wind of a possible murder charge in Paris, if that happens things could get messy.

Katarina has been checking amongst her underworld friends and has come up with some interesting information. Several days before the shooting two fellows from Athens had been making inquiries. They were looking for a couple of contract hit men, big money, no names, complete secrecy, had to be Kenzo and Lambani which places the hit squarely in the Maniot camp. It will only be a matter of time before the Stathos and Düzgün families find this out, what will result? This is not our concern. Getting Carrie out of the place is what we are concentrating on. There's Michael as well, have not heard anything from him, we don't know if he's still in Istanbul or back in Athens. How will he handle Dioni being killed, how fond of her was he?

The following day the police come calling for Carrie, they seem to be convinced she's somehow implicated, that her toilet visit was part of the assassination plot. This could become a problem, how can we convince them she had nothing to do with it. We advise the police that we want to go back to Athens and that Carrie will be staying with Detective Galani, she will be available at his place should they want to question her further, they reluctantly agree. This police suspicion of Carrie has me worried, is there something we've missed? We need to talk to Kenzo, see if he has detected any straws in the wind, perhaps lay it on him that he arranged the hit, see how he reacts. I discuss it with Nico.

Kenzo will not want to talk, will not want it known that he was even in Missolonghi, Nicos's take on it. Well what was he here for? I suggest Nico gives Kenzo a call, he will have his number and he knows that Nico knows he's here. Perhaps a meeting, just the four of us. It happens, Kenzo agrees to meet Nico, Christo and myself, Taverna Ziro in the morning.

'Kenzo, what, if anything, can you tell us? The reason we're worried is the local police are convinced Carrie was involved.'

'You're asking me to open up to you guys, possibly incriminate myself, and I emphasize, *possibly.*'

'Kenzo, no we don't want you to compromise yourself, we just want to divert suspicion away from Carrie, no way was she involved. She was passed a note just before the shooting, 'leave the top table and go to the ladies' room,' what's your take on that?'

'Ok you guys, there are things I know, things that could possibly get me dead. I have to ask myself how trustworthy are you guys, can I let you in on some privileged information?'

'Kenzo, what we hear from you will go no further, we are only interested in Carrie's welfare, what these families do to each other we want no part of. You are probably involved in their interfamily machinations but we don't want to know, you can trust us.'

'Ok, as you probably know, myself and Lambani are in the Maniot camp, it's not a happy place, there's a power struggle going on, one of the sons wants to take over, he also wants to get rid of the Stathoses and the Düzgüns, take over their businesses. This fellow contracted myself and Lambani to hire a couple of local hit men to take out the top table at the wedding, all the Stathoses and Düzgüns.

When we shopped around we discovered there was already a contract out, another party wanted the same thing, some very murky possibilities. Was it someone in the Stathos camp? or perhaps the Düzgün lot wanting to take over, or was it the Maniots? if it was the Maniots we should have been aware of it. Who warned Carrie? If it was someone in the Stathos camp how come Leonidos was not killed, perhaps his survival was not intended. What will happen now? probably a lot of blood letting. Lambani and myself are clean, we know this but others don't, we could be targeted, but by who? It would be wise for us to distance ourselves.'

'Kenzo you paint a grim picture, these people are ruthless, we need to keep right out of it, grab Carrie and clear out.'

'Yep, that would be wise, Lambani and myself will be disappearing as well.'

'There is one thing Kenzo, we need something to help clear Carrie of this suspected murder charge in France, we don't know if it's real or just something Leonidos has come up with to keep her in line. He's badly injured apparently, could be brain damage, could be he won't be doing anything for a while so we could probably get her out of Greece without any trouble from the Stathoses but the worry is that Interpol could come looking, murder is an extraditable offence. There are two parts to this, first there's a murder charge, and second, can we get the fellow who was complicit in the murder and now in the care of the Düzgüns, to put something on paper saying she did not do it.'

'Frank you are asking a lot here.'

'I know Kenzo but you are our only conduit into this den of inequity and we need your particular contacts and skills. We've got to get Carrie off the hook and we need you to achieve this, how about it?'

'Ok, I think Lambani is the contact for the hit man who's now with the Düzgüns but what the scene will be in their camp after this

shooting is an open question. I think the Düzgüns spend most of
their time in Istanbul, that's probably where this fellow is, might be
necessary to go there. I'll see what I can find out, see if we can make
contact and whether he will cooperate. The murder charge? you will
need to find out from the French Police if there is a charge. I can't
help you with that one, talking with the law is not my strong point.'

'Thanks Kenzo, I'm in your debt, don't know what we would do
without your help. Things are different where I come from, family
vendettas don't happen. We will be going back to Athens, staying
with Christos and Karisa, Carrie will be with us, we'll be keeping a
close eye on her.'

Kenzo gives me he his cellphone number and takes his leave.

'Keep in touch Frank, I'm interested in Carrie's welfare, she's a
nice girl whose been dealt a bad hand, look after her. I'll get onto
Lambani about the Paris hit man, perhaps we can do a bit of arm
twisting, get a result.'

Well it really is a can of worms, there will be fallout. We don't
want any part of it. I get onto Christos about the murder charge. He
has a couple of mates in the Athens Police who he can trust, who
have not been compromised by the Stathoses, well as far as he
knows. Can they determine if there is a murder charge in France
against Carrie, it's imperative we find out. We can't go to Interpol,
they gave us the cold shoulder when we first made inquiries and
Christos does not have a contact there. In the meantime let's get out
of Missolonghi, back to Athens.

A week has passed, we are at Christos and Karisa's place. We have
feelers out for information about the murder charge and we are
hoping to hear from Kenzo about the Paris hit man. Carrie and
Dimitra are with us. Myrine comes around every day to see Carrie,
they are very close. Michael has been contacted, he's back in Athens
under the eye of what's left of the Düzgün family, we get him to

come over. He has a bit more freedom now that the Düzgüns have been devastated.

'Dimitra this is my boy Michael.'

It was instantaneous, both Dimitra and Michael were literally speechless, the mutual attraction palpable.

'Michael I want you to walk out on the Düzgüns right now and come here to Christos's place, the way things are at the moment it should be possible to make the break, then we can think about getting you back to New Zealand, can you do it?'

'Will Dimitra be here?'

'Yes I will, I've been thinking about moving back home with Dad and Karisa, suddenly it seems like a very good idea.'

'Carrie's here as well Michael, I don't know where you stand with her, however, if you can move in here your relationship will, I'm sure, resolve itself.'

'Where is Carrie?'

'I think she's out in the garden hobbling about on a moon boot, go and find her, have a talk, you'll have a lot to talk about.'

Michael's away a long time; Dimitra's looking a bit thunderstruck.

'Mr Conchie, Frank, that's your son? I'm blown away, he's the most handsome man I've ever seen. He's the fellow who came over here to find Carrie right, now that he's found her where to from here?' Where to indeed, what will the relationship between Michael and Carrie be now? Best give them space, let them sort themselves out.

Around midday Myrine comes over, she's a daily visitor since we got back from Missolonghi, very close to Carrie. I'm beginning to suspect the two of them could be a little different, could be a couple, how will Michael react to that. There's Dimitra, her initial reaction to Michael was something else, as was Michael's. The wedding, Carrie is now married to Oziris, he survived the shooting but he's badly hurt.

'Frank, let's just leave the youngsters to sort themselves out,' it's Karisa. 'I've got something for you, a lady, you need a lady Frank, can't have you shrivelling on the vine, you're too good a man to allow that to happen, I know!'

'Karisa what are you up to, what mischief are you planning; a lady?'

'Yes Frank a real lady, Ariana, good friend of mine, you'll like her, she'll certainly like you. How about we organise dinner for this evening, just us, Christos, and Ariana, you on for that?'

That evening it's just the four of us. We leave the youngsters to themselves, they have plenty to keep them occupied sorting out relationships.

Ariana is a stunner, there's a quickening of the pulse. A dark haired blue eyed beauty, late thirties, early forties, with an incredible figure, the sort of woman you fantasize about, good friend of Karisa's. The devil, she's figured I would be smitten, she's not wrong. We enjoy a top-notch meal in an upmarket restaurant. Ariana's English is flawless. I'm smitten all right, this lady is my kind of girl, we get on just great. How come she's available? I'll quiz Karisa later in the meantime enjoy the moment, fill you boots as they say. Ariana's an executive with an oil company based in Athens, a high flyer, an asset for the company. She's got presence, the x factor, and she's got my absolute attention. The conversation gets around to New Zealand, the suggestion comes up that when our 'problem' is sorted Karisa and Christos should think about coming out to New Zealand, take in the South Pacific as well. Ariana comes alive when this is mentioned, well she was very much alive before this but now she's really interested.

'Can I come too. Frank could you see your way clear to carry me off to the South Seas, the romantic South Seas with a handsome man; you Frank; please?'

'Ariana I'll book it in the morning, leave the day after, you on for that?'

'Yes Frank, on for everything with you.'

What am I hearing this lady is not just a pretty face, she's a feisty character as well, I'm in trouble with my testosterone.

'Right, done, ah, hang on, we've got to sort the kids out first, can you hang fire on the South Seas for a bit Ariana?'

'You mean you cannot carry me off right now, I have to wait Frank, not sure I can wait, how long will this 'wait' be?'

'Ariana,' it's Karisa, 'give frank a break, he'll burst his pants if we keep this up, give him a bit of time, then he can be all yours.'

'Can you promise Frank, please promise, not sure how patient I can be. The exotic South Seas with a handsome man, now that's something.'

'Ok girls, enough,' it's Christos, 'we'll get our problem here sorted then it will be New Zealand, you too Ariana.'

It was quite an evening at that restaurant. Ariana? I want to see her again, a lot more of her. I get onto Karisa.

'Ariana must have a man?'

'No, not at the moment, there was a husband, a friend of my husband Nikias, he was murdered around the same time my Nikias was, we suspect they were connected. Never solved but we have our suspicions, justice will be served one day Frank, we both have long memories. Ariana has remained single. She loved her husband, no children, which is a real downer, but neither have I. Ariana plays the field, the fellows line up, you can see why. I think you could be in trouble there, she has taken a real shine to you, I can tell, I know Ariana.'

'Thanks for the insight Karisa, yes I'm mightily impressed, she's quite a girl and I'm a free man, there's no one back home. Getting her to come out to New Zealand is a great idea, do you think we can hold her to it?'

'Oh yes Frank, Ariana has already made up her mind, I know her, she's set her sights on you which is a bit of a bugger, sort of limits my opportunities.'

'What do you mean Karisa?'

'Well you know the loose arrangement Christos and I have in this area, it does not go as far as deceiving people. I don't think Ariana will be disposed to a loose arrangement like we have so that will sort of cut me out, pity, you were great in bed Frank, I envy Ariana.'

'Whoa there Karisa, what do you think I am, I'm not going to race her off at the first opportunity, show the lady a little respect.'

'You may not but she will, Ariana will have you in the sack in no time, she likes you Frank. She's a sexy lady, you'll not be saying no.'

'Thanks for all that Karisa, you've got me aroused now. You're right I will not be declining any advance she may make but enough of this let's talk about more serious things before I get to the stage where I can't help myself and want to rush you into the bedroom.'

'Really Frank, you want to rush me into bed right now, possible, would be nice, but there are other people in the house so, no fucking today.'

The kids, what decisions, what life changing arrangements have been arrived at? what's the relationship between Michael and Carrie? Myrine and Carrie? Something I was beginning to suspect has surfaced, Myrine and Carrie come right out with it, yes they are a couple, they want to be together. It started in Paris where they first met, a gay nightclub. Carrie was running wild, out of control, doing everything and what she discovered about herself at the gay nightclub surprised her, awakened feelings she was not even aware of, she was attracted to other females. She found Myrine, there was a strong mutual attraction. At the time Carrie was deeply involved with Pierre Gorbet, her sugar daddy, his sex toy, and drugs, she was 'out of it' for long periods at a time. Everything changed when Pierre Gorbet was murdered. Now all she wants is to be with Myrine, move in with her. Myrine has an apartment in Athens, she's a high flyer in the fashion industry.

Michael, what's his reaction? Surprisingly he takes it in his stride. His recent life has changed him, he's still fond of Carrie but the strong feelings he had when they were in New Zealand have withered, discovering Dimitra has affected him enormously. It's only been a couple of days but he's fallen for her, she's pretty keen on him as well. Things are working out for Michael and Carrie but there are obstacles. Carrie is married and Dimitra has a boyfriend, a possessive boyfriend, Filipe.

Carrie is concerned about her new husband, the husband she did not want. She does not know how badly he's hurt, there is some feeling, after all he is her husband; how to find out? We do not want the Stathoses getting their hands on Carrie, it would be wise if they did not find out we have her, what to do? It'll have to be our underworld contacts again. Kenzo and Lambani have vanished, gone into hiding, avoiding any nasty repercussions from the massacre. They were not involved but the risk of being suspected and targeted is very real. We get onto Nico, two things, what are the extent of Oziris's injuries and how badly has Leonidos Stathos been hurt, we've heard he's wounded in the head. The news is both good and bad, depends which side you are on. Oziris is gravely ill, not expected to live and Leonidos is brain damaged, how badly is not known but there's every possibility he'll be a vegetable. The news about Oziris upsets Carrie but she handles it, after all she wanted no part of the wedding, it now looks like there will be no husband. The possibility of Leonidos becoming a brain damaged vegetable could let Carrie off the hook, no longer tied to the Stathos family. It was Leonidos who had the power with the murder charge thing, will need to get some clarification on that from the French, could be tricky.

Dioni? killed in the shooting, how is Michael dealing with that? how fond of her was he? Michael has not said anything. I decide to have a heart to heart, several matters need clarifying. Michael is a changed lad, it's Dimitra, I think he's fallen in love, Dimitra certainly seems to be rapt over Michael, these things could have changed Michael's thinking.

'Michael tell me, what's on your mind. Your world has changed, I think there's a chance to get you out of the mess you're in. The Düzgüns will be in disarray, the head of the family, the big boss, is no more, could be an opportunity for you to cut your ties, get back to New Zealand. Dioni? I gather you were rather fond of her? she's gone, that must be hard.'

'You make some good points Dad, yes I have changed. Dimitra, she's pushed everything else out of my mind. Dioni? it was never serious. Her being killed is awful but I can handle it. Carrie, well suddenly I feel estranged, weird I know but the things she's been involved in, her behaviour, and now her taking up with Myrine, it's cooled my feelings, I still like her, but the passion's gone. The Düzgüns? there's a lot of discontent within the family. I think one of Andreas's lieutenants has ambitions to take over the family business, it could have been him that ordered the hit, we will never know. There's a similar situation within the Stathos family. Dioni let a few things slip. So who did it? what will the fallout be? can I make the break? Suddenly I want out. Dimitra, why would I want to be tied to a gang when I could make a life with Dimitra? About going back to New Zealand? Dimitra, she lives here, early days I know, could come to nothing in which case returning home makes sense but right now the only thing I want is to be with Dimitra, that's how I feel Dad.'

'Michael everything you've told me makes sense. Distance yourself from the Düzgüns, now. Could be difficult defecting, well you're not defecting, you were not that involved, just the messenger.

'Yep, I was not privy to any of their dealings. I was aware of the business they were in but I had no real knowledge, my roll was to bed Dioni, find out what I could about the Stathoses. Now that contact has gone, perhaps I can be gone as well. I need to give it some thought, you don't just walk out on people like the Düzgüns.'

Some clarity is emerging. The Paris murder business, that's the one thing we have to resolve. Christos has this contact in the Athens police force, perhaps he can find out what the situation is with the French regarding Carrie's involvement, if any? Is there a murder charge involving Carrie? is she a person of interest or has Leonidos just created a situation where Carrie believes she's in trouble.

'Nico, we need Lambani, he's disappeared, probably wants to stay that way, he's got the contact in the Düzgün camp. We need to contact the hit man involved in Pierre Gorbet's murder. Not sure it's something we can pursue, probably require the skills your friends possess to convince this fellow to help us. We need something on paper saying it was not Carrie. May never need to use it, there may not even be a murder charge, but we need to cover ourselves. What do you reckon Nico, think something's possible?'

'Everything is possible, it's just some things are difficult to achieve and this one could be very difficult, it's a challenge, I like a challenge. Leave it with me, I'll get back to you Frank.'

I have a talk with Carrie, it's now more than a week since the terrible events at Stamna. The police have not been asking questions so it's beginning to look like she's no longer a person of interest. The leg is healing nicely, the moon boot allows her to get around and Myrine is a daily visitor. Now that their relationship is out in the open there's a better atmosphere all 'round.

'Carrie, when this business is settled we'll need to get you back to New Zealand, what are your thoughts on that?'

'Frank, there will be no going back to New Zealand, I'm moving in with Myrine, staying here in Athens. Myrine's well placed in the fashion world, she's confident there's a place for me in the business. I'm aware I'll be in Stathos territory and that could become a problem however my problem is with Leonidos, I don't think I have a problem with the rest of the family. Should Leonidos survive it's doubtful he will remain head of the family business, it appears there's been a leadership coup, should not be difficult severing my ties with them.'

'A new life Carrie, living in Greece? you'll have to break it to your folks, how will they take it?'

'Probably badly, they are 'small town' as you know but that's the way it is. My wild life has ended, my curiosity to do everything, experience the extremes, has been satisfied, it's over, it got me in deep shit, I won't be going there again. I'm in love, yes Frank, in love, bit hard for a heterosexual to fathom perhaps but that's how I am and I'm very happy. By the way, talking about affairs of the heart, Ariana? I have noticed your reaction when she's around, a lovely lady, I get good vibes from her as well, she's the one for you Frank.'

'That all sounds good Carrie, some stability, normality. About the potential problem, and I emphasise, potential, the Paris murder thing.' I tell her what we are doing to try and resolve it, we need something in case the problem comes up in the future.

'Thank you Frank. I'm thinking about moving in with Myrine in the next couple of days, the leg in healing nicely, no problems. Myrine is sounding out the fashion business, finding a place for me. I know all this is a major change away from what you had planned but that's what it's going to be, ok with you Frank.'

'Yes it is, the reason we wanted you out of here was the Stathoses hold over you but it looks like there's been a dramatic change there, you quite sure about remaining in Athens?'

'I will be severing all ties with the Stathos family. I think I know who will be taking over from Leonidos. Even if Leonidos survives he will no longer be the big boss. I suspect this individual could well have organised the hit at the wedding. I know this fellow, he's quite friendly towards me and the more I think about it it must have been him who passed me that warning note which implies that it was him who ordered the hit. I see no problem breaking free, except for Leonidos. We will have to wait and see how he fits into the new order, that's if he survives and the way these people operate, that's doubtful.'

Things are falling into place, all that's left now is getting something from the Paris hit man then we can think about leaving Athens, myself and Michael. Hang on, Ariana and Dimitra, what's the rush, two lovely ladies, a father and son, both smitten, could be a change of plan here. What's the rush to return home, no one's waiting for me and my wanting to get Michael away from the bad company he was involved with has done a complete reversal; a rethink is required. Still need to get some clarification from the French police and something from that hit man but suddenly there's no rush. I tackle Christos on the murder charge thing. He will ask his police contact to try to determine if the French have anything on Carrie. In the meantime we have Nico working on the hit man, just have to wait for developments.

Michael has made the break. He's told the new head of the Düzgüns that he wants out and this fellow has agreed. It's a surprising outcome and very welcome. Michael's reading of the scene, the Düzgüns are reorganising, there could well be some blood letting. The new head of the Düzgüns who was organising a coup was beaten to the gun by a similar situation in the Stathos family, now he's taking advantage of the situation. Those who had been faithful to Andreas & Hestia Düzgün are being removed, replaced by a new order. Michael has been allowed to go, he had not been faithful to any of them, was only in their camp because of the threat of violence. Time to buy a Lotto ticket Michael. It's a fortuitous outcome, now there's no pressure to leave Athens.

'Dad, I need somewhere to live, I'm free of the Düzgüns, I need new digs.'

'What you are saying Michael is, Dad what are the chances of me moving into Christos and Karisa's house; right? but what you are really saying is, dad what are the chances of me moving into Dimitra's house?'

'Ah, something like that, I'm absolutely rapt, I just have to be near her, what do you reckon?'

'I'll ask, I'm sure it won't be a problem.'

'Michael wants to move in here?' it's Dimitra, 'How long for Frank? can you make it forever.'

'Who knows Dimitra, the world's a changing place, could all be different a year out from now, will be different.'

'Well it's a no brainer, I'm moving home, I'll get my things right now. Mr Conchie, Frank, I've fallen for your hunky son, you're not bad yourself.'

'Cheeky, but it will be nice to see Michael with a real interest in life, I think he likes you Dimitra, likes you a lot!'

'Good, because I think he's great, the man I've been waiting for, I go all funny in his presence, what's that tell you?'

I approach Christos and Karisa, not a problem, there are four bedrooms, enough for all of us, will be a pleasure having people in the house and having Dimitra home will be nice. There's no slowing down, Dimitra moves home that afternoon. She's been flatting with a couple of girls in the city, no problem getting another girl. Carrie moves in with Myrine and Michael brings his things around. He can have his own room until he decides what he wants to do, return to New Zealand perhaps, perhaps not? Suddenly he's got a different outlook on life.

We're in the taverna around the corner, dinner time, Christos and Karisa, myself, Michael and Dimitra.

'Frank, you're the odd man out, call Ariana, invite her to our taverna, dinner with Frank, see how long it takes her to get here.'

She's around in a flash and plants a big kiss squarely on Frank's lips.

'Ah, gulp, evening Ariana, bit remiss of me not calling you earlier, I do apologise.'

'No apologies needed Frank, my handsome man from New Zealand, just be nice to me,' another big kiss. God she's sexy I can feel it in my loins, where will this lead.

Another great meal, always is, wine, bit of unwinding, several problems have been resolved, a bit of relaxation. There's a lot of wine and the conversation flows. New Zealand comes up, the general consensus is we're all going. Carrie will probably want to stay in Athens with Myrine but all of us can go. Dimitra really lights up at this suggestion.

'New Zealand with Michael, yes please.'

The two of them are a bit stary eyed, it's nice to see a couple of youngsters smitten with each other. I'm happy for Michael, his world has taken a turn for the better.

'All of us Frank,' from Ariana, 'I'm included? you want to carry me off to the South Seas but I've only just met you, we may not get on, then again we might. I may not be able to control myself, we need to find out sooner rather than later.'

I try to ignore the 'come on' after all we have knocked back quite a lot of wine. Ariana is a sexy woman, I'm strongly attracted, it's only a matter of time before we finish up in bed and that time could be approaching fast.

'Michael, we need to find something for you here in Athens so you can stay here with me, how about that?' Dimitra's take on the situation.

'What do you do, what are you good at, everyone's good at something, what's your forte Michael?'

'Well I graduated with an architectural degree and was employed as a structural architect before I came over here.'

'My firm can use you,' it's Ariana, 'we use architects, in fact if my memory serves me we had a New Zealand chap a few years ago, he was head hunted by the opposition. I'll make inquiries, could be an opening for you, what do you think about that Dimitra?'

'Make it happen Ariana.'

Things are changing, falling into place, a new order, Athens is looming large, perhaps I should think about moving here. There's nothing holding me in Auckland, looks like Michael will not be returning to New Zealand either, well certainly not in his present state of mind, it's so nice to see him really happy, Carrie appears to have found her niche and that's in Athens as well. The immediate future revolves around a trip to New Zealand and Ariana wants to come along. The Islands would be a good add on, something way outside their comfort zone. Tonga, Vava'u, that's the place, about as far away from the world as you can get.

'Well it's six for New Zealand and the South Seas, you'll like Tonga and you'll really like Vava'u.'

It's a great evening, good food, a lot of wine and a much happier atmosphere, suddenly the problems confronting us do not appear so insurmountable. Time to leave the restaurant, Ariana indicates she's off home, early start in the morning.

'Frank you go home with Christos and Karisa, I could rush you off to my place but not tonight and thanks for inviting me out for dinner, I'm free tomorrow night if you're interested.'

Christ what does that indicate, of course I'm interested, I want to see a lot more of Ariana.

'She's playing you Frank,' Karisa's take, 'you're off the hook tonight but I don't think you'll need to hold your breath for long.'

'Come on Karisa what do you think I am some sort of sex

maniac?'

'Yes.'

New Zealand, the only thing holding us back, Carrie's French problem and we have feelers out on that one just have to wait for some response, in the meantime what to do. Karisa suggests it would be an opportune time for me to get closer to Ariana. If she's serious about travelling half way around the world with me, and she's certainly indicated that's what she wants, then we had better get to know each other a little better.'

'Frank, take her off for a few days to a romantic Greek Island, Santorini, jump in the deep end, she'll love it, so will you.'

'I'm in the same boat,' it's Dimitra, 'I need to get a bit closer to Michael after all I'm coming to New Zealand as well, so is Michael, right Michael?'

'Yes Dimitra, Dad, that's right isn't it? Dimitra and myself are included?'

'Yes you're both included.'

So what's been decided, me taking Ariana to Santorini for a 'get to know you' few days, what about Dimitra and Michael? should I suggest they come along as well, dad and son taking two lovely ladies away together, why not. I suggest it to Dimitra and Michael, the response is wildly enthusiastic.

'Mr Conchie, Frank, you are suggesting that Michael and myself come along with you and Ariana to Santorini for a romantic holiday, an exotic Greek island, father and son, of course we're on, does Ariana know yet? what if she says no? stupid question, when do we leave?'

It's settled, only loose end, invite Ariana. I give her a call.

'Taverna, six tonight, I've got something to put to you.'

It's straight out of a fairy tale picture book, high cliffs enclosing the harbour, Santorini, the sunken caldera of a super volcano. There's snow on the cliff tops, look, lots of bright white snow right along the tops of the cliffs. It's late afternoon, we are on a fast ferry that's brought us from Piraeus. The setting sun is lighting up the whole scene, it's spectacular; snow? There are buildings all along the cliff tops, vivid white buildings, the resemblance to snow is extraordinary.

*Iconic Santorini*, a Boutique Cave Hotel, been recommended, we've booked two rooms. I'm blown away, so are Ariana, Dimitra, and Michael. It's way upmarket, absolutely spectacular, set into the top of the caldera wall it feels like we are hanging out in space, the harbour way below. Everything is white except for the roof tops, they're blue, pretty much the standard colours for the whole of Santorini. I have trouble taking it all in, not experienced a place as exotic as this, ever. Two double rooms, four days, where will this lead. There's an infinity pool, a spectacular infinity pool, very private.

'Come on' it's Ariana, 'into the pool, order the champagne, lets revel in the luxury.'

Ariana and myself are in this big luxurious bedroom the idea being to change into swimming costumes and hit the pool, it doesn't happen, well not right away. Ariana just steps out of her cloths and embraces me, quite naked. It's no contest we are on the big bed in a flash and it happens, she's quite insatiable.

'That's so nice Frank, you've really got me aroused, four days, that's a lot of bed time. Once more, then the pool, your son might be wondering, but there's Dimitra, perhaps we may not be seeing them for a bit.'

We front the pool, Ariana in a G string, incredibly sexy, I'm thinking why bother with even a G string, she has an incredible figure and she knows it, she's tormenting me, the devil. No sign of Michael and Dimitra. Dimitra's a sexy girl and in this exotic setting I can't imagine them restraining themselves. It's over an hour before they appear, Dimitra's also sporting a G string and looking absolutely radiant, Michael, well what can I say, stunned mullet comes to mind, he's certainly a very happy lad.

'We won't ask and you don't have to tell, the champagne is in the ice bucket. A toast to a lover's get away, I think we can safely say that.'

It's well into evening, the sun's dropped below the horizon, the temperature and atmosphere is perfect in the hotel's infinity pool. There's another bottle in the ice bucket, how good does it get.

'Would you lovely people like us to set up for dinner poolside?' it's the maître d'.

'Yes please.'

An incredible meal in a fabulous setting, a memory that will stay with me forever, and the company, Ariana and Dimitra, two truly beautiful women, willing sex partners, and all ours. The girls had 'dressed' for dinner, well they had both donned skimpy gowns that did little for their modesty, I found myself being constantly aroused by the glimpses the loosely fitting gowns afforded, Dimitra in particular, I think she was 'working' on Michael, he looked quite uncomfortable at times squirming in his seat, I think all he wanted to do was rush her off to the bedroom again. It's going to happen, however, in the meantime there's this superb meal and more wine at this poolside restaurant at the top of a cliff in paradise. The restaurant staff are real professionals. The place is way upmarket, everything's as good as it gets.

It's late in the evening when we retire, a memorable introduction, a get to know each other exercise. Any doubts there may have been quickly dispelled. Not exactly any reluctance about rushing into bed as soon as we arrived, now we were retiring for the night, anything goes, and that's what happens. Ariana has an incredible sexual appetite. It's a long time before we have sated our mutual desires and descend into satisfying sleep. Michael and Dimitra? I'm sure they are both revelling in having found each other.

# *Athens*

The sun is streaming into our cliff top room in the *Iconic Santorini* Ariana is still sleeping, exhausted by the night's love making, a murmur, a hand stroking my thigh, an instant erection.

'Morning darling, my my, what's this, stay there, don't move.'
She straddles me, starts moving her body slowly up and down, it's an incredible sensation, please don't stop.

'Morning again darling, what a nice way to wake up, perhaps we can spend the whole day in bed, you on for that?'

'Could be, Dimitra and Michael might wonder a bit if we don't show but they'll not be too concerned, they'll be deep into each other not worrying about the rest of the world.'

An hour later, we decide breakfast out by that infinity pool would be nice.

The hotel staff are understanding, very accommodating, but when I think about it they probably see this scenario played out every day, it's that kind of place. Michael and Dimitra make an appearance, Dimitra looks a million dollars, Michael looks worn, I think they've had a good night, know each other a little better now. Our impending trip to New Zealand is starting off on the right note. We do get on well together.

I suggest a walk, that's what you do in Santorini, it's all alleyways and white stone steps, little boutiques, handcraft places, coffee shops, very touristy but it's all done in a nice way. There's the donkey ride down to the harbour as well, that's a must do. There are a lot of people out and about, all tourists, after all that's what the place exists for, what keeps the economy going. Down in the harbour, way way down, there are several big cruise ships, the place is a mecca for cruise boats from all over the world. Thousands of cruise boat passengers pour through the place every day. We wander around the myriad little alleyways, all very colourful, fascinating, all sorts of languages. I notice Dimitra and Michael holding hands, that's nice, bodes well for the future. I'm holding hands with Ariana, what's happened, what chemistry is at work here. We stop for coffee at a little picture postcard place looking out across the harbour, the volcanic caldera. There's a small island out in the centre, it's an active volcanic spot, quite hot and rising slowly, food for thought; when's the next eruption?

'I remember this coffee shop,' it's Dimitra, 'I came here with Filipe, the place does not hold good memories, this time it's different, I've found Michael, a huge difference.' Dimitra plants a big kiss squarely on Michael's lips, 'I think I'm in love.'

Well that sets the tone for the day. I too feel a bit funny, it's Ariana, she's having a powerful effect on me. It's the first time since Ginetta succumbed to cancer that I've felt like this. Perhaps Ariana could feature in my future life, I'm strongly attracted and it's not just sex. We wander on eventually arriving at the top of the donkey trail that goes down to the harbour four hundred meters below. It's a long way down the cliff to the water, five hundred and eighty-eight steps. The Karavolades Stairs, it finishes at a small port called Fira. It's smelly, the donkeys are very smelly. They are not all donkeys there are some mules as well and they are all cantankerous, too many stupid tourists in their lives.

'You all on for a ride down the cliff, have to do it, a bucket list thing, don't know when opportunity will present itself again. Well for these lovely ladies it's almost on their doorstep but us lads from far away, have to do it.'

It's smelly and the animals are cantankerous, very. There are a few yelps from the girls but the sheer spectacle of the thing, a must do. At last, the bottom, definitely a oncer, bit hard on the bottom. Fira, an exotic little seaside place, we find a waterside café and order some beer, it's needed, the donkey ride has left us hot and grubby. Sitting in the sunshine down at the water's edge, the caldera walls towering above, *snow* at the top, a spectacular setting, another bucket list thing. The big cruise ships anchored just offshore, a lot of them, this place would have to be the pinnacle of the cruise business.

Ariana broaches the subject, something we have all had at the back of our minds.

'Dimitra, tell us about Filipi, Michael may not know about him?'

'Ah yes, the boyfriend, Filipi, well he's no longer the boyfriend, the possessive boyfriend. I was never that keen on him in the first place, don't know why I went along with it, very controlling, very possessive, but he's out of my life now. I've not actually told him, however, it will be the first thing I do when we get back to Athens. I suspect he's got wind of Michael, the new man in my life, this hunk from New Zealand who I have fallen for, who I think I'm in love with, no that's not right, who I *am* in love with. How he will react I've no idea, but he does not figure in my life anymore. There now, it's out in the open. Michael I was going to tell you in the next day or so, you deserve to know and now Ariana has made it easy for me; thank you Ariana.'

'Good, I'm glad I've helped clear the air now all that's left is to let ourselves go, get right into a completely hedonistic few days, a forerunner of our visit to the South Seas.'

The tone of this conversation has strong sexual overtones, a strong desire to rush Ariana off to bed is clouding my vision.

'Another beer perhaps, then we can take the cable car, the gondola, back to the top.'

It's late afternoon before we make a move, the little café in Fira is such a delightful place, there's an aura about it, the towering caldera walls, the dead flat ocean right in front of us, the big cruise ships, it's just an exotic place to be and with our two beautiful girls in tow I am really feeling the urge, it's the beer. I notice Michael and Dimitra are holding hands again, there's real chemistry at work there, I'm feeling a bit the same way.

'Come on, back to the *Iconic Santorini* I need to lie down.'

'Good idea, a lie down before dinner,' from Ariana, a big wink and a squeeze of the hand.

I notice Dimitra and Michael looking at each other, desire written all over them, the beer perhaps, no, the beer's got nothing to do with it.

It's an exciting ride on the cable car, straight up the cliff face. The gondolas seem to be hanging out in space disconnected from earth, bit scarry. The girls are clinging to us, that's nice. I can feel every luscious curve of Ariana's lovely body and that's getting me even more aroused, back to the hotel.

'The pool in five.'

Fat chance, the door is hardly closed, the cloths come off and we are right into each other, it's lovely and it goes on and on.

'The pool, we need to tear ourselves away from this big bed, well for a while anyway.'

We front the pool, Ariana's in the G string again. I've just had her, really had her but the sight of her in that G string gets me going again, the bulge in my swim shorts is almost embarrassing. No sign of Dimitra or Michael. We splash around for a while trying hard, well not that hard, not to fondle each other but there's no one else in the pool so what the hell.

Dimitra and Michael appear, she's also wearing a G string. Seeing it on her young perfectly formed body really gets me aroused. It does not escape Ariana's attention. She moves closer to me in the pool and puts a hand on the enormous bulge in my swim shorts.

'Frank, you're not a dirty old man surely, here let me give it a bit of a squeeze see if we can make it to go away.'

No way, between them the two girls have got me into a terrible state, but it's nice, enough of this, time for a poolside drink.

We order some wine and retire to a spot beside the pool. It's sunset and like everything else about Santorini it's spectacular. The girls have covered themselves with those skimpy gowns again, the ones that do nothing for their modesty. Michael and Dimitra are happy, that's nice, and I find myself very much at ease in Ariana's company. I think I've found someone I want to spend a lot of time with. A couple of bottles and we decide to dine out here by the pool. It's a top of the line restaurant the *Iconic Santorini*, why would we want to go anywhere else, the clifftop setting is as good as it gets.

It's quite a meal, there's an intimate atmosphere amongst us, two couples who are suddenly very close. The restaurant staff pick up on it. We are the only people dining out by the pool and the waiters are super attentive. It would have to be one of the nicest dining experiences I have ever had.

Three days, three more glorious days, three more unforgettable nights, two couples suddenly in love, yes love, I've fallen for Ariana. Michael and Dimitra, what can I say, it seems they can't get enough of each other, Santorini is working its magic.

Eventually it's time to go back to Athens, to Piraeus. There's a choice, two ferries, fast or slow and the option of a stop at Mykonos.

'Let's stop at Mykonos, never been to the *party island*,' my suggestion. 'Never been to Greece and I like what I've seen so far.'

It happens, we get off the boat at Mykonos and wander along the foreshore to Little Venice. It's an area where the houses and shops are right on the water, hanging out over it, just like Venice. We seat ourselves at a waterfront café, great atmosphere. Just up the hill are the iconic windmills you see on the tourist brochures, and Zorbas, the place made famous by that landmark movie. 'Let's stay the night, no rush to get back.' There's what looks like a boutique apartment place just across the square from the café. We enjoy a bottle of wine then wander over. Yes, it is an accommodation place and yes they do have a room; one room, oh!

It's a big one with one very big bed, perhaps we can all share it? We look at each other, 'can we?'

'You will find it difficult finding somewhere, Mykonos is full right now.' The girl behind the reception desk has a twinkle in her eye, trying hard to get our patronage. I glance at Ariana, her eyebrows are raised, a 'why not' look on her face then Dimitra chimes in with, 'we'll take it.' It is indeed a big room, and the bed, the one bed, is huge, how will this play out. Bit of a generation gap here, all in the one bed, not quite the normal father son relationship. Ariana breaks the ice.

'Ok you lusty fellows here's the deal, you two will sleep in the middle, Dimitra and myself will be on the outsides. I suggest we stay up late and enjoy what Mykonos has to offer, don't want too much bedtime tonight it might be too much to handle, ok with that?'

It develops into a great evening, we go along to Zorbas. It oozes character. I can imagine Anthony Quinn dancing around smashing plates on the floor. We stay several hours eating and drinking, really enjoying each other's company. I'm particularly impressed with Dimitra, she's such a lovely girl, I just hope it works out with Michael, looking good so far. Eventually bedtime, not a problem, not much privacy either, none actually. Not a problem but I do find the sight of Dimitra in her knickers very disturbing. Into bed, separation, sleep. It's difficult and Ariana is no help, she keeps playing around getting me aroused, 'not now Ariana.' I suspect similar things are going on in the other half of the bed how long can I hold out, not long enough and it's Ariana who initiates things. She slides on top of me and it's all on. Michael and Dimitra take it as a green light and suddenly they are right into each other, oh well!

Morning, feeling guilty? not really, great night, 'not quite a father son thing but what the hell, it was a lot of fun,' Dimitra's take on the night's activity. 'Frank you are a very understanding father, sexy beast as well.'

Shower time, need to shower after the night's activity, well decorum goes right out the window, nudity all round. I think we really are getting on just great together, there's precious little left to the imagination.

'How was it?' Christos is asking, we are beside his pool having a drink.

'Seriously good Christos, no problem with the impending trip to New Zealand, we are all very compatible. I think you might be getting a son in law in the not too distant future, what do you think about that?'

'Sounds good to me, now I've got something for you. The French Police are interested in Carrie, she's not a prime suspect but she is a person of interest, that means she could still be implicated in the murder. Their thinking is she was set up knowingly as bait which makes her an accessory. Leonidos Stathos took her into protective custody with the understanding that he would make her available should the French require it. This is not a good scene, we definitely need something from the hitman currently in the Düzgün camp. I've got Lambani working on it, he's hopeful he can get something for us. The other thing, the boy Oziris is not expected to live, Carrie might like to know that. Leonidos is in a bad way, serious brain damage. What we need to do is sort out the hit man, then perhaps we can escape to New Zealand. Carrie will stay here in Athens with Myrini. The French Police have not said anything, however, I feel that if she were to leave Europe then Interpol could well want her back, so if she just stays put, as she wants to anyway, there should not be a problem, how's all that sound Frank? and how's Ariana?'

'Ariana's great, we are very compatible. You've been a busy boy Christos. That all sounds ok, well not that ok, the French Police thing could bite us on the bum, need to get something together on that as soon as we can.'

'There is another matter that needs to be resolved, Filipi, Dimitra's ex. He was around here the other day breathing fire and brimstone demanding to see her. I indicated that perhaps he was no longer in favour, he did not accept that. He's a very possessive dominant type and I suspect he's going to make trouble. I'll discuss it with Dimitra and we'll decide what to do, by the way I've never seen Dimitra so happy, your Michael has done something to her, something nice.'

Mid-afternoon, we're in Christos's pool, myself, Christos, and Karisa, another hot day, great climate, perhaps I should move to Athens, nothing's binding me to New Zealand. My daughter Rebecca is deeply involved in the fashion business in Auckland, quite independent from me. Michael may move to Athens, there's Dimitra, looks like it could work out for him. Ariana is quite sure she can find employment for him. I'm strongly attracted to Ariana, makes sense for me to be here not on the other side of the world. At the moment Dimitra and Michael are meeting with Filipi, want to clear the air in a civilised way. Make it clear to Filipi that he's no longer a part of Dimitra's life. She wants to do the decent thing, introduce him to her new man. Risky, from what I've gathered I doubt if Filipi will accept this in good grace. A phone call, Dimitra, she's at the local hospital with Michael, there's been an incident, they are both injured, shit!

Casualty department, Dimitra and Michael are both sporting bandages, 'what's happened?'

The meeting had been at a café, apparently Filipi exploded when Dimitra gave him the bad news. He had attacked them both with a knife threatening to kill and managed to inflict several wounds. Fortunately there was an off duty policeman in the cafe, he was quick off the mark and stopped Filipi before he could carry out his threat. Filipi finished up rather the worse for wear at the hands of the policeman and was now in jail. The 'damage' was not that bad, surface wounds, nothing too serious, but if it was not for the intervention by the policeman it could have been fatal, Felipi went right off his trolley. So a few quiet days while the wounds heal, not the greatest welcome home from what had been such an enjoyable holiday.

We're in Nico's bar, the Carrie problem, we need to progress the matter. Nico advises that Lambani has a mate in the Düzgüns in Istanbul. Lambani will advise him about our problem and what we are wanting from this fellow in the meantime Lambani has to remain invisible. Things are very tense between the Stathoses and the Düzgüns, each suspect the other of orchestrating the massacre in Stamna, then there are the Maniots, did they have a hand in it. All three families are undergoing leadership changes, there will be some bloodletting, it's a certainty. Nothing more we can do right now, need some feedback from Lambani.

# *Michael*

The knife wounds are not that bad, the policeman was quick off the mark. I don't want to think about what might have been. Dimitra; I feel for her. Here she is doing the decent thing, trying to make the break as friendly as possible, and Filipi explodes, no understanding whatsoever, just blind rage. I think he would have killed us. It's over, I still have Dimitra, I really do have her, how lucky can you get. Yes I'm in love, the girl just takes my breath away. It was never like this with Carrie. Even better, I think Dimitra's in love with me, it's not just a passing infatuation, she really does love me, life is complete.

Dad? he's got the hots for Ariana, she's quite a lady, just what dad needs. He's been a lost soul since Mum passed away, hit him really hard, he loved Mum. I think there's a good chance he will move to Athens, why not? there's nothing to hold him in Auckland. Rebecca is very independent, she will not be too upset not having Dad around. She's deeply involved in her career and I think there's a man in her life as well. It's no big deal living on the other side of the world, jump on a big jet and you're there. Good excuse to take frequent trips, catching up with family.

Me? suddenly I want to live here, I want to be with Dimitra. Ariana mentioned she may be able to find an architectural job within her organisation, probably be a better deal than something similar in New Zealand so it's a bit of a no brainer. My life has changed in the last few weeks, how did I let myself slide so far. The leadership change in the Düzgüns and Dioni being killed has allowed me to extricate myself. Dimitra, a huge incentive to get back on top, back into the civilised world. Carrie? life has dealt to her big time. Her adventurous spirit, her inquiring mind. The girl I had been in love with fell into a big black hole that consumed her, almost destroyed her. There is hope, she's discovered herself, her real self, I think she might have found a soul mate as well. When I think about the past year, the things I did, how could I have let myself do that? Fear, it was fear of what the Düzgüns would do if I did not toe the line.

It started a couple of years ago when Carrie disappeared. Her letters home stopped. I had to find her, been too long without a word, something's wrong, very wrong. I loved the girl despite her going off to Europe by herself. Did not want me there, wanted total freedom. It hurt, why did she do that? Was it me? did I do something that altered our relationship? She was an adventurous girl always on for something out of the normal, wanted to experience new things, extreme things. Perhaps she wanted some freedom to satisfy her desires without my restraining influence. How far would she go. Europe could be a dangerous place for a young girl who wanted to experience 'things.' I had to find her. She had intended to sound out the luxury yacht crewing business, could be dangers there. Had she fallen into bad company her curious mind taking her into places where she did not want to be. The more I thought about Carrie the more convinced I became that all was not well, I had to find her. Paris, that's where she went originally, that's where I'll go.

Where to start. Paris, was overwhelming, way outside my comfort zone. Nightclubs? Perhaps if I asked around, a young New Zealand girl? It was going to be the luxury yacht business, perhaps clubs with a nautical connection could be a starting point.

I checked into a cheap hotel, Hotel Du Havre, near the centre of the city and inquired about clubs or night spots with a nautical connection.

'Try Le Bateau monsieur, a lot of yacht people frequent the place.' Le Bateau, members only.

'From New Zealand you say, a girl interested in crewing.' I was talking to the receptionist, a young fellow. He was not exactly throwing me out because I was not a member, he was showing a genuine interest in my inquiry.

'A girl from New Zealand? There was a girl about a year ago making inquiries, I think she was from New Zealand, I don't know what happened. I did not meet her, another fellow, the receptionist at the time, had something to do with her but he's long gone. Just a minute I'll page Monsieur Charles, he's from New Zealand, he might know something.'

Monsieur Charles turns out to be a Kiwi from Auckland who lived in Paris.

'Bob Charles, glad to meet someone from Auckland, come in, be my guest.'

It was an upmarket place, a lot of wealth there. Bob Charles turned out to be a nice guy. Had a yacht down at Monte Carlo, obviously well off; he had not heard of a Carrie Gray. He did suggest a couple of nightclubs I might try, places that might attract a young girl from New Zealand. He would keep an ear open, if he heard anything he would pass it on. He gave me his phone number and suggested I call him from time to time.

It was a start. The next couple of evenings I went along to some of the nightclubs Bob Charles had suggested, no joy and my inability to speak French did not help. I did attract attention from some rather nice girls, the accent. Most of them spoke English, then on night four I got lucky. 'I know Carrie Gray.'

She was a dark eyed brunette, Greek, extremely attractive. There was a fellow with her but when she cottoned on to me, from New Zealand, the boyfriend got the push, I was a lot more interesting.

Dioni Stathos. Her family lived in Athens and she spent her time chasing around Europe having a good time. She was curious about my inquiring about Carrie Gray, what was my connection. She heard me out then hit me with a bombshell. Carrie Gray was in Athens, nanny to Dioni's two young half sisters.

They had met at a nightclub in Paris, Carrie was high on something and Dioni had taken her under her wing, she was a real party girl according to Dioni. They saw quite a bit of each other in Paris, went to a few wild parties. Both were into drugs, well it was the norm in that environment. Not long after they met Carrie took up with a Pierre Gorbet and Dioni did not see much of her after that. She did hear Carrie was on a yacht in the south of France and was into everything, drugs, wild sex, perversions. Pierre Gorbet was her benefactor, she was his sex toy. All this was a bit hard to take. I suspected Carrie wanted to 'break out,' it was why she wanted to go to Europe by herself. Dioni was quite sympathetic towards me, my girlfriend going right off the rails. She suggested I go home with her, she needed company?

It was a very upmarket pensione. We were hardly through the door before the cloths were coming off, Dioni wanted sex.

It was the start of my involvement with her, she was a nymphomaniac, just sex, sex, sex, I could not help myself, had not experienced anything like it before. When she told me Carrie was working as a nanny for her family and suggested I come back to Athens with her, it was a no brainer, the sex thing had possessed me and Dioni was a contact for Carrie. I went to Athens with Dioni and checked into a cheap hotel. Dioni suggested that would be best. She did not think her father would be impressed if he became aware she was having an affair with a foreigner. I also suspect she was not going to let Carrie find out she was being screwed by her boyfriend. Not long after I arrived in Athens the Düzgüns approached me with an offer I could not refuse. My close association with Dioni had been noticed. Keep screwing Dioni, find out all you can about their meth business. If you don't something awful will happen to Carrie. That was it, I was forced into being a foot soldier for the Düzgüns. It was all downhill from there. The big boss, Andreas Düzgün was the most ruthless person imaginable, his demise in the massacre was a blessing. The fellow who has taken over is Yiannis Stavrou. I suspect he may have been responsible for the massacre. I got on quite well with him. When I made an approach about clearing out he did not object, my role in the organisation had ceased when Dioni was killed, so where do I stand now? I'm not being threatened anymore, I'm free to do my own thing. Going to New Zealand and up into the Pacific with Dimitra is foremost in my thinking at the moment, then coming back to Athens and moving in with Dimitra perhaps. Looks like dad will be moving to Athens, probably move in with Ariana. Carrie? has she appears to be settled, that's nice, the girl I used to love has found her niche.

There is one loose end, Carrie's problem with the French police. There are promising moves there and my friendship with the new head of the Düzgüns could be advantageous, we'll need to tidy that up before we take off for New Zealand.

# *Pay Back*

We're back in Nicos's bar, there are developments. The blood letting has started, a three-way vendetta. The Stathoses, Düzgüns, and Maniots are at each other. Each family suspects the others of complicity in the Stamna massacre, there have been several killings. Nico's two mates are lying low, however, Nico is in contact with Lambani, he has news about the Paris hit man. The Düzgüns have found out that Leonidos Stathos ordered the murder of Pierre Gorbet, they want to use that piece of information to incriminate him. To facilitate this they want to get the hit man, now under their control, to put pen to paper, failure to comply could have unfortunate consequences for him. The idea is for him to say that Leonidos ordered the hit, he will also say that it was his mate who actually did it, that gives him an out, whatever the outcome it's good news for Carrie. We will need to use Michael's friendship with the fellow who now heads up the Düzgüns, Yiannis Stavrou to get it in writing.

Oziris has succumbed to his injuries, Carrie is now a widow. Leonidos will probably survive but he'll be a brain damaged vegetable, how this will affect his apparent close relationship with the French Police is an unknown. The French are interested in Carrie because they suspect she was used to set up Pierre Gorbet. If we can get something in writing that implicates Leonidos and then convince the French that Carrie did not even know Leonidos at the time of the murder then Carrie should be off the hook. Michael will need to approach the Düzgün boss.

'Dad, perhaps you can come with me when I meet with Yiannis Stavrou, he's quite a nice fellow, not your usual thug in fact if you did not know otherwise you would not pick him as a crim, very intelligent fellow.'

It happens, Michael sets up a meeting in a café in downtown Athens. Yiannis Stavrou is quite an impressive chap, very different from what I was expecting. This is real progress, here we are talking to the head of a powerful crime family. Yiannis has a couple of bodyguards with him, big rugged guys, hard as nails. There's a gang war going on, people are being murdered, we are lucky to get to meet Yiannis. He is a nice fellow, smart, really interested in us.

'All the way from New Zealand. I would like to visit New Zealand, get away from this place for a while, too much violence here, however, right now there are problems, I need to be here. About your problem with the French. I've met Carrie, lovely girl, those Stathos animals have sure screwed her up, however, I hear she's found a new life, found some happiness, that's nice. What exactly is it you want for Carrie?'

We spell it out for Yiannis the major thrust being that Carrie did not set up Pierre Gorbet, that she did not even know Leonidis Stathos until he pulled her out of that French jail. She was not the killer, the hired hit men did it.'

'I will talk with the fellow we have, I'm sure he will comply with what you are requesting.'

'I'm in your debt Yiannis, this should release Carrie from being a person of interest to the French, allow her to get on with her life, the only possible problem could be Leonidos Stathos. Should he come up with a different story implicating Carrie, which is apparently what he has done, then things could turn sour.'

'Leonidos? I don't think so, from what we have heard he's unlikely to rejoin the world of the normal, could be we might hasten him on his way to join his wife. No, Leonidos will not trouble Carrie again.'

A good outcome. If Yiannis follows through on his promise it should give Carrie all she needs should problems arise further down the track.

It's not long, a couple of days, a courier delivery, a legal looking document witnessed, stamped, and signed by a JP detailing all that we had asked for. I did not see any bloodstains on the paper, perhaps they were on the floor, who knows; thank you Yiannis.

It's all over the morning papers, a shootout between rival gangs in downtown Athens. Typical news media coverage, sensationalise it, make it appear worse than it is but perhaps the media did not need to embellish this story, the pictures are horrific enough. Bodies sprawled all around the inside of a café, shit it's the same café where we met Yiannis, time to clear out of here. We call on Nico for a beer, just Michael and myself.

'Detective Conchie, out unescorted, bit brave, there's a nasty gang war going on, careful where you poke your nose. Ok here, Nico's bar is neutral territory. Bandages Michael? I heard about it, I also heard that the fellow who sliced you up, Felipi was it? had a bit of bad luck. He was found in a back alley the other day badly beaten, broken bones, not nice, but then if you go and attack a detective's daughter you're not going to get VIP treatment from the local police.'

'Nico we need to thank you for all you've done for us, our problems are resolved and it was your input that brought it about. Both Michael and Carrie are off the hook, free to do their own thing. We will be returning to New Zealand shortly but we will be back, it's just a holiday visit. We are taking Christos, Karisa, and Dimitra with us.'

'What about Ariana Frank, not leaving her behind surely?'

'Nico, what don't you know, yes Ariana is coming with us.'

'I bet she is, I hear you are rather smitten.'

'Yes Nico you are hearing correctly, I am very keen on Ariana, that's why I will be coming back.'

'Can't go wrong there Frank, that one's a beauty, a really nice lady, you're a lucky man.'

# New Zealand

Our business here is finished, start planning the holiday. We'll break the trip at Dubai, worth a look, three days perhaps. Do all the tourist things, then direct to Auckland. Emirates, they offer a good through flight in a big A380.

It happens, good to be out of Athens, out of Greece. My Mediterranean experience was a real eye opener. A mixed bag of experiences, it did have its moments. Finding Ariana, and Santorini, what can I say, it's changed my life. I've sent a message to Rebecca. Six of us, perhaps she can open up the house, it's a big place in Parnell. I just locked up and left so it might need a 'smarten up.' Rebecca does not live there she's shares a flat in Parnell with some other girls, all models I think. There'll be plenty of room for the six of us. Handy for showing Auckland to our guests from Greece, well hardly guests, intimate friends would be more appropriate.

As we get closer to Auckland the girls get quite excited, way outside their comfort zone, the other side of the world, Ariana is loving it. When I actually put it to her, 'come to New Zealand with me,' she jumped at it. I don't think she was sure I would actually go through with the suggestion, now she's almost there her excitement is palpable. A strong bond has developed between us, you could say we are a couple.

Perfect Auckland arrival, a bright sunny morning. Rebecca meets us, she's got a mini bus, she's even organised our local Parnell restaurant to lay on a catered breakfast at our place. Great first impression for our Greek guests, no, our intimate Greek friends, welcome to New Zealand.

'Here's the plan.' We are enjoying the excellent breakfast out on the balcony at my place. 'I suggest a bit of a rest then we'll go down to the Viaduct Basin and soak up the waterfront atmosphere New Zealand style, could stay down there for dinner, it's a nice place, tomorrow we will go over to Waiheki on the ferry, visit a couple of vineyards, how's that sound?'

'Sounds great,' from Ariana, 'whatever you say goes Frank, we are on your turf now, you're the boss.' She's cuddling up to me as she says this, I think she's in a sexy mood, careful now Frank, later. There are several sun loungers on the balcony, it's a perfect day. A snooze in the sun might be a good idea, there's a pool as well. Rebecca's had it serviced, good girl. It gets very warm lying in the sun and the girls start shedding their cloths. Rebecca's gone off to work which is just as well, not sure she would be comfortable with the degree of intimacy that exists in our happy group. It's not long before the girls are down to their knickers, us fellows? well we are down to our briefs and it's a bit embarrassing, bit obvious.

'Swim time, need to cool off.'

'Yes Frank you certainly do,' from Ariana, 'you'll be bursting out of those briefs any moment.'

We're all fooling around in the pool, bit of cuddling, bit of groping and it's nice, the travel fatigue is disappearing fast. Dimitra and Michael excuse themselves and disappear inside the house, hmm!

We had stopped off at Dubai on the flight out, stayed at the Pullman, sheer luxury, did all the tourist things, well as much as you can in three days. High Tea in the Burg Al Arab was a highlight and the ATM that dispensed gold bars in the Burg Khalifa; different. Dinner on a dhow on the Dubai Creek, the Desert Experience, all fabulous, needed a lot more time there.

Mid-afternoon, our jet lag is disappearing fast, well I think it is, perhaps that bottle of sav in the sunshine by the pool has done it.

'Come on, let's walk down to the waterfront and along to the Viaduct Harbour, you'll like it.'

'All these big yachts, where do they come from Frank?'

'Mostly local, Auckland's a yachties paradise, some are visiting from far away, this place is a drawcard for the super rich. There's the Americas Cup thing, that brings a lot of super yachts to Auckland, it's a popular place.'

We wander on, over the drawbridge to the Western Extension, all the bars and restaurants.

'I'm thirsty, how about you, all this walking in the sunshine.'

We seat ourselves at an outdoor bar and order some beer and chilled white. It's a beautiful afternoon, Auckland at its best, doing a good job at impressing our Greek guests. It's very pleasant sitting in the sunshine, there's an atmosphere about the place, far removed from the scene back in Athens. Pity Carrie's not here, she would like it. There are a couple of buskers doing their thing, adding to the atmosphere. The big yachts, some of them Americas Cup contenders, being dealt to outside the team bases lining the waterfront. The next cup challenge is just a few months away, activity is ramping up.

'Frank, what's the Americas Cup?'

A revealing question. In New Zealand the Americas Cup is huge, however, elsewhere in the world, most of the world actually, it does not mean a thing. I take some time and give our Greek guests a rundown on the Cup, its history, and why it's so big in New Zealand.

'Frank I want to go sailing on your Waitemata harbour, get the feeling of what sailing means to you people, I get the impression it's big here.'

'Big! it's huge. The kids in Auckland start early in life, sailing is very popular amongst the youngsters. Tell you what, I've got a mate who's a sailing nut, I'll give him a call and organise a bit of sailing for us all, that ok with you girls?'

'Is it ever.'

Late afternoon has turned to evening. We wander back over the drawbridge to the Viaduct Basin and front the Portofino, an Italian restaurant, it's good, well it was, been a while, not done much eating out since I lost Ginetta, lost interest, but now, suddenly, I've got a new lease on life, a new lady. We are seated outside under a big canopy overlooking the Basin, all the boats, quite a romantic setting, we order up big. Portofino is upmarket and yes it's still very good.

'My shout tonight, welcome to New Zealand and welcome back to the fold Michael, good to have you here.'

'Good to be here Dad and with this lovely lady Dimitra, guess what? we are thinking about getting engaged.'

'Wowee, that was quick, no mucking around eh!'

I leave the table, 'bathroom,' well not quite. I seek out the maître d'.

'Does the restaurant have a procedure for engagement announcements?'

'Yes sir, champagne and a fellow with a violin. Just give me a nod when you would like it to happen.'

Our first meal in New Zealand, it's good, seriously good, the Portofino has not lost the touch, we get to talking.

'Tell me Frank,' it's Christos, 'are you going to settle back here and start something or are you thinking about coming back to Athens? From what I've seen so far your Auckland is a pretty nice place, be hard to pass it up for somewhere else.'

'Yes it is nice, I've lived here most of my life, a change would be quite something but then life is an ever changing canvas. Just recently someone has crashed into that life, Ariana, suddenly Athens looks very attractive.' I give Ariana a big hug.

'Frank I could come and live here with you or we could divide our time between the two, food for thought.'

'Christ you make it sound like a done deal Ariana, how long have we known each other?'

'Long enough Frank, you are coming back to Athens with me, there will be frequent visits back here, how's that sound.'

I need to change the direction of this conversation, we are making commitments. I'm wondering if all the wine we've been drinking, are still drinking, is clouding our judgements but I do like the tone of the conversation. I catch the eye of the maître d' and give him 'the nod.'

They do it well, the Portofino. A fellow comes along singing a romantic song and playing a violin, there's a magnum of champagne in an ice bucket, the wine waiter makes a real show of opening it and pouring for Dimitra and Michael, they're blown away, completely unexpected.

'Is this an engagement?' it's Ariana asking.

'I don't know, we've not thought about it have we Michael, but it's a nice idea.'

'Back off, please,' from Michael, 'give us space, I'm in love, no doubt about that, but will Dimitra have me?'

'Have you, are you serious Michael, of course I'll have you, I've had you already, and I liked it, could make it a permanent thing, here, a toast to the future, it's looking good right now.'

We continue eating and drinking late into the evening, it's a relaxed atmosphere, very different to the scene in Athens. Six happy souls, four on the verge of life changing decisions, what will the next few weeks bring, it can only be good. We are due for something nice to be happening in our lives. Eventually we Uber back to the big house in Parnell, bedtime. Ariana is an animal, she's in a good frame of mind. The novelty of being in New Zealand, the other side of the world, and an excess of wine, she goes right off her trolly and rapes me, quite out of control. I love every minute of it.

Breakfast on the veranda by the pool, another warm sunny morning, Auckland is laying it on for our guests. I busy myself in the kitchen doing the necessary. Michael and Dimitra appear, they are happy, could be the start of a lifelong relationship, who knows. The vibes last night certainly suggested that. Morning folks, it's Christos and Karisa, she looks radiant, perhaps it's been a night of sexual excess in this far off land that's done it.

'Today we are taking the car across to Waiheke on the ferry. I'll show you around that lovely island. There are lots of vineyards, restaurants, and some good beaches.'

Vino Vino's for lunch, a spectacular view, hanging out over Oneroa beach, then on around the island. I've brought the old Holden wagon, Waiheke's no place for a good car, some of the roads are pretty rough, the 'rusty wagon' accommodates six as well. We drive down to the 'bottom end' as it's known, leave the main 'around the island road' and go down a dirt track to Owhiti beach, deserted, always is, it's the most beautiful beach, completely private. It's hot, a swim perhaps in the crystal clear water.

It's all a bit much for our Greek girls, everything comes off and they fling themselves into the water completely carried away with the sensualness of it all. It's an arousing sight, irresistible. Off come the cloths and the three fellows join the girls. It's a delightful experience swimming around naked. The beach completely deserted the only possible intrusion would be the arrival of someone's pleasure boat but there's no sign of that, it's all ours. The sight of the naked girls is causing me problems, I think Christos and Michael are having the same trouble, what to do about it, nothing at the moment. I don't think 'sex in the surf' would be quite appropriate just now. How very far away we are from those bad things that happened in Greece, just a fading memory.

It's a pretty intimate scene, the olds and the youngies, father and son, father and daughter, the very beautiful daughter, all running around with no clothes on, I'm finding it very hard. I keep getting an erection, I notice Christos and Michael are having the same problem. Have the girls noticed, of course they have, will we be able to restrain ourselves? what are the girls thinking? I've brought some big beach towels along, we spread these out on the fine white sand and settle in for a bit of sun bathing.

'Frank, it's too much, I have the urge, what do you think, will they be offended if you fuck me right now?'

As Ariana lays this on me I notice Michael becoming very intimate with Dimitra, Christos is doing the same with Karisa, I think we are all getting close to having sex. It happens, Ariana sets the tone, she pushes me onto my back and mounts me, the effect is almost instantaneous. We are all right into it, to hell with everything, sex on a remote beach in the South Seas, great.

After a while, quite a long while, we have exhausted ourselves, sex in the hot sun, we need another swim. Into the water, we fool around some more, bit more intimate this time, Karisa is giving me a bit of attention, not sure about that, what will Ariana be thinking?

'Let's walk along the beach, it's all ours, should anyone show then I guess we'll just swim back.'

Four of us set off on a naked beach walk, the youngsters hang back, I suspect they want to enjoy each other's bodies for a while longer. It's a long beach Owhiti with a lot of pohutukawa trees at the far end, it's quite secluded. Karisa and Ariana are revelling in it, I guess it's far removed from anything they've experienced in Greece, the enjoyment of no clothes. It's having quite an effect on me as well. I suspect Christos is feeling the same.

'Another swim,' in we go and this time Karisa is quite open about her fooling around with me. She keeps massaging my erection, it's incredibly arousing, how can the others not notice? Does not seem to bother them in fact I notice Christos giving Ariana some attention. Out onto the sand, no beach towels, we move further up onto some grass under the pohutukawas. Karisa lies down beside me, Christos is a little further along on the grass with Ariana, we get to talking.

'You know you can take me right here if you want Frank, Christos will not mind, not sure about Ariana though, she's a bit straight laced about some things and I don't think she's one of Christos's girlfriends, she may not be impressed if you fuck me right here in front of her.'

As she says this Ariana is being very attentive to Christos, they are playing around with each other and Christos is sporting a mighty erection.

'Interesting, Ariana's a good friend of mine, I don't think she would do anything that would offend me, she's sexually active as you know Frank, but very discreet, there's no partner swapping with her however right now on this remote beach on the far side of the world who knows.'

As she says this it happens. Ariana is on her hands and knees and Christos is thrusting into her, she's quite worked up, there's a lot of moaning. It triggers an immediate reaction from Karisa, she pushes me onto my back and goes down on my bulging erection, it's magnificent, then she mounts me and we go at it like there's no tomorrow.

What a revelation, suddenly we have a foursome, I would never have thought it, what does this imply for our impending trip to the Islands?

We are back in the old Holden rattling back up the dirt road out of Owhiti. The atmosphere has changed, there's a general feeling of sexual familiarity amongst us, the youngsters included. There were no secrets down there on the beach. Ariana was a bit apologetic about her behaviour, she had not done anything like that before but this place, this South Seas beach had got to her, left her a little embarrassed, Christos was feeling the same way.

'Don't worry, we all know where we stand now, could make our impending holiday all the more enjoyable,' Karisa's take on it.

'Right, Man O'War vineyard.' Right on the water in a garden setting at 'the bottom end.' We sit at trestle tables on a big lawn under some pohutukawas and enjoy the excellent Man O'War whites, cheese board and nibbles if you want. Man O'War bay is a popular anchorage. Drop the pick and come ashore. Can be difficult getting back to the boat at times, it's very tidal.

'Frank, Frank Conchie, it is you? been a few years.'
A blast from the past, an old mate, Steve Coultard. He's seated with a group at one of the tables and he's well on the way, the whole group are, it's that sort of place.

'And where did you find the ladies you old dog, come over here and join us.'
Well it was all downhill from there. Steve's friends were a fun lot, they had put away a fair amount of wine and were showing very obvious signs.

'How did you get here, drive? We've got the boat, out for a few days, bit of fishing but it's hard to get past Man O'War as you know Frank. Pete has his boat here as well in fact most of these people are from his yacht. Tell you what, why don't you come out to our boat for dinner, there's just the two of us, myself and my good lady Rachel, you remember Rachel? Talk about a blast from the past, Rachel, an old girlfriend from yesteryear, wonder if Steve knows that?

'Frank Conchie, the man I never married;' she plants a big kiss right on my lips.

'Hello Rachel, been a long time, good to see you again.'

'Hands off Frank, Rachel's mine, we're married, you've brought your own harem I see, not bad either.'

We get into the wine and the whole scene deteriorates into what is a frequent occurrence at Man O'War, far too much wine in the hot sun but it's such a nice place, why not. I have to drive all the way back to the ferry at Kennedy Point then into Parnell. It's now late afternoon and I've had a few, more than a few, not good.

'Frank, you're getting pissed, why don't you and your friends spend the night on our boat, you don't really want to go all the way back to the city do you, we can do a bit of fishing in the morning.

'There are six of us Steve.'

'Not a problem, it's a big Maritimo, three state rooms, extra sleeping in the lounge and then there's the fly bridge, what about it Frank? bit of catching up to do as well.'

'You have a way with words Steve, these people are from Greece, enjoying a New Zealand experience, out on the gulf would have to be right up there.'

Straight out of the Keystone Cops, getting out to Steve's boat. It's early evening when we make the move and the tide's gone out, way out, Man O'War is very tidal. We drag Steve's rubber ducky out across the mud and shell until there's a bit of water then attempt to row, can't use the outboard, too shallow, well actually there's hardly any water at all and the best efforts of the oarsman results in much scrapping of mud and little progress, it's all pretty painless though, all that wine. Eventually we get into deeper water and four of us make it out to Steve's big Maritimo. I go back for the remaining four we left standing in the mud. A repeat performance and we're all on board, need a drink after all that exertion. Another drink is what we don't need but what the hell, it's a lot of fun. Our Greek contingent are looking a little bewildered.

'Is this the way people in New Zealand carry on?' 'yep!'
Rachel, bless her, has retained a little sobriety and busies herself producing nibbles and more wine. It's a beautiful evening, great sunset and eight happy souls.

'Steve tell me, what have you been up to all these years? been a long time since you stole Rachel away from me, more than twenty five years. Ginetta came into my life about that time, just as well or I might have had murderous intentions.'

'Frank, I did not know you cared that much,' from Rachel, 'now tell us about these lovely ladies from Greece.'

I give Steve and Rachel a 'sanitised' summary of what I've been doing in Greece then turn the conversation around, get away from Greece, don't really want people knowing about those unsavoury goings on.

'Steve tell me, what have you been doing?'

'I got into plastics Frank, injection moulding, one of the first in New Zealand and it's paid off big time, pretty comfortable these days, and I have Rachel, wife, lover, business partner, life has been kind, couple of boys, engineering, Canterbury university.'

We linger on for some time enjoying the ambience of the place. There are quite a few boats in the bay, it's a popular anchorage. There's the sound of revelry from several of them, ours included. After a while Rachel excuses herself and disappears inside the cabin.

'Dinner in thirty minutes.'

Ariana, Karisa, and Dimitra, are not saying much, I think they are finding the 'Kiwi experience' a bit overwhelming, they certainly look happy. True to her word Rachel comes up with a superb meal. Some keen divers had given them some scallops and crayfish the day before. Crayfish split open, grilled, served with a caesar salad. Before that kokoda and scallops, and of course more wine, the girls are mightily impressed, so am I. Rachel is a good girl to have onboard.

'This is so nice,' it's Dimitra, 'I think I want to live here.'

'We do this every day Dimitra,' I say tongue in cheek thinking how different it can be when there's a howling sou'wester.

'Tomorrow Steve will show us how we catch fish, real fish, big snapper, ok Steve?'

'Yes I'll do that, the fishing's been good recently.'

'Would that be the fish Frank boasted about on his cellphone back in Missolonghi?' from Christos.

'Been boasting Frank, let's see your phone.'

'Oh, they're just little ones, we'll show you some real fish in the morning.'

It's a lovely evening, the gulf at its best, no wind and a full moon. We are very relaxed after Rachel's magnificent dinner. I don't think the girls had experienced anything quite like this before, Christos is impressed as well. The conversation is wide ranging, Steve is interested in my career as a detective. He eventually figures that it was that that had taken me off to Greece. Bringing these lovely ladies back to Auckland has really caught his attention.

'You're a bit of a charmer Frank, always were, Rachel told me.'

'He's a charmer all right and he's mine.' Ariana's input.

'And Michael and Dimitra, what gives with you two?'

'Who knows,' from Dimitra, 'early days but right now Michael is lighting up my life.'

'We are thinking about going to Europe, the grand tour, it's what you do when you've been successful in this part of the world. You go out and splurge it. Greece will be on the itinerary, always wanted to go there.'

'You could be in luck Steve, could have some contacts there. I'm thinking about moving to Athens, it's the lovely Ariana, she's won my heart.'

'Wow, different, Greece? Ariana what have you done to this man?'

'Do you really want to know Steve?'

'Ah no, can we change the subject perhaps.'

The conversation flows till late into the night. There's more wine and a general sense of enjoyment of the circumstances we find ourselves in, eventually it's time for bed.

'You'll find everything you might need in the two staterooms. Michael and Dimitra I'd suggest the flybridge, the big seat up there pulls out to a bed, it's quite an experience sleeping out under the canopy.'

Ariana's in a dreamy mood cuddled up to me in the big bed.

'Is this what life's like in New Zealand Frank, you're so lucky to live here, would you really want to come and live in Athens? It's a very different life style to what you have here. Oh, by the way, what happened back on the beach at Owhiti, that's not me, I've never done anything like that before, it was the exotic surroundings. It's not that Christos is just anyone, I've known him and Karisa for a long time. I know what they are like, their sexual freedoms. I just got carried away, the heat of the moment, it's not something that will happen again, believe me Frank, it's you I want, only you.'

'Don't worry Ariana, I was doing the same with Karisa, you may have noticed. Christos does not appear to be concerned, it was the openness of it on this occasion that was different.'

'Frank do you think they might want a sharing relationship?'

'You mean a foursome Ariana, I don't know, no idea, it would change the whole dynamic of our relationship, is that something we want, something we could live with?'

'I have no idea either, I've never considered anything like that in my life, besides you are the only person I want, let's just let the matter lie.'

Breakfast out in the cockpit, another perfect day. There's plenty of room on Steve's big Maritimo. Rachel is doing the honours again, a good girl on a boat. I remember way back, in a previous lifetime, I had a boat, a modest little yacht, Rachel was always a gun in the galley. We had some great times out in the gulf but that was a long long time ago.

'Fishing: today we'll catch some big snapper, give some truth to those bullshit pictures Frank's been flashing in Greece. We'll drift fish out in the Firth of Thames. There have been some good catches recently, introduce the girls, and Christos, to real fishing.'

It starts off promising enough, plenty of bites, a few snapper but they're all throw backs, under the legal limit, this causes a bit of consternation amongst our guests.

'But that's a big one, big as they come in Greece and you throw them back!'

'Yep, we do, hopefully we'll show you a real fish shortly.'
The words are hardly out of my mouth when Ariana's rod bends right over and line rips off the reel.

'Help, what do I do?'

'You hang on Ariana, let it run for a bit then tighten up on the drag a little, here I'll show you.'

It's something big, probably a kingfish, that's a good start for someone who has probably never caught a real fish in their life. I show her how the drag works, how to lift the rod up then wind down, she catches on real quick. It is a kingfish, this will be interesting, kingfish are not easy to land. She does well, ten minutes and the kingi's at the back of the boat, we get a gaff into it and haul it aboard, a big one, around fifteen kgs.

'Wow, I caught that,' she's beside herself with excitement, she grabs me and plants a big kiss right on my lips.

'Where's that camera, my baitfish picture,' wait till we get a really big one.

'Oh Frank this is so exciting, I've never been fishing in my life.' There's real excitement now, bang another good strike, Christos this time, he hauls in a good snapper around five kgs.

'Get this on your camera Christos, we'll go back to Missolonghi and show that fellow in the fish shop.'

It's all on, the snapper are on the bite, everyone hauls in a good one, no 'put backs.'

'Frank, is it always like this, these are monsters, I've never seen anything remotely like this back in Greece.'

'I wish Christos. No this is a good day, there are bad days.' We continue fishing then we notice a 'work up,' the Gannets are really working not far away.

'We'll go over there, show you something else, Kahawai.' We put out a couple of lures, both are hit immediately, big ocean going Kahawai. We put Karisa and Dimitra on the rods, they are beside themselves with excitement. They do well but lose both fish at the boat, disappointment, not to worry, out go the lures again, another couple of strikes. This time both fish are netted and brought aboard.

'This is so good Frank, I like New Zealand.' Dimitra is quite carried away. I must admit the fishing is good but not that unusual in the gulf. We keep going, don't boat anymore, just release them after all what would we to with a lot of big Kahawai but it's a lot of fun catching them, these big ones are real fighting fish.

'Had enough? We've got several good feeds here, let's go inshore and have some lunch,' from Steve, the boss!

An idyllic bay on the west side of Rotoroa Island, big sandy beach, good swimming. We are enjoying fresh snapper lightly pan fried in butter, Rachel again, a chilled savvy, our guests are in heaven, it is nice. The weather is being kind, not always like this, a fresh south westerly and it's a whole lot different.

'Frank,' it's Steve, 'I suggest you people stay on board for another night then I'll drop you off back at Man O'War tomorrow, how's that fit with you?'

'Yes please' from the girls, they are right in their element, lapping up the New Zealand experience.

Mid afternoon, we are lounging around full of snapper and quite a bit of wine, it's hot, the sun is beating down, 'a swim perhaps?'

'Ah, no swim costumes, anything on board Rachel?'

'No, why? do you need something Frank, I seem to remember swim costumes did not feature back in the days of your little yacht.'

'Geez Rachel you've not changed, what the hell, just jump in,' skinny dipping off the back of the big Maritimo, Steve and Rachel are into it as well.

It's all a bit erotic, two youngsters and 'the olds' all fooling around in the warm gulf water. Getting out and showering requires a bit of self-control, I mean four naked ladies, four attractive naked ladies, 'not now Frank.'

Another idyllic evening, another perfect meal, kokoda this time, marinated raw kahawai, then kingfish steaks, how good does it get.

Steve and Rachel are staying out for another couple of days, the forecast is good, taking advantage of the good weather. We'll go ashore in the morning and continue our trip around the island.

Bedtime and Ariana is all over me, she's in an incredibly sexy mood, the love making goes on and on far into the night. The day has been so perfect, so far removed from the happenings in Greece. I've found my soul mate as well.

Rattle, rattle, bang, crash, the rusty Holden is bowling along on Waiheke's gravel road heading for Peacock Sky, a vineyard, winery and restaurant up on high ground in the centre of the island next to the airfield, I've been there before, it's good. They do a very original and imaginative wine tasting and the open-air dining is first class. Our guests from Greece are lapping it up, they're impressed. There are spectacular views, constantly changing as we make our way around the island. The hidden valleys with their micro climates that make the wines from Waiheke so distinctive. The panoramic ocean views that suddenly appear and just as rapidly disappear giving way to large areas of vineyard, an ever-changing panorama. It's a lovely place Waiheke.

'From Athens?' it's the fellow running the wine tasting, 'my home town. I'm backpacking, most of the staff here are backpackers, New Zealand is a popular destination and the wineries here on Waiheke love us.'

Dimitra had started a conversation with the handsome young man. He was putting on quite a show for us demonstrating his extensive knowledge of the local wines, real or imagined, who knows, but it was a good act.

'You people will be some of my last customers, I'm off back to Athens, I'm wanted, family business undergoing some changes, pity, I like New Zealand. I'd like to stay but when the family calls I guess

I've got to go.'

'That's a shame, been here for a while?' Dimitra asks.

'About a year, had to get away from Athens, family problems, not my scene, but they want me back, so that's the end of it.'

'Well my name's Dimitra, Dimitra Galani, I live in Athens and this fellow here is Michael, my New Zealand fiancé, you are my fiancé Michael, right?'

'Galani, that sounds familiar, I'm sure I know that name from somewhere. I'm Elios Maniot, my family live in Athens.

I'm party to this conversation, when he says he's a Maniot I really pay attention. Surely not 'that' Maniot family. Family problems, wanted to get away, and now he's wanted back in Athens. Could it be the problems we had in Athens are making ripples in far off New Zealand. I say nothing, not sure if Dimitra is aware that the Maniots may be involved in our Greek problem. I notice Christos is paying close attention to this conversation.

Elios puts on a good show, a wine tasting with a difference. I think he was rather taken by Dimitra, who wouldn't, she's a beautiful girl and a strong personality.

*She also runs around secluded beaches with no cloths on. Cut it out Frank, you're becoming a dirty old man. No I'm not, it's just that she's such an arousing sight with no clothes on.*

Just as well I had Ariana and Karisa at Owhiti, the sight of the naked Dimitra was a bit much to take.

We seat ourselves at a trestle table under a big awning and enjoy a Peacock Sky lunch, it's good, a large selection of cold dishes. There are spectacular views in all directions from the hilltop location and again our guests are blown away, some chilled savvy, life is complete.

'Frank, I think I want to live in Auckland with you, would you like that?'

'All things are possible Ariana. We could live in both places, now there's a thought, what's this living with me bit though?'

'Frank, I want to live with you, I really do.'

This could be life changing, and for the better, Ariana is 'my kind of girl' and living a solitary life is not the greatest. I've been lonely since losing Ginetta, need to give it some serious thought.

We're back in the old Holden rattling our way to the ferry, back to the city, a lovely trip on the boat, another of Auckland's attractions. It's hot again, we'll need that pool when we get back to the house in Parnell.

It's G strings and topless, we're in suburbia but it's very secluded. There's an air of familiarity, intimacy almost, and it's nice. The Waiheke experience was a good insight into the New Zealand life style, well the Auckland lifestyle, the guests from Greece loved it; more please.

'Now then, how about a trip down country, Rotorua, all good visitors go to Rotorua, it's a 'must do,' different. We could crack off in the morning.'

Rebecca appears, 'Whoops, bit daring, you girls will be getting these fellows all worked up.'

'Could be Rebecca, want to join us?'

'Not really, just dropped by to check. The house has been empty for a couple of days, no idea where you were, have a work assignment, can't stay, didn't bring my G string either.'

Another enjoyable afternoon in the pool, the skies stay clear and it remains hot, bit unusual, Auckland is notorious for its changeable weather, 'every day is different.' We are into the wine again. Later we go along to one of Parnell's better restaurants. We're doing a lot of eating here in Auckland, but it's good, why not.

'It's all so green.' The big Merc this time, same car as Christos's, seats the six of us. Do all retired detectives drive big Mercs? We're on our way to Rotorua, left the motorway at Pokeno, we're now on state highway twenty-seven, our guests are impressed by the greenness of the countryside, Waikato, dairy country.

'All these cows, there are so many, and all the grass, different to Greece, very different.' Karisa is impressed.

We check into a motel, 'right, the sights. We'll do the tourist thing, they do it well in Rotorua, you'll like it.' I'm looking forward to it as well, been a while, need to catch up.

Another good day, Maori kids diving off a bridge for coins, boiling pools, hot mud, geysers large and small, the all permeating sulphur smell, a walk through a traditional village with a Maori guide, all good stuff and the best bit, a cultural show, a good one. Plenty of singing, poi twirling, ferocious hakas, dancing, I thoroughly enjoy it all and our guests? stunned mullet is an expression that comes to mind.

That evening we buy into a Maori hangi and again it's well done, nothing touristy about this one. It's late when we get to bed. Ariana's in a sexy mood, another night of excess, yes I want to live with this lady.

Breakfast, we wander along to a nearby café that's been recommended and while I'm enjoying eggs benny I notice a glaring headline on a nearby newspaper stand, *Brutal Murder On Waiheke,* Christos notices it as well. Don't want to upset the girls, could be anything, not our concern but there was a Maniot on Waiheke, that's why it's caught our attention. I go over to the newsstand, buy a paper and tuck it away, I'll read it when I get a chance. Apparently someone has been murdered at the Peacock Sky winery in a particularly gruesome way. Don't want to put a dampener on the day but shit, what's happened. That was a Maniot boy working at Peacock Sky, possibly a member of the Maniots we're interested in, we need to find out some detail. I'll get onto my police contact in Auckland, see what he knows. If it is the Maniot boy does this have any significance for Michael, is he in danger?

'Ok girls, today we're going to Taupo, it's a lovely drive. When we get there it's a jet boat ride and a cruise on the lake, you'll like it.'

I'm finding it hard to concentrate, that newspaper headline has got me worried, I need to talk to my police contact in Auckland.

It is indeed a lovely drive to Taupo, all green and lush, our visitors are impressed, again. We book a ride on the Taupo Rapids Jet Boat, a real blast, screaming stuff, and the girls certainly scream; they love it, so do I. Lunchtime. While our group are enjoying lunch I get on the phone, it's not good news. My contact in Auckland CIB is not very forthcoming. At this early stage not much is known but it appears to have been a contract hit, very professional. The victim, Elios Maniot, a Greek national. Shit, it is the Maniot boy. Apparently the victim had been strung up by his feet in the winery tasting room, disemboweled and his throat cut, it appeared the killer had gone to some lengths to make the killing as gruesome as possible. Shit it's a hit alright, probably connected to the gang war resulting from the wedding massacre. I tell my contact some of what I know about the Maniots and their rivals in Athens, he sounds surprised, suddenly he's very interested.

'Frank, we need to talk, can you come and see us as soon as you can, you probably know a lot more about this than we do, we need to pick your brains.'

Suddenly doing the tourist thing takes a back seat, we need to get back to Auckland, how can I put it to them?

'Now then after lunch we'll do a trip on the lake, there's some rock carving on a cliff at a place called Ngatoroirrangi Mine Bay, can you get your tongue around that one? Bit of trout fishing but you'll probably find it a bit ordinary. You'll catch trout but it's not in the same league as those snapper you caught out on the gulf, and your kingfish Ariana, that was something. Tomorrow we need to go back to Auckland, something's come up that requires my attention. We can start thinking about our South Seas holiday as well, how does all that sound?'

We're back in the pool, late afternoon, we've just driven up from Taupo, another hot day. I have a meeting with the police first thing in the morning, they want to talk to Michael as well. Interpol are in on the act. I'm wondering if that's good or bad. Will have to tell the others what's happening after all they are party to the terrible events that happened in Stamna, the events we are trying to distance ourselves from.

'Murdered,' Dimitra is shocked, 'how can that be?'

'No idea Dimitra, should know a bit more tomorrow.'

'But he was just a young backpacker, how could he be involved in that business in Stamna?'

'Looks like he's a member of *that* Maniot family and I suspect there's a gang war being waged right now in Greece.'

'Is Michael in danger, is he involved?' Dimitra is becoming quite distraught.

'Unlikely but gang fallouts can result in indiscriminate killing, anyone on the other side. The sheer brutality involved in this one is probably meant to send a message, but who to?'

Dimitra's upset, the young fellow she had been talking to at Peacock Sky, the lad who did such a good job of entertaining us with his wine tasting, strung up and butchered in the most horrific way. Michael, is he safe? will they come after him, and why? He has no allegiance to any of the warring parties his only involvement was with the Düzgüns and only because he was under duress, but would the other parties know that or would he be just another Düzgün, another target. We need to contact Nico in Athens, get the inside story.

'Christos, we need you to get onto Nico if that's possible, we need to find out who's killing who, see if he thinks Michael could be in danger? and what about Carrie?'

'You're right Frank, you folk enjoy yourselves in the pool, if that's possible, I'll get onto Nico.'

The fun's gone out of the day, even the girls in their G strings no longer cause a stirring in the loins. Bugger, how can we shake ourselves free from this Greek business.

'Frank Conchie, what have you been up to in Greece?' It's an old mate in Auckland CIB, Peter Culpan. 'This your boy Michael?'

We spend the next hour giving him a full run down of what has taken place in Greece, all the unpleasant detail, the killings, the drug dealing, the stand over tactics, what we know about the Stathoses, Maniots, and Düzgüns, we also indicate that we have an 'in,' an information source in the Athens underworld. He takes it all in, information that would not be available to him if it was not for us. The Auckland Police's problem is that this brutal murder has happened on their patch, they are obliged to solve it, our input is invaluable.

'Ok, now you tell us, what do you think has happened in this case?'

'Well officially I can't say, please don't repeat what I am about to tell you. You've given us so much information that I feel obligated to reciprocate. It appears it was a professional hit with maximum violence, intended to send a message. The killer has left the country, gone before the murder was even discovered. We've been able to identify him, surveillance, immigration cameras, and facial recognition gear at the airport did spot him however this fellow was a true professional, almost evaded the lot. Radul Jaksic, a Serbian contract killer, known to Interpol. Who hired him? well you tell me. Motive? If there's a gang war going on who needs motive.'

'Thanks for that Peter, makes sense, nasty business and on your patch, I would never have thought an Athens gang fallout would reach this far, an innocent party perhaps, just belonged to the wrong family. We might have more information for you, our contact in Athens. It will be privileged information for you only, give you a better understanding of what's going on. Our contact would not want to be identified, that ok with you?

'Yep, anything will be helpful and yes we can be discreet.'

That's about it for the time being. Nico is sniffing around in Athens. Christos has spoken to him but he did not know anything except that there was indeed a nasty gang war going on. Exactly who is killing who was not clear, a lot of bodies showing up. Nico will get back to us when he's got something. Is Michael in danger, unlikely, he's not affiliated to any of the Athens gangs, and this is known. What we can do now is plan our Island holiday.

# *Michael*

Home, Auckland, been a while, now there's Dimitra, I'm in love. It was never like this with Carrie but how was I to know what real love was like? Was it sex? well that was a big part of it, but Dimitra? it's a whole new experience. With her it's fantastic but there's a lot more than that, real emotional involvement, the sex, it's on a whole new level, there's a huge amount of feeling.

The trip over to Waiheke was something, that beach at Owhiti, running around naked with the olds, seemed such a natural thing to do, no one was embarrassed, god I love that girl. The fishing and the night on the boat up on the fly bridge under the stars, Dimitra was an absolute demon, quite out of control.

Going back to Athens? yes, I've got to be with this girl. Ariana is quite sure she'll find me employment in her organisation, probably better prospects than here in New Zealand. I'm pretty sure dad will be moving as well, he's smitten with Ariana, she's quite something. Seeing her running around with no cloths on and dad having sex, got me quite aroused, she's a sexy lady.

The killing at Peacock Sky, am I in danger? I'm not attached to any of those families in Athens, why would I be a target? I've not done anything to piss them off, but gang wars? there's always collateral damage. Will it be safe for me to go back to Athens? Is Carrie, safe? probably, why would she be a target? The Auckland Police fellow, Peter Culpan, was really interested in everything that had happened to me in Athens, I think he's trying to get the big picture. My friendly relationship with the new Düzgün boss, Yiannis Stavrou, should put me out of danger. Carrie's in the same position. Yiannis is aware of her circumstances. He did us a huge favour getting that statement about the Gorbet murder, but a gang war, there are some senseless killings. The idea now is to take off for Tonga, Vava'u is the place. Mounu Island for a few days, a true South Seas hideaway.

# Tonga

We phone Nico again. A couple of days have passed, a couple of very pleasant days. Auckland is being kind, warm and sunny, plenty of time by the pool, eating out in Parnell and down at the Viaduct. Took the ferry across to Coromandel and the dolphins laid on a show out in the gulf. Now, about the unpleasantness in Athens.

Nico's been busy. It's not clear who was the perpetrator of the massacre. Each of the three families suspects the other two, there's been a wave of killing. Nico's opinion, it was Yiannis Stavrou, the Düzgün fellow who master minded it. Elios Maniot's murder in far off New Zealand made big headlines in the Athens papers, there were a couple of gruesome pictures. The Stathoses have no leader. There were rumours that one of Leonidos's lieutenants was responsible for the massacre, had grand ideas of taking over, however, this fellow was found in an alley with his throat cut. The killing has slowed but there's an ominous development. Leonidos has a brother, Janus, he's Paris based and he's into all sorts of crime. Janus has turned up in Athens. The word is he intends to take over the Stathos family business, there's been an attempt on his life already.

'So, you people down in the South Seas, stay there; it's a can of worms in Athens, why would you want to be here.' Nico's advice.

'Ok folks, the Islands, Tonga, specifically Mounu in the Vava'u group, the most romantic spot in the South Seas, believe me, I've been there. Give me a day and I'll organise it.'

There's going to be a delay, Mounu's full. There are only four fales on the small piece of corral that is Mounu. They're all booked for the next seven days then there's a five day opening, we'll take it, three fales. Onto the airlines, bookings, all done, seven days here in Auckland before our South Seas odyssey.

'I've got an idea, a mate of mine has got a place at Pataua, a small community out on the coast just past Whangarei, it's a great spot, a real Kiwi bach, you'll like it, different.'

We're sacked out on the big ocean beach at Pataua, the waves are crashing in, it's windy, there's grunt in the waves. The sound of the ocean, the seagulls screeching overhead, it's great.

'Come on, into the water, let's get pummelled by the surf.'
The big waves toss us around, so refreshing. I don't think the girls have experienced anything like this before, they're loving it. It's a long wide beach backed up by sandhills, wild and rugged. A walk, you can walk for miles along this beach, it just goes on forever. There's a rocky outcrop at one point covered with mussels, green lips, the good eating one. We pull some off and bundle them up in a beach towel one of the girls has brought along, supper later. We continue on, it's just so lovely, remote, not a soul in sight.

'Come on, into the tide again, everything off,' it's Karisa. Being so close to nature has turned her on. It's a good idea. Being thrown about in the surf naked is quite a sensation, and the girls, the very attractive girls, are a sight to behold.

The afternoon passes quickly, time to go back to the bach, cocktail hour. Behind the sandhills are some large pipi beds in a tidal lagoon. We stop and puddle around with our feet dredging up some pretty good pipis, it'll be shellfish tonight.

A great meal, green lip mussels in the shell, all you can eat, pipi fritters, as many as you can handle, all cooked on a big black Shacklock wood burner, an institution in a true Kiwi bach. Sitting out under the stars after dinner with a beer Christos and myself get to talking about the situation in Athens.

'Christos what's your take on the Maniot lad being murdered, does not seem to make sense, who was the message intended for?'

'Could be any of several scenarios. If either the Stathoses or the Düzgüns suspected that the Maniots were wanting in on the meth business then sending them a strong message makes sense. Which family it actually was, your guess! If the massacre was the work of rogue elements within the Stathoses or Düzgüns then it could be a message to tell the Maniots to stay out of it while they sort themselves out but really who cares, the more they kill each other the better.'

Janus Stathos, Leonidos's brother, what's his involvement, is he just trying to capitalise on the situation or was he involved in the massacre. The more we think about it the more possibilities there are, but really why are we concerned? Well there's Michael and Carrie. Could the current bloodletting extend to them? unlikely, but common sense can be the first casualty in situations like this. We are going to be away from Athens for some time our only real worry is for Carrie, but what can we do?

'Let's change the subject Frank, tell me about Mounu, it's going to be way beyond anything I've experienced by the sound of it.'

'It's different alright, very different, you'll love it Christos and I'm sure it will send Karisa right off her trolly, reinvigorate your relationship perhaps.'

'Dosen't need reinvigorating Frank, believe me, we get on just fine but I must admit seeing Ariana running around naked does cause my blood pressure to rise, very tempting but she's yours Frank, you lucky fellow. I think Karisa might just be a little envious, she fancies you, but tell me more about Mounu.'

'Well Ginetta and I had a holiday there some years ago, it's one of the world's premier whale watching places and that's a tremendous draw card. Each year humpbacks migrate from the Antarctic to Tonga to give birth. The lagoon around Mounu is one of the places where it happens. You can swim with the whales right there in the lagoon. It's what draws whale watchers from all over the world. We're lucky to get accommodation, the place has very high occupancy for most of the year. A lot of the action happens right in front of the little resort. You can sit on the deck with a beer and watch humpbacks and their calves cavorting around right in front of you, not many places in the world where you can do that.'

We enjoy two more days at Pataua, do a bit of fishing off the beach and would you believe Christos lands a really big snapper, right out of the surf.

'Get this on your iPhone, have to live up to those bullshit photographs.'

'No bullshit Christos.'

More mussels, pipis, fish, more being pummelled by the surf, a bit of sex in the sandhills behind the beach. Ariana loves it, reminds me of my youth, the sandhills behind New Brighton beach in Christchurch, then we head back to Auckland.

There's a call from Nico, not good news. Janos Stathos is making waves. Leonidos has made a slight recovery, he's been talking to his brother. It appears Janos could be taking over the Stathos family operation. There'a another wave of killing, this time a turf war with the Düzgüns. The other thing, Carrie. Leonidos is still alive, will he try and exert his influence over her again, or will he convince Janos to use her? does not sound good. We do have the sworn admission absolving Carrie, we could be needing it. I tell Nico about how Yiannis Stavrou, the new Düzgün boss, had indicated to us that he could possibly hasten Leonidos's demise. In light of this new development perhaps it would be helpful to Carrie if this happened, does Nico have any influence? No he doesn't. Yiannis is favourably disposed towards Michael and he's aware of Carrie's situation, he also appears to be a nice guy, well if you can stretch your imagination; a ruthless gang leader being a nice guy.

'Nico, can you make something happen?'

'Doubt it but all things are possible.'

Nico's call is a bit of a dampener, only he and myself are privy to what's been said. We decide to keep this new development to ourselves, no need to worry Michael or the girls.

We have a few days before we head off to Tonga, what about a trip around the Coromandel, real scenic New Zealand, great beaches, forests, impress our guests, great idea.

We set off early next morning in the big Merc and the weather changes, cracks up big time, heavy rain, bit of hail, some thunder and the wind, a howling nor-easter, remnants of a tropical cyclone that's come down from the north, it's hammering the east coast.

'Whoops, sorry about this, won't last long, these things usually blow through in a day.' *I hope.*

We drive to Thames in heavy rain, not the greatest, then the Kopu-Hikuai road through the Coromandel hills closes, slips and road subsidence, the heavy rain continues, we'll need to spend a night in Thames.

'Have I got an experience for you, a night in an original old goldmining hotel.'

Well that's not quite true. Thames still has a few old wooden hotels from the goldmining days back in the eighteen hundreds. There used to be more than a hundred of them. The Brian Boru on the main street, an eighteen-hundreds classic. Big two story wooden building with a tin roofed veranda right around, big rooms, high ceilings and big fans, no ensuites, it's down the hall, shared. Three adjacent rooms on the first floor and a shared veranda, all the guests share the big veranda, it goes right around the hotel. Our Greek guests look a little taken aback, bit different alright, not quite the *Iconic Santorini.*

No ensuites but there are room bars, different. We sit out on the big veranda, six of us in old cane lounge chairs and enjoy a drink, the rain is pouring down, drumming on the tin roof, welcome to the Coromandel, it rains a lot. The big veranda is all ours, there do not appear to be any other guests.

'Well Frank, this is different, rather nice,' Ariana gives me a hug.

'There's a big iron framed bed in there, wonder what that will be like?' another hug and a cheeky smile.

Dimitra is quite enthusiastic. 'This is so different, I like it, so green and natural and there's gold in those hills behind us?'

'Yes there is and what's more you can get yourself a genuine goldminers pan at the local store and have a go in the local streams, there's every chance you might find a little gold dust. A lot of gold was taken from around here in the eighteen hundreds and the locals would have you believe there's still a lot more to be had.'

The rain continues. We enjoy a few more drinks on the veranda then it's early evening, we seek out the hotel dining room. A big last century affair and surprisingly there are quite a few diners, locals, the Brian Boru's dining room has a good reputation. It is a good meal, roast lamb, they know how to do it in Thames. Real Kiwiana, our Greek friends love it.

'Frank, about the weather,' it's Christos.

'The moment the rain eases the local council will be right onto reopening the road, it's a frequent occurrence here. I think we'll find the Hikuai road will be usable by midday tomorrow.'

She can't help herself, I'm loving it as well. Ariana's just got to make love in the old iron bed. There's a big soft mattress and the iron frame creaks and groans a lot as we go at it. I think Ariana is a bit carried away by the pioneer atmosphere of the place. Eventually we're spent, lying there enjoying the glow, the aftermath of sex. There's this noise coming from the next room, a bed creaking and groaning, bit like ours, hmm.

A fine warm morning, the bad weather has moved on down the coast but it's left its mark, the Kopu-Hikuai road is in bad shape. Not a problem, well it will be a bit of a problem, however, the local council are familiar with this and are right onto it. There are several slips and a section of road is half washed away but we are able to negotiate our way around the mess with the aid of some very helpful council workers. Our 'tourist' friends are quite impressed with the helpful attitude of the road workers, welcome to the Coromandel!

Tairua, across the estuary from Pauanui, we stop for a coffee and a look around. The wild weather has generated a big easterly swell. The Tairua bar is looking dangerous, more so than usual. While we are watching a big launch heads out into it, he's taking a risk, the Tairua bar is notorious. Over the years many boats have broached attempting to cross it and today it looks really dangerous. The fellow helming the launch must know a thing or two. The big boat rears up at some crazy angles but the skipper manages to control it and gets across the breaking seas out into calmer water, quite a display of seamanship.

'You Kiwis are crazy.' Christos's take on it.

'You could be right Christos but we do have big fish and they bite right after bad weather.'

We drive on up the coast, green and bush clad, lots of ferns and pongas, little bays, panoramic views of bush, beach and ocean, our guests are loving it, turn right for Hahei, a beach community with a spectacular rock formation, Cathedral Cove.

'Come on we'll do the bush walk along to the Cove, bring your swimming gear, there's a good beach and usually a lot of tourists, no skinny dipping.'

It is indeed spectacular, a big hole, bit like a cave, that goes right through a rock promontory projecting out across a fine sandy beach to the ocean. We walk through the hole, it's huge, and marvel at the sight. I'm enjoying this, been a while since I visited the Coromandel. It's hot, a swim's the story, careful, there can be undertows. There's quite a bit of surf, leftover from the recent bad weather and the waves really whack us around, great. Back along the bush walk to Hahei.

Whitianga and a motel that's been recommended, only one unit left, two bedrooms, one bathroom, we take it, modesty no longer a consideration.

The Mercury Bay Game Fishing Club, incredibly popular, the 'go to' place. We get cleaned up, showered etc, one bathroom. The girls running around with nothing on, well virtually nothing, I think they are doing it deliberately, slightly amused by the boys reaction. Along to the Club.

'Frank,' an old police mate from Auckland, 'what are you doing here and who are these lovely ladies?'

Introductions all around. Bob Simmonds, ex Auckland CIB. He's a handsome fellow Bob, I recall how popular he was with the ladies.

'All from Athens Bob, Christos is ex Athens CIB so we have something in common.'

'Interesting Frank, but Whitianga? what brings you all to this place?'

'Tourists Bob, showing them New Zealand, I've been over in Athens enjoying their hospitality, returning the favour.'

'Christos,' it's Bob, 'Athens CIB? you'll know all about their criminal underworld, tell me what's your take on that murder on Waiheke the other day, it was a Greek fellow from Athens, I hear he was a member of a Greek crime syndicate, that true?'

Whoops, better close this conversation down; not to worry Christos is onto it.

'Don't know Bob, I'm out of it these days, don't want to know either, pretty nasty business by the sound of it.'

'Yes it was by all accounts, not the sort of thing that happens here, I guess all will be revealed one day. Now then how about a beer or two, and the ladies, what's it to be girls?'

That was the start of it. The Game Fishing Club was indeed the 'go to' place. It soon became packed, nearly all locals. Bob had a bach in Whitianga so he qualified as a local. In no time a big school of drinkers had gathered around our group, I think our ladies, our very attractive ladies, had something to do with it.

'Right, listen up.' A chap was up on a table commanding everyone's attention. 'Toss the chicken time.' 'What?'

Bob explains. The idea is to buy tickets in a raffle that's circulating amongst the crowd, when all the tickets are sold there's a draw. The lucky number holder will be somewhere in the crush of people, he shouts out and the fellow on the table chucks a frozen chicken in his direction. 'Chuck a chook,' he's expected to catch it, usually fails. It's a frozen chicken, quite heavy, there's plenty of potential for physical damage. There are several draws and quite a bit of 'chucking' with varying degrees of success. An air of hilarity engulfs the place. Our visitors are a little wide eyed at all this, New Zealand is different. There's food and we manage a bite or two in amongst the crush.

It's a great evening, a lot of drinking, it's that kind of place. The girls are right into it. Numerous fellows strike up conversations with them, who wouldn't, they are very attractive, they love every minute of it.

'Frank, these people are so friendly, this is such a fun place, we could live here couldn't we?' Ariana's a bit carried away.

Dimitra was really attracting the boys, just as well her relationship with Michael is rock solid, these lads were trying hard.

Back to the motel, bit tipsy, we decide the boys will sleep in one bedroom the girls in the other, keep things respectable, and that's what happens.

'We'll spend today at the beach, Otama, one of the best around, not far, a spectacular drive as well.'

We get some picnic things from the local supermarket. Black Jack Road, not for the faint hearted. More panoramic scenes of valleys and coastline and eventually Otama, a fine white sand beach, gentle surf, pohutukawa trees the full length, and not a soul in sight.

'All over tan, ok with you fellows?'

The girls strip off and stretch out on some beach towels, this could be difficult.

Toot, toot, another car, we're going to have to share our beach. A group of young people. They notice us and move along to the far end, our privacy is restored. No need to worry, I notice they're all stripping off. It's not long before there are sounds of hilarity coming from the interlopers, they're all fooling around in the water naked. What are we going to do? I'm having trouble, the usual trouble that girls with no cloths on cause. Into the water, some vigorous swimming, it works, I'm able to rejoin the sunbathers. The sun is warm, it's a lovely environment, an erotic one as well., how long will I be able to control myself, Ariana looks so sexy lying there naked.

Another car, more people, the beach is a bit too popular, some decorum is needed, the girls solve the problem, they don G strings, it does nothing to reduce my blood pressure, they look even sexier. Mid-afternoon, we are enjoying a wine or two, I get talking with Ariana, her life before I came on the scene. There had been a husband, Alain, a friend of Karisas's man Nikias, they had business dealings together.

'A few years ago now. Nikias was murdered, never solved but it's suspected he was involved with the Stathoses meth business. Karisa is pretty sure that Leonidos was responsible for Nikias's demise. Alain was found drowned shortly after. He was a good swimmer, his drowning does not stack up, foul play was suspected but never proven. How well these two deaths were investigated is a moot point. The Athens Police have been compromised by the Stathos family for a long time. Karisa has not let the matter go, she wants revenge for Nikias's death and I too want Alain's drowning solved. There was a large payment made to Karisa shortly after Nikias was killed, adds fuel to the fire, why was he murdered? I know Karisa has feelers out. She has gathered a lot of information about both deaths, there will be a day of reckoning.'

'Another swim folks, then we can think about tackling the Black Jack again.'

Lukes Kitchen at Kuaotunu where the Black Jack joins state highway twenty-five, a must visit, great pizzas and locally brewed beer, Riwakasaurus Rex, we eat up big. It's well into evening when we get back to Whitianga, a couple of beers out on the balcony and we get talking again.

It's Karisa. 'You people are so lucky living here, why would you want to come and live in Athens?' why indeed, she makes a good point.

'It's you girls, you've got us hooked, Michael and myself. Does not have to be all Athens, we have the place here, all you have to do is jump on a big jet. We can live in both places, you too, and Christos.'

'Food for thought, a lot of thought, thanks for the offer Frank.'
'There's a lot more to do here yet, big game fishing up north, down south the Marlborough Sounds, the West Coast, but right now we need to get back to Auckland, Tonga, remember, we're going to Tonga, a whole new experience.

Tua'amotu Airport on Tongatapu, we've arrived in Tonga. The big jet has brought us here, now a little aeroplane will take us to Vava'u away to the north. There will be a delay, the little aeroplane has not showed and it's a bit difficult trying to find out when it will be here. Slow down, Tonga time, stop worrying, it will be here, sometime. A couple of hours later the little aeroplane arrives, good we're off. Not so fast there will be a further delay, a fault that has to be fixed. Another hour, right we're off. Not so fast, there has to be an air test, no pilot. Another half hour, a pilot arrives. Not a place for the impatient.

Finally we're airborne. The pilot advises we'll be stopping at Ha'apai to pick up a passenger for Vava'u. Different, never been to Ha'apai. A lot of very good All Blacks come from Ha'apai, must be something in the water.

No passenger, further delay, 'the truck broke down.' Finally, many hours after arriving in the Kingdom of Tonga we land at Vava'u. A rattly old truck left over from the war takes us into Neiafu the local town, the only town. It's suggested we kill an hour or so at the Bounty, a waterfront bar 'with character.' The boat from Mounu will be along to take us to the island later.

Character alright, straight out of last century, all that's missing, a couple of real pirates but looking at the people in the bar perhaps there are real pirates here. It's an old tumble down wooden building on a bit of high ground overlooking the waterfront, the view? rusty tin roofs, overgrown alleys and a lot of rubbish strewn around, the interior was not much better but the place had character, a real South Seas dump. We get some beers from the wild looking fellow behind the bar, seat ourselves, and absorb the ambience of the place. A whole new experience for me, what our guests were thinking I can only imagine. The view out over the waterfront into the late afternoon sun however is quite spectacular, the real South Seas.

A boat arrives, a big tinnie with an even bigger outboard motor. Mounu written all over it, must be ours. The character driving it, is he for real? A scrawny looking chap of indeterminate age sporting the biggest beard I've ever seen, a shaggy grey mass stretching down to his waist with two wild looking eyes buried in the mass of whiskers, black singlet, scruffy shorts and bare feet. He looks up and spots us in the Bounty.

'You the folk I'm looking for? stay there, I'll be right up.'
Larger than life, character to burn, Hollywood could not match this fellow. When he enters the bar he totally dominates the place, his 'presence' is incredible.

'I'm Allan, I'm you host for as long as you're here, another beer?' Allan's waving his hand at the barman, 'lazy bugger, needs a rocket up his arse, place has gone to the pack since he took over from me, used to be the smartest bar around.'

The folk from Greece are 'gobsmacked,' that's the best description I can think of.

Allan owns Mounu, started it from scratch, it's now the leading whale watching operation in the Pacific. Allan's a Kiwi, spent years shark fishing on the Kaipara harbour, now he takes tourists out to watch the humpbacks and their calves right in front of his little island paradise. Behind the rough exterior there's a real character. Smart cookie Allan, an extremely likable fellow, bodes well for our sojourn at Mounu.

We're zipping along in the big tinnie, Mounu is some distance from Neiafu, on the outer fringe of the Vava'u group. Allan has a unique driving style. He's standing on the helmsman's seat with his head stuck up through a hatch in the canopy top, he's steering with one foot and wasting no time.

'Welcome to paradise, mocktails or the real thing?' it's Lynne, Allan's wife, they run the place. It's paradise, well it's how I imagine paradise to be. The quintessential South Seas coral island, Mounu, a patch of coral covered in coconut palms, four fales, a central bar and dining room and a big veranda, walk right around the island in fifteen minutes, heaven on earth. It's all ours, only one other couple and they are leaving tomorrow, I wonder how the girls will react, the place is incredible, far removed from the rest of the world, exotic!

'The idea is to do whatever you want,' it's Allan giving us a briefing. 'There are four others on the island, three staff, all locals, and Kirsty, our daughter, our tearaway daughter.' The words are hardly out of his mouth when Kirsty arrives, an attractive girl, mid-twenties, she has 'presence,' bit like her father.

'What have we here,' Kirsty's first words, 'some handsome men and some beautiful ladies, could liven things up a bit.'

What does that mean, what's Kirsty got in mind?

We spend an hour on the big veranda looking out over the lagoon as the sun sinks into a spectacular sunset.

'Dinner will be when you want it, an hour or so perhaps, that ok?' Lynne asks.

We go along to our fale, there are only four of them, spread around the island, total privacy. Each has its own patch of perfect beach and crystal clear water. There's no stopping Ariana, the cloths go flying and she's into the ocean. We fool around for a while, Ariana's quite carried away by the atmosphere, so am I. We retreat to the fale, a big bed surrounded with mosquito netting, quite a setting for our first love making in paradise.

'Five days of this Frank, can we just make love for five days, do we need to do anything else, this is so nice, the nicest thing I've ever experienced. I think I'm falling in love; with you Frank.'

Dinner out on the veranda under a perfect tropical night sky, every sort of seafood imaginable. We're a bit late getting along to dinner, it was hard dragging ourselves away from that big bed, we are not alone, the others are a bit late as well, guilty looks all round. Our hosts were not in the least put out I reckon they see this all the time. I mean how could you not be carried away; five more days! We sit out on the veranda for several hours, put a dent in the resort's wine cellar. The other couple on the island, the ones leaving in the morning, are honeymooners, been here four days and chastising themselves for not making it four weeks.

'It's just perfect,' was their take on the place.

'Tomorrow I suggest you might like to go across to the sandbar, dog will show you the way.' Allan's suggestion.

'Dog?'

'Yes dog, loves the sandbar, swims out there frequently, likes company. You can wade across, it's not far. We'll give you a picnic hamper, you'll love it and so will dog.'

It just gets better, a big sandbar in what appears to be the middle of nowhere, it's a given, no cloths required. Quite a day, several hours on the sandbar frolicking around naked. There's wine in the resort's hamper, quite a lot, it's necessary to keep the body hydrated. Too much wine, hot sun, secluded sandbar, not sure what dog must have thought, a lot of intimacy, couldn't help ourselves.

'God I like the South Seas,' an opinion expressed by all of us.

Around mid-afternoon Kirsty bursts on the scene, she's kite boarding and makes a fast pass by the sandbar.

'Hi there, what are you folks up to, perhaps I can join in. Don't be embarrassed all our guests do it, how could they not. On second thoughts perhaps I won't, don't see a spare man.' She speeds off across the lagoon. 'Cheeky.'

Dinner that evening, another seafood banquet out on the veranda, Kirsty joins us.

'Enjoy your day on the sandbar?' There's a provocative edge in her voice.

'Yep, sure did, you should have joined us Kirsty, we could have pulled you pants down.'

'Bugger, missed opportunity.'

Allan arrives, 'here's something you folk might be interested in. I've had a call from Nuku'alofa, they want me to check on a volcano.'

'Excuse me Allan, did I hear correctly, check on a volcano?'

'Yep, you heard correctly. There's some underwater volcanic activity about fifty miles northwest of here, a vast area of pumice has been reported floating on the ocean surface, they think it's associated with an underwater eruption and they want me to check, see what I can find, if anything, interested?'

'Well that is something, of course we're interested, fifty miles you say.'

'Yep, it's quite a way but our tinnie does forty knots on a calm day and the sea is flat right now, should not take long, want to come along?'

'Do we ever, exploring live volcanoes in the South Seas, different.'

We're rocketing along, Allan's tinnie really does do forty on a calm day, and it is calm, dead flat water, the girls are with us.

'What a story when we get back to Athens.'

Pieces of pumice start appearing on the surface and this rapidly becomes a dense raft stretching to the horizon, there's a strong smell of sulfur. We slow down, the pumice is quite abrasive on the hull. It's an incredible sight, I've never seen anything like it in my life.

'What's your take on it Allan?'

'There's been an eruption alright, quite recent I'd say, I've seen this before, a couple of years ago. This pumice raft will be around for a couple of weeks then gradually disperse, it's a navigation hazard. Nuku'alofa want all the information we can gather.'

We work our way to what appears to be the edge of the pumice raft and try and get some idea of just how extensive it is.

'Allan, can't Nuku'alofa get access to satellite imaging or aerial surveillance,' I ask.

'Money, Tonga is broke and we are at the end of the earth. No one cares what happens down here, not much charity in the international community. NASA will have all the satellite imagery you could ever wish for but they are not great on sharing, would give away too much about their capability. Nuku'alofa want as much information as possible so they can alert shipping about the potential danger.'

We run around for a couple of hours estimating the size of the pumice raft, it's big, around twenty kilometres across and there's what appears to be steam hanging around near the centre, there's still some underwater activity.

'That's enough, won't hang around too long, this thing's still active, don't want to be here if it goes bang.'

The girls are fascinated, they gather up several pieces of pumice. What a souvenir, a piece of rock just ejected from an active underwater volcano in the South Seas, great conversation piece back in Athens.

Back to Mounu, it's been a long day, as we approach the Island there are two humpback whales and two calves close to the beach. This is what the world comes to Tonga to see and here it is right in front of the little resort.

'Hop in, it's quite safe,' from Allan, 'believe me, the whales know there's no threat from humans, just swim around normally, that's if your nerves let you, let the whales come to you.'

No swim costumes, we strip down to our underwear and hop over the side, it's a sexy sight, the girls in their knickers but this time the whales put those thoughts right out of our minds. It's incredible, the two calves are inquisitive and come in quite close. The two adult whales keep a discreet distance, let the calves do their thing. It goes on for half an hour or more, the calves swimming around us apparently fascinated and us just hanging in the water hardly able to believe our eyes. Eventually, their curiosity satisfied, the whales move away and leave us hanging in the water struggling to comprehend what has just taken place.

Back on the big veranda, need a beer, it's been a long day. It's hard to take in everything that we have experienced. Out in the lagoon the whales are still swimming around, what a place, I think our Greek visitors are gobsmacked, again, so am I.

There's a yacht moored just off the beach, visitors, Italians, walking around the island at the moment, will be back here shortly. They are doing the 'sailing the Pacific' thing, heard about this place, want to stay for dinner. The Italians are hard looking dudes, two middle aged couples. They appear to want to keep to themselves, not that keen on joining us for a drink however they are forced into it, it's not a big veranda, we get to talking. Bit vague about where they have been and where they are going which is unusual, most blue water sailors are keen to talk about their travels. Not getting good vibes from the Italians. I notice Allan is keeping his distance, not like him. I corner Allan out in the kitchen.

'What do you make of the Italians.'

'Not good, I got a message from Nuku'alofa a couple of days ago to keep an eye open for a yacht with Italians on board, could be somewhere near Vava'u, apparently it's being monitored by Interpol. Sailed from Colombia a couple of weeks ago, your guess is as good as mine. It's not rocket science, got to be cocaine. I'll be talking to Nuku'alofa shortly, they want all they can get on what we discovered today. The Italians? that will get their attention as well.

Let's engage the Italians in conversation, you can try your detective skills, so can Christos.'

We invite the Italians to join us for a drink, they can't say no, it would be too unusual but they are not comfortable. The girls and Michael know nothing about our suspicions and ply the Italians with questions, I mean sailing the Pacific in a yacht, that's Hollywood stuff. 'Where have they come from, where are they going.' Not many answers forthcoming. About an hour on and the Italians have a bit of a meeting, they decide they no longer want to stay for dinner.

'That's a pity,' it's Lynne, 'we've catered for an extra four guests, sure you don't want to stay?'

'No, no, we have to go,' and they pick themselves up and leave abruptly. Christos gives me a look, 'crooks, written all over them.'

Half an hour later they up anchor and sail off into the night.

'Hope they know what they're doing,' from Allan, 'would not catch me sailing around here in the dark, bad enough during the day, too many uncharted reefs.'

Another magnificent feast, Lynne and the local girls who help around the place can certainly cook. We sit up late into the night, it's been such an eventful day. An undersea volcano, all that pumice, and the whales, it was all so far out, incredible memories for life, great stories to tell. The Italians, what's the story there? Allan has been talking to Nuku'alofa, they are very interested in the Italians. There's a patrol boat headed our way, they want to catch the Italian yacht in Tongan waters and search it. Bit of drug running by the sound of it. 'Hey we are supposed to be distancing ourselves from that sort of thing.' We keep it from the girls, don't want to spoil things, besides it does not involve us.

Early morning in paradise, Ariana and myself are swimming around in the lagoon just outside our very private fale, nothing on, it's that sort of place, sex on the beach if you want? we want.

'Frank, what's that way out there, looks like a yacht on its side.'

It's a long way out and yes, it is a yacht, looks like it's come to grief on a reef, got to be the Italians.

Allan, Christos, and myself are zipping along in the big tinnie heading for the yacht, it appears to be hard up on a reef, yes, it's the Italian's boat and it's well and truly stuck on a coral reef. The water is flat at the moment but any wave action is going to cause major damage. The way it's stuck will make any salvage attempt extremely difficult if not impossible. There's precious little capability at Vava'u to attempt salvage. No sign of life and the dinghy's missing. They did have a decent sized rubber ducky when they came ashore at the resort. We get in close then wade over to the yacht, it's deserted. There's a hole at the waterline near the bow, I think this boat's days are numbered, destined to become a wreck stuck on a coral reef in the South Seas. We climb aboard, no sign of life, looks like they've taken off in the dinghy, but where to and why? Inside the cabin there are a few things lying around. We have a really good search, bit suspicious about what they had been up to but there's nothing to find, if they are smugglers then they've taken whatever it was with them. Our conclusion, and remember, apart from Allan, we are experienced in these matters, drug running from Columbia. They've taken the goods and scarpered, but again, where to? Vava'u is a long way from anywhere and a rubber ducky won't hack it. My guess, they'll try and steal a yacht, that could put people in danger. These Italians are probably ruthless. Suddenly this business has taken a potentially dangerous turn. Our South Seas holiday is turning into something else, something we are trying to distance ourselves from.

'Ok, back to Mounu, we need to put out a general warning to all boats in the area, that's going to be difficult. A lot of yachts cruising around here are out of contact with the outside world. I'll get onto Nuku'alofa, this is now a police matter.' Allan has taken command of the situation.

'We won't tell the girls, nothing to be gained, it would take the edge off their holiday.'

Nuku'alofa advise their patrol boat will be at Mounu next morning, they suspect drug running, there will be a sniffer dog on board. There's a general warning out on marine radio about the Italians, do not approach, dangerous, but there will be some yachts that will not get the message. There are countless little bays and anchorages all around Vava'u, delightful places, but completely out of radio contact. What do we do now, well nothing much, just continue to enjoy all that Mounu has to offer.

'Come on, what did you find, don't tell us there's nothing to be concerned about,' it's Karisa. So much for our bright idea to keep it from the girls.

'Ok, you win.' We give the girls a sanitised version of what we think the situation is, playing down the possibly dangerous aspect.

Lunch, another feast, at this rate the weight will be piling on. We decide to spend the afternoon lying on the beach doing nothing, a bit of snorkelling perhaps, there's magnificent coral everywhere. The place is booked out in a couple of days' time, we'll have to give it all up and go back to Auckland. That's a pity, I could stay here for ever and I think Ariana thinks the same way. What's in store for us when we do go back, not thought about it really. Do we stay in Auckland for a while then think about moving to Athens, don't know, don't want to think about it, just want to stay in this paradise with Ariana. I think I'm in love.

It's all temptation on the beach, the girls in their G strings and so secluded, I mean we can do whatever we want, indulge our wildest fantasies. The sun beating down, real warmth, adds to the ambiance of the place, raises the sexual tempo, those G strings. Michael and Dimitra move away, go further around the island, I don't think they can control the urge any longer. I'm having trouble as well, have a snooze, get your mind off sex, a sleep in the sun, away with the fairies. Frank and Karisa excuse themselves, same problem, need a little more privacy, they move away. I'm dozing, dreaming, it's lovely, this wonderful creature is upon me, moving her body sensuously up and down, the most wonderful sensation, I'm in heaven being made love to by an angel, the tempo increases, my dream angel is mightily aroused. The dream fog clears, it's real, it's Ariana, she's astride me and she's worked herself into a real state, really going at it, I find myself responding in kind. It's magnificent sex, something to be savoured. The intensity increases and I explode into her just as she reaches an intense climax.

'Oh Frank, I can't help myself, I've just got to have you.' We collapse in a heap on the sand, exhausted, the sun's beating down, this remote spot in the South Seas, this incredible sexual experience, no it's not a dream, it's real.

It's the following morning, the patrol boat from Nuku'alofa is anchored just off the beach. Two police officers come ashore, they want to talk to us. They are pleased when they find out we are retired detectives, can talk the same language, understand what goes on in the underworld. We fill them in on what we know, what we suspect, it appears we're not far off the mark. The Italians are suspected drug runners, and yes, it's probably Colombian cocaine. They want to have a look at the wrecked yacht, let their drug dog have a sniff, however, even more importantly, where are the Italians right now and what will they do. Probably try and steal a yacht, that could mean real danger to some unsuspecting yachties. We go out to the wrecked yacht in Allan's tinnie and put the dog aboard. Yes it's cocaine alright, looks like there was a lot of it. The Italians little boat will be well loaded, four people and a considerable amount of cocaine, they won't be going far.

Back to Mounu and the Police swing into action. They've got good radio gear on board and a search is initiated for the Italians' small boat. There's no aerial surveillance available, too far away from everywhere however they do indicate to us that NASA have been helpful in the past, hopefully they might come to the party on this occasion. NASA's satellites see everything but they are loth to give too much away, but drugs, that's serious stuff, here's hoping. In the meantime they are going to spend the rest of the day checking on some of the many anchorages around the Vaua'u group of islands.

Well that releases us from doing anything more in the matter, the police have it in hand, what will we do with the rest of the day?

'The Japanese coral garden and Swallows cave, you'll love it,' Allan's suggestion, 'not far from here, bring your snorkel gear, let's go.'

On one side of Kapa Island not far from Mounu there's a big cave in a cliff face extending down into deep water, crystal clear and teeming with fish, an incredible sight. We don snorkel gear and hop over the side. The cave extends in for quite a way, brightly coloured walls and very colourful underwater, we can see all the way to the bottom. We just hang in the water mesmerised. Overhead, right up in the top of the cave there are swallows, hundreds of them, it's a nesting place. We linger on in the water, it's such a remarkable place we don't want to leave.

Next, the Japanese Coral Garden, it's just around the corner on the east side of Kapa. Don't know why it's called Japanese however it's one of the best coral gardens I have ever seen. Again we just hang in the water marvelling at the sight, every type, shape and size of coral formation, and the fish life, extraordinary, billions of little coloured reef fish darting in and out of their hidey holes. Eventually we clamber back onboard Allan's big tinnie. There's food and drink, what a good host, what an extraordinary day. Unfortunately it's all about to end, we're booked back to Nuku'alofa then Auckland in the morning.

Back on the big veranda, late afternoon and the humpbacks are active out in the lagoon. It's going to be a spectacular sight in the sunset and we have to give it all away, bugger.

'Ok folks,' it's Lynne, 'there's been a cancelation, the group who were going to arrive tomorrow afternoon have pulled the plug,' she's looking at us expectantly. 'Tell you what, how about you people stay on. The group who've cancelled forfeit their deposit, that's the way it works here. You people can have their fales, half price, interested?'

It's a no brainer, one thing though, the air travel back to New Zealand, I raise this with Lynne.

'Leave it with me, how long do you want to stay, one year or two?' If only!

How good does it get, we can stay on, probably for as long as we want. The group who cancelled had booked for three weeks. how much of this place can we take? Right now I can take as much as I can get and I'm pretty certain Ariana and the others feel the same way. There is a heaven and we have found it.

The following afternoon the boat from Nuku'alofa shows up again, two policemen come ashore.

'Thought we would bring you up to date, we know you're interested. It's not good.'

There's a body, a local found it floating in an anchorage not far from Mounu, a male with a bullet wound in the head. No identification however the police boat has some pretty sophisticated gear on board, facial identification capability given to them recently by Interpol. The body is that of a Swedish yachtie who had been sailing around the world with his Swedish girlfriend. They checked in with Nuku'alofa when they arrived in the area three weeks ago, no sign of their yacht, or the girl.

These Italians are dangerous, what should we be doing? what can we do? Just continue our holiday and keep a sharp lookout for any yachts that might show on the horizon. The police boat will be staying in Vava'u waters for the time being. Allen organises a radio link with them in case we want to make contact. What do we do? continue our holiday, chances are this unfortunate business will not be our concern any more.

'Tomorrow I'll take you over to Valeloakakau Island Lagoon, it's a little west of here and quite unique. A large expanse of ocean trapped in a big lagoon with just one narrow entrance to the ocean, the sea rushes through this entranceway with considerable force, it can be quite a sight.'

Another dinner out on the big veranda, we get to talking about the Swedish yachties. It appears they've been murdered and their boat stolen, this is terrible, how can this sort of thing happen in such a lovely place. We are trying to distance ourselves from that sort of thing. Out in the middle of the Pacific and crime catches up with us. The police from Nuku'alofa will sort it out, and soon.

Next morning. 'There's been a development,' it's Allan, the police have been on the radio. They've had a frantic call from the Blue Lagoon Resort, a small place over by the entrance to Valeloakakau Island Lagoon, the place we are planning on visiting today. It's been attacked, two people have been shot and the resort's food supplies looted, got to be the Italians. The police have asked Allan to go over there, we are the closest people to the place. Can we possibly track the Italian's boat, don't get too close, just track it, they'll be there as soon as they can.

'Boy stuff; girls you don't want to be there, could be a downside.' Allan's taken control.

'I'll take this along as well.' it's a twelve gauge shotgun.
When pushed the big tinnie will do close to fifty, Allan is pushing. Michael is along as well, 'man stuff Dad, I want in.'

We spot a yacht just west of Valeloakakau, got to be them, heading due west, leaving Vava'u, probably Australia. That's what the raid on the resort was all about, need food for a long ocean voyage. We keep well clear and get the Police boat on the radio, they're on the way.

'This is good stuff Allan, drama on the high seas; no extra charge? We are going to be staying with you for some time by the look of it, what else can you rustle up to make our holiday more memorable, you've done remarkably well so far.'

'There's fishing, makes New Zealand look ordinary, we'll have a look at that when we've sorted this business.'

The police boat advises they are not far away, they have us and the yacht on their radar. They will approach the yacht from the north with the intention of boarding it. When we see them approaching they would like us to close in from the south, distract the Italians, but be careful, there could be danger, these people have already killed.

We hear the police loud hailer.

'Police, come up on deck, hands in the air, right now.'
The response is immediate, four people appear hands held high. The police boat closes in and we see them going aboard, we edge a little closer.

Two Australian couples, terrified, 'what have we done?' Bugger, where are the Italians? Where indeed? Suddenly the situation takes a worrying turn. From what we know it appears the Italians have killed the Swedish sailor and probably his girlfriend, stolen their yacht and shot two people at the Blue Lagoon Resort. We don't know at this stage whether that shooting has been fatal. What now? The police suggest that we get back to Mounu and concentrate on looking after the place, these Italians are on the loose, armed and very dangerous, anything could happen. The police will get additional resources from Nuku'alofa, the situation has now escalated into a serious manhunt.

Back to Mounu, the humpbacks are in the lagoon. There's a yacht moored just off the beach, no sign of life, where are the girls, where's the welcoming committee? shit! We radio the police boat, they're on the way. We edge up to the yacht. Allan goes aboard with the shotgun. There's a girl trussed up in the cabin, terrified, it's the

Swedish girl, no sign of the Italians, they must be ashore, shit. They've probably got the girls bailed up. We talk to the police boat, a plan is hatched. We'll make a bit of a fuss that hopefully will keep the Italians focused on us. The police boat will make a wide detour and approach Mounu from the opposite side the idea being to get ashore undetected, high risk but it could work, it's got to work. We release the Swedish girl, she's still traumatised. We bring her up on deck and make a bit of a show for the benefit of the Italians who must have seen us by now, get their attention.

The police are ashore, they've succeeded in getting five of their people onto Mounu, apparently undetected, they are armed. Next thing it's the loud hailer ordering the Italians to come out onto the beach, hands in the air, nothing happens, there's a scream, a very loud girl's scream, shit, what's happening, shots, several shots, we can't see anything. It's too much for Allan, he's over the side and splashing his way ashore. A man rushes out from the undergrowth, got to be an Italian, there are no other men on the island, he's got a handgun and he's pointing it at Allan, foolish move. A twelve gauge shotgun is a formidable weapon, especially at close range and this fellow is quite close to Allan. Both barrels, no contest, the blast literally cuts him in half, terrible mess, silence. The police landing party emerge from the trees, three prisoners, handcuffed, one bleeding profusely, a female. One of the local girls who works at the resort has been critically wounded as well.

It's over, we're on the veranda, late afternoon, we're in shock. We hear one of the staff at the Blue Lagoon has succumbed to their injuries. People have been killed, murdered, in this island paradise. The police boat has gone up to Neiafu with the three surviving Italians. They've taken the local girl who's been wounded and the poor Swedish girl as well. The fellow Allan shot? self defence was the senior policeman's assessment, his body has gone as well.

The humpbacks are cavorting about in the lagoon and there's another spectacular sunset, our idyllic South Seas holiday is anything but.

'Bastards,' Allan's summing up, 'how dare they invade our fiefdom. Don't like their chances, these killings happened in Tongan waters, they hang people in Tonga.'

The yacht is still moored out from the beach, the police will pick it up later. They have taken the cocaine, a huge amount, probably destined for the Australian market, could have been in transit to elsewhere. It appears the Italians did not find enough food at the Blue Lagoon, they were looking for more. They had come ashore and threatened the girls with guns but they did not get Kirsty, she had vanished into the undergrowth and was planning a rescue operation with some locally devised weaponry, spears, bows and arrows. Just as well the police arrived, the Italians might have come to a nasty end if Kirsty had been able to get at them.

Two days later, things have returned to normal, an idyllic sleepy South Seas coral atoll, the nasty things that happened a fading memory, well not quite. The girls have a hell of a good story to tell when they get back to Athens. Should be able to dine out on it for weeks but right now it's all sun, sand, surf and sex, it's great. Our relationship, Ariana and myself, has grown stronger by the day, we are meant for each other, want each other's company. Will definitely be making the move to Athens, there'll be a lot of time in Auckland as well, we're both agreed. The odd trip to Tonga, nostalgia. Michael and Dimitra are head over heels in love, he's definitely moving to Athens. In the meantime they are just getting as much of each other as they can. Christos and Karisa have found a new spark in their relationship, maybe they'll not be going outside their relationship so much in the future, Tonga has been good for all of us.

'Fishing, I promised you folk some real fishing.'

It's another evening on the veranda, another sunset, another banquet, another hole in the belt. Allan wants to take us fishing.

'Girls, you're included, some real fishing, none of that ordinary New Zealand stuff, we've got real fish here in Tonga.'

'That should be interesting,' from Karisa, 'I thought the fishing was pretty good in Auckland but go ahead Allen, impress us.'

Next morning, we're rocketing along in the big tinnie heading for deep water outside the main reef that encloses the Vava'u group of islands. It's another picture postcard day, not a cloud in the sky and smooth water. We're there, Allan's spot, out go the lures, we start trolling slowly, it does not take long, 'bang,' line peeling off a reel.

'Dimitra, you're first up.'

Dimitra's not done this before, it's not something you do in Greece. Not a problem, we strap a rod harness onto her and turn her loose.

'Pull up, wind down, pull up, wind down,' she catches on immediately.

It's a wahoo, a big one, puts up quite a fight, eventually Dimitra has it alongside, gaff into the shoulder and we haul it aboard, a big long thrashing silver fish with big teeth. Dimitra's awe struck with what she's done, she's beside herself, incredibly happy, she throws herself at Michael, wraps her legs around him kissing him passionately.

'They'll never believe me back home, quick, pictures.'
The fishing's good, everyone has a turn, more wahoo, then a really big strike, a screaming reel, 'Christos, your turn.' It's a mahi mahi, the dolphin fish, a big one, this will be a test, mahi mahi are not easy to land. Christos is up to the task, puts on a good display of how you do it and is rewarded when a really big mahi mahi is boated. It's as long as Christos is tall.

'Get this on your iPhone Christos, you might go back to Missolonghi one day and seek out that fellow with the fish shop.'

We continue dragging lures, several yellowfin tuna and some more wahoo.

'That's enough, this lot will fill the freezer, reckon you can better this in New Zealand?'

'Ok, ok, Allan, you win, the fishing is certainly good here in Vava'u, but it's a long way from town.'

'Yes it is and I like it that way.' Time for a beer on the veranda. It's been a great day, real fish and plenty of them.

Back at Mounu there are a couple of new arrivals, people from Athens. They had contacted the resort from Sydney on the off chance there might be a vacancy, they were in luck, one empty fale. Athens, small world. Angelica and Fabio Giuliani, mid-forties, travelling around the world, ticking the boxes on their bucket list. Tonga, Vava'u, they had heard about it, and the humpbacks. They're over the moon they were able to get accommodation.

Another session on the veranda, another sunset, the new arrivals have joined us, they are impressed, so far out of their comfort zone, enthusiastic about being on a South Sea coral atoll, they just can't stop talking.

'It's awful in Athens right now, shootings, murders, there's a gang war going on and it appears to be beyond the police to control it.'

We keep our silence, don't want to give anything away after all the whole point of our being here is to escape all that. Don't want the new arrivals to find out about our association with these things.

'There was a terrible massacre in Missolonghi, a gang wedding, dozens killed and the violence has spread to Athens.'

We glance around at each other, stories do get embellished in the telling, we wonder what else is forthcoming. We don't want the new arrivals to associate us too closely with Athens. They soon pick up on the fact that four of our group are from Greece.

'We live in New Zealand most of the time, go back to Greece occasionally.'

'New Zealand, there was an article in an Athens paper the other day about a horrendous murder on an island in New Zealand, apparently connected to the gang war in Athens, do you people know about that?'

'Not really, don't get to hear too much about the outside world here in Tonga.'

We need to shut down this conversation before we compromise ourselves.

'Tell us about your travels, a bucket list you say?'

'Yes, a bucket list, the sort of thing you dream about but never do, can't afford to, then a windfall, a big lotto win. I'm a lawyer, legal firm in Athens, several partners, they will have to get along without me for now. We plan on taking our time going around the world, maximise our good luck.'

'A lawyer,' from Christos, 'what's the name of your firm, I might know of it.'

'Aetos, Giuliani, and Papadakis, we specialise in criminal law, how come you might know about us?' Whoops, Christos has left himself a bit exposed.

'Athens police, I'm a retired detective, spend most of my time in New Zealand now.'

'What did you say your name was again?' from Fabio.

'Galani.'

'Galani, rings a bell, I think I might have defended some people who were of interest to the police but it would have been a long time ago, that deserves a drink, we were probably adversaries in yesteryear, definitely deserves a drink.'

The ice is broken, we can let our defences down a little, Fabio and Angelica are a neat couple not likely to go prying into our lives.

Lynne and the two local girls who have survived the earlier fracas deal with our catch, the results are extraordinary. Rum cocktails, marinated raw wahoo, tuna sashimi, and pan fried mahi mahi followed by a paw paw and mango combination with home made ice cream and cream. The new arrivals are mightily impressed, so am I. Such an abundance of good seafood. Perhaps we can go fishing with Allan again.

The following morning the police boat shows up again, a couple of officers come ashore This gets the attention of Fabio. We had not told him anything about what had happened a few days earlier. The police just wanted to thank us for our help in the whole unfortunate business. The local girl who worked on the island is ok, should be back in a couple of weeks. The Swedish girl's not so good, very traumatised. She's in hospital in Nuku'alofa and will be repatriated to Sweden when she's recovered. Some good news. The story has made headlines in Sweden and a bunch of fellows intend to come out to Tonga and take over the yacht the Swedish couple had been sailing around the world, the trip that ended so tragically. The idea is to sail it back to Sweden. In the meantime the police are keeping an eye on it up at Neiafu. The cocaine had been intended for South East Asia, part of a well organised worldwide smuggling operation. The Italians? in jail in Nuku'alofa and likely to remain there. Several countries wanted to extradite them however the Tongan government intended to make a point. Smuggling a large amount of cocaine through Tonga was bad enough, add a couple of murders and you will feel the full weight of the law Tongan style, we hang people in Tonga. Fabio was party to this conversation.

'What's been going on?'

We fill him in on the smuggling, after all there was no downside for us, nothing to do with the goings on in Greece.

'Action and intrigue in the South Seas, how romantic, something straight out of a story book, real Hollywood.'

More idyllic days doing very little, we had to be a little more circumspect, Fabio and Angelica were not the type who would embrace running around the place naked indulging in sex at every opportunity, well that's the impression we got however Angelica did make an appearance on the beach one morning in a very brief bikini, she's a good looking woman too, great figure. Then one morning when Ariana and myself had just come out of the water after our regular morning swim and were indulging in some sexual foreplay on our little bit of private beach Fabio and Angelica appeared, walked right in on our intimate moment. 'Can we join you?' Not waiting for an answer they shed what little they were wearing and lay down on the beach right beside us. It was an arousing sight. I was already sporting a mighty erection, Ariana had that effect on me every time and the presence of Angelica with nothing on just reinforced it.

'Want to share?' What am I hearing. There was no stopping Angelica, she had her hands on my erection and was trying to drag me on top of her, Fabio was all over Ariana, I caught her eye, what do we do? what can we do, just go with the flow, we did, just let ourselves go. She was a magnificent fuck, Angelica, really got into it thrashing around on the sand moaning loudly as I thrust into her, what the hell. There was lot of moaning coming from Ariana as well, Fabio was really dealing to her.

What have we done? this sort of thing was never intended, sharing with others, it's not our thing.

'Look you two, we don't do this, it's not us, I don't know how this has happened,'

'Nor do we, it's this place, it's so far removed from anything we have ever experienced, it arouses such an incredible sexual urge and the sight of you two playing around with each other was too much, we just had to.'

'What now? what indeed, let's put it behind us, not to be repeated, it's this island, ok!'

'Ok; now how about breakfast.'

It was weird, out on the big veranda enjoying an exotic breakfast, fruit of every kind, more fish lightly pan grilled, coffee, toast, anything you want, trying to ignore the fact that we had just been screwing the new arrivals. It did not happen again, did not even think about it, not something Ariana or myself wanted. There were some subtle changes though, Angelica did front in a G string, a very sexy G string, but so did all the girls, that was it, there were no come-ons, no little provocations.

The days pass quickly, there's more fishing, more exploring of the outer islands. Angelica and Fabio depart, continue their round the world trip. I wonder if their little dalliance with us on the beach that morning features on their bucket list. Fucked by a stranger on a remote South Sea island, who knows. I suppose we should be thinking about returning to Auckland, there's no rush, there are no pressing issues requiring our attention.

Some decisions are made, I will close up the house in Auckland. Well not completely, Rebecca will be there, she will keep the place 'alive.' I will move to Athens, how long for, no answer to that one. Ariana will stay in Auckland with me for a while then we will move to Athens together, I will move in with her. Christos and Karisa will spend a few days in Auckland with us then return to Athens but they will be back, oh yes, they will be back. Michael and Dimitra? they're hopelessly in love, they'll move back to Athens and probably set up house together. Ariana is quite certain her firm will employ Michael. The immediate future is clear all that remains is to extricate ourselves from this jewel of the South Seas, there's no rush to do that.

# *Carries' Story*

'By yourself?'

'Yes Michael, by myself, it's something I want to do, have to do, and I have to do it alone.'

'But why Carrie, what's possessed you?'

'I don't know, it's this feeling I have, I need to discover myself, my real self, I don't know what I want, something's missing, there's a hole in my life. It's not your fault Michael, it's me, I love you but I need to get away for a bit, to look at myself from outside, re-evaluate my soul. I'm going to Europe, to Paris, I have to experience other things, find out what it is that's missing.'

Poor Michael, what am I doing to him, he's distraught, devastated at my decision, but I have to do this. I feel stifled here in Auckland, committed to Michael, he loves me, I know that and I think I love him, but it's not enough, there's something missing, I need to find out what it is, perhaps in Paris. It's not sex, definitely not sex, we are very active sexually, no it's something else, what?

Money, how will I provide for myself in Europe? My sailing skills? that's a saleable commodity. Crewing on a mega yacht, a rich man's mega yacht, perhaps I could take up with a rich man, someone who could show me another life, pamper me. What am I thinking, I'm sounding like a whore. Perhaps that's what I'm hankering for, do I want to be a whore, a rich man's whore? his sex toy? Sex, plenty of that with Michael but it's not fulfilling, somethings missing, I don't know what, but something.

Paris, it's overwhelming, can I cope, take it all in, where do I start? I've checked into a small pensione in the 10$^{th}$ arrondissement, a cheaper part of Paris. Is this where I want to be? not really but it's a start. I've got no contacts, no 'in' on the mega boat world. Take it easy for a bit, soak up the ambience, worlds apart from Auckland. Wandering around the 'city of light,' an extraordinary experience, real atmosphere. There's a place pushing Mediterranean cruises on a mega yacht, they might know about crewing, I'll ask.

'Ah mademoiselle, you come from New Zealand I can tell, we see quite a few people from your country, always interested in the sailing, are you a sailor?'

'Yes, I'm interested in crewing on a boat in the south of France, do you know anything about that?'

'Non, it's not our field, we are an agency selling the cruises, you will have to go down there to find out about crewing. There is one place here in Paris where boating people gather, a club, Le Bateau, members only. A pretty girl like you might be able to get past the doorman. People who own expensive boats in the south of France frequent the place. You might be able to get a lead on something there.'

Le Bateau is in an upmarket part of Paris. It has an expensive look about it. How will I do this? Perhaps if I tell the doorman I'm looking for someone and come up with a name, that might work.

'I'm from New Zealand, I've been asked to look up a Pierre Gorbel by some French friends in New Zealand, he's a sailing man and I understand he frequents this club.'

The reception area in Le Bateau is very smart, the whole place is rather exclusive. I've got the attention of the fellow behind the desk, the very handsome fellow.'

'Pierre Gorbel, I'm not familiar with that name, sure it's correct?'

'I think so, could be wrong.' Shit this is not going to work, I'm going to be turned away.

'Just a minute, I'll have a look at the members list, see what I can find. Why don't you go through to the bar while I do a bit of searching, I'll come and find you when I've got something.'

I'm in, for how long though, surely they would not ask me to leave now if there's no Pierre Gorbel, and there probably is no Pierre Gorbel. It does not take long, pretty girl alone at the bar.

'Mademoiselle, all alone, surely not, where's your man?'

He's a real hunk, definitely a boaty, plenty like him in the Auckland sailing scene, usually good guys but I'm not in Auckland, I'm all alone on the other side of the world totally exposed, exposed to what, is this what I'm looking for?

'Ah, not quite alone, I'm looking for someone who's usually here.'

'You're from New Zealand, that accent. I've met a few Kiwis, they come over here chasing crewing jobs, pretty good sailors most of them, what brings you to Paris?'

'Chasing a crewing position, I've been told to look up a Pierre Gorbel, he's a member of this club.'

'Pierre Gorbel? doesn't ring a bell, there's a Pierre Gorbet, a middle aged fellow, very wealthy, has a yacht on the Riviera, nice fellow but not your type, you need a young fellow like me, now let me get you a drink.'

That was the start of it, my long slide down a slippery slope. André was a charmer, he plied me with drinks, and I suspect they were not ordinary drinks. The handsome fellow from reception sought me out at the bar and advised, yes Pierre Gorbet was probably the person I was looking for. He was not in the club that night however he was there frequently, he would let him know that a pretty girl from New Zealand was looking for him. Shit that won't wash, Pierre Gorbet will have no knowledge of me.

The evening passed in a haze, the reception fellow joined us at the bar, there were a lot of drinks, then blackout, I don't remember the latter part of that night, but I do remember the next morning.

*Where the hell am I and what's been going on.*

It was a big bedroom, I was naked. Both the fellows I had been drinking with were in the bed with me, also naked. It was pretty obvious there had been a lot of sex. I could not remember a thing. André roused himself and started to grope me, he wanted sex. Shit this is terrible, no way, I have to get out of here, where are my clothes? I scrambled around the room looking for my things. The two handsome fellows? bloody rapists, were comatose on the bed. Out in the street, no idea where I was and in a terrible state, welcome to Paris and the big wide world. Is this what I'm looking for? shit.

I stayed in bed and cried for two days, what had happened. I was sore, very sore, those two fellows had really worked me over, naïve little me. Want to go to Europe all by myself and look what happens. Day three I venture out, coffee in a kerbside café. A young couple at the next table strike up a conversation, excellent English, suddenly realisation that I'm in a foreign land and I don't speak the language. Fortunately just about everyone speaks English but I must make an attempt, learn French.

'Nouvelle Zélande, we want to go there one day, come join us, we can pick your brains about your lovely country.'

They are a lovely couple and they invite me to their place on the outskirts of the city for the day, see what a French household is like. It was a cottage, very neat and tidy. When they find out I am staying in the 10th arrondissement they are concerned.

'That's not a nice neighbourhood, not the place for a girl from far off Nouvelle Zélande, would you like to stay at our place until you can find better accommodation.'

It happens, I get my things and move in with my new friends. I'm getting good vibes from them, particularly the girl, Monique. That evening I dine with them in their cottage. It's a pleasure to be able to relax after that horrible experience a couple of days ago, bedtime.

*'Would you like to sleep with us?'*

What? what am I hearing? please oh please not another bad experience.

'Relax, I'll sleep in the other bedroom,' from Antoine, Monique's husband.

'Monique likes sleeping with another girl, it turns her on more than I do.'

This sounds interesting. I feel my emotions stirring, what's happening? We're in a big bed, I guess it's normally where Monique and Antoine sleep, do whatever it is they do to each other in bed and at the moment I'm beginning to question what that could be. Monique is pressing up to me, she's not got anything on, quite naked, it's embarrassing but nice, what's happening? Her hands are down on my tummy sliding down to my pubic area, the place that was horribly violated a couple of nights ago, well I think it was. I feel myself becoming aroused, but it's a girl, another female. Suddenly I feel strongly attracted to Monique and my hands are now down on her pubic mound playing around with her vagina, what is happening? Is this what I've been missing, subconsciously craving, the thing Michael had not been providing, am I attracted to girls? yes I am. It's an erotic night we do all sorts of things to each other, there's a pent up desire on my part that's crying out for fulfilment. Monique rises to the occasion, I get extreme satisfaction from her masturbation efforts on me and she likewise, it's a wonderful night.

'Morning Monique, that was such a nice night.' I've discovered a part of myself I never even suspected was there, thank you for awakening me.

'Carrie, we would like you to stay with us for a while, how does that fit with you. Antoine thinks it's a good idea and it will give me some real satisfaction having you in my bed, help us keep our marriage together, how about it.'

This is a giant step for me. The experience with Monique has blown me away, I've discovered just what my sexual orientation is. I think I want to explore it further.

I stayed with them for two weeks, two whole weeks with

Monique in the big bed. doing all sorts of things to each other, I absolutely revelled in it.

Time to move on, I need to find somewhere to stay, don't want to outlive my welcome. I go for a walk, wander into the city.

'Carrie.'

Shit it's André, the bastard who took advantage of me at Le Bateau, he's right there in the street, I can't avoid him.'

'Carrie, you just took off the other morning like you were scared of something.'

'Too right I was scared, what did you bastards do to me?'

'It was nothing Carrie, just a little meth, you seemed to like it. When we made suggestions you went right along with it and we all finished up in bed, you seemed to be a willing participant.'

'Well I wasn't, I've no recollection of what happened, I don't do things like that, ever, you bastards took advantage of me.'

'Well you certainly gave no indication that group sex was not your thing, quite the opposite in fact, you appeared to be having a great time in that big bed, a very willing participant.'

Shit, what have I done, what have I let myself in for, André thinks I'm just another groupie, a wild party girl.

'You've got it all wrong André, you drugged me. I had no idea what I was doing, I doubt if I was even conscious, you're nothing but a bloody rapist preying on naïve girls like me, bigger fool me for letting it happen.'

'Carrie, I apologise, I had no idea. A lot of girls come into Le Bateau on the make, trying to hook up with wealthy men, what can I say? When you indicated that you were looking for Pierre Gorbet, well he's just another wealthy man.'

I'm learning fast, the situation was all of my own making, naïve me.

'Ok, ok André, the drugs, it was your intention to render me helpless, right? make it easy for you and your mate eh? don't you have a conscience? feel any remorse? how the hell do you think I felt when realization hit me the next morning?'

'Carrie, we got it wrong, we've done you a terrible disservice, you're totally different to the girls who usually come into the club, but that's the way it is here in Paris, probably a far cry from what you've ever experienced, what can I say? I admit I've been a real bastard in your eyes and I'm sorry, really sorry. Tell me, how do you know Pierre Gorbet?'

'I don't, I picked the name out of nowhere, a ruse to get me through the door, it worked, it got me raped, great ploy!'

'Don't be so hard on yourself Carrie. Pierre Gorbet is a nice guy, very wealthy with a big yacht in Monte Carlo, he employs quite a few transient yachties as crew, perhaps I can get you an introduction. You did tell us the other night that you were looking for a position like that, remember.'

'No I don't remember, I don't remember anything.'

'He might be in the club right now, he's quite often there around midday. I could take you along, allow me to make some reparation for the other night.'

'Ok, no drinks, I don't trust you André, could be weasel words, sure he will be there?'

Am I being foolish? is André for real or is he conning me? don't know, I'll go along with it, could be an opportunity.

Pierre Gorbet, big, handsome, around fifty, a likeable guy, I feel relaxed in his company. He's interested in my boating background, been to New Zealand, an Americas Cup fan. His yacht is on a marina in Monte Carlo, Yvette, eighty feet of pure luxury, ten deck hands, three of them Kiwis, and yes there will be a vacancy coming up in five days time, you're hired.

Just like that, I've got what I came to Europe for, got raped in the process though.

'Get yourself to Monte Carlo and be at the boat in five days time, in the meantime would you like to have lunch with me here at the club?'

Would I what. André has disappeared. I got the impression he was uncomfortable in the presence of Pierre Gorbet.

It was an upmarket dining experience in Le Bateau, the very best. Pierre Gorbet was a charmer. He plied me with food and wine, the perfect gentleman, very different to my previous experience at this club, drugged and raped by a couple of opportunists. The deal on Yvette is a six month renewable contract, live on board, everything provided, and a modest salary. Be available at all times and whenever the boat leaves Monte Carlo for other places, which is quite often. It all sounds great, what I've been hoping for and now it's fallen in my lap, well it did involve getting raped. I went back to Monique and Antoine's place.

'Could I stay for another four days?'
Could I what, Monique is delighted, I too looked forward to another four nights in her bed. Loving another woman, well that's what it is, loving, doing all those things that lovers do to each other, it's just different doing it with another woman. Antoine was not offended, I wondered if all the moaning that went on in our bedroom upset him. I suspect he had a sexual interest elsewhere, he did spend a lot of time away from the house some nights.

The TGV, a very fast electric train to the south of France, 320kph. Along to Monte Carlo in a bus, down to the yacht harbour.

Yvette, big and modern, three masts, yes it actually was a sailing boat, powerful engines as well. I made myself known and was welcomed aboard. I was the replacement for a New Zealand girl who had moved on when her contract finished, there was some hesitancy amongst the crew when they mentioned this, interesting. It was late in the afternoon by the time I had settled in. When the owner was not on board the custom was for the crew to gather on deck for a few drinks. It was a pleasant environment but I detected an undercurrent, not sure what but there was something. Gabrial, the girl who had left had been a favourite of Pierre Gorbet's, they had been lovers. She was a drug abuser, there had been problems, interesting. I wonder what the culture is on this boat.

Day one, general cleaning and polishing, a couple of hours off during the afternoon, then more cleaning and polishing. Eating out away from the boat was allowed but it was not popular, the shore restaurants were expensive. The waterside bars, however, did get some patronage from the mega boat crews. The other New Zealand crew members, a young fellow and a girl, were from Auckland, they had been on the boat for several months. I was enjoying a drink with the young chap, Peter, when I got my first inkling of what went on. Apparently Pierre Gorbet was in the habit of descending on the place with a whole bunch of friends, mainly attractive ladies, and throwing wild parties, very wild parties, everything was on, drugs, drink, uninhibited sex, all sorts of debauched behaviour. They could be one night affairs or they could last a weekend, occasionally the boat put to sea during one of these parties and it could go on for several days.

'Really, what have I let myself in for, tell me about Gabrial.'

'Ah yes Gabrial, well she was Pierre Gorbet's girlfriend, she was not on the boat that often, spent most of her time in Paris or tripping around the world with him. She was a drug addict, I think Pierre liked it that way. There were several occasions during wild parties on the boat where she went right off her trolly, high on cocaine, had sex with anything in pants and quite publicly. I think Pierre got fed up and dumped her. Don't get me wrong Pierre is a nice guy, he does not have a problem with girls getting high and going right off their trollies, in fact he encourages it. There's always plenty of drugs available at his parties, anything you want. Crew members are not encouraged to participate is these orgies, however, it's not discouraged either, particularly if you're a girl.'

Food for thought, how will I react when people are high on drugs and deep into sex, could be tempting.

'Well, I would not have picked that, how do you handle it Peter.'

'I try and keep out of it, particularly the drugs. There have been occasions however when a gorgeous girl has thrown herself at me high as a kite, insisting on sex; hard not to.'

'Naughty boy Peter but I can understand the temptation. Seems hard to reconcile Pierre's promoting this sort of behaviour when he appears to be such a nice guy.'

'He is a nice guy and he's got a lot of money, he just likes having a wild time, anything goes, does not worry too much about the drugs although he did get fed up with Gabrial. She was his favourite, his sex toy. She became addicted to meth, he threw her out a couple of weeks ago.'

'Where does the money come from Peter?'

'Good question, you tell me? Rumour has it he's a kingpin in the drug smuggling world but I find it hard to believe, he's not the type you would expect in that business, he's just a nice guy. The girls certainly like him and he's very good to them, not averse to suggesting a bedroom dalliance with some of the girls who crew the boat but there's never any coercion, definitely their choice.'

Peter's a nice guy, good to have a fellow Kiwi who I get on with. He's not the sort who will put the hard word on me either, well I don't think so. Good looking fellow but as I've recently discovered I don't think I'm that interested in boys. I've been put in a two berth cabin with another girl, Anna, from Latvia, she's a real long legged beauty. Two bunks, one up, one down, I get the lower one.

That evening I go ashore with Anna and Peter. We visit a couple of bars, I just lap up the ambiance. Monte Carlo, very upmarket, very exclusive, very expensive!

'Carrie, do you have a boyfriend,' Anna asks.

I explain about Michael back in Auckland and how I need to have a break for a while, do my own thing.

'He must be very understanding your Michael, will you be going back to him after you've done your thing?'

'Of course, well I'm pretty sure I'll go back but there's a lot I want to experience before that.'

'Really Carrie, want to investigate all the options, your orientation in life, boys or girls perhaps.'

Peter intervenes. 'Back off Anna, what are you suggesting, do you think young Carrie here is going to fling herself into some of Pierre's wild sex parties?'

'Could be, very tempting at times believe me.'

'Yes I did notice you at that last affaire Anna, but it was a girl you were being rather intimate with, right?'

What am I hearing, is my bunk mate attracted to girls, this could be interesting. I feel a stirring in my loins, what will the night bring forth?

'Yes Peter I was giving that girl a lot of attention but only because you gave me the brush off, I rather fancied getting you into the sack that evening but you were not playing along. I wanted to piss you off.'

'Okay Anna, lets stop it there, Carrie will be thinking we are a lot of sexos.'

They're not wrong, there's a definite sexual inuendo in all these conversations. I don't find it offensive, rather stimulating. I'm beginning to wonder what does go on aboard Yvette.

Back on board, bedtime. Anna is down the companionway in the ablution block. I put on a nighty and hop into the lower bunk. Anna appears in the doorway, knickers only, an incredibly erotic sight, suddenly I'm mightily aroused.

'Can I get into bed with you?'

I'm overwhelmed with desire.

'Please do.'

It's all on, we caress each other passionately. She's got a magnificent body, very long legs that she wraps around me, I feel myself bursting with desire, quite an extraordinary sensation, I've never felt this way before. Way beyond anything I ever experienced with Michael. We stimulate each other in every possible way far into the night and eventually fall asleep.

What's it going to be on this boat, am I in love with Anna, can we leave each other alone, the attraction is incredible.

'Carrie you are magnificent. You've probably figured out that I'm a lesbian, boys don't interest me. We've got a week then my contract is up, I'll be leaving the boat.'

It hits me like a train, I'm shocked. I think I've just found love and the rug's pulled out, shit.

Next morning, Anna is concerned about my devastation.

'Here snort this Carrie, a little meth.' She's offering me some crystal meth. I take it and feel much better. We start fondling each other again and it's all on, stimulated by meth we reach even greater levels of enjoyment.

'It's the meth Anna, it really turns me on, where did you get it?'

*That was a turning point, lesbian sex and crystal meth, it was to plague me for the rest of my life.*

It was a week before Anna left. We were relentless, in bed the whole time, I think the other crew members noticed. Anna had a good supply of meth, one of the crew was supplying her. She was not addicted but certainly a heavy user, me? it increased the pleasure I experienced enormously, I had to have it. Lesbian sex and crystal meth.

The day Anna left the boat was a disaster, how will I cope? I've got to have her, and I need some meth. She told me to look her up when I was in Paris. Le Depot was the place, a gay's club. Meth, where can I get some meth, what am I saying, what do I want crystal meth for?

Later that day the owner, Pierre Gorbet, turned up, he wanted to take the boat out to sea for a couple of days and he wanted to go immediately, he seemed to be up tight, afraid of something.

'Carrie, my new crew member from Nouvelle Zélande, how's life aboard Yevette?'

'Different, enjoyable, yes I am having a good time.'

'I hear you're a bit down now that Anna's gone. She did not renew her contract, has something in Paris she wanted to follow up. Why don't you have dinner with me this evening, my private suite. I'll try to cheer you up, take your mind off Anna, you ok with that?'

'Yes of course, I'd love to dine alone with you, away from the prying eyes of the crew.'

Shit, what has Pierre learnt, does he know about my infatuation with Anna, my using crystal meth, no secrets on a mega yacht.

He's a gentleman Pierre Gorbet, dinner in his private quarters is something else, it will also be the hot topic amongst the crew.

'Carrie, you appear to be nervous, would you like a little meth?'
Shit, he does know I've been snorting crystal meth with Anna, no longer a secret, who else knows? probably everyone, what the hell.

'Yes Pierre I would.'
It was not the smartest thing I've done. We both snorted meth and both became very relaxed, it also turned me on. It may not be another female but Pierre Gorbet suddenly looked very attractive, very sexy, but he's a male, what the hell, does it matter, a little more meth.

That was the start of it, I think I initiated the move to the bedroom, there was certainly no coercion from Pierre, he let me take the lead. Perhaps he was wondering just how far I would go, I went a long way. There was more meth and I think it was me who raped him. It descended into total debauchery, every sort of sex act you could imagine, and I revelled in it. The latter part of that first night is just a hazy memory. I stayed in his private suit for the whole two days we were at sea, high on meth, Pierre had plenty of it. Continuous sex and I loved it, well I thought I did.

'Carrie, this boat is not the place for you, come back to Paris with me. I'll set you up in your own apartment, look after you, how about it?'

An offer far too good to refuse, being looked after by a wealthy man, being shown a good time, something I had fantasized about. A sugar daddy, well not really, Pierre Gorbet was a good looking fellow in his prime, fantastic in the sack with a ferocious sexual appetite, will I be able to handle it?

It's quite something, an apartment in the 7th Arrondissement, a very desirable part of the city. Pierre came along with me to ensure it was everything I would want, everything? shit it was way over the top, absolute luxury.

'All yours Carrie for as long as you want, I will be a frequent visitor, you are my lady now, my lovely sexy partner from Nouvelle Zélande, how does that sit with you?'

'Sit with me? hell how good does it get, I've never experienced anything like this in my life, how can I ever thank you Pierre?'

'Having you in my bed is thanks enough Carrie, you give me immense pleasure, sure you are still interested in other females?'

'I don't know, it's just a recent thing but after that session on your yacht, in your bed, I'm not so sure any more.'

'Ok, here's the deal. You are your own master, do whatever you want, the only thing I want is your company, and I think I will be wanting your company a lot. You're a fun person to have around Carrie, not just in bed, in every situation. I want to show you off, my lovely girlfriend.'

'Charmer, you're flattering me now Pierre and I like it.'

'Ok that's settled. I'll be out of town frequently, business. There will be periods where you will be on your own, do you think you'll be able to handle that?'

'I'll do my best, will you trust me in your absence?'

'I'm not your master Carrie, feel free to do what you want when I'm not here.'

The rules are in place, my life is complete, hedonistic pleasure, nothing is off the cards, the only cloud, my growing desire for crystal meth, what can I do about that? Should I ask Pierre about obtaining some, will he be unhappy if I ask?

'Yes Carrie I can fix that, cocaine as well if you want, however, I would urge restraint, that first night on the boat, you went right out of your mind, it was nice though, we both had a great time. I will be out of town for the next three days, you'll be on your own, can you handle that?'

Three days, no restraints. Anna said Le Depot was the place I might find her.

It's a lively place, chocka with gays. I venture in and find the bar. I'm hit on immediately, a big blond affair with a lot of makeup, not sure which gender. I display total indifference, she? it? moves away only to be replaced by another, a pretty brunette, hand on my thigh straight away and moving up, shit what have I let myself in for.

'Want a snort?' she mumbles, high on something.

'Buzz of Chérie,' it's another blond, a good looking one, definitely female, there's a fellow with her, a hunky good looking chap.

'Hello, meet us, Rachell and Bruno, not seen you here before, what are you after, boy, girl, both, double, triple, what's it to be sweety?'

'Well actually I'm looking for a girl called Anna, know of her?'

'Yep, sure do, she's not here tonight, wild thing that Anna, how come you know her?'

'I crewed with her on a boat in Monte Carlo.'

'Your name's not Carrie by any chance?'

'It is, wow, Anna's told us all about you, come, we've got a table over in the corner, I think we need to get to know you.'

Get to know me? Out comes the meth pipe. It's not long before we're all puffing away, a lot of other patrons are doing the same. There's a bit of coke snorting too. The place is a drug den, shit. Do I want this, bit late now, besides, I'm enjoying the relaxed sensation, drugs agree with me. It goes on for a couple of hours, well I think it does. Meth, I like it, try some coke, sensation's different, better perhaps. My new found friends are right into it, heavy users. It's not long before they appear to be detached from the world, I'm feeling the same way, well I think I am, don't know. I'm not a druggy, not yet. Another fellow joins us. 'Hello Claude.'

We're in a taxi, four of us, no idea where we are going, having trouble staying with it. It's a big room, a big bedroom and a very big bed. There are four of us, naked, all playing around with each other, boy, girl, whatever, does not seem to matter. I'm having sex with Claude, he's really giving it to me, it's lovely, well in my drugged state I think it's lovely, now it's the girl, Rachell, she's fondling me, her fingers deep in my vagina, that's lovely as well and Claude is down on Bruno, I think he's giving him a blow job, I've never seen that before, fascinating, I wonder what it's like.

'Here let me try.' I push Claude aside and go down on Bruno's bulging penis taking it right into my mouth, he clamps his hands around my head and moves it up and down furiously. I'm dizzy, not quite with it, what am I doing, oh yes giving Bruno a blow job, it's nice, a first for me. What's this, there's white goo all over my face, christ he's ejaculated all over me, shit! I'm fading, my lights are going out, it's the meth, bit too much perhaps. Rachell's got me again, she's got a vibrator, she pushes it into my vagina, another first, it sends me to heaven, then blackout.

Light coming through a window, where am I? A big bed, naked bodies, who are these people, what's going on?

'Morning Carrie.'

It's a girl, a blonde girl, she's got no clothes on, she's embracing me very affectionately, kissing my nipples, sucking on them, it's nice. I seem to remember her, last night, she was the girl in the club, Le Depot, now I remember. I tied up with some gays, we finished up in bed together, it was an orgy, shit, what have I been doing? My head is throbbing, I need something.

'Here Carrie try this, cocaine, it'll help you feel good again.'

I don't need this, don't want this, I'm not a drug abuser, sure about that? The last few days have involved a lot of drug taking, drug abuse, you're a druggy Carrie, can't stop, shit!

I'm back in my apartment, the lovely apartment Pierre has given me. I wandered out of the place where I found myself this morning, got a cab. I remembered where I lived, that's about all though. Am I being unfaithful to Pierre, I'm his girl now, well I think I am, what will he think if he finds out what I have been doing in his absence, will I tell him? Will he ask?

A lot of coffee, some serious reflection, where have I gone wrong? Well just about everywhere. I like drugs, Anna's fault, damn her. Stop making excuses, you could have said no but you didn't, wanted to experience it, remember, you want to experience everything, well now you've experienced something that you can't control, where to from here? I'll make a stand, no more meth, dry out before it's too late, get my act together before Pierre gets back, be a bit more discerning about where I go, who I associate with. Now, more coffee, go for a walk, clear the head. All that sex, lesbian sex, any sort of sex, I enjoyed it all, I think. Was it the drugs or was that me? the real me, the liberated me. Have I got a sex problem? am

I a nymphomaniac? Hang on it's the girls I like, well I like the boys too but it's the girls who get me turned on the most, perhaps I'm bisexual, how can I find out? do I want to find out? What if I discover I really do prefer girls? how will that sit with Pierre? after all, gentleman though he is, he's expecting me to be his sex partner, his sex toy. Those two days on the boat, all that sex, it's pretty obvious he wants plenty of it, and he wants it with me.

Early afternoon, a long walk has cleared my head, realisation of what happened last night is sinking in, I'm disgusted with myself. Keep away from the gay bars, you can't handle the temptation.

'Hello, mind if I sit here.' An attractive girl, mid-twenties, I'm sitting at a kerbside café deep in thought, reflecting on my recent life, my rather unsavoury recent life, experience everything, yeah right, look where it's landed me.

'Yes, of course, I'd like some company, feeling a bit down right now.'

'English?'

'No, New Zealand.'

'Nouvelle Zélande, I'm Greek, Athens, here for a few days, business, what brings you to Paris?

How do I answer that? Here to indulge in a wild sex life, boys, girls, drugs, everything, life on the edge, anything goes, is that what I'm here for? Has this girl's simple question caused me to focus on that very question.

'The big OE, something young people in New Zealand do before life makes too many demands on them.'

'That sounds exciting, where has your OE taken you so far?'

'I've only been here a short while, crewed on a boat in Monte Carlo, now Paris, not sure what my next move will be.'

'Thought about Greece, a lot of young people from your country visit Greece.'

'No, I haven't, tell me about it; by the way my name is Carrie,

Carrie Gray, and you are?'

'Myrine Paganos, I work in the fashion industry in Athens, I'm here for a few days checking on the opposition, spying actually. Coffee? you look a little down, lonely in the big strange city?'

'Yes I am, life in France has been a bit fast and furious, I'm feeling the pace.'

'That's not good to hear, what have you been up to?'

No way am I admitting to a stranger what I've been doing, I'm disgusted with myself.

'Well I've found a benefactor, a rich man who's keeping an eye on me, that doesn't sound good does it but this chap is a genuine good guy, only trouble he's out of town quite a lot.'

'You need a female friend Carrie, someone who can show you the feminine side of the city of light. I've got a couple of days free, let me take you in hand, show you around.'

What am I hearing, I don't know this person, is she for real or am I being set up again?

'Ah, not sure Myrine, my man might be back today.'

'Tell you what, if you find yourself free this evening come along to the Mix Club in Montparnasse, it's a fun place, you'll find nice people there. I'll be there this evening around seven, been there several times and I like it.'

What to make of that, Myrine makes it sound attractive. I don't want to get ambushed again, the last two club visits were disastrous, drugs, sex, perversions of all sorts, I don't want that again, well I don't think I do. Snap out of it Carrie what are you thinking. Is there a dark side to you that's taking over, get a handle on yourself. What Myrine has suggested could open a door to a nicer night life. Give it a try, can't be any worse that what you've experienced so far in the city of light. Pierre will be back soon, well I hope he will, perhaps he will show me the nicer side of Paris. He'll probably ply me with drugs and indulge in wild sex as well; hmm that could be nice. The

Mix Club, looks good, lively crowd, all young people, disco, continuous stage show, getting good vibes.

'Carrie, you did come, you'll like this place, over here, we've got a table, meet my friends.'

They look like decent people but you can never tell, those 'nice fellows' in Le Bateau finished up drugging and raping me. These people appear to be different, I might be safe here. I'll stick close to Myrine, no sign of drugs.

'Come on Carrie dance with me.' Myrine's, onto the disco floor dragging me along into the centre of the pulsating crowd, great atmosphere. She's hugging me, really close, it's getting me aroused, what's happening? I'm responding to the hugging, hugging her right back. Myrine's looking right into my face, suddenly she's kissing me. I feel a little dizzy, I'm kissing her right back, shit I want this girl, I really want her. We whirl around in the crush of people our bodies pressed together, her loins hard up against mine and it's heavenly, so much nicer that what I have been indulging in recently, and no drugs. A break, we go back to our table.

'What were you two up to out there?' It's one of the fellows. 'Myrine have you fallen in love perhaps, I rather fancy Carrie myself but if you've staked a claim, well bugger, that's me out.'

'Take no notice of Rolf, he fancies all the girls but I suspect he fancies the boys more, right Rolf.'

'Perhaps, but Carrie here is a stunner, I think you might be going to rush her off Myrine, right?'

Suddenly it's out there for all to see, Myrine is a lesbian and she's taken a shine to me, that's rather nice because I am reacting strongly to her.

It's a great night, no sign of drugs, just regular people, a lot of gays, I feel safe, nothing bad is going to happen here at the Mix Club. It's now one in the morning. Myrine and myself have been together all evening, now it's time to go home. I don't want to let go,

I think she feels the same.

'Myrine why don't you come home with me, I've got a big apartment in the 7th Arrondissement, I'm there alone.'

'Yes.'

That was the start, we spent a long time in bed doing just whatever we wanted, it was fantastic, completely unaffected by drugs, able to enjoy every tender moment and there were many very intimate moments. Myrine had a fantastic body and a huge sexual appetite that I was only too pleased to satisfy. I too got extreme satisfaction from our lovemaking, far more than a man could provide.

'Athens, yes I'll definitely be going to Athens Myrine.'
Little did I know just then. I would be going to Athens but the circumstances would be very different to what I envisaged.

'Carrie, I've missed you.' Pierre, has wrapped his arms around me in a huge embrace.

'My lovely Carrie, I need you, I'll not go off and leave you again.'

He's being very attentive, possessive, is that a problem? no, it could keep me out of trouble, I'm not very good on my own, can't resist the temptations that abound in this place. I've not handled Pierre's absence very well at all, what do I say if he asks? Going to wild night clubs, getting screwed by people I cannot even remember, boys, girls, well it's true, that's what I've been doing, will I tell him? I don't think so. Myrine, a ray of sunshine, she's made me realise what my real sexual orientation is, how can I convey this to Pierre? do I want to or will I fake it? pretend to enjoy sex with him. Actually I do enjoy sex with boys, I enjoy all sex, perhaps I'm bi-sexual, perhaps I'm a bi-sexual nymphomaniac, is there such a thing?

Midafternoon, 'Carrie we'll go out to dinner this evening, some fine dining, a welcome home celebration, let me show you off, my girl, the love of my life.'

What am I hearing, it's nice but is it for real, the love of his life? I'm sure there have been many loves before me.

'You're a charmer Pierre.' I plant a big kiss squarely on his lips, he hugs me tightly and starts breathing heavily.

'The bedroom Carrie, a little bedroom dalliance before we go out.'

Shit, I've got him aroused, he wants sex and he wants it right now. I'm not in the mood but I daren't show it, my recent activities have sated my desire, particularly my liaison with Myrine. I don't want to be fucked by a man right now.

'Carrie, what is it, you're not letting yourself go, not your usual self, perhaps a little stimulation.'

We're going at it in the bedroom but I cannot work up any enthusiasm, can't get aroused, just fucking like some whore, is that what I am, a whore, Pierre's whore.

'Here Carrie, snort this.'

Shit, it's a line of meth, I know it's going to turn me on, Pierre has figured that as well. It's the thin end, drugs. I don't want drugs, well you had better snort this lot or you might put your relationship with Pierre in jeopardy he wants sex right now, serious sex, not just some mechanical fucking. It works, I feel some arousal, some enthusiasm, some more meth perhaps, yes that's it, plenty of meth, now I'm away, I'm giving Pierre a real working over, starting to enjoy it, he's really fucking me and I'm responding with mounting enthusiasm. More meth, I'm losing it, I'm reaching some sort of climax, more, more, suddenly oblivion.

'Morning Carrie, how's the head?'

The head is ratshit, pounding away, let me die, bloody meth, it'll be the end of me, 'what happened to the fine dining?'

'You were magnificent last night Carrie, right over the top, sex with you is something else, something fantastic, thank you. The dinner? didn't happen, to-night perhaps.'

A watershed moment, the use of drugs is necessary for me to get right into the sex thing, well it is with men, with Myrine it's different, no drug stimulation require. It's becoming clear I'm a lesbian, girls are my thing, how will this sit with Pierre? best if he does not find out. Have to fake it, have to use drugs, bugger. Don't want to lose Pierre's patronage, his support, how would I get along in this place without him? Judging by my experiences so far; badly. Perhaps if I get out of Paris, move to Athens, take up with Myrine. She would not be averse to such a suggestion, well I don't think she would, certainly get me away from the drug scene here. I need to do something before I become too dependant. Staying with Pierre means drugs, possibly a lot of drugs, I want to stay with Pierre, he's my ticket to a good life style, can I fake it?

Fine dining, L'Arpege on the Rue de Varenne, way beyond anything I've ever experienced. There are no restaurants like this in New Zealand. The menu, out of my league and all in French. Pierre is at his best, the perfect gentleman, not so sure about the bedroom though, bit of an animal there. He asks a few questions about my likes and dislikes then orders, it's seriously good, several courses, champagne, incredible desserts, yes I like this lifestyle. I'll need to keep Pierre satisfied, indulge his desires, fake it, can I manage that without drugs, don't know, I guess I'll be finding out.

'Pierre Gorbet, hello.' A hard looking character appears at our table. Suddenly Pierre looks uncomfortable, 'Marcial Crabaire, have not seen you in a while.'

'No you haven't Pierre, been avoiding me perhaps?'

'No, no, out of town a lot, business.'

'Ah yes business, and how's your business doing?'

'Well enough considering the competition.'

'Ah yes the competition, be careful there, the competition's not very happy with you, better watch your back, now then why don't you introduce me to this lovely girl.'

'Carrie, meet monsieur Marcial Crabaire, my friend; I think. Are we still friends Marcial?'

'Perhaps, keep out of my patch and we can be friends.'
What am I hearing, my patch, what does that imply, sounds like a warning, what business is being referred to here, something outside the law perhaps. Pierre looks decidedly uncomfortable. Marcial Crabaire gives Pierre a slap on the back and moves away from our table.

'Pierre, I can't pretend that what happened just then did not happen, what was it all about?'

'You don't want to know Carrie, give me some time and I'll tell you, right now I think we're finished here, we can leave now.'
We are not finished but Pierre is obviously troubled, wants to be out of the place, we up and leave. Pity, I was really enjoying that restaurant, nice company, excellent food, oh well.
Back to the apartment, the bedroom, the bed.

'Want to tell me?'

'No, but It would be ridiculous for me to try to pretend all was well. It's my business Carrie, it's competitive and there are some rather unsavoury people involved.'

'It's drugs, isn't it Pierre?'

'Yes Carrie it's drugs, it makes me huge amounts of money but it's dangerous. Right now there's a bit of push and shove going on but you don't want to be troubled by that. Tell you what, tomorrow I have to go to Athens, why don't you come with me, you'll like it. Athens is a pretty exciting place, you on for it?'

Athens, I wonder if Myrine is back there yet, how can I find out? Hang on you can't go running around after Myrine, you're with Pierre, think girl, don't go spoiling what you've got. Pierre looks out of sorts, that Marcial Crabaire fellow has upset him, the smart thing to do right now is to cheer Pierre up a little.

'Yes Pierre I'm on for Athens and right now I want you to fuck me, you'd like that right?'

'Yes I would, let's spice it up with some meth.'

Shit, how can I avoid this constant drug use? I can't! give in. You like what it does to you, the tremendous sexual high, that's what Pierre is looking for right now. There's a pipe, we cook up a brew and inhale heavily, in no time we're both high and right into each other. Sex with Pierre is enjoyable when meth is involved the more meth the more enjoyment, the greater the sexual high. I love it, I'm fast becoming a druggy. Perhaps this is the way it has to be when I'm with Pierre. Do I want that, not really but that's the way it is.

Athens, what does Pierre have to deal with? something to do with his business, must be urgent. He's just returned from wherever he's been, now he has to be in Athens. Did the unexpected appearance of that fellow at the restaurant, Marcial Crabaire, have something to do with it.

We check in to a nondescript pensione in a rather unsavoury part of Athens, Pierre uses a false name. I notice he has a passport in the same name.

'Going to tell me about it Pierre.'

'No Carrie I'm not, it's not your concern, you don't need to know. We'll not be here for long, just a day or two. Why don't you go out and have a look around while I do what I have to do, see you back here around four this afternoon, ok?'

I'm on my own, wonder if Myrine is here, how can I find out. She's in the fashion business, perhaps a discreet inquiry at one of the fashion house head offices might turn up something.

'Myrine Paganos, yes, she's here, just a minute, I'll check her office.'

How's that for luck, first shot and it pays off. I'd asked the maître d' at a kerbside restaurant if she knew of any of the leading fashion houses in the city and struck a mother lode of information, she knew them all. When I told her about my chance meeting with Myrine in Paris she came up with the name of a fashion house that might be a possibility, she was right.

'Carrie, have you followed me here? please say yes. I've missed you terribly, realised you're the person I want in my life, are you here for long?' She's hugging me passionately as she comes out with this. We're in a small reception room away from prying eyes. Myrine's hug is a bit more than a hug, her hands are all over me her thighs pressed hard into mine.

'I wish. I'm here with my benefactor Pierre, I think it'll be a short visit.'

'Let's go out for lunch, I'll take the rest of the day off, god it's good to see you. The nights have not been the same without you in my bed.'

Oh dear, Myrine really has taken a shine to me, that's nice, I have strong feelings for her as well. Perhaps I should break away from Pierre, forget the life he is offering and move in with Myrine here in Athens.

Lunch is great. The afternoon passes quickly. Myrine is quite emotional, she's making her feelings very obvious and I find myself responding in kind. I'm strongly attracted, it's more than that, perhaps I'm falling in love, could that be? I thought I was in love once before in my life, Michael, but this feeling I have for Myrine is different, very strong.

'Have to get back to Pierre, promised to be there by four, how about I contact you when I'm free. Do you have a card, phone numbers?'

It's an emotional parting, Myrine is all over me hugging and kissing and I'm responding, strongly, what is happening?

'Pierre, what's happened?' he looked a mess, there was a bruise on his face and a bloodstain on his shirt, I noticed the knuckles on his right hand were missing some skin. There was another fellow with him in the pensione, a real hard looking dude, he looked roughed up as well.

'Bit of trouble with our business here, nothing we can't fix.'

Shit, this could be dangerous, do I want to be associated with this sort of thing? no, I don't. Perhaps staying with Pierre, enjoying the lifestyle he is offering is not such a bright idea, there could be a downside.

'Carrie, we have to go out tonight, business to attend to, can you look after yourself for the evening?'

What kind of business? I sense something violent. The fellow with Pierre looks a real thug, perhaps I'll keep my nose right out of it.

'Yes dear, I'll be ok, see you later in the evening perhaps?'

'Perhaps, I might be late, don't wait up.'

Myrine, where's that card.

'That was quick, I'm still at work, come 'round in half an hour.'

'We'll go back to my place Carrie, some time together, private time.'

I sense Myrine wants some intimate time, so do I, the desire is very strong. Myrine's apartment is big, in a lovely leafy suburb. We sit out on the balcony and enjoy a wine in the late afternoon sunshine, just the two of us, a totally different world from the drug scene I was becoming all too familiar with, it's nice. This is the life I want, I don't need men, their sexual demands, their drug use, I want Myrine. It's a passionate evening, we do all sorts of things together, all sorts of lovely intimate things, very different to the plain old fucking that men seem to want. It's late, do I need to go, no, bugger it, I'm staying here with Myrine, I'll go back to that scungy pensione in the morning.

They're both there, Pierre and the hard looking dude. It's around eight in the morning. It had been a memorable night with Myrine the only downer, she had to go to work otherwise I doubt if I would have bothered to come back to Pierre.

Shit they don't look good, Pierre is very pale and the hard looking dude is bleeding, there appears to be a wound in his abdomen.

'Good, you're back, we're out of here. We'll drop Carlos off at the hospital on the way to the airport, we're going back to Paris right now, grab your things.'

There appears to be an air of urgency, shit, what's happened? what's happened to the hard looking dude Carlos? do I want to know? no I don't and I don't think I want to continue my life with Pierre either.

We're back in the lovely apartment in the 7th Arrondissement, I've got a lot of doubts in my mind but I dare not question Pierre. I'm beginning to think he's not a gentleman at all but a hardened criminal, a nice one, easily mistaken for a gentleman.

'Carrie, I need you right now, I need some release, it's been a trying time, take this, we'll both get high, enjoy some sex.'

A moment of truth, I'm just his sex toy, something to release his tensions, he wants sex and he wants me high on meth, give him some real release, enable him to rape me every which way, the worrying thing is, I like it when this happens, really enjoy the fucking; until I pass out.

Morning and I'm feeling disgusted with myself; again, sliding further down the shit hole I've fallen into.

'Pierre, I want to talk, I'm not happy, I need to know just what you are up to for my own peace of mind. I'm not going to blab about whatever you choose to tell me, you can trust me on that but I want you to tell me; now. This sex thing, seems you just want a sex toy you can get high on meth then get to satisfy your every sexual perversion, right?'

'You're a perceptive girl Carrie, you're right, I'm not a very nice person, however, I do like you, like you a lot. The sex thing? yes I do like a lot of sex, I think you do as well, particularly when assisted by a little meth, you turn into a real animal.'

'Well Pierre I'm not into fucking, I do it because you're my meal ticket, I prefer girls, but that's something I only recently discovered in myself, now I'm just leading you on, I never knew until recently. Athens? what was that all about?'

'In confidence Carrie, not a word to anyone, could be nasty consequences. My supplier in Athens was being leant on by the opposition. You have probably figured out that I deal in meth, there's competition. It was an intolerable situation that had to be addressed, Carlos and myself addressed the problem. Unfortunately Carlos suffered a knife wound in the process. That's it Carrie, that's what happened in Athens; business.'

'Shit, you killed someone?'

'I did not say that Carrie and it's dangerous to assume too much, I'll say no more.'

I'm in a dangerous world here, I want out, what to do? Go along with Pierre for a while until I see an opportunity to make a break.

'Dinner this evening Carrie, some fine dining, our previous outing was soured a little for which I apologise, let me make it up to you.'

He's trying, give Pierre some credibility. He likes me and it would be very hurtful to abuse that but keep in mind that after the fine dining he'll want sex. It would be sensible for me to indulge him by snorting a bit of meth, quite a lot perhaps, really get me in the mood, remember I too get a kick out of fucking when I'm high on drugs. It will not be a continuing thing, I'm going to bail at the first opportunity.

It's a great dinner, another of Paris's finest restaurants. Sure enough it's into bed when we arrive back at the apartment, out comes the pipe and we cook up a brew, quite a big brew, we indulge heavily and the resulting sex is something else. It goes on and on Pierre can not get enough of me, I really enjoy it, multiple orgasms. Getting dizzy, Pierre's still on top of me, still thrusting into me, I'm loving it, really enjoying being fucked by my man, perhaps it's not so bad after all being Pierre's sex toy; blackness; my lights go out.

What's up where am I? oh yes I'm at my place, Pierre, shit, what's this, blood, there's a lot of blood, shit it's Pierre's, what am I seeing? It's Pierre, he's covered in blood, the whole bed is covered in blood, shit Pierre's throat, something's not right, shit, his throat's been cut, torn open, a gaping wound, *he's dead.*

A police cell, a cold concrete police cell. I've got blood all over me, Pierre's blood, why am I here?

'Mademoiselle Gray,' it's a French Police officer, 'do you have anything you might like to tell us?'

'Tell you, what do you mean?'

'Your screaming this morning attracted the attention of the neighbours who called us. We found you in bed with a monsieur Pierre Gorbet, he was dead, his throat cut, can you tell us about that?'

'I've no idea what happened, I was in bed with monsieur Gorbet, there's nothing untoward about that, when I woke up I found this terrible shambles, I have no recollection of anything.'

'Are you sure you do not want to tell us what really happened?'

'What do you mean, I've just told you what I remember.'

'Come now mademoiselle Gray, a man has his throat cut while he's lying beside you in bed and you've no recollection, don't you find that rather hard to believe.'

'Well that's what happened, I had passed out the previous

evening.'

'Passed out, why was  that, were you using drugs?'

'Yes.'

'So your story is you were using drugs the night before with monsieur Gorbet in bed and you passed out, when you came to the following morning you discovered that monsieur Gorbet had been murdered in the same bed and you have no recollection of it.'

'Yes.'

'Perhaps mademoiselle Gray you might like to think long and hard about what you have told me, we will talk again in a few hours.'

They think I murdered him, these stupid police think I murdered Pierre, how can they think that. Shit I'm in trouble, who can I call? Who indeed, I don't know anyone here. I need to get cleaned up, I've got Pierre's blood all over me, it's awful, I've got to get cleaned up.

'Anyone there, help, I need help, anyone there.' I'm shouting at the top of my voice, someone must hear me.

'Mademoiselle you are making a lot of noise, what do you want?' It's a policewoman. She looks the kindly sort, that's if a policewoman can look kindly.

'I want to get cleaned up, this blood, I want a shower, I want something clean to wear, please?'

'Of course, bit remiss of us not to think of it, men. The people who interrogated you have no feeling, no thought for your wellbeing, here come with me. I'll have to keep an eye on you, can't have you running off, they think you're a murderer.'

'I'm not a murderer, it's ridiculous, how can you people be so stupid.'

A long hot shower, the water's running red, Pierre's blood, shit, how can this be, what has happened? Pierre no more, it's awful, my benefactor gone, just like that, I'm alone in a strange country. I'm falling further down that shit hole, how has it come to this?

Late afternoon, the worst day of my life. I'm dressed in prison garb, stripped trousers and top, just like the movies, the French movies. It's the same police officer who interrogated me earlier in the day, the fellow who made me feel like a liar. I get bad vibes, very bad vibes, from him.

'Mademoiselle perhaps you have a different story to tell me now?'

'How the hell can I have a different story, I told you what I know, do you want me to make up a different story just to satisfy you, don't be so stupid.'

'Now then mademoiselle no need to get angry. It appears to us there was no one else in the apartment last night, just yourself and monsieur Gorbet so who else could have done this?'

'I have no idea, that's what the police do, find the bad guys, not simply accuse an innocent party. How could I have done this, you think I tore his throat out with my bare hands, get real, where's the murder weapon, why aren't you doing some real policework?'

'We are mademoiselle, we are looking at all possibilities.'

'Good then perhaps I can expect to be out of here soon?'

'Afraid not mademoiselle Gray, we need to keep you here until our inquiries are complete then a decision will be made about your future detention.'

'How long?'

'Can't answer that at the moment but it will take us a while. Perhaps you can tell me what you were doing in bed with monsieur Gorbet.'

'That's a personal matter.'

'I'm sure it is and this is a murder investigation, you need to answer all my questions, all of them. Now what were you doing with monsieur Gorbet in bed last night?'

I feel I'm being stripped naked in front of an arrogant French policeman, he's expecting me to tell him all about our drug use, our lovemaking, how do I answer these questions? Perhaps a direct frontal assault, hit him with the facts, what the hell, it's murder, all the niceties have gone.

'Pierre Gorbet is my lover, we had been using meth, quite a lot of meth, we like the high it gives us, the huge increase in sexual pleasure. Do you know about things like that inspector? do you enjoy sex? got a responsive sex partner have you? or is it just a frowsy old wife stuck at home.'

Careful Carrie, you'll antagonise him, not the brightest thing to be doing right now. Stuff it I don't care anymore these people are out to get me, implying that I'm telling lies. I can't get in any deeper so I need to defend myself, get stuck into him.

'We were fucking, really fucking each other, we like doing that especially when we're on a meth induced high, ever experienced that inspector? do you do things like that with you wife? I think not. My last recollection of last night is Pierre on top, really giving it to me and I was loving it, then blackout, my lights just went out, too much meth. That's it inspector there's nothing more I can tell you.'

'That will be enough for today mademoiselle Gray, we'll talk again tomorrow when perhaps you can be a little more civil.

Shit, shit, shit, I'm deep down that shit hole.

Next morning, terrible night, terrorized by nightmares, le guillotine, off with her head, lots of blood, cheering crowds.

'Mademoiselle Gray, wake up.' It's the nice policewoman, 'you're being moved.'

'Where to?'

'I don't know but you are being moved out of Paris, there's a van waiting for you.'

I'm in a plane, a corporate jet sort of plane, there's no one else in the cabin, just me, I'm handcuffed to a seat, what's going on. I'm past caring so I scream out.

'Anyone there, what's going on.' No response so I scream even louder and start stamping on the cabin floor. It works, a door at the front of the plane opens and a man comes in. He's about sixty and looks as hard as nails.

'What the hell's going on, where am I?'

'Calm down mademoiselle Gray, you're on your way to Athens.'

'Athens, what the hell for, got another trumped up murder charge have you?'

My mind flashes back to Athens, Pierre and his offsider Carlos, the hard looking dude, they had been involved in something violent. I mean there were bloodstains, skinned knuckles, a knife wound, had there been a murder? was Pierre involved? were the French police onto it? Why am I being taken to Athens? Do the Athens police want to talk to me? I'm sliding even further down that shit hole, I need a fix, meth, I'm dependant on it, I'm a druggy.

'Allow me to introduce myself, Leonidos Stathos, I live in Athens. Here let me remove these handcuffs. The French police insisted on them. You have been released into my care while they conduct further investigation into the murder you were involved in. You are a person of interest in that matter. I have given them an undertaking that you will remain in my care for the time being. There are a couple of reasons why I have done this. First, the French police are not the nicest people when it comes to matters like this. I understand you are a recent arrival from New Zealand, you probably don't have any friends here in Europe to offer some support. I have two young children at home in Athens in need of a nanny. A few months ago we employed a girl from New Zealand, it was a very agreeable arrangement. Girls from your country make good nannies. Unfortunately for us she married so I am actively looking for a replacement, preferably someone from your part of the world. When your situation came to my attention I made an offer to the French police, they accepted. The situation now is that you remain in my care, primarily in Athens, and look after our two children until such time as the French police have resolved the murder of Pierre Gorbet. There could be some travel involved, my family spend time in Istanbul, we have a house there. Should the French police require you back in Paris then I'm obliged to comply with their request. Now then Carrie, how does all that sound?'

Is this for real, how can a Greek just pluck a murder suspect out of a French prison on a promise to return her if the French police require it, there's more to it than Leonidos Stathos is telling me. On the positive side, I'm out of that awful prison cell, away from those rather unpleasant, no, very unpleasant, French police. This nanny business, possible travel to Istanbul, things are looking up, but this Leonidos? he's a hard looking dude, what's the quid pro quo. Am I being marketed, is this some sort of white slavery, I've heard about that sort of thing, surely not, there's got to be a better explanation.

'Sounds a lot better than a prison cell but I didn't do it, I did not murder Pierre Gorbet. He was my lover, my sugar daddy, my meal ticket, why in hell would I murder him?'

'The French think you had a hand in it, that you set him up, they are very suspicious.'

'That's ridiculous, set him up for who, what, why, he was very good to me why on earth would I betray that trust, the very thought is objectionable.'

'Your Pierre was not exactly a knight in shining armour, how much do you know about him, where all his money came from?'

'A little, he had confided in me but nothing of any real consequence, I know he dealt in meth.'

'Yes he did, he was a major player, ruthless in dealing with people who got out of line. He had a lot of enemies.'

'So? do I want to know all that? he was very good to me and I respected him for that.'

'The French police suspect you were used to set him up, that you were not the faithful lover you make yourself out to be, that you are in the employ of others, rivals, what do you say to that?'

'Absolute rubbish, there's no truth in it. How come you seem to know so much about this business?'

This Leonidos fellow is another bad egg, he's obviously got the Paris police compromised, I mean how could anyone get a murder suspect out of jail and out of the country? I'm sliding even further down that shit hole.

'Ok Carrie let's not dwell on it, a bit of forward thinking. You'll like our family, the two children are pretty well behaved, they got on really well with your predecessor. You'll be under my wing, I'll be looking out for you.'

I'll hit him with a pointed question, it will give me an indication about what I'm beginning to suspect.

'Tell me monsieur Stathos what business are you in?'

'Spice, our firm is the major spice trader in Athens, we have substantial interests in Istanbul as well.'

I'm sure that's all kosher but my guess is he's into drug trading and Pierre was a rival, could be he's the villain in this mess, better watch my back.

It's a big house in an Athens suburb. There's Zoe, Leonidos's wife, she's an even harder looking affair than him, two young children, seem nice enough, and a daughter from an earlier liaison, Dioni, an attractive girl around eighteen. It all looks ok, anything's better than a police cell. What will life be like here? and for how long. Myrine, will I be able to see Myrine? the one ray of sunshine in my life.

I settle in. I've got a nice room overlooking a garden, the two children are ok. Not sure being a nanny is quite my thing, however, I'd better go along with it, there is no alternative right now. There's quite a lot of coming and going at the Stathos residence, all sorts of people, some shady looking characters. I pick up from overheard conversations that a family with the name Düzgün are a problem, could be the competition in the meth business that I increasingly suspect the Stathoses are involved in. I'll keep my ear to the ground, see what I can find out. Can I leave the house? I'll ask. Yes I can but I have to promise to be back by a certain time. Each absence will come with a curfew that I must observe. Nothing is said about the consequences for not sticking to the curfew, however, I guess Leonidos feels obliged to the Paris police to keep me under close supervision. Myrine, I'll make contact, I've got her number.

'You're living here.' Myrine's surprised, then I tell her the circumstances. We are in a café in downtown Athens. I'm allowed out for two hours.

'That's terrible Carrie you've got to get out of this mess, clear your name. How is that done? where do we start? I've got some friends in the private detective business here in Athens, I'll see what I can find out about these people you've fallen in with, in the meantime it appears we can only see each other for short periods. I guess a night together is out of the question.'

A pattern emerges, short periods away from the house to see Myrine, a lot of time looking after the two children, then after a couple of weeks a trip to Istanbul. Istanbul, that exotic Middle Eastern city. We are going there for three weeks to attend to the family spice business but I suspect there's a lot more than spice involved. A private jet, the same one Leonidos used to get me out of Paris, perhaps it's his, definitely a lot of money involved, spice? I'm sure it is!

Istanbul, the sights, the sounds, the call to prayer, the smells, it's all extremely exotic. It would be a lot more exciting if my circumstances were different, however, here I am. I'll get whatever enjoyment from it I can.

It's a big house near the airport surrounded by high walls, 22 Papalya Street. A big gate electronically operated, the place is a fortress. I'm not to leave the house.

'Hang on, that's a bit tough, not allowed out, come on, allow your nanny a little freedom. I've never been to this exotic city before, I'd like to have a look around.' I lay it squarely on Leonidos.

'Ok, perhaps I'm being a bit too strict, yes of course, I apologise. There's a young fellow I would like you to meet, perhaps he might like to show you around, Oziris Düzgün.'

What am I hearing, a Düzgün, they're the opposition, what intrigues am I getting involved in. Careful I'm not supposed to know anything about the illegal things the Stathoses do or that there is opposition, go along with what's being offered, could be a ticket to get out and about, see Istanbul.

'Carrie,' it's Leonidos, 'Oziris will be around in the morning, he would like to take you out for the day. He's from an old established family here in Istanbul, nice lad, you'll like him.'

What game is being played, Leonidos speaks with forked tongue. If the Düzgüns are the competition what's with the apparent olive branch? Don't ask questions Carrie, go with the flow remember you are not your own master right now, far from it.

He is a nice lad, good looking, polite, thoughtful, not the brightest though, oh well. I'm not exactly in a position where I can be choosy. We do a few of the famous places, Blue Mosque, Hagia Sophia, Topkapi Palace. Oziris is good company, nice lad but I don't think he's going to light my fire, not sure if any man can do that now, not since I've found Myrine. A little meth could set me off perhaps, in fact I'm sure some meth would help in my present circumstances but where am I going to get crystal meth, do I want to? Yes I do, I think I need it, shit I've become dependant, I'm a druggy. It's a shock realisation. I'm dependant on meth in fact I'm craving it right now.

Late afternoon, been a pleasant day with Oziris. He's suggested dinner, that's nice, keep me out late though, hope he's checked with 'mother,' bit like childhood days. It's a lovely restaurant in Istiklal

Street, Istanbul's restaurant row, the meal is excellent. Meth, I need some meth. This is something new, I've not had a craving like this before, well I've got a craving now, what can I do?

'Oziris, have you ever used crystal meth?'

'Ah yes I have but I'm not a user.'

'Do you have any with you?'

'No I don't.'

'Can you get it?'

'No, not right now, why do you ask, do you want some?'

'Yes Oziris, I need some right now, I really do.'

'Ok, ok, I'll see what I can do.'

He gets on his cellphone. Half an hour later a shady looking character shows up. Oziris has a word with him, there's an exchange and I'm given a small packet.

'Here you are Carrie, a gift from me.'

I rip the packet open, crystal meth ready to go. Into the toilet, I snort some, then some more, the effect is immediate. Suddenly Oziris looks pretty sexy, I wonder, will he? our first date. I'll leave it to him to make the first move, no sign of it, perhaps I can initiate something.

What the hell am I thinking, what's wrong with me, I'm a raving nymphomaniac, it's the meth. Get a hold of yourself before you slide even further down that shit hole.

The following morning. Nothing happened last night, Oziris did not satisfy my drug induced sexual urge, I don't think he even recognised it, bit of a wimp. Will I be seeing him again? Can't say I'm excited about the possibility but he could be my ticket out of this house, this prison. I do need to get out and about, I mean it's Istanbul, I want to see it all. Leonidos questions me.

'Carrie, how was it with Oziris, he was pretty smitten with you, wants to see you again soon, I would like that.'

'Bit of a ho hum I'm afraid Leonidos, did not exactly bowl me over, nice lad but not my type I'm afraid.'

'Carrie, I want you to see him again, get to like him, get him into bed, get him to go for you in a big way, understand.'

'Excuse me Leonidos, you want me to prostitute myself because you say so?'

'Yes Carrie that's exactly what I'm saying. You owe me remember. The French police are still very interested in you. I can send you back there whenever I like so you will do whatever I tell you and right now I'm telling you to get Oziris hooked.'

'That's slavery Leonidos, white slavery, it's disgusting.'

'Carrie do you appreciate you circumstances? you're a suspected murderer, the only thing keeping you out of a French prison cell is me, do you realise the enormity of that?'

Shit, I'm his slave, he wants, no he's demanding, that I seduce Oziris, where will that lead? Why does he want me to do this. Oziris is a Düzgün, is it an attempt to forge closer links with them? Why me? he's got a daughter, Dioni, why not use her, she's family, I'm a nobody, a foreigner, I don't get it. How will I handle this? Do I let on what I suspect, that Leonidos is in the drug smuggling business, that the Düzgüns are the opposition, that he wants to forge closer links, perhaps present a united front to any others who may have ambitions in the drug business?

'Look I don't much care for Oziris and you are telling me, no ordering me, to bed him, to get real close, why Leonidos?'

'Carrie I think I need to tell you a few things about myself to enable you to better understand what is going on, perhaps you might have figured some things out already; have you?'

'Yes.'

'Tell me.'

Shit, how do I answer that, how much do I divulge?'

'Come on Carrie, you're a perceptive girl, if you've figured things out I'm not going to hold it against you, could be we can use you in our organisation. Tell me what you know, or think you know.'

So I tell him, what the hell, might get a bit more respect, not just be his prostitute for hire.

'Hmm, more than I thought. Carrie, we can use you, remember you are beholden to me for your future wellbeing.'

'Unfortunately for me you're right.'

'Don't be like that, we can be friends, it will make things easier. I want you to get close to Oziris, find out about the Düzgüns drug dealing operation, pillow talk. It's amazing what is revealed in the extasy of sexual climax, can you do that Carrie?'

'No, I'll need help, specifically a regular supply of crystal meth, it's the only way I'll ever be able to bed Oziris and retain my sanity, can you arrange that?'

'Of course.'

*A pivot point in my life, I've just committed to being a paid prostitute who needs to be high on drugs to ply her trade. Have I hit rock bottom or is there no end to my degradation.*

I do bed Oziris, not the greatest experience of my life, far from it. I get high on meth and push him to do the same, we finish up in bed. I just about have to instruct him how to do it, I think he's a virgin. Our 'affair' develops, Oziris becomes a bit of a sex fiend, wants it all the time, not a great experience for me. I'm frigid when it comes to sex with Oziris. The meth helps, even manage to climax occasionally but I find myself using a lot of meth, I'm totally addicted, shit! As for finding out anything about the Düzgüns and their operation, nix. I don't think Oziris is privy to their innermost secrets, he's not the brightest fellow.

There's quite a bit of coming and going at 22 Papalya Street. Some pretty dubious characters. Occasionally I deliver packages to people in the city. I guess I'm now a drug courier, why me? what if I get caught? am I expendable? I'm also doing the nanny thing, that's the nicest part of my current life, the two youngsters are a real relaxation for me.

There is an incident that frightens me, terrifies would be a better description. A meeting at the house. I think it's some of the big players in the drug business. I was in the nursery a couple of rooms removed from where this meeting was taking place, there are raised voices, some shouting, it goes on for some time then a gunshot, shit! A bit later there's movement outside the nursery window. I glance out. Two men pushing what looks like a body into the back of a van, shit, am I witness to a murder? what else am I going to encounter as I slide further down my shit hole.

Back to Athens, the private jet again. Perhaps I'll be able to see Myrine, something nice in my life, get away from Oziris, he's becoming very possessive and it's not nice.

I open my heart to Myrine, she's very understanding. Her suggestion, go along with the present situation, an opportunity to escape will presents itself, something will happen, the drug dealing world is a pretty volatile place.

My strange existence continues. I'm doing minor delivery jobs around Athens and going out with Oziris. He's moved to Athens and he likes to show me off. Unfortunately he also wants to fuck me at every opportunity, it's not a pleasant experience. I find myself using increasing amounts of meth that Leonidos is happy to supply. I think he wants me to become a hardened addict, compliant. One day Leonidos's daughter Dioni shows up, she's got a man in tow, Michael, *Michael!* It turns out he had gone to Paris looking for me and found Dioni instead. He's taken up with her. It was a shock seeing him, an even bigger shock to discover I no longer had any strong feelings for him.

Michael? it's hard to get to talk. Dioni knows about our previous relationship, however, she now considers him her man and keeps him away from me, strangely I'm not upset. There's just no opportunity for us to have a serious talk. He's not living in the Stathos house. I don't know that he's been recruited by the Düzgüns, their mole in the Stathos camp via Dioni. Bit like what I'm supposed to be doing for the Stathoses with Oziris.

My strange unpleasant life continues, there's collusion between the Stathos and Düzgün families. It's been suggested Oziris and myself should get married, *what? no way.* Michael calls around occasionally, deliveries of some sort, I'm not allowed to talk to him. The marriage thing comes up again. Leonidos wants me to marry Oziris; *no way.*

'Carrie you will marry Oziris, he likes you, more than just likes you, he's totally smitten, and he's a Düzgün.'

'No Leonidos I will not marry Oziris. What's with the Düzgün bit anyway, you don't like the Düzgüns.'

'Carrie you realise that if I want I can put you back in that French police cell and I will if you don't go along with this, is that clear. As for his being a Düzgün, that's no concern of yours, there are reasons for this marriage, it will happen.'

'No, no, no, I will not marry Oziris.'

*It's a stunning blow, flashes of light, stars and wiggly things, I'm on the floor, my head's exploding.*
  *'You will marry Oziris.'*

A few weeks on, another move to Istanbul, the private jet again. Certainly a nice way to get around, an OE with a difference, unfortunately with nasty strings attached. Leonidos has shown his true colours, he's a nasty piece of work. The Düzgüns are also in

Istanbul, they spend a lot of time there. I suspect they are the major suppliers of crystal meth and they source it in that city. I don't know where Michael is, probably Istanbul. I suspect he's a Düzgün man now. I wonder if the Stathoses know that? Of course they'll know. What does it mean? Who's spying on who?

A phone call, it's Michael, '*Michael!* where, how, you've got my number, god at last we can talk.'

I tell my 'minders' I'm going for a walk, I'll be two hours. It's a restaurant in Istiklal Street, Michael, his dad, and another couple are there. Michael and I move away from the others, we talk, I tell him everything. It's a huge relief just to be able to talk to someone. I tell Michael about Myrine, about my feelings for her, how my feelings for him have changed, he appears to accept it all. The wedding. I tell him about that as well, how I want no part of it, how I have no choice. The French thing, how my life is shit. Sorry Michael but that's my lot right now. We join the others and after a bit I say farewell for now, have to get back to the people who own me.

# *Auckland*

Back to New Zealand, not ready for it, 'can't we just stay.'

'Afraid not, there have been a lot of enquiries, the place is fully booked again, you have to go but you can always come back.'

We're giving voice to our thoughts. The whales are making it harder, cavorting with their calves out in front every day. We've been swimming with them, it's almost like they welcome us, quite incredible, where else in the world?

Could make a stop at the Bounty on the way to the airport, well the grass field that passes for an airport. The place has so much character, straight out of a South Seas adventure story. *This is a South Seas adventure story.*

Feeling a bit down, we stop by the Bounty, did not do it justice when we arrived. Allan had plucked us out of the place and taken us off to his island paradise, Mounu is definitely paradise. There's a cruise ship anchored out in the harbour, the tourists will be all over Neiafu, experiencing a slice of the real South Pacific, they won't be disappointed, Neiafu is something else. Several people from the ship are in the Bounty, eyes popping, they had good reason. Several locals were in there drinking, I think the locals were making a thing about being a bit over the top, impress the visitors, Hollywood's perception of South Sea Swashbucklers, they certainly succeed. We were pretty impressed as well. Allan was with us, the wildest looking fellow there, his enormous beard and those eyes. The locals act it up, a lot of drinking, plenty of raucous laughter, a general sense of mayhem.

The little aeroplane is waiting, is it working? Yep. We're on our way, back to Nuku'alofa.

'Why don't we stop in Nuku'alofa, there's a big jet back to New

Zealand every couple of days, the opportunity may not come up again.'

'Done.'

Nuku'alofa, Tonga's capital, it means *abode of love,* really, our sort of place. Somewhere to stay for a couple of nights?

Fafá Island Resort, a fast ride in a small boat just to the north of Nuku'alofa, thatched roofs on little intimate fales, restaurant and bar, great South Seas atmosphere. Hang on we've just come from a place like that. Look at this as a continuation of our South Seas experience. No whales but everything else about the place is great. We wine and dine in their little restaurant. It's all ours, just a handful of guests, mostly honeymooners, we're in good company. A couple of days sacked out on the sand, pretty much all over suntans now, the nights, well it's a romantic place. The fales are spread out around the little island and the beds are huge.

It's a pleasant break in our trip back to New Zealand, gives our Greek friends a look at another South Seas paradise, they love it, 'we'll be back!'

Auckland and it's pouring, bitterly cold sou'wester, Auckland at its worst, welcome home, 'sorry about this folks.' There's hope, every day is different in Auckland, and it is, the following morning dawns fine and warm. The wet day does have a silver lining, best place to be? bed.

'Right Athens; do we have to?' What's this, 'want to stay in Auckland a bit longer?'

'It's a thought, all that unpleasantness seems so far away, so far removed from what we've been enjoying, do we really have to?'

'Ok, here's the plan, we go back to Athens and establish our new living arrangements. We get Carrie off the hook and Michael into a job then we can think about another trip out here, no rush. Some more time here perhaps before we move, what do you think?'

'Frank, you've just planned our immediate lives for us, great job.' Ariana's summing up.

'How about lunch at Vino Vino's on Waiheke again, we'll get the ferry over to Matiatia and walk up to Oneroa, on for that?'

It's another great meal at Vino Vino's always is. I notice Michael is uncomfortable, something's troubling him, certainly not Dimitra, she's all over him, pretty much the norm these days, that's nice. Lunch over, down to the beach for a walk in the surf, bit of hand holding, it's just so nice on Waiheke. The ferry back to the city in the late afternoon.

'Dad, that fellow in the restaurant with the gorgeous girl in tow, did you notice him?'

'He did look vaguely familiar. She was quite an eyeful, how could I not notice her.'

'That was Yiannis Stavrou the new Düzgün boss.'

It hits like a bomb, of course, I had met him, in Athens, it's just the mind-set, not programmed to see him on Waihehe. What the hell is he doing here in New Zealand.

'Did he see you Michael?'

'Probably.'

The Maniot lad murdered at Peacock Sky, got to be that, but why would it bring the Düzgün boss to New Zealand? Perhaps a word with Peter Culpan the Auckland CIB fellow, might be a good idea. Yes indeed Peter Culpan would like to talk to us again.

Next morning we leave the girls at the pool, another lovely day. The fellows go along to Auckland Central, there's a high-powered collection of police people keen to talk to us. The presence of Yiannis Stavrou in Auckland is not known to the police, it's assumed he's using an alias. Michael is in no doubt, it was him in the restaurant and he thinks he was spotted, could this have consequences?

The Düzgüns are drug dealers, that's cause for concern. The Peacock Sky murder? Was it intimidation, part of the gang war raging in Greece, or was the young lad part of something here in New Zealand? Are the Maniots into the New Zealand drug scene? The New Zealand Police did have intelligence that a major drug smuggling operation was establishing itself in Australia and New Zealand and the presence of the Düzgün boss lends credence to that information. Where would the drugs be sourced? Not Europe, Istanbul, not practical, got to be South America. The Vav'au thing, that was cocaine from South America and they were Italians, does not necessarily mean there's not a connection. Perhaps the police can pick up Yiannis Stavrou for questioning, if they can find him, the alias thing is reason enough. Suddenly the scene has changed, the nasty world that Michael and Carrie are involved in appears to extend to New Zealand.

We decide to stay a bit longer in Auckland, there's no real rush to get back to Athens.

'Well yes there is,' from Ariana, 'there's a job that requires my presence, can't stay away forever but I will, it's too nice here and there's Frank, can't just leave him all alone, not now.'

The police are unable to find Yiannis Stavrou, they think he's left the country. If he thought Michael had spotted him then his cover would be blown. Interpol would have him on their watchlist but the New Zealand police had not been advised, perhaps he had evaded Interpol's surveillance. So just what was he doing here? The police go back to Waiheke. The Peacock Sky is now a place of interest. What was the young lad from Athens up to, an innocent backpacker or something else, something sinister?

It turns out quite a few people had called on young Elios Maniot at The Peacock Sky, rather unsavoury looking people. There was a young girl, another backpacker from Greece, she seemed to be close to him. She had disappeared soon after the murder. In the course of their investigation it is revealed that young Elios had been supplying several of the staff with cocaine, where was he getting it? Was he part of an organisation distributing cocaine in New Zealand and was it the Maniot family? The young girl who had been close to him, where does she fit in? She's disappeared, was she involved in some way? Could it be the Düzgüns want in on what is a Maniot operation and had made their intentions brutally obvious, there are a lot of possibilities.

'Can we give it another week before we move, how's that fit with you Ariana?'

'For you Frank all things are possible.'

I was thinking there could be developments here, we could assist the police, our knowledge about the Athens scene. It appears two of the Athens crime families are active here.

A couple of days go by then Peter Culpan calls, 'we need to talk, can you people come in.'

The police have been busy, spurred into action by the Waiheke business. Apparently there's an active cocaine distribution network in Auckland but the police do not know at this stage who the bad guys are. Young Elios Maniot had been involved, he had access to considerable amounts of cocaine and appeared to be running things which makes it look like the Maniots. His brutal murder and the presence of Yiannis Stavrou in Auckland suggests that the Düzgüns want in and have made their intentions clear. There's been another murder, the police have played it down. The young Greek girl, Elios Maniot's friend, had been found in a ditch in south Auckland with her throat cut. The Maniot operation in Auckland is definitely being targeted, got to be the Düzgüns.

'Michael, you know this fellow Yiannis Stavrou,' Peter Culpan asks, 'what can you tell us about him?'

'Not much, he only came to prominence after the Stamna massacre, I know very little about him. He's not you archetypical thug, he's a nice guy, well he appears to be a nice guy, he let me off the hook when I found myself tied to the Düzgüns, however, I'm quite sure he will of doing whatever it takes to keep control of his organisation. I think we've seen a bit of that already.'

'Thanks for that Michael, looks like we're dealing with an Athens based crime syndicate, possibly two, it's cocaine at the moment but it could encompass meth, who knows, meth is their stock in trade in Europe. Who heads up the New Zealand operation? we don't know. It appears there's been a takeover, a brutal takeover.'

Peter Culpan then tells us about another development that's causing concern. Three weeks ago a yacht, a Beneteau 40, was stolen from Bucklands Beach. It was found five days later abandoned on a deserted northland beach. There were signs of violence, bullet holes and a lot of blood. The police put their drug dog aboard, the yacht had been carrying a lot of cocaine.

The police take on the situation. The stolen yacht had made a pick up out at sea, probably cocaine from Columbia. They had run into trouble when they landed it in northland. It appears the people wanting in on the New Zealand cocaine business, probably the Düzgüns, got wind of the shipment and highjacked it when the yacht made landfall. Judging by the number of bullet holes and the blood, there had been a shootout, probably some fatalities.

'Sounds a bit like Athens, this sort of thing does not happen here, it's what we're trying to distance ourselves from. Can we help you Peter?' I offer.

'Yes, we need to find out all we can about the Düzgüns. It appears they are going to become our problem. At the moment it's coke from Columbia and that brings up another matter, your encounter with the Italians up in Vava'ua. The Tongan police have given us a detailed account of what happened. They appreciate what you people did to assist. It was Columbian cocaine. We don't know where or who it was destined for, could have been New Zealand.

There might be, probably is, an organised crime ring involved, that means problems for us. We need to find out all the background we can. You people can probably help, you are closer to the goings on in Athens than we are. Michael, you could be a point of contact, your friendship with Yiannis Stavrou.'

'Wow, hang on, he's not my friend. The only dealing I had with him was my request to be released from the organisation that he took over after Andrias Düzgün was gunned down. I have no desire to have anything to do with him or his organisation, he's a dangerous man.'

'Ok, I understand your reluctance but it's a possible avenue that could be explored. What we want is information, anything about the Düzgüns could be helpful, enable us to better understand how they operate.'

'I'll keep it in mind but don't pressure me, I like being alive.'
Back to the house in Parnell, the girls will be asking questions. There's nothing to hide, they're party to what's been happening. We fill them in on the details, well nearly all the details, then set a date to go back to Athens; three days from now.

'Frank we haven't been sailing, you did mention it, remember?' it's Ariana, 'If I'm to put my job on the line, absent without permission, the least you can do is take us sailing on your magnificent Waitemata, ok?'

Steve Coultard, as well as having a big Maritimo, has got a yacht, an Oceanis 60, a big Beneteau. Must be money in plastics, should have got myself into that.

'Frank you rascal you want to get the ladies out on the water in a yacht, my yacht. I suppose you'll want to be there, keep an eye on your harem, wouldn't want them getting all carried away again? Hang on, that's not a bad idea, Rachel would be a starter, but you know that. How about first thing in the morning, a full day's sailing, we could stay out for the night, you on for that.'

'Done deal Steve, I'm in your debt.'

Early morning Half Moon Bay, a lot of big pleasure craft in the new marina development, including Steve's big Beneteau. We sail down the Tamaki estuary out onto the Waitemata, a perfect day, good run of weather, not always the case in Auckland. Steve's an experienced yachtie and it all comes back to me as well. I used to do a lot of sailing in yesteryear, 'remember those times Rachel?'

We get right into the sailing bit, there's just enough wind to make it viable, swishing along at peace with nature, no noise, just the relaxing sound of water sliding along the hull and the slight rustling of wind in the sails.

A secluded bay on the north side of Waiheke, we drop the pick, 'lunchtime,' Rachel does her thing. Athens seems so far away, on another planet, the sun's beating down, it's hot.

Lunch, another excellent spread, she's quite a girl, always was, memories from long ago, could have been the same bay. We used to do a lot of sailing, Rachel and I, nostalgia. The girls go up front with Michael and Christos, spread themselves out on the big deck sunbathing, Steve and I get to talking.

'Frank, tell me about Athens, pretty obvious your tied up in something, I mean these lovely ladies, your boy Michael, and Christos, he's a detective, right?'

'You don't want to know Steve, another world, not a nice one either, the good news, I've found Ariana, I think I'm in love, going back to Athens to be with her.'

'Come on Frank, you're a detective, a good one from what I've heard, what's with the Athens thing, I won't tell, trust me.'

'Trust you, the guy who stole my girl, no that's not right, lack of attention on my part, that's what happened; anyhow Athens, in confidence Steve, seriously, no telling anyone.'

I give Steve a sanitised version of all that's happened including the unfortunate things that have occurred right here on Waiheke, he looks stunned.

'Shit, glad I stuck with plastics, and stole Rachel, sounds exciting though, real James Bond stuff. I think it's about time Rachel and I did something about that bucket list, Athens could be a good starting point, plenty of action.'

'No Steve you don't want that sort of action, settle for reading about it in the papers.'

'Frank, the cocaine business here in Auckland, I think I might know a bit about it. It's a recent thing, the past year or so, become trendy, well it always has been but a lot more so these days. From what I've heard, and I hear a lot, there are two main suppliers, a local fellow and a Greek chap, I think the Greek chap is the kingpin, I also hear the Greek chap has disappeared.'

'Anything else Steve, anymore straws in the wind? ask your supplier, you are a user, right?'

'Er yes, we do snort a bit of coke occasionally, socially, no I'm not a user, it's the trendy thing to do in Auckland society these days, bit stupid though.'

I ask Steve, 'the Peacock Sky murder, the fellow was a Greek, a Maniot, could he have been the kingpin?'

'That fellow was just a kid, a backpacker, doubt he would be the boss man, he must have had good access to the stuff though.'

We let the subject drop, time for a drink, no need to move, this little bay is a known anchorage, we'll spend the night here.

'Steve, Steve Coultard.' A loud voice, another yacht, another Beneteau, has invaded our space, mates of Steve. They tie up stern to stern and come aboard, two couples, middle aged, look like party types.

'What have you got here Steve, where did you find these lovely ladies?'

'Imports from Greece Colin, they come with minders, these two big guys, and an apprentice.'

'You're kidding me, Greece, what sort of business are you running Steve?'

'Cut the bullshit, allow me to introduce these people. This is my friend Colin Petrou and his party friends from Auckland. Colin these people are visitors from Greece, names, you'll forget them as soon as I tell you so I'll leave it up to you individually to get acquainted.'

The new arrivals look like fun people, how will this develop. Colin Petrou brings a case of champaign over from his boat and it's all on, could be some heavy drinking.

It's late afternoon heading for a glorious sunset, we are spread around the spacious cockpit on Steve's big Beneteau drinking Colin's champaign, it's not long before the suggestion is made, 'what about a little coke?' This is going to be difficult, we are not users, not even occasionally, not sure about Steve and Rachel, just go with the flow. Our visitors are right into it, look like heavy users. Long lines of the white stuff disappearing up their noses, hope this does not get messy. I'm sure Steve will keep a lid on things. Steve broaches the subject.

'Tell me Colin where do you get this stuff?'

'From the mother lode Steve, right from the top.'

'Top of what.'

Colin is a bit spaced out, a glazed look in his eyes, slurring his words, his friends are fast approaching the same state. Bit of a worry, not experienced this before, our girls look a bit apprehensive.

'From the big boss, the new man from Athens.'

Shit, alarm bells, what have we come across, what's with this Colin Petrou, stay cool Frank. Christos has zeroed in on the conversation, very alert, he's not participated in the coke snorting.

'The top top Steve, the new man. The incumbent got the bullet, vanished, the new guy is number one. Heaps of the stuff, price is right too, I'll introduce you if you want.'

What the hell have we stumbled onto, does Colin know the new man at the top of the cocaine distribution ring here in New Zealand? is he a Düzgün? We need to tread carefully, very carefully. Humour Colin, see what we can find out. I glance at Christos and Steve, they both realise what we've uncovered, the need for caution. Steve takes the lead. After what I've told him I think he realises we may have a goldmine of information here in Colin.

'Colin tell me, how do you actually obtain your coke?' it's Steve asking.

Colin snorts another long line of the stuff, he's away with the fairies, could be ripe for the plucking. Can we take advantage of the situation, pick his brains? What about the others in his party, will they get suspicious? don't think so, they're a bit beyond it, heavy users, let's go for it.

'Who supplies you Colin?'

'I supply myself, get the stuff in bulk and distribute it, help myself to as much as I want.'

Shit, he's a dealer, a major distributor perhaps. We're in dangerous territory here.

'In bulk, what do you mean Colin.'

'Just that, this Greek fellow, just arrived on the scene, replaced the previous chap, he gets the stuff from abroad, don't know where, I distribute it, big money.'

This is getting dangerous, if Colin remembers what he's been telling us we could be in real danger, he appears to be a major distributor for the importer. I suspect that importer is tied up with the Düzgüns, could be a Düzgün. His predecessor was probably a Maniot and probably dead. There's been a takeover, that would explain the presence of Yiannis Stavrou in Auckland, setting up his own organisation, more bodies will be turning up.

'Who is this fellow Colin?' A dangerous question, if Colin realises we are milking him things could change.

'Mr No Name, these fellows don't have names.'

I think it's time to drop it, don't want Colin getting suspicious, we have enough information, the police can deal with it from here. What have we just learnt? A lead on the Düzgüns head man in New Zealand, should not be too hard for the police to nail him. Will involve putting the squeeze on Colin and that might expose us as the informants. The police will need to be careful on that one, don't want to endanger ourselves. It could compromise us back in Athens as well. The police will need to be very careful. The Düzgüns are a ruthless lot. If they found out Colin was the cause of their downfall in New Zealand, well hard to know what they would do but it would not be nice. Colin is a mate of Steve's, what have we done? well nothing yet but if we take this to the police then it's possible Colin could be in danger, what to do? If Colin continues snorting the white stuff at the present rate I doubt he will have any recollection about what we've been talking about.

The party continues, well not really a party, the fun's gone out of it. Colin and his friends are high on coke, how long will they last? We have a couple of drinks and start to think about how we can extricate ourselves.

'We have to get back to Auckland tonight, need to think about moving,' Steve's input. Good one Steve, but bugger, the idea was to stay out overnight and enjoy another day's sailing tomorrow but we need to get away from Colin's lot, they're turning into a disaster area. Steve bites the bullet.

'Ok we're off, have to get back to the city, how are you people fixed, need a hand to get back aboard your boat?'

Need a hand? an understatement, they need all the help they can get, they're legless and in charge of a big yacht. I don't think they will be moving anywhere tonight.

We help them return to their yacht then we're off, along the Waiheke coast to another little bay, there are plenty of them. Pity, that one had fond memories, myself and Rachel back in yesteryear. Colin's turning up has put a bit of a dampener on things, not to worry, still plenty of evening left. Another idyllic bay, let's have a relaxed wine and perhaps a bite to eat. The rest of the evening is a lot more enjoyable but what we've learnt has left me deeply disturbed, there's no escaping the nightmare we're involved with in Athens.

Another glorious day's sailing, been a while. Did a lot of it years ago, then it became family, work, career, all sorts of distractions and not much sailing, should get back into it. The girls are wildly enthusiastic, all new to them, wonder if Ariana would make a good yachtie? Perhaps a share in an Auckland based yacht, go sailing when we visit Auckland, good excuse to spend time here, lots of time perhaps, food for thought. Then just to round the day out, a pod of dolphins close in on the bow, rolling under the hull, leaping out of the water, putting on a great display. I don't think our visitors had seen anything like it before.

Back onto the marina and home, that was great, thank you Steve, you've won some Greek hearts. Some good contacts when you visit Athens, that bucket list, ticking those boxes.

We are booked back to Athens the next day, better alter that, we need to confer with the police, put the travel back a few days. I get on to Steve, I think he needs to be fully in the picture, after all the big break through happened on his yacht. If his mate Colin comes unstuck with the Greek supplier then it could implicate Steve. We arrange a meeting with the police for the following day.

Myself, Christos, Michael, and Steve go along to Auckland Central. The police are pleased to see us, it seems we are their main source of information. What we had to tell them confirmed what they already suspected. They had spent a lot of time investigating cocaine distribution in Auckland, already had tabs on the new *Mr No Name*. It would not be necessary to involve Steve in the matter, no reason for his name to be mentioned. Steve's mate Colin? His involvement was news to them, a major distributor, that could get messy.

Back to Parnell, pack the bags, nothing more to do here, all in police hands now. Athens and a new life, a life with Ariana.

# *Athens*

Athens, do we want to be here? what happens now? hopefully just our domestic arrangements, who lives where.

Ariana comes right out with it, 'Frank, you're moving in with me.' It had not actually been discussed, an unsaid understanding, however, Ariana has now made it definite. Michael moves into Christos and Karisa's house with Dimitra and they start looking for their own place. No rush, Christos and Karisa rather like having them at home. Ariana starts looking for a position within her organisation for Michael, does not take long. There's a vacancy coming up in a couple of weeks for a structural architect in their head office in downtown Athens. There'll be an interview, however, Ariana's quite sure he'll land the job. Her firm had employed a Kiwi some time ago, it was a happy association.

'Frank, we'll call on Nico, get the lowdown on the war.' Christos' suggestion.

'He's in hospital, some bastard shot him,' Zinovia tells us. 'Gang wars are not too particular about who gets targeted, why Nico? He's in Athens General Hospital.'

'Nico, why? who have you pissed off?'

'Don't know, probably a lot of people over the years. The guy who did this has taken advantage of the current falling out to get me, make it look like collateral. Shot two others in my bar, killed them. I saw it coming, ducked for cover, got away with a bullet in the guts. Bastard; I know who it was, he'll need to watch his back.'

'How's the war going Nico, who's winning?'

'Well it's not the Stathoses, they've lost a lot of people, bodies turning up all over town, the public are pissed. Lot of pressure on the police to clean the place up, stop the killing. I think the Düzgüns might have the edge, don't know about the Maniots. Kenzo and Lambani have dropped right out of sight. There is one worrying development, Janus Stathos, Leonidos's brother, real bad dud, turned up from Paris, looks like he will head up the Stathos family, that's if he survives the current wave of killing. I hear there have been a couple of attempts.'

'Not good Nico, getting yourself shot, need to tread carefully. Us? well hopefully we're out of it, just Carrie's Paris thing but I think that could well have blown over. We've got the necessary to get her off the hook should anything develop. I'll be living here for a bit, Ariana. Michael's here as well, Dimitra. He's going to be a permanent resident.'

'Well welcome to Athens perhaps we'll see you in my fine establishment from time to time. What are you going to do Frank, apart from keeping a smile on Arianas's face, anything in mind?'

'Not at this stage Nico.'

Nico has raised a good point, what am I going to do? Not given it much thought, not given it any thought. I'll need something to occupy my time, can't just vegetate.

'Christos, I need to be doing something, how do you handle retirement, what occupies your spare time?'

'Nothing in particular Frank, just enjoying all the free time but I'm getting restless.'

We're both in the same boat, can't just sit on our bums being retired, that's not good, the brain will atrophy. What skills do we have, what can we offer the world? Well we're both experienced detectives that should be a marketable commodity, how's that done? A private detective agency, that's how. Hang on we're retired, don't want to be working our butts off.

*Well don't work your butts off, be selective in what you take on, low profile, plenty of time off, work at your pace not at the whim of others, how does that sound?*

'Sounds like something that might work for us.' Christos's take on the idea. 'Galani & Conchie - Private Investigators, how's that sound?'

'Not a silly idea, doing something we enjoy without the pressure of a police environment. Private clients, steer clear of the criminal underworld. The more I think about it the more it makes sense. If we're any good there could be money in it. Our own masters, take off to New Zealand whenever, suddenly the idea has a lot of appeal, 'what do you think Christos?'

'I like, let's think about it before we put it to the ladies.'

'Carrie, we'll catch up with her, how about tonight at your local taverna.'

There are eight of us, the happy travellers from New Zealand plus Carrie and Myrine.

'How's it going Carrie, how's your new life? No moon boot I see?'

'Good and bad, mostly good. Myrine is now my boss, I'm working for her in the fashion business and I really like it. Got tabs on a yacht at Piraeus so there's a bit of sailing as well. I'm teaching Myrine how to sail. I'm the boss at weekends.'

'Sounds great, free of the other business?'

'Drugs you mean Frank? yes completely free, Myrine's all I need these days.'

'So what's the bad?'

'That bastard Leonidos has not carked it, trying to exert control apparently. I got a note from him the other day indicating he wanted me back in the fold.'

'Jesus Carrie, that's real bad, what did you do?'

'Nothing, nothing at all. It was three weeks ago, I've just ignored it. I also hear he's no longer the boss, his nasty brother Janus is.'

'Shit, excuse me, did not want to hear that Carrie. Why would he want you back, what possible use can you be to him now? Sounds like there's not much of his organisation left anyway. Try not to concern yourself about Leonidos. We have the wherewithal to deal with the French Police should that business come up.'

'Yes Frank, I see it that way as well. I'm not worrying, my new life has no room for worrying, let's change the subject. Michael, what have you been up to? Don't worry Dimitra, Michael's very much the ex, stop giving me that look.'

'Ok, ok Carrie,' from Dimitra, 'for a moment I thought I might have competition, silly me, we can all be friends especially now we're all living normal lives here in Athens, well I hope they'll be normal lives.'

'Working in the city for Ariana's company, very happy too, been given a major design project. I think they're testing me.'

Four weeks on, Galani & Conchie - Private Investigators, a registered company, discretion is our byword. At this stage it's a post office box number, if there's interest we'll think about an office. Michael's enjoying his architect job. Nico is back in his bar, fully recovered. I would not like to be the fellow who put the bullet in him. The gang war has quietened down, no more bodies turning up. Perhaps our lives can continue on like this, normal, if only! Michael gets a note from Yiannis Stavrou, he wants a meeting.

'What do I do Dad, ignore it? I don't think he'll allow that. I want nothing to do with him.'

Not a good situation. Michael is right, people like Yiannis Stavrou cannot be ignored. What can he want from Michael, only one way to find out.

The decision is pre-empted the very next day, Michael is

kidnapped. A witness tells us a black van pulled up next to him, a couple of fellows grabbed him, shoved him into the van and took off. What do we do, call the cops? don't think so, probably Yiannis Stavrou. Michael had not responded to his request for a meeting. Perhaps Nico can put us onto Yiannis Stavrou, we can confront him. Doing nothing is not an option. Dimitra is beside herself, quite hysterical. Christos and myself are at the flat consoling her late the same evening, Michael walks in, he does not look good, there's a cut on his face and he's holding his ribs, it was Janos Stathos, why?

'He want's me to work for the Stathoses. I'm in the Düzgüns camp according to him. If I don't agree it will not go well for Carrie.'

Shit the thing we were afraid of is happening. It's obvious Leonidos has put Janos in the picture, they want to use the hold they have over Carrie to their advantage. I'll have to think about that. What hold? Leonidos is bluffing. After the massacre Carrie had severed her connection with the Stathoses. Put it this way, we had taken her into our protective custody, the French would know this. They had not said anything to us, so although Carrie may still be a person of interest they do not seem to be concerned that she's not in the care of Leonidos but has moved in with Myrine. The French would know this as well, know where to find her should they want her.

'Dad I tried to explain I had severed my connection with the Düzgüns, they did not believe me, they claimed I was friendly with Yiannis Stavrou. They want me to nurture this friendship. Carrie's welfare is at stake. They will come after Dimitra as well. Dad they beat me up. This Janos Stathos is a real bad bugger.'

Problem, a big one. Perhaps we should approach Yiannis, we need help, not sure we can deal with this ourselves. Michael has not responded to Yiannis's request for a meeting, now could be a good time, put him in the picture. Perhaps the situation can be turned to our advantage. Give the Düzgüns an avenue to feed the Stathoses misinformation. Could suggest it's time to deal to Leonidos and his brother. Yes, but there will be a price for whatever Yiannis might agree to. The only real fix for us would be the removal of the threat to the girls, what would be Yiannis's price?

The meeting happens, whatever it was that Yiannis wanted with Michael is overshadowed by this latest development. Yiannis sees numerous advantages. Michael can be a conduit to feed misinformation to the Stathoses, disrupt their operations, allow the Düzgüns to strengthen their position. Removing Leonidos and Janus is another option, one that will eventually be carried out, but not right now, the price?

'Michael I want you back in the fold, a Düzgün man, there are things you can do for us, our New Zealand operation. You saw me in Vino Vino's, I'm sure you've got it figured.'

'No way Yiannis, I'm out of it. I don't want any connection with either of the families, seriously. I'm happily employed, I want it to stay that way.'

'Michael, you don't want Carrie or Dimitra being threatened, I can help you with that but there is a quid pro quo. Auckland is your home town, we can use you there, not right now but at a future time. Right now you can go along with the Stathos's belief that you're a Düzgün man, you can pass on information for us, can you do that? It will ensure the safety of the two girls.'

Shit shit shit, an impossible situation, go along with Yiannis, feed the Stathoses false information, remove the threat to the girls. What if they cotton on to what I'm doing? what if I don't agree to Yiannis's request? will he harm the girls? possibly, and the suggestion about New Zealand, I want no part of that.

'Dad what shall I do?'

'Right now go along with the Stathos's request but what are they expecting? you're not privy to what the Düzgüns are thinking, you're an outsider. You need to question Janos Stathos on that point, what sort of information does he expect from you? More to the point, what will they do if you don't go along with it? Bit of a lose-lose situation right now.'

'Ok, I'll sound out Yiannis, find out how he wants to use me, I've got a day job now. I don't want to be associated with any criminal elements but the threat to the girls, and from both sides, can't ignore it.'

# *Michael*

Athens, my new home, my new life with Dimitra. We've found a place to live and Ariana has come through with a job. Bit of competition, the previous fellow from New Zealand must have made a good impression, they seemed to like me at the interview. Living with Dimitra, I mean living full time with her, like a married couple, it's incredible, I've never been so happy, then *whamo* the past arrives back in our lives, shit.

It's a note from Yiannis Stavrou, he wants a meeting, why? What possible interest can he have in me. Vino Vino's on Waiheke, he saw me, or more to the point I saw him, is that it. Can't ignore the request, you don't ignore a thing like that, give it a couple of days, some thinking time then perhaps a meeting.

What the? I'm out walking, thinking. Crash, two rough looking types grab me, shove me into a van, slam the door and take off, shit.

'Michael Conchie, the Düzgün lackey,' it's a bad looking dude. 'Allow me to introduce myself, Janus Stathos, I run things now.' Shit, what does he want with me.

'My brother Leonidos has filled me in on your old girlfriend, the lesbian bitch you thought you were in love with, the bitch who murders people, the one the French want to lock up and throw away the key, still feel for her do you Michael?'

Geez this bastard sure knows how to get a guy riled up.

'What makes you think I'm a Düzgün man?'

'Don't insult my intelligence, you've been working for them for quite a while. What we want from you is information about their operations and don't tell me you don't know anything. You're a buddy of that asshole Yiannis Stavrou and that puts you close to the centre of things.'

'Afraid you've got it wrong, I've severed all connections with the Düzgüns and' --- my words are cut short by a savage blow to my stomach.

'Don't piss with me you young prick or your girlfriend will have her face rearranged, you're a Düzgün insider, don't try to bullshit me.'

Shit I'm in big trouble, antagonising this fellow is not a smart thing to do right now, he looks the sort of lowlife that's capable of anything, better go along with whatever he's going to lay on me, not much choice.

'You are going to get close to that bastard Yiannis Stavrou and find out what he's planning to do in Paris, we know he wants to expand his distribution business there. We want to know how big an expansion? Got that. I'll give you two weeks to come up with something; or else! Do I make myself clear!'

'How the hell do you expect me to be privy to the Düzgüns innermost secrets, I'm an outsider' --- another sickening blow to my stomach, this Janus is a real nasty bastard.

'Just do it, your girlfriends good looks are at stake.'

I'm in the back of the van again, crash, they push me out right outside our flat, the one I share with Dimitra, bit close to home.

How do I handle this, doing nothing is not a good idea, these Stathos animals are quite capable of making good on their threats. I'll have to enlist Yiannis's help, open my heart to him, the problem is he's a crook, just like the Stathoses, there will be a price. There is one thing going for me. The Stathoses have laid it on me in no uncertain terms that they want information about Yiannis's intentions. They've opened a door that will allow Yiannis to feed them dud information,

I should be able to capitalise on this. If I help Yiannis cripple the Stathoses, and their vicious ultimatum has opened the way to achieve this, then I could ask him to remove the threat to the girls. That's a big ask and would probably involve murder. Shit, what am I thinking? how far am I being drawn into the Athens underworld.

It's hard to concentrate at my new job. They've given me part of an oil berthing terminal to design. It's fascinating and something I'm comfortable with but this Stathos Düzgün business, it's worrying me sick. It's been a week since the kidnapping, a week of serious thinking. I think I've got a plan sorted in my mind. I need to meet with Yiannis and figure out how we will feed the Stathoses dud information. He will be on my side, after all he wants to stick it to the Stathoses and they have obligingly made it possible. The grey area? How can I convince them that I am privy to such sensitive information. It would have to start with unimportant stuff and slowly escalate but it won't be me stealing information, Yiannis will be right there regulating the flow. This could work, will have to work, the stakes are high. I set up a meeting with Yiannis.

'Michael I'm impressed, the lengths you've gone to to win the confidence of the Stathos lot, kidnapped, beaten up, it would be stupid not to maximise the opportunity that's been presented.' I'm talking to Yiannis, filling him in on what's happened, he's delighted.

'We'll play this real low key for a while, just enough to keep those bastards on the hook without endangering your ladies, they are lovely and I appreciate a lovely lady.'

Yeah right, weasel words, I would not trust Yiannis in any situation, he's a crook albeit a nice one. Well if you're on his side he can be nice but cross him? I don't want to think about it. So what happens now?

'Ok Michael, here's the plan. We'll do nothing for a couple of weeks then I'll give you some bullshit story that you've overheard, about us sending a man to Paris to reorganise our distribution chain. The story will mention the disappearance of a Stathos operative in Paris. Their Paris man will vanish about the same time they get your story, will authenticate it, you ok with that?'

Shit they are going to murder someone just to establish my credentials, do I want to be party to this? no, do I have a choice? no, do I divulge what I'm getting into to anyone? Dad perhaps, have to think about that.

It's a worrying couple of weeks, I immerse myself in my new job, try not to think too much about my other life, the life on the fringe of the criminal world. Fringe, bullshit, you'll soon be donkey deep and it would be a good idea to tell Dad.

'I've been waiting for you to tell me something Michael, they did not beat you up for fun, they want something and you will have to deliver, what you deliver will have to be believable. What you have just told me is believable, that's what these people do. You'll have to go along with it, keep the faith with both sides. Right now I can't see any other option. The new detective agency on the block, Galani & Conchie – Investigations, will be sniffing around for any straws in the wind. The danger for you is twofold. If the Düzgüns prevail they will probably want to keep you on, you'll need to sort that out with Yiannis, you'll need a release agreement. If the Stathoses suspect you are misleading them that could be very dangerous and you could well be on your own, Yiannis may not protect you. If he did it would expose you as a Düzgün sympathiser, a traitor in the Stathoses eyes. It's a bad scene Michael, not sure how you can free yourself from it either.'

Well Dad's in the picture, I've got some moral support but shit I'm back to square one, back in the Düzgün camp. I really am in a lose-lose situation. If I want to break free from the Stathoses then really Leonidos and Janus need to be gone, what's that involve? The same with the Düzgüns, Yiannis needs to go. Between a rock and a hard place takes on a whole new meaning.

Snap out of it getting depressed does not help, think of your new life with Dimitra, how good is that, the girl loves you. The pendulum will swing, life's like that, you'll get lucky sometime. I found Dimitra, how lucky was that? Can I have some more good luck? In the meantime get on with the life you have, perhaps not quite what you want but it's what you've got. Do what's being asked of you and do it carefully, there's danger, a lot of danger.

'Let's get Carrie and Myrine 'round for dinner, not seen them for a while,' my suggestion to Dimitra, 'have a meal at our place, give the taverna a miss, check out your cooking skills Dimitra.'

'You'll be surprised Michael, not had much of a go in the kitchen recently, not since taking up with you, hopefully you'll be pleasantly surprised. I attended a cookery school a couple of years ago, not had much chance to put it into practise of late.'

She sure can cook, might give the taverna a miss for a while, Dimitra's meal is fabulous. The conversation at Dimitra's dinner party is wide ranging. Our Tongan adventure holds centre stage. I think Carrie's a bit regretful she was not there however we make the point that both her and Myrine are more than welcome to come to Auckland any time. Another holiday in Vauv'au could be on the cards. It's a pleasant evening and the two girls leave around eleven.

Half an hour later there's a panicky phone call from Carrie. Their car has been run off the road and they've been threatened by a couple of bad looking dudes, Stathos people.

'Message for that young shit Conchie, we want something and we want it now, pass it on.'

'Michael what's that all about?'

There's no escaping, my criminal connections are going to haunt me. Best if I get on with it, do what they want and keep an eye open for an escape opportunity. It's a bloody repeat of what happened not that long ago, back to square one, bugger. I'll get onto Yiannis, need to give the Stathoses something.

'Ok Michael, let's put our plan into action.'

I'm in a café downtown with Yiannis. The story is that I've overheard a couple of conversations. It appears the Düzgüns are putting a new man into Paris, their operation there is to be ramped up. There was mention about getting rid of somebody and that's all I heard. The inference that hopefully the Stathoses will take from this bit of misinformation, well perhaps it's not misinformation, I don't know, is that the Düzgüns are about to expand their Paris operation. The bit about getting rid of someone, who? the incumbent Düzgün man or an opposition Stathos fellow? I have no idea. I'm not party to the Düzgüns inner circle how in hell could I be expected to find out these things. How do I communicate with the Stathoses they've not told me how to contact them, perhaps I'll just front their house. It works, I'm admitted and confronted by Janus.

'Ah, the Düzgün asshole.' Nice guy Janus. 'What do you want?'
I give him our prepared story.

'Is that all, we want real information from you not this low grade crap, if you don't want your girlfriends harmed you'll need to do better than this, now piss off.'

A real nasty piece of work however, he has eased the way for me a little. He will be receptive to more detailed information that he will think I have had to take risks to obtain. I get onto Yiannis and fill him in on the meeting.

'That's good Michael, yes that Janus is not a nice person. I've not met him but I've heard about his charming mannerisms. Perhaps a bullet in the head would make the world a better place. His confidence will be dented in the morning when he learns about the disappearance of his boss man in Paris during the night.'

Shit, did I want to hear that, does this make me an accessory to murder, no way, that would need a big stretch of the imagination but shit it's indicative of what I getting mixed up in.

# *Frank*

There's no respite, the crap we were caught up in before the welcome break in New Zealand continues to dog us. Michael's been sucked back in. The Stathoses have forced him to work for them, they're convinced he's still a Düzgün, they want a spy in the Düzgün camp. They've threatened Carrie and Dimitra. Michael's confided in Yiannis Stavrou and Yiannis sees an opportunity to feed the Stathoses misinformation. It's a dangerous game, if it blows up it could be fatal. Michael has to tread carefully, one misstep and who knows?

Michael does have another life, a very enjoyable one with Dimitra, and there's the job he's landed, it's right up his alley.

Our 'new life' in Athens continues. Galani & Conchie pick up a couple of jobs, watching philandering husbands. Cuckolded wives, as we soon find out, are good payers. Should be safe too, the people involved are regular citizens not underworld thugs. Michael's world is not so secure, his day job is great, he's enjoying it and living with Dimitra is working out just fine, it's the other stuff that's the problem. He's keeping me in the picture, relying on my worldly experience for advice. The first bit of information he passed on to Janus Stathos was factual. The Düzgüns did put a man into Paris and the fellow who was running things for the Stathoses vanished. Michael's credentials are established. He will need to keep it up though to survive. If he can manipulate the situation to a point where it would be in the best interests of Yiannis Stavrou to liquidate Janus Stathos then Michael's situation, and the girls, would be a lot safer. With Janus gone how much of a threat would the handicapped Leonidos be? Perhaps we can lay it on Nico, see if he can find out how brain damaged Leonidos really is. Would he be capable of threatening Carrie with the French police thing. It's an empty threat, we have the necessary evidence to clear Carrie and there is no actual murder charge. Janus is in charge of the Stathoses now and his hold over Michael is the threat of violence to the two girls. Michael's got another meeting with Yiannis, another poisoned chalice for Janus. What clever bit of misinformation this time?

'Dad, give me your opinion on this, I think it involves killing people. I have to pass on some information that will set it up. Shit, this is real high stakes stuff, bloody dangerous, I don't have much choice. If it comes off it could enhance my standing with Yiannis.'

Michael fills me in. He's got to convince Janus that he's overheard Yiannis Stavrou briefing his cronies about a delivery of meth to a Paris address, it's a high value delivery and there are details of the time and place. Yiannis has stressed that the time and place are the important bits he wants to get across.

'That's it, that's all I've been told. What's your take on that Dad?'

'It's a hit, he's sucking them into a hijacking. He intends to take out some of the Paris distribution people and he's using you to set it up. If it happens you could be implicated. There is one thing working in your favour, these people do not like any police involvement. If people are killed it will be just about impossible for the police to determine who did it. Bloody risky Michael but you've got to do it.'

'Christos can your police contacts track gang activity in Paris? I'm asking because there may be a gang shootout in the next few days and it would be in Michael's best interest to know what happens.' I tell Christos about Michael's involvement, the proposed misinformation, and the suspected outcome.

It happens. A week later the Athens papers headline a story about a gangland massacre in Paris, a lot of bodies and some gruesome pictures, shit! Christos is able to get a lot of information from his contacts, and with Michael's input, we piece together what has happened.

Michael had passed on the prepared story about the meth delivery. Janus had been suspicious and Michael had a hard job convincing him that what he was telling was only what he had overheard, what he had pieced together from several conversations. It appears that Yiannis had set up a sophisticated hit designed to deal a mortal blow to the Stathose's Paris operation. The delivery had gone ahead and sure enough the Stathoses had hijacked it. There were four Düzgün people making the delivery, they did not put up any real resistance. One was shot dead and the remaining three allowed themselves to be trussed up and dumped in a ditch. What the hijackers did not know was the delivery was just bait, there was a lot of crystal meth in the delivery. A Düzgün hit team was observing this. They followed the hijacked van to a warehouse, apparently a distribution base. There was a shootout, real bad, there were a lot of people at the warehouse. It appears the hit team were successful, a lot of fatalities, mostly drug distributers. The warehouse was set on fire. When the police arrived the place was well ablaze with people locked inside.

Understandably Michael is worried, and with good cause. He's kidnapped off the street again, shit, it will be Janus. I'll need help, Michael could be in real danger this time. Janus will suspect he was party to the Paris hit, had to be, his life could be in danger. I'll approach Yiannis, how can I, I've not got a contact point, Nico, he knows everything.

'Yes Frank I can contact Yiannis and we need to do it right now.'

It does not take long, I'm soon talking to Yiannis, asking, begging, for his help, get Michael please. I tell him how Michael has been confiding in me, that we figured out that Yiannis must have master minded the business in Paris and how worried we are that Janus might take revenge on Michael for his perceived betrayal. We've got to get Michael now.

'Ok Frank I hear you. I like Michael, he's achieved something for us in Paris, perhaps the time has come to deal to Janus and his charming ways, leave it to me. Don't you try anything, I'll sort it. You go and keep an eye on the lovely Dimitra she'll be beside herself with worry.'

We're at Dimitra's place with Christos and Karisa. Dimitra's a mess, worried sick. It's early evening, a knock on the door, it's Yiannis, not expecting anything like this. He's got Michael with him and he does not look good. Yiannis is the perfect gentleman, a real ladies man.

'Here we are, your Michael, bit battered but intact, with my compliments. I won't stay, I'm having a busy night, give the lad here some tender loving care and he'll be right.'

Dimitra cracks up completely, crying and hugging Michael. Poor girl this was not expected when she fell in love with him. Michael's got some cuts on his face, he's limping, holding his ribs, and there's blood on his shirt, shit, this is not the life we want.

Michael's story. Kidnapped off the street, dumped in a small room, and beaten severely by a couple of Janus's thugs. Couple of hours and Janus shows, wants to know how come I sold him a shit story, would not accept that I knew nothing about what subsequently happened. I'd just told him what I'd overheard, he would not accept that. Another beating, real bad this time, I was beginning to fear for my life. It was some time later, not sure how long, I was starting to lose it. There was some shooting, the door bursts open and a couple of fellows pick me up, carry me outside and put me in a car. I noticed a couple of bodies as I was caried out. Yiannis is in the car, we are driven here, that's it, all I know.

More gang violence, glaring headlines, when are the police going to put an end to it, the citizens of Athens are fed up. There had been a shooting and several gang members had died. Janus Stathos whose family are prominent in the spice trading business was also killed. What is his connection, if any, is not known to the police however it is rumoured he was active in Paris's criminal world.

It could all be over, Janus is gone, he was the only real threat to Michael. Yiannis has made good on his suggestion that the world would be a better place without him. He got his bullet in the head, but, and it's a big but, there will be a price. Michael's usefulness to the Düzgüns is no more, no conduit to the Stathoses.

Nico gets the latest on Leonidos. Severely brain damaged, not life threatening but he's pretty much a vegetable, not capable of doing much at all and quiet irrational. He's no longer a viable threat to Carrie but he's still alive, something that does not go unnoticed by Karisa, she's got a long memory. The Stathoses appear to be leaderless. I'm sure Yiannis will ensure things stay that way, leave his empire unchallenged. There are the Maniots, they don't appear to be active at the moment, however, I'm sure there will be bad blood over their New Zealand cocaine operation. From what we gathered in Auckland there had been a takeover, most likely the Düzgüns.

Things are quiet, the unsavoury events that had made things so difficult are no more, hope it stays that way. Michael can get on furthering his new architectural career and enjoy the deepening relationship he has with Dimitra. Me, I'm really enjoying living with Ariana and playing detective with Christos. Carrie and Myrine seem happy enough living together. It's an enjoyable period, will it last?

It's too horrible to even think about, Dimitra fails to arrive home from her job one day. By seven in the evening Michael is really worried and goes to the police, a missing person situation. Not much joy, the police think it's a lover's tiff that will resolve itself by the following day. The following morning Dimitra has not come home. Carlos gets into the act and leans on the police to do something. They do. Dimitra is found in an open drain in the city, her throat cut.

# Retribution

Michael falls apart, he's distraught, his grief destroying him, he loses interest in staying alive, suicidal. Frank stays with him day and night, afraid he will do something precipitate to himself or to whoever he thinks did this. Christos is devasted as well and after a couple of days of unbelievable grief he resolves to take matters into his own hands. His mood is dangerous and Frank fears something even more terrible could happen. Who's responsible? has to be the Stathoses, but who? Yiannis Stavrou calls around to the Galani house to offer his condolences. Not a good look, a gangland boss calling on an ex member of the Athens police. It's a genuine visit. Yiannis is deeply shocked that something like this could happen to an innocent girl who was not involved in any way in the nasty underworld goings on. He will find out who has done this and let Christos know. What will Christos do should Yiannis come up with a name? What will we do? What can we do?

It's got to be a Stathos, who else would be motivated to do such a terrible thing. It appears it was directed at Michael, retribution for the killing of Janus, Leonidos is probably behind it.

The very next day Carrie comes 'round. She's had a message from Leonidos, he wants her back, to work for him, the nanny thing and to run errands otherwise Michael might meet the same fate as Dimitra. It's pretty much telling them that Leonidos is responsible. He's obviously not 'all there,' why would he admit to anything? We need to do something before the situation deteriorates any further and we need to do it now. Karissa is party to all this, aware what chaos Leonidos is causing. She makes it known that she wants Leonidos 'taken down,' her husband Nikias avenged. She's certain Leonidos ordered his murder and Ariana's husband as well. Now is the time for retribution. We make Yiannis aware of our wishes, perhaps he can deliver up Leonidos.

It's a disused abattoir on the outskirts of Athens. I'm there with Christos. Yiannis has delivered up Leonidos. There had been a shootout at the Stathos home in Athens. Leonidos has been dragged out and delivered to this abattoir. Yiannis had also brought along his Serbian hit man, Radul Jaksic.

'I'll leave this scumbag with you, I think your two lovely ladies might have some ideas of how justice should be administered. I believe he's responsible for both their husband's deaths and we're pretty sure he ordered Dimitra's murder. Radul here knows how to deal with people like this. Let me know when you've done whatever it is you are going to do and I will arrange a 'clean up.'

It's the following day, Leonidos is hanging by his heels from a meat hook terribly mutilated, blood and gore all over the concrete floor, entrails hanging from a slashed abdomen. He's not quite dead, a flicker of life, the eyelids. He has been tortured to the point of death, his life ebbing away.

'Come on you murderous bastard, we know you killed Nikias and what about Ariana's man? did you drown him as well?'

'Fuck you.'

His tormentor has an electric drill with a big auger bit, he places it in front of his right eye.

'Last chance, did you order the hits?'

'Fuck you.'

He plunges the drill into the eye, the scream is sickening, blood and brain tissue sprays around the room, his suspended body convulses, shudders then goes still, he's dead, the auger deep inside his brain.

# *Michael*

I don't want to live without Dimitra, why has this happened? What did Dimitra have to do with any of the nasty things I was involved in? Nothing. Life can be so cruel. Some criminal lowlife exacting revenge for something that had nothing to do with her, trying to punish me. It's my fault. If I had not become involved with the gangs Dimitra would still be alive. It's my fault. How can I ever reconcile myself to the fact that I'm responsible for her death. Dad is worried, worried I might do something foolish. He's right there day and night, I'm rarely out of his sight. He did tell me the person responsible, Leonidos Stathos, has been taken care of in a particularly brutal way. Karisa and Ariana also had good reason to see him gone from this earth.

My job? Not been to work for several days, lost all interest. I mean what's the point, my whole reason for being in Athens has gone, just like that. Suddenly I don't like this place, perhaps I need to go back to New Zealand, perhaps I don't want to live anymore. Dad is worried.

It's now two weeks since Dimitra's murder and Nico has come up with some startling information. He's heard on the grapevine that it was not Leonidos, but a completely unrelated party, her possessive ex, Filipe. Yiannis has heard the same story, not much he does not know. Yiannis has approached me with an offer. He wants me in New Zealand to help with an operation he has going there. Shit that will be his cocaine smuggling business. Do I want to be involved, what the hell, I don't want to stay in Athens, not now. Suddenly the place is one horrible memory. Should I confide in Dad or should I just tell him I want to go home? Yiannis has added that if I take up his offer he will see that Filipe is dealt to. I'm finding it difficult to accept that Filipe could do such a terrible thing, must be something mentally wrong with the guy. The more I think about it the more acceptable the whole situation becomes. I help Yiannis's with his New Zealand operation and he deals to Filipe. Dad does not need to know. Don't want him knowing I'm doing something outside the law. Could get a job in Auckland, architecture, good cover. Working for the Düzgüns, that would put me in conflict with the Maniots. Apparently they were operating the cocaine business in New Zealand before the Düzgüns moved in, would there be conflict? Kenzo and Lambani are Maniot soldiers, would not want to be up against them. But they are in Europe, long way from New Zealand. Dad will be staying in Athens, Ariana, I can't see him moving back to Auckland anytime soon. Going outside the law, should I do that? What the hell, I've been there once and when I came in from the cold what happened, a couple of months of bliss then I get slammed in the worst possible way. I'll do it, I'll move back to Auckland. I set up a meeting with Yiannis.

# The Offer

'Michael, here's the deal. I want you in Auckland, no rush, take your time. Make it appear you can't stand Athens. That will be genuine as well, people will understand. Get a job in Auckland, lead a normal life. I won't be imposing on you right away, however, a couple of months down the track I will want you to take up a role in my organisation, nothing nasty, an administrative role. You've probably worked out that we have replaced the Maniots in the New Zealand cocaine business. You've already had a brush with our organisation, the Tongan business. That cocaine was destined for Auckland. I don't want to force you into anything that you are uncomfortable with however I can use your talents, not in the unsavoury side of the business more of an administrative role, you will be well rewarded. The cash will be hidden in an offshore account and I will guarantee Carrie's welfare here in Athens, I know you still have feelings for her. Take a couple of days to think about it and we will talk again.'

What to make of that? do I want to be involved in criminal activities? What Yiannis is offering is an administrative role, is that criminal? Of course it is, anything to do with cocaine smuggling is a criminal activity, don't fool yourself. What if I don't go along with it, will Yiannis accept that or will he put the pressure on. He's a crook, don't fool yourself. He's got people like Radul Jaksic, the Serbian hit man working for him. There's a very nasty side to Yiannis that I've not really seen, not wanted to see. He's not the nice guy I'm imagining. How safe will Carrie be if I refuse? Yiannis is responsible for numerous murders, how many were there in Paris? the Maniot lad on Waiheke? Leonidos Stathos? How many more I don't know about? I need to sound him out about what exactly he will want me to do in Auckland.

'You will be my personal spy on my own organisation, reporting directly to me. The people I employ can be pretty violent, you know that, unpredictable as well. The business I'm in needs these people to make it viable. I need to keep a close eye on them. That's where you come in. You will observe, and keep me informed, particularly if you suspect they may not be acting in my best interests. You will also organise things, oversee importations and the like, no direct footwork. You will be well rewarded. You'll need to keep your involvement at arm's length and you'll need a cover, a normal day job. I believe architecture is your thing.'

Yiannis has laid it out, do I want in? do I want to be a criminal because if I commit, that's what I'll be, a common criminal. How will Dad react if he finds out? What if I decline? will Yiannis put the pressure on. Carrie? that's a worry. What if he threatens her? Could I handle that? I couldn't.

'I don't know Yiannis, I just don't know, it's not me.'

'Michael you don't have much choice in this, I want you working for me in Auckland. If you decline then I cannot guarantee Carrie's wellbeing and Filipe will be getting away with murder.'

That's it, he's spelt it out in no uncertain terms. Yiannis's true character is showing. I do as he wants otherwise he will go after Carrie, shit. If I agree, Carrie will be safe and I will be responsible for a murder, shit. It's a lose lose for me, how has it come to this?

# *Frank*

There's been brutal retribution. Leonidos got his comeuppance in a terrible way and a mutilated and headless body was found in the same ditch where Dimitra's body was dumped; Filipe. Nico tells us he's heard it was Filipe who murdered her, not the Stathoses. Who had dealt to Filipe is not known but it looks like the work of Radul Jaksic. Michael has withdrawn from everything and wants to go back to Auckland, there's nothing to keep him in Athens.

Dimitra's murder has cast a terrible pall over everything. Christos is very depressed and Karissa is finding it hard to cope. I feel I'm responsible. If Michael had not gone to Europe in his search for Carrie, and if I had not followed him, then none of this would have happened. Why have things turned out this way? Have we done something wrong? Life can be so unfair at times. Ariana is a tower of strength. I find myself deeply reliant on her, and even more in love. Michael is a lost soul, just wants to go back to New Zealand. I fear for him.

It's now a month since those terrible events and life is slowly returning to normal, well not really, there's a huge hole and a lot of hurt. Our venture into the private detective business, 'Galani & Conchie - Private Investigators,' or 'GC Investigations,' is attracting a bit of business. Easy stuff, nothing nasty, all at our discretion and at our pace. Michael has gone back to Auckland, a very sad and depressed young man. I worry for him, hope he does not do anything foolish.

GC Investigations has been approached by an Athens legal firm, Aetos, Giuliani and Papadakis. Small world. Angelica and Fabio Giuliani, the couple we had that brief sexual encounter with on the beach at Mounu, are the firms principles. They would like to engage our services in a couple of low profile investigation on their behalf. Angelica contacts me, she wants a meeting. It happens in a down town coffee shop. She's a sexy lady and appears to be on the make, not sure how to handle this. She tells me our dalliance on the beach at Mounu has aroused a dormant desire in her for illicit sex, am I interested?

'Angelica you are a dark horse, what man would not be interested in bedding you, me included, but I'm in a happy relationship right now. You've met my Ariana, I'm in love with her.'

'That's a bugger, I would love to hop into bed with you. Perhaps you and your good lady might be interested in a foursome sometime, Fabio would be a starter.'

'Not to be Angelica, group sex is not our thing, but it's a tempting offer.'

'Oh well, guess I'll have to live with your refusal but should you ever weaken, call me.'

Well that was out of left field, I did not pick her as being like that, but then Mounu. When I think about it it makes sense, they were certainly keen to fuck on that beach.

Christos and myself are in Nico's bar, we feel we owe him and patronising his bar is our way of saying thank you. Nico is very sympathetic. Dimitra's death has upset him and he feels sorry for Christos. Nico has news. The Stathoses a spent force, no leadership. The Düzgüns are cleaning out what's left. There are continuing murders, and now defections. There's a new player in Istanbul in the meth business. Not much is known about them however they have been going after the Maniots meth business. Apparently Pierre Gorbet's murder had not been ordered by Leonidos Stathos but by this new gang. Pierre Gorbet had been doing business with them and there had been a falling out. Leonidos just capitalised on a situation he was presented with. Pierre Gorbet's killers were not Stathos men at all but free 'killers for hire' under the protective wing of the Stathoses at the time. The new crowd are upsetting the status quo. It's now the Düzgüns, Maniots, and this new crowd. Nico has also got wind that the Düzgüns are expanding their empire to encompass cocaine out of Columbia. That's interesting. Cocaine, Tonga, Yiannis seen in New Zealand, the Waiheke murder, there are several straws in the wind. Michael going back to Auckland and Dimitra's killer being dealt to by Radul Jaksic, a Düzgün operative. Is Michael somehow involved? He is friendly with Yiannis Stavrou and he heads up the Düzgüns. We need a break, all the benefits from our South Seas adventure have been dissipated by recent events.

We're in the taverna 'round the corner from Christos and Karissa's, not quite the usual happy atmosphere. Carrie and Myrine are with us.
    'What about a cruise around the Med, there are plenty on offer. A week on a boat, absolutely nothing to do, what do you say?'
    'Yes, you too Carrie and Myrine.'

The Silver Cloud, a boutique cruise boat operated by Silver Seas, an upmarket cruise line operating out of Venice. We will fly to Venice, board the boat, cruise down the Adriatic Coast, the Greek Islands, Turkey, up through the Dardanelles to Istanbul then fly back to Athens, six of us.
    Early start. Arrive in Venice late morning, drop our gear on the boat and spend the day wandering around the city. A first for me. Venice, and I like what I see. The place is awash with tourists but that's ok, they are a friendly lot and give a certain something to the place. We find an open air café under the Rialto Bridge. It's a warm day, a cold Peroni in a tall frosted glass hits the spot. Atmosphere to burn, hard to put a finger on it but the place oozes charm. I'm loving

it and so is Ariana. Carrie and Myrine seem to be happy. Christos and Karissa? Christos is hurting and so is Karissa. Dimitra was an only child and to lose her in such a terrible way must be devastating. I feel for them both.

We wander around amongst the crowds in the late afternoon sunshine, down back alleys, little secluded courtyards. Venice is a lovely place for walking. All the leaning towers? I don't think the Venetians were very good at foundations in yesteryear. Back on board our luxury boat, out on deck, cocktail time. We sail down the Grand Canal in the setting sun, Venice's spectacular waterfront, it's a stunning experience. We stay on deck, another cocktail, it's just so nice. Dinner will be late, it's that kind of boat, eat when you want. I can feel myself unwinding. This cruise could be just what's needed particularly for Christos and Karissa. It's quite late when we get cleaned up and changed for dinner and that's another experience. Very elegant dining and the waiters are all over us, superb meal. A whole week of this, how good does it get?

The Croatian coast, Pula, Split, Dubrovnik, coastal cities, all quite extraordinary. Ashore each day wandering around, soaking up the ambience. A wine or two sitting in the sunshine, it's very romantic, therapeutic, particularly for Christos and Karisa. They are more relaxed, finally putting their grief to rest. Carrie and Myrine are loving it, holidaying with the olds, it's working.

It happened on day two. Stretched out on a sun lounger, eyes closed.

'Frank, Ariana,' it's Angelica and Fabio Giuliani, small world. Ariana suddenly looks a little apprehensive, memories of Mounu come flooding back, that fleeting tryst on the beach.

'Well hello, what a coincidence.'

Shit how are we going to handle this, don't want to get too close, don't want Angelica suggesting sex again. She's certainly 'got it,' tiny bikini, great figure. Memories of Mounu, she was a great fuck.

Ariana is giving me a curious look. The sight of Angelica is causing a stirring in my loins, Ariana will notice, she's well attuned to me these days. I'm wondering how she will react to Fabio's presence. She's never said anything about the Mounu interlude, perhaps she might be reconsidering, re-evaluating her attitude towards group sex. Do I want to go down that track, no, not with Ariana and I'm pretty sure she feels the same way. Perhaps we'll just go with the flow, it may not come up, if it does we'll play it down. Christos and Karisa do not know about Mounu, well I don't think they do, how would they?

'Angelica, Fabio, this is a surprise, escaping from Athens for a bit?'

'Yes we are, not a very nice place these days. We heard about Christos's daughter, hard to comprehend, why? The ex turning up dead in the same spot, makes you wonder what's going on.'

Fabio's doing the talking and I feel he's probing for information. He's in the legal business, a criminal lawyer. He will be well aware of what goes on in Athens, will probably know about Michael's relationship with Dimitra. Has he connected us with the bad things that have been happening?

'It's hard Fabio, Christos is hurting, so am I. My boy Michael was living with Dimitra, her murder absolutely devastated him, he's gone back to New Zealand.'

'Yes I did hear something, why Dimitra? Was it a rejected lover thing or are there deeper reasons?'

He's definitely probing. Fabio knows a lot more than he's letting on. Perhaps I can draw him out, see what I can find out. There's little downside for me, I've not done anything naughty and besides he's a client of GC Investigations so there is some common ground.

'Fabio what have you heard on the grapevine?'

'Frank, both you and Christos are ex detectives, good guys, and I'm a criminal lawyer. I'm party to a lot of bad things. My clients tend to be bad people. Your boy Michael got himself involved with a couple of criminal gangs and apparently managed to piss off one of them. Dimitra's murder appeared to be pay back however I also hear that this may not be the case. It was the ex.'

'Fabio, we're on the same page, that's what we think happened as well. Tell me about these gangs and Michael's involvement?'

'Frank, client confidentiality, I can't do that, however in this case because your firm does work for our firm and because you're a good guy and because we've both screwed each other's ladies----'

'Wow there Fabio, what's with the screwing?'

'Well that's what it was Frank, fucking on the beach, it was wonderful, when can we do it again?'

'We're not; nice thought though. We're not into group sex, sorry to disappoint, but I must say you've got a great sex partner in Angelica.'

'Oh well, lose some, win some, such is life. About the gangs. We defend some unsavoury characters at times but that's the business we're in Frank. I'm sure you know quite a lot about the Stathoses, Düzgüns, and Maniots, Christos will have filled you in and your underworld mate Nico as well. I get to hear a lot of things. I know your Michael was in the Düzgün camp, still is from what I've heard. Our firm get to defend Düzgün people from time to time. I believe Dimitra's killer was dealt to by a Düzgün operative and the quid pro quo was that Michael would be their man in New Zealand.'

*It hit me like a bomb, surely not, Michael would have said something, he would have told me, it can't be true.*

'What are you saying Fabio, Michael in the pay of the Düzgüns? You must be mistaken, he would have spoken to me, asked my advice. I think you've got it wrong?'

'Ok Frank, I'll let you in on a few secrets, I like you, you're a good guy, most detectives are good guys. Our firm do a lot of work for the Düzgün family, we know a lot about their smuggling business. You could call it unethical but we are a legal firm, the idea is to make money and where we draw the moral line is a variable. Yiannis Stavrou, you know him, runs the show, he's not all bad, ruthless when he has to be, however, he has taken a shine to your Michael and intends to set him up in Auckland. How do I know these things? Yiannis sleeps with Angelica. I don't have a problem with that, we both sleep around, a lot. As you know she's quite magnificent in the sack and she has quite an extraordinary effect on Yiannis. She is able to arouse him to such an extent that he divulges all sorts of secrets during periods of sexual frenzy. Don't look so shocked Frank, it happens and it can be quite beneficial to a business like ours. By the way she has set her sights on you.'

I'm reeling, having trouble comprehending what Fabio has told me. Michael in the pay of a gang who think nothing about killing people. Not a word about it to me? no asking my advice? Well I guess he realised there would be no support coming from me. Going back to Auckland apparently to engage in a smuggling operation, shit!

This conversation with Fabio happens just out of Ariana's earshot, well I hope it is, don't want her being upset. This cruise is supposed to be therapeutic, healing the wounds inflicted in Athens. Suddenly it's anything but. Michael in the employ of criminals, shit, my worst fear. He's going to do something stupid, dangerous even, and he's far away in Auckland. I have to do something, what?

Ariana senses all is not well, she's on a sun lounger nearby looking her normal gorgeous self.

'Darling what's up, you're upset, I can tell. I thought it was plain lust, the sight of Angelica in that bikini, but no, it's something serious. Tell me Frank, what's Fabio been telling you?'

'This is a rest and recuperation holiday Ariana, I'm not going to spoil things by unloading my concerns onto you.'

'Frank, I heard a bit of what Fabio said, it was not nice, the guy's a crook. Lawyer for the mob! I guess a lot of legal firms are like that and to think I enjoyed sex on the beach with him. What are you going to do Frank? Get Michael out of another black hole?'

'Ariana, let's keep this to ourselves, don't burden Christos and Karisa with this latest dump of shit news. We'll enjoy this cruise as if this conversation with Fabio never happened. I'll figure something out before we get back to Athens.'

'You'll be going back to Auckland, you'll have to. I'll come too; support.'

We leave our sun loungers and go down to our cabin, our big luxurious cabin. Ariana drags me onto the bed shedding her cloths as she does so. The resulting sex is almost therapeutic.

A couple of days, several picture postcard ports of call, and we are amongst the Greek Islands, Santorini. Ariana and I don't go ashore, don't want to be reminded of our previous visit, the romantic interlude with Michael and Dimitra. The others do and are suitably impressed. They too finish up down in the little waterside café in Fira. We see a bit of Angelica and Fabio on the boat but keep them at arm's length. Don't want to get too familiar. Angelica's penchant for group sex is a bit of a worry. Don't want to go there, and her stated desire to bed me? no thanks, especially now I know she sleeps with a gangland boss, a murderous one. Carrie and Myrine keep to themselves, infatuated with each other, that's nice. We dine with them most evenings and they do their own thing during the day which includes a lot of lying around on the sun loungers out on the deck. They are both good lookers and they have some very brief bikinis, G strings sometimes. They get a lot the attention from the younger fellows on board, hmm! I can imagine the frustration, what a waste!

Christos and Karisa are enjoying the cruise. They're concerned I'm not my usual self. Ariana and I have not told them anything about what we've learnt from Fabio, don't want to spoil things for them. It's certainly spoilt it for me, worried sick about Michael. I need to do something, and soon. Turkey, Kusadasi, Emphasis, Canakkale again, all great tourist places but I cannot enthuse about them. Through the Dardanelles, the Sea of Marama, then Istanbul. This time we are just passing through. Onto an aeroplane, Athens. It's not been the 'unwinding' I was hoping for. The others however, possibly not Ariana, thoroughly enjoyed it all. Christos and Karissa are almost back to their normal selves again.

'Come on Frank, what is it? you've been a sad sack the whole trip,' it's Christos asking.

'You don't want to know Christos, my cross to bear, I don't want to burden you with my concerns.'

'Not good enough Frank, I want to know? It was that Fabio, right, he's told you something bad. You're my business partner Frank, we do work for Fabio, tell me.'

'You won't like it, I don't like it, and I don't think it's fair after what you've been through.'

'Tell me.'

So I tell him.

'Shit Frank, we need to do something.'

We've been back in Athens for three days and I'm wracking my brains about what to do about Michael. Ariana is getting concerned about my state of mind. She's a tower of strength, I'm a lucky man to have her. I've made up my mind. I'll confront Yiannis, ask him, no, tell him, I want Michael out of his business, just leave him alone in New Zealand. He's in a pretty fragile state of mind. His search for Carrie, and subsequent involvement in the unsavoury goings on in Athens, then the murder, have destroyed him, he needs time out, right away from the Düzgüns. I get a message to Yiannis, I want a meeting.

It happens in a downtown taverna, Yiannis hears me out. He's curious to know how I became aware he would be requiring Michael to do things for him in Auckland, had Michael confided in me? no? then how did I know? was I guessing? This was awkward. Fabio had told me in confidence. I'm not going to reveal my source to Yiannis, he's a crook capable of very nasty things. I'm in a hole here.

'Frank I think you have the wrong end of the stick, why would I want your Michael doing things for me in Auckland, he's not beholden to me for anything. I think you worry unnecessarily.'

'Yiannis I want to believe you but I've picked up on a few things that say otherwise. Filipe, that had to be your man Radul Jaksic, there would be a price for that.'

'You know about Radul, interesting, how do you know about him?'

Shit I'm getting in deep here, Yiannis is no fool and he's sensed that I know more than I'm letting on.

'Frank, let's stop being nice to each other, let me lay it on the line. I have recruited Michael into my organisation and he is going to be my man in New Zealand, nothing nasty, my personal spy. Keeping me advised about how my people are handling things. Yes Michael owes me; Filipe! He won't be directly involved just an admin and observing role, *and he will do it!*'

Shit, Yiannis is threatening me, implying that if Michael does not go along with what he wants there could be consequences. He's not a nice guy at all just appears that way. I worry that Yiannis might try to figure out how I know about these things, where did my information come from, have I compromised Fabio? What if Michael has to advise Yiannis that there are problems with his New Zealand operation, that 'changes' are required, could Michael be party to murder. The Maniot lad on Waiheke, Yiannis can be ruthless.

'Ok, ok Yiannis, I get the picture. I'm asking, would you consider releasing Michael from his obligation to you as a personal favour to me?'

'No Frank, I owe you nothing. You're a detective right? and you've been snooping around. I suggest you keep out of it. Michael works for me. There are few favours in this business and if you persist with this there will be consequences. You are vulnerable. Carrie, Myrine, Christos, Karissa, and your very own Ariana. Perhaps the best thing you can do is go back to New Zealand. There's nothing more to talk about Frank, go home.'

It's a disaster, my olive branch approach has gone up in flames and I've put everyone in danger, what possible redress do I have? Short of liquidating Yiannis nothing at all, shit.

I'm shattered. I confide in Christos, he knows more about how things work in Athens than I ever will. I cannot just accept Yiannis's ultimatum I have to do something. I gather that Michael will not be required to do things in Auckland right away, there will be a break, time for me to figure something out. There are the Maniots, sworn enemies of the Düzgüns. It was their operation in New Zealand that the Düzgüns have forcefully taken over, the Waiheke murder, the change in the cocaine distribution set up in Auckland. We have an in to the Maniot family, Kenzo and Lambani. Perhaps we should confide in Nico, he's our contact. Could we enlist their aid in dealing with Yiannis?

A couple of days later. Christos and myself have done some serious thinking. There's only one way to resolve Michael's problem, get rid of Yiannis. That's a huge ask and something that could backfire with fatal consequences. It would involve murder and would put all of us in serious danger. High stakes, very high stakes but right now I can't see any other way. We need to enlist Nico's help, he knows the Athens underworld, knows who would like who 'gone.' There will be people out there who want Yiannis gone, the Maniots for one.

Christos and myself are in Nico's bar and have opened our hearts to him; we have to save Michael.

'Frank, do you realise what you're implying? murder, you are sanctioning a murder. That's not you Frank, that's the sort of thing the low life who frequent my bar do, you're losing the plot Frank.'

'Shit Nico, I'm desperate, what can I do. I can't just sit on my bum and let Michael throw his life away, I've got to do something.'

'Give me a couple of days. There are plenty of people out there who would be glad to see Yiannis gone but he's a survivor. The cemetery's full of people who thought they could get rid of him. If he gets wind about what you are thinking, you're gone, Yiannis would have no reservations about taking you down, and your family. You're into very dangerous territory Frank, take care.'

'Nico, how about Kenzo and Lambani, they're Maniot people and Yiannis has taken down the Maniots New Zealand operation, the Maniots must be approachable on this?'

'I'll sound them out, not a silly idea. Not seen Kenzo or Lambani for a while, still lying low. I know the Maniots are hurting over the murder of that lad in New Zealand, leave it with me. I'll get back to you when I have something but let me warn you Frank, don't go stirring things. If Yiannis gets a whiff of this you're gone, he's ruthless.'

It's a start, I've done something. Nico's warning though? He's right, if I make waves I could finish up dead. There's nothing I can do here to further things, better out of it; Auckland. I'll go home and confront Michael, nothing to lose. I'll ask Ariana, see if she wants to come along.

'Yes, I'll come, need to keep an eye on my lover, you're not thinking rationally.'

Another couple of days, Nico calls, he's got news.

'I've found Lambani. He's an integral part of the Maniot family and they would dearly love to deal to Yiannis. Lambani remembers Michael, nice lad, does not deserve this shit. I think we've found a like minded friend whose in a much better position to deal to Yiannis. No need for us to get involved, no need for you to sanction murder Frank.'

'Sanction murder? you make me sound like some sort of low life Nico.'

'Well you were heading in that direction, about to join the criminal underworld, however, I think you can distance yourself and still achieve the desired outcome.'

'You think it can be done Nico?'

'Put it this way, the Maniots want revenge and in this business that means killing people, can you live with that Frank? You may not be sanctioning it but you will be a fellow traveller.'

'Thanks Nico, now I really am in your debt. That's a tremendous load off my shoulders, another Mythos perhaps, unopened.'

'Cheeky. Don't get excited just yet, what's being proposed will not be easy to achieve, could take some time and there are no guarantees, however, I'm pretty sure the Maniots want Yiannis gone. My crystal ball tells me they will succeed; eventually. I don't need to tell you, zip your lip, not a word to anyone not even Ariana in a moment of passion Frank. Only us two are party to this conversation, keep it like that.'

Relief, at least we've got something going, takes a bit of the worry out of it but I do need to get back to Auckland and talk to Michael.

# *Michael*

Auckland. I've moved into the family home, lonely, depressed, nothing to live for, my life is shit. I'm back to where I was in Athens before I met Dimitra. There was that wonderful period when my life was enjoyable beyond belief, then it was snatched away, no reason, it just happened. What now? Am I about to become an underworld figure, a criminal? Can I avoid it? I made a commitment, can I backout? no. Well you could but you've seen first-hand what happens to people who get offside with the gangs and it's a gang you're going to be working for, a gang who murder people if they get out of line. It's not going to impact on me immediately, Yiannis did say it would be a month or two before he would require my services. I need a job, a cover. Architecture, that's my field, get onto it. Go for something good, something that will occupy my mind, get me focussed on other things. I need company, no good moping about the place feeling sorry for myself. Perhaps I can make this work, downplay the cocaine thing, immerse myself in a proper job, keep well clear of the unsavoury side of Yiannis's cocaine operation. Don't get totally caught up like you did in Athens.

Bach Architects Ltd., a big Auckland outfit and there's a job vacancy in the Herald. Impressive office in the city and a very attractive receptionist.

'Michael Conchie? One of our principles will see you in a minute, would you like a coffee?'

'Conchie, sounds familiar. I'm Bob Bach. This firm is my baby and I do the hiring. Tell me about yourself, your experience and why you want this job.'
I fill him in on my past job in Auckland and how I left to go to

Europe. I tell him about the job I had in Athens, working with a team on an oil terminal project for a large Athens company.'

'Why are you back in New Zealand Michael, sounds like you had a good thing going in Athens?'

'It's not a nice story, I don't want to burden you with it but briefly my Greek fiancée was murdered and suddenly Athens was not a nice place for me.'

'Oh dear, do not want to pry, that's just awful, I feel for you. Conchie? Your father's name is not Frank by any chance?'

'Yes it is, he's a retired detective.'

'Frank Conchie, my best mate at school, what's he up to these days?'

I tell him about Athens in a bit more detail, how Frank is living there, about Ariana, about GC Investigations, how he will be in Auckland from time to time with Ariana.'

'Small world, will need to catch up when he's here next. What I'm doing now is figuring out if you're the right person for this vacancy we have. I have a team designing a large factory for an engineering firm and one of the key men has been head hunted by the opposition. It's a team effort. You say you were working in a team in Athens on an oil terminal, sounds like you're the man we need, when can you start Michael?'

I'm gobsmacked, perhaps my luck's turned, well anything's got to be better than my present miserable lot.

'Mr Bach, I'm lost for words, thank you, I can start tomorrow if you want.'

'Ok, eight in the morning, be here at the office, and say hello to your Dad for me. Let me know when he's coming to Auckland, we need to catch up, and call me Bob.'

I'm quite light headed, my life has taken a big upward swing. I go out through the front office and on a whim I ask the receptionist if she would like to go out for dinner tonight.

'Yes I would.'

Her name is Ayla a blue eyed blond, she's lovely. I take her to Swashbucklers down in the Viaduct. I've always liked the place, best fish in town but perhaps I've made a mistake. Last time I was here was with Dimitra, and not long ago either. Memories come flooding back. I guess it's something I'll have to live with.

'I'm flattered Michael, do you do this often, ask girls out on a whim?'

'No, but your boss had just offered me a job and I felt on top of the world, plucked me out of depression.'

'Depression, why would that be?'

'I don't want to go there Ayla and you don't want to know, it's not a nice story. Here, some more savvy, another bottle perhaps, we'll be ok, there's Uber.'

'Michael you've got me curious, what's with the depression, tell me, perhaps I can help.'

Ayla appears genuinely concerned, perhaps I should open up, keeping grief bottled up is not good, but I hardly know the girl, I only met her this morning, she's a fun person. We demolish another bottle of sauvignon blanc.

'I know what it's like, depression, experienced it myself recently. There was a boyfriend. I was keen on him but he became very possessive, tried to restrict me in all sorts of ways. It became a problem, I like my freedom. He was the boyfriend but he did not own me. We split up a few weeks ago, I've been a bit down.'

'I can understand that Ayla, I've suffered a similar sort of thing. I was living with a girl, my fiancé, in Athens. There was a possessive ex, he murdered her just a few weeks ago.'

Ayla looked shocked, having difficulty comprehending what I had said.

'You lived in Greece? what are you doing back here?'

'Distancing myself, suddenly I could not stay another minute in

Athens, the whole point of being alive was snatched away.'

'Michael that's terrible, you need support. You're living with others I hope, not good being alone.'

'No, I'm in the family home, big place in Parnell. Dad has moved to Athens, the house is empty. There's a sister Rebecca but she's a very independent girl, fashion industry, flats with her mates.'

We've put away a fair bit of wine and I'm feeling quite relaxed, warming to my date, my 'impulse date,' Ayla. She's lovely, I think I like her, I do like her, and it's not just the wine talking.

'Michael, it's not good for you to be alone in your grief, how about I come home with you tonight?'

I feel a surge of lust, she's a very attractive girl, sexy as well. What the hell, she's laid it on the line, she wants to bed me, it would be stupid, almost insulating not to go along with her suggestion.

E-mail from Dad, he's coming to Auckland in a week's time, bringing Ariana. What's prompted this, why would he want to come back here so soon.

My circumstances have taken a turn for the better, the architect job is working out fine and 'Bob' has put me on a good salary. Ayla, the lovely Ayla. She stayed two days after that first date and she's around at the house just about every night, she's lovely, I really like her and it's not just sex, well the sex is a big part of it. She's extraordinary in bed, can't get enough of me and I like it.

There's been no contact from Yiannis, he did say a couple of months. It's a worry, an unpleasant fact of life, beholden to the Düzgüns, but that's the deal unless something changes, unless something can be made to change. Why is Dad coming to Auckland so soon? has he found out something, wants to talk?

'I thought we were on the same page Michael now I find out

you've sold you soul to Yiannis, you're going to carry out his wishes here in Auckland, become a common criminal, why the hell did you not confide in me?' Dad is not happy.

Shit, what can I say? why did I not confide in Dad? how did Dad find out? have I stuffed up again? Did I really think I could handle it alone, protect the girls, my family, my loved ones by becoming Yiannis's lacky? another bad life choice. I seem to be vulnerable to making bad choices.

'Dad, he threatened me, threatened our whole family, there's no room to move. It's not all bad, I'm his inside man, spying on his employees, or I will be, that's his plan. Nothing's happened yet. I will not be directly implicated in the bad stuff, just observing, staying at arms length.'

'Michael, don't delude yourself, it's the thin end, you'll be donkey deep in no time and the police will be looking, is that what you want?'

'Of course not. How can I prevent it Dad? Yiannis is ruthless, he kills people.'

'Ok Michael, here's the plan, it's dangerous and there's the possibility it could backfire and put us all in real danger. That's the way it's panning out right now. When Yiannis makes contact go along with what he requests, be careful, keep your involvement minimal. From what he's said so far you will be an observer, looking out for any untrustworthy people in his organisation. That's the dangerous bit, people who get offside, or try to cheat, finish up dead and you want no part of that, don't want to be an accessory to murder. Gather as much information as possible and don't commit anything to writing. Eventually everything you know will be passed on to the New Zealand and Greek police. Do not contact the New Zealand police, security of information cannot be guaranteed and just a whiff of disloyalty could be fatal. The intention is to take Yiannis down, the Maniots will be working towards that end. When it happens you will hand over all you know to the police. Again, that will be dangerous. If the police think you are deeply involved then you could be in trouble, so don't get deeply involved. With Yiannis out of it the threat to us should be removed but you never really know. That's the scene Michael, the ball is in your court. Don't be stupid, and keep me advised.'

'I hear you Dad, my mistake, no, my stupidity to think you would not find out. I guess the stakes are right up there now. Your plan could work, will work, the downside is too awful to even think about. Now I want you to meet a friend, a girl who has been helpful in my getting over Athens, she'll be around here in a couple of hours. Ayla, she's brightened up my life.'

'Michael, you are a dark horse, did not take you long to re-join the world.' It's Ariana. 'We'll be seeing a bit of Ayla I presume?'

'Could be, she's lovely and she's sorted me out.'

# *Frank*

Auckland: Ariana and I arrive on a fine warm morning, good start. It's going to be a 'difficult' visit, confronting Michael. He's been holding things back, not being up front with me and I suspect he's got himself in a hole again. It's a dangerous game being played here, I just hope Michael can see that. He's had two girlfriends murdered in Greece, don't want him involved in any more killing. He's curious about why we are back in Auckland so soon, I think he suspects I may have found out about what he's up to. I decide not to beat around the bush, get straight to the point.

'Michael I know what you're up to. I've confronted Yiannis and he's revealed his true character, the price he's extracted from you for Filipe's demise. He's threatened our whole family and it's not an empty threat either, he expects you to fall into line. The suggestion you can keep your involvement at arm's length is bullshit. You'll find yourself deeply involved in his cocaine business, a criminal as far as the law is concerned. There is a possible out, something that could save you ass when it all turns to custard. Go along with his wishes and do your best to distance yourself from anything nasty. Gather as much information as you can on the cocaine business in New Zealand and play it close to your chest, confide in no one. It may not be for very long. The only thing tying you to this business is Yiannis, if he's gone you're off the hook. There are moves in train to make this happen.'

'Dad, what can I say, I've let myself be taken in again, blackmailed. I've not been contacted by Yiannis yet but it'll happen sometime.'

'You're right, all you can do is wait until he comes calling, lets you know what he wants. Keep me advised. Don't object, I'm your father, I want to know what you're doing. I'll be staying here in Auckland with Ariana for a couple of weeks then going back to Athens. Could stay longer, need to see how things develop. When we do go back you will contact me in Athens, keep me advised. Nothing in writing, no phone calls. There's a code, several codes, depends which day of the week you send a message. Use e-mail and encode it using one of these codes. I've used this system before and it's good but don't send anything that's likely to cause trouble should it be intercepted. Now then Michael let me get off your back and take you out for dinner, your choice.'

'Swashbucklers Dad, there's a girl I would like to bring along. Ayla, she's lovely, you'll like her. She's been a real comfort to me since I arrived back here.'

'Didn't take you long Michael.'

We're in Swashbucklers, there are other restaurants, heaps of them, but Michael is keen on this one. Ayla is a revelation, she's lovely. Ariana strikes up a conversation with her.

'The receptionist, and young Michael hits on you at your first encounter? Bach Architects? rings a bell. I work for an architectural firm in Athens. We keep tabs on similar firms around the world, probably where I've heard about Bach Architects.'

Ariana is in conversation with Ayla and I hear 'Bach.'

'Ayla, would that be Bob Bach?'

'Yes, I'm the receptionist, Bob Bach's my uncle, bit of nepotism.'

'Small world, Bob Bach was my good mate at school and now he's employed my son, more nepotism perhaps. I'll have to look him up.'

It's a great dinner, Michael is more at ease than when I last saw him in Athens, Ayla must be a good influence. I just hope the business Michael's caught up in does not cause her problems, he's not got a good track record with girlfriends.

We Uber home dropping Ayla off on the way. I sense she wants to come home with Michael but he's playing it cool, trying to make a good impression on me perhaps.

Ring ring, early morning, Michael answers, who can it be?

'For you Dad.'

'Frank, Peter Culpan, CIB. I heard you were back in the country with your lovely lady, can we meet?'

'Of course, but what for?'

'Want to pick your brains about the latest in Athens. We suspect there's an Athens based operation here in Auckland, you might be able to help us.'

Oh shit! what does Peter Culpan know, and does he think I know something. Of course I know, a hell of a lot, but does he know that I know. Can I tell him anything? Hell no, dangerous, very dangerous.

Auckland Central, Peter Culpan and Bob Simmonds are both present. Peter Culpan leads.

'Frank, Athens tell us they suspect the cocaine business in Auckland that was the preserve of the Maniot family has been forcefully taken over by the Düzgüns, have you heard anything?'

Is he putting me on the spot, testing my loyalty? What else does he know?

'Not really, I'm not party to what goes on in the Athens underworld, the odd snippet but nothing substantial.'

I don't think he's buying it, the body language says otherwise.

'Frank, your lad Michael, he's back here in Auckland. Our information is that he's friendly with Yiannis Stavrou, the Düzgün boss, we also believe that his girlfriend's murder was avenged by a Düzgün operative, the same fellow we want for the Waiheke murder. Why is Michael here?'

Now he's really putting me on the spot.

'Michael was devastated by Dimitra's killing, he wanted to get out of Athens, wanted to go home. He's done that and now he's got a job here in Auckland. He's getting over the trauma of it all but he's still pretty fragile.'

'Ok Frank, I don't want to call you out for withholding information but we believe that your Michael is a Düzgün operative involved in cocaine smuggling, what's your take on that?'

'News to me, if Michael has become involved with the Düzgüns I'm sure he would have confided in me. His return to Auckland was purely to distance himself from the terrible events in Athens, nothing else.'

'Frank, I'm not going to push it, you're a good guy and your loyalties must be sorely tested by recent events, however, I must make you aware that we are watching Michael. Back in Athens he worked for the Düzgüns for a while, we understand it was under duress. There was the liaison with the Stathos girl, Dioni. That was encouraged by the Düzgüns, a spy in the opposition's camp.'

Shit the New Zealand Police know a lot more than I figured. I think we need to reconsider how we handle the mess we're in.

'Frank, I'm not going to pursue this any further at the moment but I suggest you have a word with Michael. If he is involved then it would be sensible for him to think about keeping us 'in the loop,' could make things easier for him in the future. We'll leave it like that for now but I suggest Michael gives serious consideration to what I've suggested. Dangerous I know but so is the business he's become involved in. He needs to think about saving his own skin. How about we meet again in a couple of days and bring Michael. Better still we'll meet somewhere neutral, a coffee shop perhaps, don't know how far the Düzgüns have infiltrated this place.'

It just gets worse. I will talk to Michael. The best thing we can do is bite the bullet and take Peter Culpan into our confidence. If he can guarantee the security of anything we tell him and not initiate any precipitate action which would reveal a 'leak' then perhaps we can make it all work, the alternative is too horrible to think about. Michael is alarmed that the New Zealand Police know so much. Bit pointless pleading ignorance, trying to keep it hidden, doing that will only make his situation worse. After a bit Michael realises there's little option for him and agrees to go along with my suggestion, it's dangerous. Just a whiff of a leak and Michael's in extreme danger. There is one thing going for us, this situation may not go on for very long. There's only danger as long as Yiannis is running the show. We need the Maniots to make good on their intention to remove him, sooner rather than later.

Another meeting with Peter Culpan, this time a downtown coffee shop, Michael comes along. The arrangement we hammer out is that Michael will deal with Peter Culpan only, no one else in Auckland must be involved at this stage. Absolute secrecy is essential for Michael's survival. As long as Yiannis is alive the Police will not take any action. When, and if, Yiannis is eliminated the police will take down the whole New Zealand operation. They already have Mr No Name, the Düzgüns new man in Auckland, under observation.

'Ok' from Michael, 'I'll cooperate with you, but Peter, you've got to be honest with me. No one is to know anything about this business until the Yiannis thing is settled. I would appreciate your continued silence about your source. Yiannis will have mates, they may come looking. So far there's been no contact but I'm expecting something soon, some instructions about what is required from me. I'll keep you informed.'

We now have a plan, it's got to work. Security will be the problem, no leaks, not even a suggestion. I'm pretty sure Peter Culpan will honour it. What now, wait for some contact from Yiannis. What will Ariana and myself do in the meantime, go back to Athens? No, I need to stay here, keep an eye on Michael, he'll need support, need advice as things develop, I definitely need to stay here. Ariana is not party to all this, I've kept her out of it, why cause extra worry. She knows we are in Auckland to 'sort out' Michael but she's not privy to the unpleasant detail. I'll need to level with her.

I give Ariana a sanitised version of the situation stressing the potential danger for Michael and how she needs to say absolutely nothing, not even to her closest friends, it's just too dangerous.

'Don't worry Frank, I can keep a secret especially when the stakes are this high. I won't be saying anything. I know you have not 'told all,' but I don't think I want to 'know all,' don't want to be a worry wart. Now then what are we going to do?

'I need to stay here until this thing is resolved, leaving Michael on his own is not an option, how long? don't know but my instincts tell me not that long. It all depends on the Maniots, how long will they tolerate Yiannis?'

'Ok Frank, I don't have to rush back to Athens, I've got quite a few brownie points to my credit, what better way of using them than being with my lover in New Zealand.'

'Michael has not been contacted about what's required of him so right now there's nothing that needs doing. How about I ask my mate about Pataua?'

'Dad, you're going up to Pataua with Ariana, a few days of bliss together? do you think I could come along? When we went there last time it was so nice but then I had Dimitra. Reckon I should ask Ayla? Would it be appropriate? or would I just be burdening myself with memories?'

'Don't know Michael, how well do you know Ayla? how intimate is your relationship? Would she be embarrassed by the way we behave I mean our penchant for shedding our cloths.'

'We're pretty intimate Dad I don't think she would be offended. I like her a lot, plenty of character, an adventurous spirit. I reckon she'd be right into it.'

'Go for it Michael, make the most of the good things life has to offer, you've copped enough crap recently to last a lifetime.'

We take the big car, the Merc. Ayla jumped at the opportunity, told her uncle she would be AWOL for a few days, 'running off with your best mate's son.'

We stop off at Whangarei waterfront for a coffee, what a lovely spot. It's been years since I'd been there. My recollection? a backwater, a dump, what a pleasant surprise. Cafes to burn, spoilt for choice, good restaurants and a way-out building called the Hundertwasser Centre, an Art Deco place like no other. Ariana was mightily impressed with the Hundertwasser Centre, purchased a Hundertwasser painting, rather weird but it certainly had something. I think a little cannabis would help in appreciating what it was all about.

Pataua, the bach is all ours. I'm a little concerned Michael might have trouble handling the memories. Ayla spotted it and suggested a short rest after our car trip. The bach is quite small and Ariana and myself could not help hearing the sounds of their lovemaking behind the bedroom door. It did not take much to arouse us, the cloths go flying and we barely make it to the main bedroom.

'Frank, I don't think we need worry about those two. This break could involve a lot of sex, what's your take on that?'

'Let's just immerse ourselves in a couple of days of decadence, no need to worry about Ayla and Michael.'

It is indeed a few days of sexual excess, this little bach in Pataua is the perfect environment. Ayla is a revelation, makes no secret about having plenty of sex with Michael and she's not too worried about running around with very little on. It stimulates Ariana, well she does not need stimulating, but it reaches new heights. We find ourselves fucking each other all over the place, on the beach, in the sandhills, in the surf, not even being discreet about it in the presence of the youngsters, well they are not being too discreet either. I think it's working for Michael, no time to be a sad sack, no time for reflection or worry.

Better not stay away from Auckland too long, Michael's 'acquaintances' may be wanting him, his other life might be calling.

'Another two days, ok? you two manage that?'

'Mr Conchie, Frank, there are no secrets, I need this man, I want to move in with him when we get back to Auckland, is that ok with you?'

'Do I get a say in this?'

'Not really, we'll do it anyway but your blessing would be nice.'

I'm elated, a loving girl is exactly what Michael needs, being alone is not good when there's so much stress. I shudder a bit, this will be his third girlfriend, those affairs did not turn out well.

We stay for another two days. There's a small tinnie at the bach and we go out over the sandbar that protects Pataua lagoon, into Ngunguru Bay and try our luck with the fishing. Six big snapper just like that, we must be doing something right. Ariana is impressed again.

'This Kiwi fishing, these big fish, they just jump into the boat.'

Back across the bar, this could be interesting. The tide has turned, it's streaming out over the bar, there's a chop on the water and our tinnie is just a *little tinnie*. It is interesting, the boat rears up and Ariana takes fright.

'Never fear Frank is here.'

Frank might be here but he's fully extended controlling the situation. Bars command a lot of respect even little ones like this. We survive and make it into the lagoon, not a problem.

'Frank that was dangerous, I was frightened,' from Ariana.

Ayla comes to the rescue.

'It's ok Ariana, looks worse than it really is. These bars are common in New Zealand and boaties know how to handle them.' Ayla's a boatie.

We get the little tinnie back to the bach then go back down to the lagoon and get some pipies, there are plenty of them. It's steamed pipies then big snapper fillets lightly pan fried in butter for dinner, savvy blanc, several bottles. Life is complete, I wish!

# *Michael*

Dad's sorted me out, we have a plan, dangerous, but there's no viable alternative. We've come to an arrangement with the New Zealand Police; well with Peter Culpan. It's high risk and it's dependant on a murder. If it succeeds I will be free of my involvement with the Athens underworld, it's got to succeed!

Ayla, this lovely girl who has come into my life, helping me to get over Dimitra. It's a huge hurdle. Dimitra was extraordinary, there will never be another like her, I'm still hurting. Been up to Pataua again, last time was with Dimitra and that was fantastic, this time it was Ayla and it was pretty good. Ayla's good in bed, a keen sex partner. I'm warming to her, she's a great comfort to me.

'Michael Conchie?' An early morning phone call, a Greek voice.

'Who is it darling?' Ayla is lying beside me, naked. A couple of days back from Pataua and we've continued the sexual orgy we started there.

'I'm from Athens, I've got a message for you, we need to meet.'

Shit, the moment of truth, this will be from Yiannis.

A park bench under a pohutukawa tree at the end of Musick Point. A peaceful place looking out over the Waitemata towards Mothuie. Seagulls taking advantage of the light easterly breeze, just hanging in the air, the sound of the ocean, the wind in the trees, such a lovely spot, far removed from life's unpleasant things. *Michael your life could be like this, but it's not.*

'I've got a message from Yiannis.' A Greek fellow, a bad looking dude, shit! It had to happen, the hard word, expected, but a shock when it actually happens.

'You are to organise a pick up off the northland coast and deliver it to a warehouse in Wiri. That's it, that's all you have to do. You'll be on your own, no one else involved.

'On my own?'

'Yes, you have no knowledge of who or what's involved, got it?'

'Ok tell me what I need to know.'

This bad looking dude then gives me a lot of detail about how I will need to get a seaworthy fizz boat and go fishing off Helena Bay late on the afternoon of the 23$^{rd}$, that's three weeks from now. I'll need a good GPS receiver. I'll need to be fishing well out and I'll need to do it regardless of the weather. There will be a container ship passing close to the coast and it will be off Helena Bay around nine in the evening. Here are some co-ordinates. Be at this spot when the ship passes by. Tuck in behind and keep in mind that these ships move along at quite a speed, there'll be no slowing down. When you are spotted a package, quite a large package, will be dropped over the stern, it will be a 'floater.' Pick it up and deliver it to Wiri. You'll need a cell-phone. Call this number as soon as you can after the pickup. Just one word, a yes or a no, you've either been successful or you've failed. Weather, breakdowns, those sorts of things. There is a plan B, you know nothing about that. Got it?

'Yep, I can make all that happen.'

'Here's some cash, you'll need it to buy a boat, nothing flash, don't draw attention to yourself. An old dunga but make sure it's a good old dunga.'

He hands me an envelope. '$100,000 keep the change, any questions?'

'About plan B?'

'You don't need to know, got the idea.'

That's it, the Greek dude ups and walks off.

Well I've got my orders. So much for the administrative aspect of what I was going to be doing in New Zealand. This could get me a long stretch in a New Zealand prison. I'm out on a limb. Do I confide in Peter Culpan or do I do what's been asked and tell him later? Suddenly I'm glad Dad's in the picture.

I stay on the park bench under the pohutukawa tree for a long time reflecting, where is this leading? I've got to do it, got to free myself from the criminal world that all started quite innocently with me trying to find Carrie. A lot has happened, there's been a lot of growing up on my part. Two girlfriends murdered. Hard to comprehend in this tranquil environment, sitting on a park bench looking out over the gulf. My luck must turn, make it turn. It has turned a bit already, there's Ayla, and we have an understanding with Peter Culpan.

I tell Dad, I'll need his help. A boat and it would be a good idea if Dad did the buying. Retired fellow wants to go fishing. I'm working, my front job, can't go off looking for a boat, I need to be in the office. Peter Culpan? do we confide in him at this stage? yes to a point. We invite him around to the house for coffee. Dad, Ariana and myself are living in the family home in Parnell, Ayla is a frequent visitor. Perhaps she should move in, how would that sit with uncle Bob, Dad's best mate.

Ariana has gone off to do a bit of household shopping. I sense she's detected that Peter Culpan's visit is not something she wants to know about, very perceptive Ariana.

We tell Peter about the pickup, don't know what, but probably Columbian cocaine. It will be in a warehouse in Wiri in three weeks' time. We don't tell him the details, don't want any police involvement screwing things up and leaving me exposed, he understands. The police know about the warehouse, they've had it under surveillance for some time. They are more interested in tracing the distribution patterns in New Zealand, want to take out the whole cocaine operation. I'm party to the actual importation and that part of the operation could well collapse if Yiannis is taken out. Peter advises us to go ahead and do what's been asked. He does not want to know the detail, does not want to jeopardise things. The stakes are high and it's dangerous. He's more interested in the distribution side. We ask Peter if he's free to tell us about the distribution set up. Yes he can, confidential of course, does not want the bad guys becoming aware that the police are onto them.

'There's been a takeover. An Athens based outfit was running it. We did not know much about them until it came to our attention with that Waiheke murder. We now know it's a Düzgün operation, they stole it from their predecessors the Maniots. We also hear from Athens that the Maniots are not happy. The lad who was murdered was a favoured son, they want revenge. The takeover was a brutal business. We've found five bodies so far attributable to the Düzgüns.'

I ask Peter about the supply side, 'Columbian you think?'

'Pretty sure it's Columbian. They'll sell to whoever's top dog at the time in New Zealand so it could be an on going thing. Take down one crowd and the supplier will be looking for another. Yiannis appears to be in the driving seat at the moment, how long that lasts, you tell me?'

'Not too long Peter, my information is that he's a marked man. Killing the Maniot lad was not a smart move.'

'That's good to hear, anything else?'

'I wish, removing Yiannis will get me out of jail and I desperately want to put this business behind me.'

'Hang in there Michael, get as much information as you can, you'll be a free man eventually.'

Peter Culpan thanks us and takes his leave, 'let me know when that delivery is in the warehouse.'

'Ok Dad, a boat, we've got three weeks to establish our keen fishermen credentials.'

'Our credentials? your credentials.'

It's a well used tinnie, big, should be able to handle a rough sea, 220hp outboard, plenty of grunt. The trailer's seen better days but appears sound enough, better get out there and be seen fishing.

'What about this weekend Dad, want to come? We can use the old Holden, big V8, should handle it.'

'Why don't you and Ayla go, not sure a beat up tinnie is Ariana's thing.'

'What about it Ayla, got anything planed for the weekend?'

Ayla and myself spend two days up near Helena Bay, small motel. Have to be seen fishing. Insurance should anyone come inquiring. Unlikely, but if anyone got wind of a drug importation then it will deflect attention away from us. We get out fishing on both days and catch a lot of fish. We give most of it away to some people staying at the motel, we don't really want a lot of fish. Ayla is keen on fishing but she's more enthusiastic about jumping into the sack. It's an enjoyable weekend and we become even closer.

The pickup. Back to Helena Bay. I go alone, don't want to involve Dad and Ayla knows nothing about what we are up to. I stay at the same motel, 'fishing alone this week end?'

Weather's marginal, sea is lumpy but ok, late afternoon evening fishing. I get a few snapper and I'm at the appointed place a little before nine. Sure enough there's a container ship bearing down on me. It's huge, really getting along, containers stacked way up, quite a menacing sight in the fading evening light. Need to be careful. I tuck in behind, not too close. It's not easy keeping up, a turbulent wash as well. Shit, this is difficult don't stuff it up. There's a spotlight directed onto the water close in behind the stern. Splash, something lands in the water. I close in, it's a large white package of some sort. I grab it with a boathook and pull it alongside, how am I going to get this aboard? with great difficulty. It's heavy and bulky,

I'm uphill with this, don't capsize the boat. The choppy sea is not helping, I really need a second person. Harden up Michael, your life could be dependent on this, splosh, it's in the boat, back to Helena Bay.

'Here, want some fish, got more than I figured.' It's the hotel manager, good cover, just in case. I've stashed my 'load' well forward under the boat's dash and covered it with fishing stuff. I'll drive back to Auckland in the morning, no rush, stay cool.

'Peter, coffee at our place, we need to talk.'
He's around in a shot.

'It's in the warehouse at Wiri and I think there's a lot of whatever it is. The balls in you court now, I have no knowledge of what happens beyond my delivery. I don't think it would be the brightest thing to raid the place, how would you have known there was anything there? could focus attention on me.'

'Stop worrying Michael, we won't be doing anything precipitate. We want to track the distribution network not just get ourselves a pile of cocaine. Your delivery will probably trigger some activity in that area, we will be watching.'

Well that went off without a hitch and there's sixty thousand dollars left over. We have ourselves a big tinnie as well, what will we do with it? a lot more fishing perhaps. Have to keep it somewhere. Might be wise to keep it away from prying eyes, around behind the house, out of sight? What now, what will Yiannis be wanting next?

One week on, I'm in a Parnell coffee shop with Ayla, she's moved in with me. Dad's old schoolmate, 'uncle Bob,' is chuffed that his old mate Frank has surfaced and that his son has got together with his young cousin, his receptionist. Ayla and myself are very close now. I've kept her well away from what I'm doing, might have to level with her sometime in the future, will have to!

'Shit, it's Lambani.'

'Excuse me Michael, what did you say.'

I'd just seen Lambani walk past the coffee shop, mistaken? no, definitely Lambani.

'Michael you're pale, you look like you've seen a ghost.'

What can I say? what do I do? what the hell is Lambani doing in Auckland, a Maniot soldier.

'It's ok dear, I thought I saw someone, mistaken identity, not to worry.'

'I don't think so Michael, you're still pale, who did you 'think' you saw.'

'It's nothing Ayla, nothing at all, another cappuccino perhaps.'

She's not buying it, I'll have to come up with something.

'I thought it was someone I knew in Athens, not a very nice person, no way could they be here in Auckland.'

I'm getting a quizzical look, Ayla's no fool, she's sensed something's not right.

'Ok Michael, little white lie perhaps? I won't press it. Would not want you keeping secrets from me though.'

'Ayla, I had a life in Athens, I think I've mentioned a few things. There was a girlfriend, my fiancé, she was murdered by a jealous ex and I'm having trouble getting over it. I have mentioned it. I was traumatised, still am.'

'Michael I have sensed there are things troubling you, you can tell me all if it will help.'

'I will Ayla, not yet, the memory is still raw, soon though when I've got my head sorted.'

'Dad, Lambani's here, I saw him in Parnell, no mistake, it was Lambani. Why is he here?'

There's only one possible reason, the Maniots want their cocaine business back, shit, that's trouble big time. Lambani knows us but what will be his take on it if he knows we, well me, are working for the Düzgüns? Killing everyone seems to be the standard fix in gangland disputes, does friendship carry any weight? Do we let Peter Culpan know? It's only a coincidence that we know the Maniots are here, what if I had not spotted him? we would not suddenly be worried. We decide to do nothing, I never saw Lambani. We'll need to watch our backs. We are in the Düzgün camp, not by choice. Does Lambani know that? Is he still sympathetic towards us?

Ring, ring, early morning. 'I have another message from Yiannis.' It's the Greek fellow. 'Musick Point, 10am.'

Bugger I don't need this but there's no choice, I've bought into it. Have to get Ayla to convince my employer that I'm crook, won't be in today.

'Michael you're not sick, what are you up to?'

'Give me some slack Ayla, I will explain, but not right now.'

This is not good, telling lies, well not quite. I'll have to level with Ayla sooner rather than later.

It's such a lovely place this bench seat, the gulls soaring in the standing wave that the light easterly breeze is creating, the soft sound of the wind in the pohutukawa trees, the sound of the ocean at the bottom of the cliff, such a peaceful place. Why am I involved in a business that destroys young lives, causes untold misery, how has it come to this? how can I escape?

'It's a yacht this time. The Capilino a ketch rigged ocean going yacht. It will be anchoring at the north end of Elliot Bay late on the 23rd, two weeks from now. The beach is deserted and there's a track running in from the nearby road. The yacht's crew will use their own tender to bring the shipment ashore. You will deliver it to Wiri, ok? There's no money for this one, you've got plenty left over from the first job.'

He's gone, the messenger from hell, left me in this tranquil spot contemplating my lot in life. I need to take Ayla into my confidence. She's a smart girl, I can trust her to keep her mouth shut. It will remove a potentially disastrous split in our relationship, no lies, share the burden. The burden could be removed soon. Lambani, I don't think he's here for a holiday.

'Peter Culpan wants another meeting,' it's Dad, 'didn't say what it's about.'

'We have information that the Maniots are in Auckland, we don't know what for but it's a fair bet they want their cocaine business back. Have you two got any information?'

What do I say? do I let on I've seen Lambani? I want to keep as far away from things as possible so best if I remain ignorant, just play my role as the import man. That role is not quite what my understanding was with Yiannis. He indicated he wanted me to keep an eye on things but right now my only contact, the only person I know about, is the Greek fellow who delivers Yiannis's messages. Good, the less involvement the better. I let Peter know about the latest shipment.

'It's a yacht this time Peter, north end of Elliot Bay, two weeks' time.'

'The Capilino, we've been tracking it, from Columbia, Italians again, we'll let it land. You'll be delivering to Wiri, we'll take it from there. How and when were you advised about it Michael?'

'Yesterday, a Greek fellow. Message came directly from Yiannis.'

'Yes it seems the Düzgüns have tapped into the same Columbian supplier the Maniots were using, we're expecting trouble. Let us know if you hear anything.'

Do I volunteer what I know about Lambani? no, keep out of it.

Back at work, my day job. $60,000 in the pocket from the first pick up, well for two pick ups. Spent $40,000 on a boat and we get to keep it, proceeds from crime, we're criminals.

Work; they've put me in a team working on a big factory out at Wiri, it's quite close to the warehouse being used by the Düzgüns, small world. A major engineering company, a lot of specialised detail design, interesting. Most of it is done in the office in Parnell, convenient. Ayla and myself go to and from work together. 'Bob the boss' as he's known, is a good guy, he's dragged us into the pub after work a couple of times, got Dad and Ariana in there as well. He's happy that his niece has taken up with me. Ariana is still here, been a few weeks now, she's talking about having to get back to her job in Athens, can't push her luck too far, not sure how that will sit with Dad. He wants to keep a close eye on me and that's not a silly idea. I'm pretty much out of my depth with this cocaine business. Good to have Dad's steadying hand. The only thing binding me to the Düzgüns is Yiannis, if he were gone I'd be a free man. Perhaps Lambani's presence is significant, maybe things are about to change.

# *Frank*

'Bob the boss' is a yachtie, got a big Beneteau, popular boat in Auckland. Ayla's done a lot of sailing on it, a dyed in the wool yachtie, and guess what, 'Bob the boss' is a mate of Steve Coultard. We went sailing with Steve last time we were in Auckland, he's got a Beneteau as well. That's the time we ran across the cocaine dealer, Colin Petrou.

'What about a weekend's sailing,' it's Bob, 'I'll lay it on Steve, he reckons he's got the fastest Beneteau around, it's bullshit but he's convinced. How about it Frank? Ariana? My good lady Lydia is always a starter.'

'Done deal, the youngies as well?

'Of course, we need Ayla's expertease, makes the boat go faster.'
This will be good, get to see Steve's lady again, Rachel from yesteryear. Get us away from this cocaine crap for a while, need a break. I've got a strange feeling it's all about to go pear shaped.

Saturday morning, Half Moon Bay Marina, two Beneteaus and a competitive atmosphere. The idea is to sail, no, race over to the north side of Waiheke and find a bay for lunch, play it by ear after that. Perhaps Vino Vino's for dinner, hanging out over the water at Oneroa, I love the place. These two guys are seriously competitive. Hardly out of the marina, up go the sails and we're racing down the Tamaki estuary, ferries, weekenders, fizz boats, small dingies, look out we're coming through. Another good Auckland day, light easterly, perfect sailing conditions. Once clear of the traffic it becomes a real tactical scrap between these two, first to Matiatia gets boasting rights. Us 'passengers' lay back and enjoy it, let the very competitive crews, Steve, Ratchel, Bob and Ayla, show us how it's done. Lydia, Bob's lady, wife perhaps? I don't know, is not mad keen on the crewing bit, lets Ayla demonstrate her skills, and Ayla does know her stuff, the boat does go faster, well I reckon it does.

Swishing along through the waves, the sound of the wind in the sails, in tune with nature, it's very relaxing and peaceful, good for the soul, this is what sailing's all about. Question, why do yachties always race each other? answer, because there's nothing else you can do with the things. That's not very nice Frank! just thinking, not voicing it, don't want to finish up in the tide. We fly past the entrance to Matiatia, whose in the lead? 'We are,' 'no we are,' depends on where the finish line is! What the hell let's get on 'round to Hekerua Bay tucked in under a cliff just past Oneroa, drop the pick, lunch in paradise. Hekurua Bay is picture postcard stuff. We tie the sterns together and breakout the food and wine. It's hot, a swim's the story. A little decorum this time, we don't know each other all that well.

'That was terrific Bob, I reckon we had the edge on Steve and Rachel.'

'Bullshit,' it's Rachel, 'Frank you always claimed victory remember, way back in yesteryear, you had that winning streak, still have it I see, but who cares. Right, into the water, it's very hot and we're just blowing hot air.'

'Cheeky.'

The water's warm and crystal clear. There's a blowhole under the cliff by the entrance to a cave, not very active today, calm sea, bit of a swell causing some blowhole activity. The local kids are jumping off a ledge up above the entrance to the cave, pretty high, There's a lot of verbal encouragement for the more reluctant jumpers.

Cooled off, out, must be time for a wine. We get to talking while the girls get lunch organised.

'Steve, how's your mate Colin Petrou these days,' I ask,

'remember we came across him and his coke snorting friends last time we were out with you.'

'Not seen him since but I hear he's getting a name for himself as the 'go to' man if you want coke, living dangerously I reckon. What's your connection to that business these days Frank, you were involved in some way weren't you?'

Careful, what have I let slip to Steve in the past?

'There was some contact with the business in Athens, not nice and I'm trying to keep my distance from things like that, lead a normal life.'

'Did I hear you mention Colin Petrou,' from Bob.

'Yes you did,' and we tell him about our encounter with him during our previous visit, how he and his friends had snorted themselves into a real state.

'Yes he is a big user by all accounts. We buy a little from him, use it occasionally, the trendy thing right now in Auckland, that's right Lydia isn't it?'

Lydia's been pretty quiet so far, strikingly attractive, brown hair and strong facial features. Her eyes, unusual, large green eyes that look right through you. I got the feeling she was a very strong personality.

'We? you Bob, keeping up with your mates, trendies, it's not you, only do it to keep your good guy image intact.'

'She's right, Lydia's always right, she's good for me. We do snort a little, very little, and only when it would be rude not to, stay onside with the trendies, bloody stupid trendies.'

'You say you get it from Colin Petrou? is he the main supplier amongst your crowd Bob?'

'Yep, from what I hear he's Mr Big.'

'Where does he get it from? is he an importer?'

My question is a shot in the dark, never know what bit of information might pop up.

'Don't know, doubt it. There was a Greek fellow who was well known amongst the Auckland trendies. I think he was the source but he disappeared, now I hear there's another Greek fellow.'

What I'm hearing figures. Yiannis has probably wiped out the Maniots who were running the business and taken over, could be using the same distributors. Colin Petrou still being in business suggests that's the case. I get the feeling the Maniots are about to retake what was theirs otherwise why would Lambani be in Auckland. Is Kenzo here? how many other Düzgüns are here and does Peter Culpan know about them?

The day follows a typical pattern for a day on the water in Auckland, eating, drinking, probably too much, swimming, enjoying the sun and generally relaxing. The Waitemata harbour is such a wonderful place why would you live anywhere else, good question, why indeed?

'Ok, listen up,' it's Bob, 'we're going to have another go at racing. Down to Gannet rock and back to Oneroa, will take around two hours, looser buys dinner at Vino Vino's.'

It's around three in the afternoon and we're off. These two guys are very competitive, this will be good. Some serious racing with a couple of guys who know what they're doing. Around Gannet and back along the coast. The weather remains the same, light easterly. These Beneteaus go really fast in the hands of experienced yachties and these two guys are experienced. Ariana is liking it, a first, she's never been racing on a yacht in her life.

'Frank I could get to like this, like it a lot. We should organise access to a yacht for our visits to Auckland, there will be frequent visits?'

What am I hearing, have I found a soul mate who might like sailing, life is complete. It was a little yacht and Rachel in yesteryear.

Oneroa's coming up fast, we have not determined just where the finish line will be, it was assumed there would be a clearly defined gap between the two yachts when we arrived at Oneroa, no way it's neck and neck.

'Draw.'

'Rubbish we were in front.'

'Bullshit.'

No way is this going to be resolved without blood on the floor, perhaps we'll just split the bill before we come to blows.

We're well into dinner and as usual at Vino Vino's it's excellent. Everyone's in good spirits, the racing has got us all fired up, several bottles of wine have disappeared already. It's developing into a wonderful evening when fate steps in. Kenzo *and* Lambani walk in with a couple of attractive girls, shit! They purposely ignore our group, well only Michael and myself know who they are. I don't think Ariana has ever seen either of them before. Michael looks shocked. He had spotted Lambani in the street a couple of days earlier, however, seeing him now is a shock. We continue with our meal trying hard to remain in party mode. I'm finding it difficult and Michael? particularly hard. Kenzo and Lambani are well aware of our presence and thankfully, purposely, choose to ignore us however the worrying question, why are they both in Auckland? Maniot hit men, and Michael in the Düzgün camp. He's got a pick up in a week's time from a yacht at Elliot Bay. It was not that long ago that there had been a shootout involving a stolen Beneateau on the Northland coast. The Maniots had been running the business at the time. What if they know about the impending importation by the Düzgüns, what are the implications for Michael, is he in danger? do we enlist police help? The police are aware of this importation, do they have any knowledge of a possible hijacking? Probably not, Peter Culpan would have said something surely. If there is a hijacking will Michael be in danger, is his tenuous friendship with Lambani sufficient to save him?

We're back on Bob's boat, Michael and Ayla are bunking on board for the night with myself and Ariana.

'Come on, what's wrong? you've been on edge since dinner, what is it Frank?' Ariana can read my mood.

I level with her, all the detail, not sanitised this time, she's got a right to know. The immediate problem? is Michael in imminent danger and if he is what can we do about it?

# *Michael*

Elliot Bay. I drive there in Dad's old Holden, arrive around six in the evening. Down the dirt track to the north end of the beach, deserted. I park amongst the sand dunes and wait. An hour later a yacht enters the bay and anchors about a hundred meters off the beach. What do I do, show myself? no, wait for them to make the first move. Shortly after a rubber ducky heads for the shore with two men aboard. They step ashore and look around as if expecting someone. A couple of tough looking characters. I make the first move.

'You fellows got something for me?'

'Yeah, it's in the boat.' Italians. 'Ya want it now?'

'Yep,' not much being said.

The two fellows manhandle a large package out of the tender and dump it on the beach.

'All yours mate.' They get back into the rubber ducky and go back to the yacht. That's it, delivery completed.

I go back to the car. I'll have to drive it onto the beach to retrieve the package, it's quite big and looks heavy. Shit, there are people in the car, Lambani and Kenzo, shit, I'm in trouble.

'Settle down Michael, you're not the enemy.' It's Lambani. 'We'll be relieving you of that big package.'

'Christ Lambani that will get me killed.'

'Possibly, but we have a plan, it should save your skin. If you were a true Düzgün we'd cut your throat right now.'

Shit, I'm up to my neck in it. The police? they know about this shipment, are they in the area, do they realise what's going down?

'We'll give you a package to deliver to Wiri and we'll relieve you of this one. Your new package contains a pretty good substitute. It'll take those turkeys a while to realise it's not what they're expecting and when they do figure out who's done the dirty? well you don't need to know. What you will need to do is piss off, get clear of the place pronto.'

Lambani and Kenzo have a vehicle nearby and I finish up with a large package that they supply. They take the package from the yacht and disappear. What now? I guess I follow through and deliver it to Wiri as planned. Their comment about not sticking around at the Wiri warehouse is a worry, what's going to happen?

It's four in the morning when I get to Wiri, I'm expected. There are four people there, I recognise one of them, Colin Petrou the dealer. The fellow who appears to be in charge is Greek, perhaps he's Mr No Name, the big boss.

'Ok, that's my bit done, I'm out of here.'

'Not so fast,' it's Mr No Name, 'stick around while we test this stuff.'

Shit now I am in trouble, do they suspect something? Was not like this when I made the first delivery. Remember what Lambani said, piss off immediately. *I need to get out of here.*

'Is there a toilet?' I ask.

'Out the back.'

Out the back door and I keep going. Something, I don't know what, is going to happen in there, I just feel it. Shit I run smack into Kenzo.

'Keep going Michael, forget about your car, get away from here.'

Morning, I'm home, hitched a ride then an early bus. I tell Dad what's happened. Hardly finished telling when Peter Culpan calls, he's coming 'round. I tell him everything that's happened.

'You did your bit Michael. We knew the Maniots were here. We had two observers watching the warehouse, your arrival was observed. We did not expect anything precipitate to happen so we let whatever was going to happen play itself out. Not long after you left there was a shootout. We had the armed offenders squad on standby, too late, it was all over when they got there. The warehouse was empty, no cocaine, no Düzgüns, no Maniots, but there was a horrific message. Two bodies strung up by their heels, disemboweled, throats cut. One was the local dealer, Colin Petrou, the other the Greek fellow who we are pretty sure was Mr No Name. Payback for the Maniot lad on Waiheke. Why Colin Petrou was dealt to we don't know, could be he was perceived as being in the Düzgün camp. There were three other bodies, all shot in the head, we think they were all local distributors. It appears the Maniots have wiped out the local Düzgün lot. I've brought your Holden around, it's outside. We are not interested in it.'

*Ring ring*, Athens, Nico. It's three hours on and I'm still reeling from the horrific events that have transpired.

'Good news, particularly you Michael. I've just been told a body has turned up in a ditch here, the papers are not onto it yet but it appears to be Yiannis Stavrou.'

Shit it appears the Maniots have hit the Düzgüns with a well planned operation. What do we do with this information, advise Colin Culpan? no, keep as far out of it as we can. He does not know that we know Lambani and Kenzo are in Auckland, perhaps he did not know either. Revealing what we knew could cast suspicion on us. Nico's phone call is a huge relief, should clear away all our problems. It's a police matter now. I'm sure the Athens Police will advise the New Zealand Police about the demise of Yiannis Stavrou and the implications that will have on the New Zealand cocaine operation. Lambani and Kenzo, did they do this? probably. I saw Kenzo outside the warehouse, pretty obvious. Do I tell Peter Culpan? no, keep out of it. I did not know Lambani and Kenzo were in Auckland, I do not even know them, how would Peter Culpan know otherwise. The big question, where are they now? hopefully out of the country. Peter Culpan did say he was aware the Maniots were in

Auckland, did he know exactly who? and will there be a watch out for them.

Nothing in the morning papers but the news on the radio mentions a police raid on a Wiri warehouse that involved some shooting, details are not known at this stage.

With any luck this could mark the end of my involvement with these Greek crooks. Yiannis is no more according to Nico, he will know. I'm a free man. I guess this must be how a fellow feels when he gets out of jail, an overpowering feeling of relief. I need to celebrate.

# *Frank*

We're around the pool, Saturday morning, weekend off for the youngsters. Four of us, myself, Ariana, Michael and Ayla, another lovely day. A horrific night but the girls are not aware of it, do we tell them? Ariana will understand but Ayla knows nothing about these things, perhaps we'll keep her out of it. Suddenly Michael is a happy lad. It figures, he can see a normal life rolling out ahead of him unencumbered by the sort of crap that's bedevilled him for the past year or so. Losing Dimitra was a huge blow, not sure he's over that, doubt he ever will be. Ayla is good for him, she's no fool and I sense she's aware there's a lot about Michael she's not party to. Ariana is curious, she senses something has happened. She's not asked me directly but has implied that perhaps there's something I should tell her. I will, after all last night's developments change everything. There's no longer a requirement for us to stay in Auckland and keep an eye on Michael, we're free to go back to Athens. Can we discuss this here in the presence of Ayla?

*Ring ring,* it's Peter Culpan. 'Frank, we need to talk, ok if I call around?'

'Ayla, there is something we need to tell you, you'll find it pretty overwhelming. It involves Michael and I feel you have a right to know. A fellow's coming around, a policeman. He'll be talking to myself and Michael and perhaps you should sit in on the conversation, you'll be horrified by what you'll hear but this is no time for secrets. Ariana, you too. I've not levelled with you about the latest development but it only happened last night and I've been prepping myself to tell you. Peter Culpan coming around now has made this an opportune time to reveal all. Ayla, this will be privileged information, you must not tell anyone, absolutely no one. We may not be completely out of the woods yet and your knowing about these things could compromise you, so zipped lip, can you handle that?'

'Yes Mr Conchie; Frank; I can handle it, suddenly I am very protective of your gorgeous boy Michael.'

Peter Culpan tells us what they found at the Wiri warehouse, it's horrific. Michael had told me about running into Kenzo but that was all he knew. Peter Culpan's information was shocking. The girls are incredulous, these things don't happen in New Zealand. Well yes they do, they just have.

'Frank, I want you to level with me about just what you do know. I appreciate there are things that you might want to keep to yourself and I know you are a good guy, however, this business involves multiple murders in two countries. We have to find out as much as we can and I'm asking you to tell me what you know?'

'Ok Peter, first you tell me. What do you people know about the Maniots operation here in Auckland?'

My question is intended to find out if the police know about Lambani and Kenzo, if they don't do I tell them? These two guys have been very helpful to Michael and myself and I feel honour bound not to dob them in unnecessarily, after all we have no hard evidence that they've done anything bad apart from stealing a load of cocaine from the opposition, is that illegal?

Peter Culpan tells us that the police were aware that the Maniots were active in Auckland. They knew about Mr No Name, been watching him for some time. Colin Petrou was also known to them. He's a major distributor who deals with whoever is doing the importing. He does not appear to have any allegiance to either the Maniots or the Düzgüns. No mention of Lambani or Kenzo, perhaps Peter Culpan does not know about them. It appears the Maniots have taken over the New Zealand operation from the Düzgüns. The New Zealand Police do not know very much about them at this stage.

'That's about the extent of our knowledge at the moment. Can you add to this Frank?'

What do I do? tell him about Lambani and Kenzo? I don't think so. We owe these guys and we don't want any more involvement than we already have.

'You seem to be on to it Peter, you know as much as we do. There is one thing we are aware of and I'm sure Athens will be telling you to-day. Yiannis Stavrou is dead. Our Athens contact has just phoned with the news. It was Yiannis who had Michael on the hook. His demise changes things in our camp. Michael will be free from any obligation.'

These developments clear the air for Michael, he's now free of any involvement, well he should be? can lead a normal life? Ariana and myself can think about returning to Athens and resuming the life we had started together, divide our time between Athens and Auckland. Perhaps I should think about an interest in a yacht here in Auckland. Ariana has expressed real interest in sailing and I would love to get back into it. We could get Christos and Karisa out here from time to time as well. So that's the scene, time to celebrate our new found freedom.

# Back To Athens

We're in the taverna around the corner, jet lagged, getting back to a normal life, putting all the nastiness behind us. The police can sort out the mess, we're no longer involved. Michael has stayed in Auckland, he'll not be moving. He's living with Ayla in the big house, keeping it open, ready for the frequent visits by the people from Athens. We are recounting all that's happened in Auckland to Christos and Karissa. They are gobsmacked, the brutality, the horror, let's close the door on that chapter of our lives. It's good to be eating 'taverna style,' superb as usual, and the carafes, many carafes.

Before leaving Auckland I came to an arrangement with Bob Bach and his lovely lady, Lydia, about access to their big Beneteau. I suggested I buy part ownership the idea being to use it when we visit Auckland, something we intend to do reasonably frequently. Ariana is suddenly a big sailing enthusiast and I'm keen to get back into it. Bob is going to give it some thought. His initial reaction was positive. A spin off could be he and Lydia having somewhere to stay when they come to Europe, the bucket list thing.

During the long trip back to Greece I give a lot of thought to the future. GC Investigations will be a significant part of my life, keep me occupied, stop me 'withering on the vine.' It will produce income as well. Living with Ariana is working well, she's a busy lady, it's her nature. Our occupations allow plenty of time for both of us to do our thing whenever we decide. Travel will feature large, trips to New Zealand will be right up there. That's the plan, wonder how it will work out?

Christos has leased some office space downtown for GC

Investigations. We are attracting quite a bit of business and operating from home is no longer viable. We're having to turn down work, getting selective about what we take on, we're retired remember. Then one day an inquiry from Aetos Giuliani & Papadakis, Angelica and Fabio Giuliani's firm, they want a meeting.

It takes place in our downtown office, it's with Fabio. I've filled in Christos about Ariana and my relationship with them, the Mounu thing. He's surprised and I've indicated that Fabio and Angelica are not exactly pure as the blown snow, they have a relationship with the Düzgüns, specifically with the now deceased Yiannis Stavrou. Perhaps we will need to treat with caution anything they might propose. I am wondering if they might still be influenced by the now defunct Düzgüns. It would appear that both the Düzgüns and the Stathoses are no longer players in the drug business, it's Maniot territory now.

Fabio tells us they have been approached by a fellow from Istanbul, a Marcial Crabaire. This fellow spends a lot of time in Paris and is into the meth business, they suspect he heads up a drug manufacturing operation. Would we be interested in checking on him?

'Not really, we want to keep clear of the drug business. GC Investigations specialises in simple stuff, wayward spouses, nothing nasty.'

'Ok, I understand, however, you have a past and your Michael is not exactly an innocent party either, there's Carrie as well. There are people who think you have things to answer for.'

'That's not very nice Fabio, are you threatening us?'

'No just stating a position. We don't take sides, we are a legal firm, we defend people. We understand Marcial Crabaire was an associate of Pierre Gorbet, the murdered friend of Carrie Gray. Crabaire is dangerous. We suspect his organisation could come into conflict with the Maniots.'

'That's interesting stuff Fabio, give us some time to think about it but our initial reaction is it's not our field, we do simple stuff only.'

Well that was out of left field, what's Fabio hinting at? a past? Michael and Carrie? surely we can rid ourselves of all that. It appears this Fabio knows a lot about our involvement, where does he get his information? Well Angelica was sleeping with Yiannis, he would have been a source. Perhaps a talk with Nico might be a good idea.

'Aetos Giuliani & Papadakis, bent lawyers for the underworld,' Nico's assessment, 'don't get too close to them.'

We're back in Nico's bar, been a while. I think we need to put him on our payroll, he's such a good source of information.

'Marcial Crabaire, I've heard the name, don't know much about him, apparently he's a real bad dude.'

'Nico, give us your take on the drug scene now that the two main players have been taken out, are the Maniots going to have free reign?'

'Unlikely, there are elements of both the Stathos and Düzgün families still active, whether they survive is anyone's guess. Your mates Lambani and Kenzo are back in town. The rumour is they were in New Zealand recently, know anything about that?'

Is Nico trying us on, does he know more than he's letting on, testing us perhaps. Should we level with him after all if we are thinking about putting him on our payroll then some openness would be appropriate. We decide to take him into our confidence. We give him a run down of the events in Auckland and our suspicion that Kenzo and Lambani were the executioners. Don't know for sure, don't want to know, in fact we want no further involvement.

'Good decision, keep out of it, but, and it's a big but, you might find that just about impossible to achieve. There's no real reason why anyone will come looking for you or your family but these crooks can be unpredictable. Making inquiries about Marcial Crabaire is not a good idea, he will get wind of it and could come looking. Let me seek out what there is to know, I don't have to ask questions, the information just turns up in my bar, all I do is listen.'

Well that's sorted, for the time being. We will not be making inquiries for Fabio, it's not what GC Investigations do.

We decide to get Carrie and Myrine around to the taverna for dinner. I'm curious if she knows anything about Marcial Crabaire.

'Yes, Paris. He was rather threatening to Pierre in a restaurant and it was not long after that incident that Pierre was murdered. I suspect this Crabaire fellow may have had a hand in it; why do you ask?'

I explain how GC Investigations had been approached about investigating him and that we had declined.

'Now let's change the subject. How's the sailing? Myrine up to speed?'

'Yep, she's a natural, a real fan, should have discovered it years ago. We are out every weekend. We have access to a yacht owned by a couple of gay guys, I don't think they are real sailors, don't use their boat much, suits us. You'll have to come sailing with us, how about this weekend?'

It's a Bavaria 32, a good size for the girls and they know how to sail it. Myself, Ariana, Christos and Karissa are on board as we sail out of Piraeus with the two girls. Warm and sunny, light easterly, bit like Auckland. We sail along the coast for a while and anchor off one of the numerous beach resorts, lunchtime. We've brought along the necessary and the girls prepare some lunch, we get to talking.

'Frank,' it's Carrie, 'You have mentioned Marcial Crabaire, do you know anything about him?'

'No, it's just that we've been asked to investigate him. Do you know something Carrie?'

'Well a few straws in the wind. I first came across him in a restaurant in Paris with my man Pierre Gorbet. He was rather threatening towards Pierre. I've often thought about it and I think he might have been involved in Pierre's murder. Who was responsible has never been established and making me a suspect was a red herring. I don't think the French Police believe it was me, and we have the so called confession. That's suspect, but it does divert suspicion away from me. I would like to find out one day who it was who killed Pierre. I liked him, he was very good to me.'

'Unlikely Carrie and best left alone, there's nothing to be gained except your peace of mind. We'll keep our ears open, never know what might turn up but actively pursuing the matter is not a good idea. Can you live with that?'

'Yes I can, I've closed the book on my past, perhaps I should burn it. Now then Frank, tell me about Michael? nostalgia.'

It's a lovely day on the water. I fill in the details on Michael's recent life, a sanitised version, and I tell Carrie about Ayla, she appears to be happy to hear that. I suggest perhaps she and Myrine should think about coming out to New Zealand, great sailing, have access to a Beneteau. Myrine lights up when I mention this, she's never been to New Zealand, never travelled outside Europe. We sail back along the coast to Piraeus, Myrine is quite an accomplished sailor and obviously loves it.

I'm in the office with Christos, Monday morning, sifting through what's on our desk, what we can get to work on, earn some cash, check up on some wayward spouses, real riveting stuff.
*Ring, ring,* 'Is that GC Investigations.'

'Yes.'

'I hear you've been asked to investigate a Marcial Crabaire at the request of that asshole firm Aetos Giuliani & Papadakis, forget it, there could be unfortunate consequences.' Click, the caller hangs up.

Shit, what's that all about? Our decision to decline the job suddenly looks to be the right one however it's raised our curiosity, what's with this Crabaire fellow?

We tell Nico about the call, what motivated it? Nico has heard a few things and fills us in on what he knows.

'Marcial Crabaire has extensive underworld connections, Aetos Giuliani & Papadakis will know this that's why they want to subcontract to you, they don't want to be seen as the party making inquiries. They are being a bit naïve, of course Crabaire will know about their involvement, probably knows who wants the information as well. Crabaire controls the meth manufacturing business in Istanbul, he sells to whoever wants to buy. He's not got the market to himself, there's competition. The Özbir family, a long established and feared organisation wants in, wants total control. It's probably the Özbirs who have approached Aetos Giuliani & Papadakis but when you think about it why would they? their own organisation would have all the resources required to investigate Marcial Crabaire. So that's the story so far, could be more to come, a lot more.'

'Nico you have been busy, well you've been listening. Don't ask questions, we need you alive. We'll keep our distance from Aetos Giuliani & Papadakis, nothing to be gained there. This Özbir crowd, are they new to the meth business?'

'No, they've been dabbling in it for a while, supplying a few distributers but I think they want to take over completely, push Crabaire out of it, and that means only one thing.'

'All good stuff Nico, nothing to concern us, we'll stick with wayward spouses.'

'Mr Conchie, Frank,' it's Carrie on the phone, 'I need to talk to you, can I come along to your office right now.' It's a week on and Carrie sounds worried.

'Marcial Crabaire arrived on my doorstep last night, I was home alone, he just walked right in. Wanted to know what I knew about Pierre Gorbet's meth business, specifically how he got the stuff. What could I tell him? I have no idea what Pierre got up to, where he got his meth from, just that it apparently came from Istanbul. Crabaire was very threatening, would not accept that I did not know anything. He gave me a few days to sort my ideas out, he would be in touch. If I did not come up with something things would not go well for me. Frank I'm frightened.'

'Ok Carrie here's what I'll try to organise, a couple of bodyguards, specifically Kenzo and Lambani. Kenzo has a soft spot for you and will not be favourably disposed to anyone making threats. Leave it with me, I'll get back to you later to-day. Try not to worry, difficult I know but we'll deal with it.'

'Nico, emergency, need to speak to Kenzo and perhaps Lambani right now, is that possible?'

'All things are possible Frank, I think they are in town, give me a couple of hours.'

Two hours on, Kenzo appears at the office. He's a big boy, commanding presence and a mean disposition but he's favourably disposed towards us. I explain how Carrie has been threatened, she needs protection. Would he be prepared to move into the girls flat with them for a few days?

'You kidding me, two lovely girls and you are asking me to move in with them?'

'Yep Kenzo I am, but there's something you need to know, these two are in love; with each other.'

'I know. Perhaps I might get Lambani in on it as well, he'll be back in town tomorrow. I won't tell him about the girls being gay, see what sort of state he gets into. What do you want us to do with this Crabaire guy?'

I fill Kenzo in on the detail, how Carrie knows nothing about Pierre Gorbet's drug dealing, she was just his girlfriend. There's nothing to be gained from threatening her. She also suspects Crabaire might have been involved in Pierre Gorbet's murder.

'I get the general idea, convince him to keep well away from the girls otherwise we might seek him out. If that should be necessary then his survival might be at stake.'

'Carrie, you will have a house guest for a few days, Kenzo, you know him from Istanbul. You might have Lambani there as well. They will deal with Marcial Crabaire if he shows up again. Best if you're not present should that happen.'

It doesn't work, Carrie is snatched off the street on her way to work three days later.

'Nico, we really need your help this time, find Carrie.'
No joy, Carrie's vanished, no clues, nothing. Pretty obvious it's Crabaire, where's the bastard holding her? Two days later she turns up in a park badly beaten and drugged to the eyeballs. Crabaire's overstepped the mark this time. Kenzo and Lambani are really pissed, their bodyguard abilities have been questioned. Carrie's taken off to hospital, she's in a bad way, severely overdosed on meth, it's life threatening. Bad luck seems to be her second name, bad star sign perhaps? Another couple of days and she's coming 'round, we need to talk, find out who did this, but it's pretty obvious. Need to get our facts right before we turn the wolves loose.

Carrie tells us it was Crabaire. He would not accept that she knew nothing about Pierre Gorbet's drug dealings. He beat her up and forced her back onto meth in an attempt to get information but she had nothing to give. He did mention the Özbirs, did they supply Gorbet, no idea, more meth, blackout. She did not recall what happened after that.

Christos and myself discuss it with Kenzo and Lambani. They are hurting that Carrie had been abducted on their shift. Did they have any contacts in the Özbir camp, 'yes.' Crabaire needs to be dealt to. Perhaps they could talk to their contact, see what can be done, get the Özbirs to deal to him after all he is their opposition.

'Leave it with us,' Kenzo's comment. 'I guess we can move out of the girls flat for a while, pity, they are lovely, what a waste!'

Well that could be the end of the matter as far as Carrie is concerned, no more threats perhaps. We don't need to do anything, back to philandering spouses, riveting stuff, I wish! Two days on, a phone call, Fabio.

'You guys told me you were not interested in investigating Marcial Crabaire, right?'

'Yep, that's right and we have not made any inquiries.'

'Well he's been onto me, threatened me, about people making inquiries and you are the only people I've approached.'

'Not us Fabio, why would we however we have heard that his drug manufacturing business is being threatened, the Özbirs, did you know that? We also hear he's got offside with some Maniot heavies. Look, we are not interested in the Athens underworld and we would appreciate you not bothering us, ok!'

Will we ever be able to extricate ourselves from this quagmire of crime and now another problem, Carrie, she's back on meth. That bastard Crabaire overdosing her has tipped her back into her old habits. A week in hospital and she's 'dried out' but unfortunately the craving has returned. Myrine is worried that Carrie is sliding downhill desperate for meth but there's no supplier. Myrine is having to be with her all the time in case she does something reckless. We need to get Carrie away from Athens, complete change of scene, New Zealand perhaps? Unbeknown to us Carrie has somehow made contact with Marcial Crabaire and he is fuelling her habit, why? She's also been going on about how she suspects Crabaire of involvement in Pierre Gorbet's murder, she wants revenge. What can we do? Perhaps we can put Kenzo and Lambani in the picture, let them know that Crabaire has become a big problem. Is this wise, could this make us accessories to something awful?

# *Carrie*

Where am I? a rehab facility, a religious order, Greek Orthodox I think, why am I here? My recollection of Greek Orthodox is endless grandstanding by priests who ramble on in Latin, totally unintelligible, and being partially drowned in a barrel of water.

What has put me in this place? Has my life degenerated to a point where I have to be institutionalised? I thought I had overcome my demons, able to enjoy a normal drug free life with Myrine, what's gone wrong? why am I in this place? That bastard Crabaire, he's done this, I want him gone, I want him dead!

What am I thinking? I'm a long way down that shithole, thinking irrationally, how could I have such thoughts? Push a person far enough and this can happen. I've been pushed and I've had a gutsful, I want Crabaire dead.

The more I think about it the more obvious it becomes. Crabaire was responsible for Pierre's demise. Pierre must have been getting his meth from the Özbirs in Istanbul, Crabaire's opposition, he would have good reason to make an example of Pierre. Leonidos just took advantage of the murder to recruit me. The so called confession implicating Leonidos was probably obtained under duress. I'm sure the French Police will have figured it out. They don't really suspect me of foul play, anyway I don't care, don't give a shit. I just want Crabaire gone.

I've hit rock bottom, institutionalised in a drug rehab facility in Greece.

It started way back, an incredibly long way back in New Zealand when I decided to go to Europe. I was unhappy with my life in Auckland. There was Michael, but there was a longing for something else, I could not figure out what it was. I needed to go alone, be completely free to do my own thing, unanswerable to anyone. How naïve, I was completely outside my comfort zone. Europe devoured me, degraded me, addicted me to drugs. Unable to control myself, I fell into a deep dark hole.

Le Bateau and the two handsome guys who drugged and raped me. Discovering my lesbian cravings with a casual acquaintance in Paris, Monique. Meeting Pierre Gorbet and crewing on Yvette. Falling for Anna and her introducing me to crystal meth. Becoming Pierre Gorbet's sex toy and moving into a luxury pad in Paris. Losing it at Le Depot while Pierre was out of town and indulging in a lesbian orgy. Finding Myrine. Athens with Pierre and a night with Myrine. Finding out about Pierre's drug empire. Pierre's murder and the French Police. Whisked out of Paris by Leonidos Stathos. Istanbul and Leonidos forcing me to prostitute myself to Oziris Düzgün. Meeting with Frank, Christos, Karissa and Nico in an Istiklal restaurant in Istanbul arranged by Kenzo where I tell them everything. Observing the aftermath of a murder at 22 Papalya Street. Missolonghi, the wedding, the terrible massacre at Stamna. Oziris's demise. Then a period of peace, in love with Myrine, living with her in Athens.

Frank and company, including Michael, all went off to New Zealand and Tonga for several weeks and when they returned things were quiet for a bit then a horrendous murder, Dimitra, Michael's girlfriend. Michael disappears off to New Zealand, Frank and Ariana follow shortly after. When Frank and Ariana return there's an unsettling undercurrent in relationships. Frank wants to know about Marcial Crabaire the fellow who spoilt my romantic dinner with Pierre in Paris shortly before Pierre's murder. Then this Crabaire fellow arrives on my doorstep in Athens, threatens me, then kidnaps me off the street. He's a brute of a man, beats me up, forces me to take crystal meth, it's disastrous. Old cravings are awakened and I'm away with the fairies, right back down my shithole. Myrine is beside herself with worry seeing me slide back into my old habits and now I find myself in this place, a rehab facility, end of the line, where to from here?

I need to get a grip on myself, break this dependence on drugs. There's Myrine to consider, we're in love and I'm just a bloody useless druggy. Snap out of it, where's the willpower? That Crabaire bastard did this and I'm pretty sure he's responsible for Pierre's murder. He needs to be held to account, how is that done. Well in this place it seems there's only one fix for bad people and it's not nice but then Marcial Crabaire is not a nice person. Perhaps Kenzo might have some ideas, how can I contact him?

# *Frank*

Carrie's in a bad way, in a church run rehab centre, however, in the last couple of days there's been a change; she's determined to break her dependence on meth. There's a strong side to Carrie, she's no fool but she sure did manage to go way way off the rails when she moved to Europe. Perhaps she's learnt from her bad experiences. She wants to see me.

'Frank, my problem right now is this Crabaire fellow, he's tipped me back into my bad old habits, he needs to be dealt to. I'm sorry if I appear to be not very nice when I say these things but my recent life has opened my eyes, really opened them. Society would be better off without this prick and I would be able to get back into a nicer world, one without drugs. Get Kenzo on the job.'

'You really don't like this fellow Carrie; you're not alone, there are others who want him gone. How our lives have changed. We are talking conspiracy to murder, serious stuff.'

'Yep, serious stuff Frank but that's the way it is. Crabaire needs to go.'

Perhaps I'll get back to Fabio, he was the one wanting Crabaire investigated. Could be we can get satisfaction for Carrie without any direct involvement. In the meantime we need to get Carrie back on the rails, back home with Myrine. As long as Crabaire is around Carrie will need protection.

Carrie responds well to the treatment at the rehab centre, she's determined to sort herself out. She's a strong girl, wants back into the normal world, one without drugs. A couple of days and she's allowed to go home; protection?

'Kenzo, want to 'Carrie sit' again?'

I tackle Fabio. 'Crabaire? who wants to know his movements and why?'

'Come on Frank you know the rules, client confidentiality. You did not want to take it on, why the renewed interest?'

'He's become a threat to Carrie.'

'He appears to be a threat to quite a few people.'

'The Özbirs perhaps?'

'How do you know that?'

'We have our sources Fabio. Tell me, how badly do your clients want Crabaire gone?'

'We never said anyone wanted him gone, you assume too much Frank.'

'I don't think so, we'll watch with interest.'

Why is Crabaire hassling Carrie? He said he wanted her to find out who was supplying Pierre Gorbet. Pretty obvious it was the opposition, he would have figured that out surely. Whatever the reason he's gone too far, Carrie is quite determined to have him dealt to. Kenzo has moved into the girls flat. He's rather chuffed to be living with two attractive girls, pity about their sexual orientation. I think Carrie has laid it on Kenzo to get rid of Crabaire. Kenzo approaches me about Carrie's request. Shit this is conspiracy to murder, serious stuff that we don't want to get involved in. Kenzo has an idea that could work.

The Özbirs are the people inquiring about Crabaire, well we're pretty sure it's them, they've got good reason, he's their opposition. Kenzo tells us he has a contact in the Özbir camp. Perhaps we can get them to deal to Crabaire. Kenzo will see what he can do however there's no urgency on his part he rather likes living with the two girls. He also tells us that Lambani is pissed that he was not asked to help with the protection, ok, he can move in as well, 'is that ok girls?'

A couple of weeks on, nothing's happened. Crabaire has not shown, not hassled Carrie again. Still not sure why he did so in the first place. Kenzo has been in contact with the Özbirs and sure enough they are favourably disposed to having Crabaire removed from the scene. Kenzo has also learnt that the Özbirs have recruited Radul Jaksic, the freelance killer, into their organisation. It was Jaksic who murdered the Maniot lad, Elios, on Waiheke. Not sure how Kenzo will react to that, Kenzo and Lambani are Maniot people. The suggestion is that Jaksic be contracted to deal to Crabaire. The idea is to distance ourselves. Conspiracy to murder is not looked upon favourably by authorities around the world. I don't want to know anything about what might happen but in the Athens underworld, I'm sure a hit can be made to look like a drug deal gone wrong. Bit different to my long career in the New Zealand Police. Conspiracy to murder. That's the sort of thing I investigated, not being investigated myself. How life has changed.

When this mess is sorted I think a holiday would be a good idea, particularly for Carrie, Myrine will need to come as well, perhaps New Zealand again. I float the idea with Ariana, Christos and Karisa.

'So soon? we got into trouble last time.' Karissa's take on the idea, 'and I liked it.'

'We've got access to a yacht in Auckland, Bob Birch and Lydia's big Beneteau. I'm now a part owner and Ariana is itching to learn how to sail, right Ariana?'

The holiday idea catches on, a welcome diversion. I mention it to Carrie and Myrine, they're not sure, having trouble comprehending, a huge change for them. Get away from all the crap that's been intruding into their lives.

Kenzo advises that he and Lambani will be moving out of the girls flat, reluctantly, they liked it there. 'There's no point in our staying.' That's all Kenzo's saying, does not sound good for Crabaire.

After some prodding Kenzo tells us what has happened. The Özbirs asked Radul Jaksic to deal to Crabaire. He'd been grabbed off the street and taken to a pig farm, his gut sliced open and then he'd been left with the pigs. Radul said his screaming was pretty bad.

Suddenly we have our lives back, will it last? it should. The people who had been troubling us are no more, sounds awful, but that's the reality. We all need a break, New Zealand. Carrie and Myrine are not sure, they like the idea but Carrie needs some quiet time with Myrine here in Athens, able to do 'whatever' without having to worry about what might happen. The French Police thing? the one dark shadow. Perhaps Christos and myself should devote some time to resolving the problem, a trip to Paris perhaps, confront 'head office.'

Not a silly idea and we have an excuse. GC Investigations have a client, a cuckolded wife, who suspects her husband has a mistress in Paris. He's spending an extraordinary amount of time there on business and he's not keen on having his wife along. Let's do that. 'Girls, fancy a trip to Paris?' 'Yes please.'

The city of light, a first for me. Four of us, Ariana has taken more time off, she's pushing it, her employer must like her. Silly question, who could not like Ariana and from what I've gathered she's very good at what she does.

'Girls why don't you check the shopping, we need to tail our quarry, find out what he's up to, who he's visiting. We'll keep in cell phone contact, get together later in the day.'

We had flown in earlier and checked into a hotel. We decide to split up, girls can check the shops, boys can play detective, just one at a time observing our quarry, reduce the chance of being spotted. We pick him up leaving the hotel his wife told us he always used. A couple of cafes where he meets some shady looking characters and then an upmarket apartment building. The list of tenants in the entrance were all businesses. A couple of hours and he comes out and returns to his hotel where he remains. Not exactly the behaviour of a philandering spouse. What to make of this initial period of observation? Apart from being rather boring not much. Around five in the afternoon we abandon our detective duty and join the ladies. A restaurant along the street from our hotel, looks good and it is. Menu expensive; excellent meal, far removed from the taverna around the corner.

We decide to play it a little differently. One observing during the day, the other in the evening. If our target is a wayward spouse then we should be seeing some female company. The following evening it's me on 'night duty.' I pick up our target leaving his hotel around six, he's with another man, is this a gay thing perhaps? A nondescript restaurant and a table in a corner. I take a table near the entrance. Half way through the meal a rough looking fellow sits down at my table, he has a threatening manner about him. Both his hands are on the table under a napkin, there's a gun, shit!

'Englander; I'll tell you this in your language so there will be no misunderstanding. Piss off and stop tailing my friend. There will be unpleasant consequences if you don't.'

Shit! GC Investigations do simple stuff, well that's the intention so what's happened? A philandering husband? I don't think so, looks like a gang thing to me. I'm out of here, back to the ladies and Christos.

'What do you reckon Christos? We're not a law enforcement agency, we don't want involvement in anything criminal and I think we might have stumbled across just that.'

'I agree, let's drop it and go back to Athens, we don't want this case. Either this fellow's lady is not aware of what he's up to or we are being misled, whatever it is we don't want the business. Sorry ladies we no longer have a reason to be in Paris. Hang on what's the rush, we're here, let's enjoy the place.'

We do, three days, sightseeing, good restaurants, a show, and a substantial account for our Athens client who I think is not being honest with us.

Back in Athens we advise our lady client the detail of what happened in Paris, including the threat. We no longer want her business, here's our account for services rendered.

Two days later the police call at our office. Our former lady client has been murdered, what can we tell them?

Will we ever be clear of the Athens underworld. The murdered lady was a Stathos, was that significant? Christos knew the detective who called and was able to get some information from him. It appears what's left of the Stathos family are trying to re-establish in Paris. The philandering husband was the new boss and it could be the wife had no knowledge of what he was really up to. Her murder could have been a warning from the opposition and that could be any of several outfits.

'Christos, we only do simple stuff, how the hell can we tell what's simple? If the wife was in on it why would she want her man followed? She must have been an innocent party. His apparent philandering? a red herring.'

What the? a screech of brakes, it's a black van, I'm grabbed, a hood pulled over my head and I'm bundled into the van, shit!

'Frank Conchie, GC Investigations? why were you following that fellow in Paris? who are you working for?'
I was trussed up in a chair in a room somewhere and the fellow asking the questions had a mean disposition. I tell him that his lady asked us to investigate him, she suspected a mistress. From the little we had seen it appeared this was not the case.

I did not see it coming, a brutal blow to the head.

'Bullshit, let's have the truth, who employed you and what did they want to know?'

How can I respond, I've got nothing to tell, I'm totally unaware of what is really going on.

'His lady employed us, I've no idea what her motives were however her subsequent murder suggests it was a lot more than a philandering spouse.' Another stinging blow, shit I'm in real trouble, how can I get through to this fellow that I don't know anything.

'You've got a son, Michael, he's tied up with that Düzgün mob and perhaps the Maniots, you know a lot more than you're telling me. I'll ask you again who got you to investigate our fellow in Paris?'

How in hell am I going to extricate myself from this, it's getting dangerous, this fellow's not going to believe me.

*Crash*, the door to the room bursts open, there are gunshots. What the hell? It's the Athens armed offenders squad.

My abduction off the street had been observed by an Athens policeman. He had been quick off the mark, jumped in his squad car and followed. The address I was taken to was known to the police.

Athens Police Central.

'Frank Conchie and Christos Galani, what have you two been up to?' It's a very senior policeman asking the questions.

'Trying to run a low key private investigation business.'

'Frank Conchie, you were abducted by some serious criminals, why would that be?'

'Investigating a philandering spouse at the request of his lady, and that's the truth, that's what we do. We want nothing to do with anything bordering on the criminal.'

'Well your lady client has been murdered, as you probably know, and it appears to be gang related, sure you are telling me everything? Why would the bad guys kidnap you and why is your face so bruised?'

'You tell me? I repeat we do not take on anything that appears to have criminal connections. I suspect this lady client was either an innocent party to whatever is going on or she was deeply involved and wanted to find out what her spouse was really up to. Why was she murdered? I've no idea, we do not have any answers.'

'Ok, that's all for now, and Christos, can you just be a retired detective, much more relaxing.'

'What do you make of that Christos, low key simple stuff, yeah right! and how are we going to determine what we take on in the future. I think we need to buzz off to Auckland again, Athens is not a nice place.'

# *Auckland*

Siting in the sunshine by the pool with Ariana, Christos and Karisa, getting rid of jet lag, peace and quiet, no bad people hassling us; I hope! We don't seem to have much luck in that area. We did ask Carrie and Myrine to come to Auckland with us. They wanted time to think about it, may come later. Michael and Ayla are living in the house so everything is up and running.

We have escaped from Athens, that place is bad news. It all seems to turn to worms when we are there. We need to rid ourselves of any lingering connections, real or imagined. Hiding in Auckland is a good idea, the only possible hitch, Ariana's work commitment in Athens.

Free, unencumbered by worry, no bad guys here, well there should be no bad guys; relax in the sunshine, enjoy a drink, nothing to do, life is complete,' I hope! *Ring, ring,* it's Peter Culpan; bugger!

'Peter, we don't want to hear from you right now, we are trying to enjoy some free time away from the nastiness that's been bedevilling us, what is it? make it good news.'

'Heard you were back in town, yes it is good news, ok if I come around?'

'Peter, tell us something nice, cheer us up.'

'Michael is the winner today, he's off the hook. We've determined that his involvement with the drug importing was forced on him under duress. We don't have anything against him, however, we would like to talk to him again, we need all the information we can get. The cocaine distribution business is still active here, just a change of ownership, and Frank, we want you to tell us all you know. You've been holding back, distancing yourself. I can understand that, however, you have no connection to the people running the show now. We want you to level with us, we're not coming after you.'

So the police have not closed down the Maniot's operation in Auckland, interesting, why not? Perhaps they've not identified everyone involved. What can I tell them that they don't already know? The little I know relates to the Düzgüns and they are no longer in the business. There's been a high body count.

'Not much to tell Peter and the little I do know is Düzgün related, can't help with the Maniot's, not had any involvement.'

'Sure about that Frank? do the names Kenzo and Lambani mean anything?'

Shit, how does he know about them, what can I say? He'll think I'm withholding information.

'Ok Peter, yes I do know Kenzo and Lambani and I know they are Maniot people. Our relationship with them goes back some time to when we were having problems with Carrie Gray, the New Zealand girl who became involved with the Stathoses in Athens. They were both instrumental in extracting her from a bad situation. At the time I did not know they were connected to the Maniots. I feel obligated to them for what they did for Carrie. Since then I have become aware they are Maniot people, however, we no longer have any contact with them. That's all I can tell you Peter.'

'Thanks for that Frank, it tallies with what we know, and we know a lot. By the way did you determine who grabbed you off the street in Athens? Here's another one, Marcial Crabaire; know anything about him?'

'You have been digging deep Peter, yes I've heard about Crabaire. I believe he came to an unfortunate end and I stress, I only heard about it.'

'Tell me Peter, if you can, what's the cocaine situation here in

Auckland these days?'

'Come on Frank, you know the rules, can't tell you about that, however, I will say we have it under control, it's not going to be a problem for much longer. Your mates Kenzo and Lambani have been in Auckland recently, Maniot hit men, did you know that? I suggest you keep your distance from them.'

'Peter, they are not my mates! They helped us in Athens with Carrie Gray and we are grateful for that. We did not know of any specific gang affiliation at the time, however, since then we have become aware of their Maniot connections. I assure you we have nothing to do with them now and it's going to stay that way. About Michael? I'll let him know you want to talk but I don't think there's anything more you can learn from him. You probably know he was being threatened by Yiannis Stavrou but he's gone now and Michael no longer feels indebted.'

'Ok Frank, I think that clears the air. You've had an interesting few months, bit different to the Auckland crime scene, well what used to be the Auckland scene. It's changed recently, the Greek influence, however, hopefully, we'll clean that up soon. You staying in Auckland?'

I give Peter a brief rundown of what I intend doing. GC Investigations in Athens and a lot of sailing in Auckland, far removed from anything criminal.

'Sounds great Frank. I'll be retiring soon, could look you up in Athens, the bucket list thing, and thanks for your help. Horrific business, real eye opener for us, we'd only heard about this sort of thing and having it dumped on us, well, bit of a learning curve.'

Ok, sailing, put the nasty stuff to bed. I'm now part owner of Bob Bach's big Beneteau, need a bit of tuition. Be advisable to spend a couple of days sailing with Bob, it's been a while, there'll be a lot to learn.'

'Yep, I'm free, three days from now, how's that fit?' Bob's on for it.

'Right Frank, you too Ariana, pay close attention, how to sail a big yacht according to Bob.'

We're out on the Waitemata, light easterly, perfect sailing day. Ariana is excited and so am I, been a long time, I'm sure it will all come back. My yacht, way back in yesteryear, was a lot smaller than this Beneteau and it was another lady who was the love of my life. Inattention was my downfall then, I let Rachel get stolen away. Pay attention Frank, the sailing, you too Ariana.

Ariana has come to an arrangement with her employer in Athens. A contract has been negotiated that allows her to take up to four months off a year. They want to keep her on and this new contract satisfies both parties; no pressure to get back to Athens. GC Investigation? Well the two principles are their own masters, the rules are infinitely variable and right now Auckland is a much nicer place than Athens. Perhaps an Auckland branch? no! rubbish! you fellows are retired remember. Now pay attention, sailing a Beneteau.

Bob is a very understanding tutor and we are two keen pupils. It's more than two. Christos and Karisa are along for the ride and they are becoming increasingly interested in learning to sail. It's a good boat for beginners, well some beginners, and one who needs a serious refresher. A Beneteau is a 'forgiving' boat, you can make glaring mistakes and the boat won't bite you on the bum, it'll just 'round up' and leave you embarrassed, don't make that mistake again! It developes into a great day, a lot of learning, a lot of refreshing. Bob was a good and patient instructor. A full day of serious sailing then back to the marina, that's enough for starters.

'Tomorrow there's a stiff sou'wester forecast, be a good idea to take advantage of it. You can see what it's like when the weather's challenging which is a lot of the time in Auckland. Spray beating onto your face and cold water getting inside your wet weather gear.

See if the enthusiasm is still there? Sailing conditions are not always enjoyable.'

It is challenging, howling sou'wester, not a day to go sailing by choice, but the thinking is it's necessary to demonstrate what it's like when the weather turns against you. Poor Ariana, and Christos and Karisa; just as well Bob's experienced the boat really got whacked around and everyone gets drenched. I think the girls were frightened, however, Bob had a very reassuring manner and pointed out that the boat being tipped over at forty-five degrees while thundering along was normal and getting drenched was all part of the fun.

It was a subdued crew that returned to the marina, drenched, cold, and not sure about this sailing business.

'That will do for now, take a break, couple of days, then we'll do some more. Now, how about something different, a trip to the South Island, Marlborough, I come from Blenheim.'

'Frank, what am I seeing?'
We're flying into Blenheim, grapes, as far as the eye can see, vineyards. Marlborough is the Sauvignon Blanc capital of the world. A far cry from the dry, sunburnt, rabbit infested, useless stony landscape and dirt poor farmers of my youth. Now it's lush vineyards, wineries and restaurants. The whole Wairau valley has been transformed. I should have stayed at home and grown grapes, but no one knew about grapes when I was growing up in that stony wasteland.

'Today we'll visit some wineries and have a meal at one of the numerous restaurants. Tomorrow it's Havelock and a boat trip down the Sounds, you'll like that, different.'

We hire a car and check out several wineries. Wine tasting, very enjoyable, the Marlborough people are right up with the play. Better watch it their wine tasting is rather generous and I'm driving. Never used to be a problem, well not that I can remember, however, in this modern age it's a capital crime.

Havelock at the head of Pelorus Sound, a real sleepy hollow, a place where I spent a lot of my childhood. Aunty Mary's cottage, it's still there, little has changed. Aunty Mary's long gone but the place still looks the same. The visitors from Greece are impressed. Down to the wharf, mussels, the Mussel Pot Café hanging out over the water. Green lip mussels, they farm them right here in the Pelorus. We pig out.

'Frank, we love New Zealand.' An opinion expressed by all the visitors from Greece.

'Ok, the mail run.'

It's a launch that does a day trip down the Pelorus Sound, been doing it since I was a kid. I must have been on it countless times when I was a young chap, before I moved to the big city, became a cop and got involved in a very different life style. Should have stayed in Blenheim and grown grapes but then I would not have found Ariana, would not have found myself involved in all the crap that's bedevilling my life right now either.

'These people, they're different Frank, why?'

We are well down the Pelorus and Ariana has picked up on the appearance of the people who meet the mailboat, either at their wharf or those who row out. The mailboat delivers the mail and everything else these isolated communities require, been like this since forever. There are few roads down the Pelorus, the mailboat is their link to the outside world. Isolation has had an effect. Ariana is right, they are different, bit like stepping back a hundred years.

Nostalgia, my mind goes back to a happy childhood, much of it spent at Aunty Mary's place and down the Pelorus. Dad had a big army surplus tent and every year we went camping way down the Sounds for a couple of weeks. It was all fishing, blue cod, and shooting goats. The goats were a nuisance and the locals down the sounds, we called them 'soundsies,' were grateful for our help in getting rid of them. The cod were good eating but the goats, no! That was a long time ago when life was simple, wish it still was. But my current, 'not so good life,' has given me Ariana and the future is now looking much brighter.

We decide to spend a night in the Havelock Hotel another experience for the people from Greece. It's not changed from what I remember from childhood. Bathroom and toilet down the hall and a big rowdy bar full of noisy drinkers, gumboots and black singlets, they love it.

'Tomorrow we'll have a look at the Pelorus bridge, it's not far and there's a scenic reserve and native bush area, it's good.'

The bridge is high and the river? a rocky gorge. We used to jump off that bridge, mum never knew!

'There's gold in the river, you can pan for it and probably get a little gold dust, but the mosquitoes, they're huge, the gold dust is safe.'

Back to the Wairau Valley and the vineyards. We visit another couple of wineries and enjoy a restaurant meal at one of them.

'Ariana, this is where I come from, where I grew up. I have happy memories. The vineyards and restaurants did not exist, just hot stony worthless land overrun with rabbits, that's how it was. I had not been spoilt by the outside world and I was happy, perhaps I should have stayed.'

We decide on another couple of days in Blenheim then we'll go back to Auckland and think about going back to Athens, no rush, Athens is not such an inviting place.

'There's Kaikoura, crayfish heaven.'

'Crayfish?'

'You have lobster we have crayfish, almost the same thing but better.'

'Really?'

It's an interesting drive out to the Pacific coast from Blenheim, the parched brown hills interspersed with lush green vineyards. The grape is spreading out from the Wairau valley. The saltworks at Lake Grassmere, mountains of salt right beside the road, harvested from the sea in huge evaporation ponds.

Down the coast road to Kaikoura. A stop at the seal colony tucked into a small gulley that the fur seals have turned into their own private nursery. Dozens of pups playing in the secluded fresh water pools while their parents lie around on the rocks out on the coast.

They are big, a crayfish tail each, split open and barbecued with butter. We are seated at an outdoor restaurant in Kaikoura with a bottle of Marlborough Savvy Blanc. I remember crayfish being common when I was a little fellow, and there was whitebait. A young lad door knocking with a big kerosine can full of whitebait. Two shillings and sixpence for a big mugful. I don't think I appreciated it at the time.

The excellent meal, the crashing surf, the coastal ambience!

*Do we want to go back to Athens?*

# *Athens*

Jet lag, *again.* Back at Christos and Karisa's place reflecting on our latest New Zealand experience. We had flown back to Auckland from Blenheim and enjoyed another couple of days on the Beneteau under the watchful eye of Bob Birch. He had given us a 'pass.' Ariana and I can now sail the boat solo. Now there's real incentive to get back to Auckland whenever possible, preferably during the southern summer, winter sailing in bad weather is not Ariana's thing, not mine either. Work? A couple of inquiries on the desk at GC Investigation, appear innocuous enough. Getting suspicious now, super cautious about what we take on.

Life is normal, quiet, uneventful, could call it boring but we like it this way.

*Ring ring,* a call from New Zealand, it's Peter Culpan. My heartbeat races, shit, why would he be calling. All sorts of scenarios flash through my mind, most involving Michael. What's happened, why would he be calling me here in Greece?

'Relax Frank, it's not Michael.'

'Thank god for that Peter, I had a bad moment just then.'

'Thought it would be nice to hear it from me and not the news media. We have arrested Kenzo and Lambani here in Auckland. They let their guard down, bit too overconfident. There's an arrest warrant from Interpol as well. They are wanted for multiple murders in several countries including New Zealand. It was them who carried out the Wiri warehouse massacre. They will not be going home anytime soon. The justice system in New Zealand will prosecute to the full extent of the law, a deterrent to overseas criminals setting up shop here. We caught a couple of accomplices as well. Looks like the end of the Maniot's in Auckland.'

'Thank you Peter, that should be the end of it. Got the monkey off our backs, could you tell Michael as well.'

'Already have Frank.'

That's it, close the book and burn it. We're free to do our thing unencumbered by possible nasty consequences, well I hope so. We've been here before and it did not last, this time it looks much better.

A new *normal* life with Ariana, and it's going to be a normal life, no criminal involvement. I call on Nico.

'Courtesy call Nico, not seeking information. How is it in the criminal world at the moment? just curious.'

'Things have quietened down Frank, lack of leadership. The undertakers have been doing well but that's gone quiet as well but don't count on it, there's the Maniots. They have taken a hit in your country but it's a different story here. They are primarily an Istanbul outfit but the way things are here in Athens they could muscle their way in; then there's the Özbirs, active in Istanbul. They could well move into Athens and take advantage of the existing situation but that should not concern you Frank. You've not had any dealings with the Özbirs have you?

'None at all but I believe it was the Özbirs who had Crabaire dealt to. Carrie had made it known that she wanted him gone and that would probably have come to the attention of the Özbirs, but I believe there were plenty of people who wanted Crabaire gone.'

'That's right Frank, he was not a popular fellow. By the way talking about people 'gone,' our mates Kenzo and Lambani are gone as well, locked up in your country, looks like they'll be there for a long time, bit of a bugger, they were useful contacts.'

'Here's something that might interest you. Pierre Gorbet's yacht, Yvette, it's now tied up at Piraeus. Belongs to an underworld character who has connections to the Özbirs. I believe Carrie is familiar with Yvette.'

'She sure is and I don't think she'll want to know anything about it either. That yacht was the start of all her troubles. I wonder if Carrie knows it's here? The girls do quite a bit of sailing out of Piraeus, she's bound to see it.'

'Well Frank now that you've severed any connection, real of imposed, with the underworld I guess I won't be seeing you in my bar, that's a pity.'

'Of course you will, we'll drop in from time to time, your virtually on GC Investigations payroll and quite apart from that you're a friend. Hopefully we will not come seeking information, we are only doing simple stuff, well that's the intention, however, one of our 'simple' cases turned into a gang related one and we had to bale. Have to be real picky these days.'

# *Carrie*

I'm out, home with Myrine, my craving has declined, not completely gone but I've got no access to the stuff, going to keep it that way. My love for Myrine should give me the strength. I'll make it work. Crabaire, the bastard, I hear the pigs tore him to pieces. I should be shocked but I'm not, hope he suffered real bad.

Frank and company have been to New Zealand, *again,* want us to go sometime. We should think about it, would be great for Myrine, she's not been out of Europe. The cruise with the 'olds' worked out well, a trip to New Zealand should work just as well. It appears Frank and Ariana will be frequent visitors to Auckland, Frank has bought into a yacht there.

We are back into sailing, still have access to the gay guys boat, they don't use it at all. If we went to Auckland we could do some real sailing on a big yacht, Myrine would love it.

I've not gone back to work yet, not making a very good impression on my employer. Myrine is trying hard to smooth the way, I will need to be a lot more responsible, who wants a druggy on the payroll?

Frank wants us both to come along next time he and Ariana go to Auckland. The sailing, that's the big attraction for them. Right now though I've got to get back to work.

A fellow called around the other evening, seemed nice enough, said he had been a friend of Pierre Gorbet. Shit, I don't want any connection with my unsavoury past, nothing at all, it's gone, dead, I've burned the book. He was very polite, did not look like a bad guy. He said he was the new owner of Yvette and wanted to ask me about the boat, things he thought I might know. I know precious little about Yvette, I was off with the fairies for most of the time I was on the boat. How do I get that across to this fellow? I suggested he should seek out some of the crew who worked for Pierre Gorbet, Peter from New Zealand might be a good starting place, if he can find him. He told me all Pierre Gorbet's crew had disappeared, I was the only one he had been able to find. I thought that a bit strange, who is this fellow? is he legit? Then he asked if I knew anything about Pierre's drug business. Alarm bells, who the hell is this fellow? I told him as politely as I could that I was unable to help him. I had severed all connections with Yvette and I knew nothing about Pierre Gorbet's affairs, I would appreciate it if he would leave now.

Not a good scene, people seeking me out, making inquiries. I have to rid myself of any perceived perceptions some people may have. Who can I turn to? Frank and Christos, they have the contacts and more importantly, the knowledge about how to deal with this sort of thing. I call into GC Investigations, first time in their downtown office.

'You're right to be concerned Carrie. Our information is the new owner of Yvette is a criminal aligned with the Özbirs. He could be 'fishing' or he could think you have some knowledge about Pierre Gorbet's operation. We know Pierre Gorbet sourced his meth in Istanbul from either the Özbirs or the Maniot's. This fellow would know which, perhaps he doesn't, perhaps that's why he's hassling you. By the way, you might have noticed, Yvette is tied up in Piraeus. I'll get our 'employee' on the job, Nico has the wherewithal to find out about this fellow.'

Well that's all good, perhaps it will be the end of it. I've got to rid myself of my past. Yvette tied up in Piraeus, bit close to home, does that mean this fellow lives here in Athens?

Back to work, feeling much better, have to make a good impression for Myrine's sake. She's had a difficult time convincing our employer that I've been a bit out of sorts and that I'm ok now. That's the truth, sort of! Out of sorts is stretching it. Overdosed to the eyeballs on meth, off with the fairies and in rehab, don't want our employer to find that out. Sailing, that's what we need to do, therapeutic, this weekend, a couple of days on the water, we'll overnight somewhere.

The weather's perfect as we sail out of Piraeus and there it is, Yvette tied up in one of the expensive marina berths. I don't want to see it, too many bad memories, ghosts from my past. I don't say anything to Myrine, I've never really told her about what happened on Yvette, how I was drugged out of my mind and indulging in all sorts of wild sex with Pierre Gorbet. I've purged it from my mind, well I think I have.

Fifteen knots out of the southeast, perfect. We sail along the southern coast of the Attica peninsular to Cape Sounion and anchor in the bay under the Temple of Poseidon, an impressive sight towering above us on a clifftop, two thousand five hundred years old. It's so lovely to be alone with Myrine in such an idyllic place. I've turned a corner, this is my life now.

It's late in the afternoon, we are enjoying a bottle of wine lying in the sun on the deck, enjoying each other's bodies, when we become aware of an approaching yacht, shit, it's Yvette. It comes right up and bumps alongside, what the hell!

'Carrie.'

It's the same fellow who had knocked on my door a few days ago, the new owner, the fellow who has ties to the Özbirs, a crook.

'I'm coming aboard.'

Shit, what can we do, can we do anything? What does he want, it won't be anything nice, I can sense it. Myrine is scared, so am I. Crash he arrives on our deck. I cannot recognise any of the faces that are peering at us from Yvette, none of the old crew.

'Do you mind, you're not welcome,' my feeble response.

'That's your problem lady. What I want from you is everything you claim you don't know about Pierre Gorbet's drug business, his supplier, his customers, his enforcers, and don't pull the I don't know routine, of course you know, you were his plaything, his sex toy. You were not forthcoming the last time we met, pleading ignorance. Bullshit, of course you know all about his operation.'

Myrine looks appalled, I'm not sure she realises what my relationship had been with Pierre, I had not told her the full story, why would I, it was not nice and I did not want to sour our developing relationship. Now it was all being brutally spelled out by this crook, poor Myrine.

'I've told you I don't know anything about Pierre's business, can't you comprehend what I've said.'

'I suggest you refresh your memory Carrie, do you think I'm stupid? You'd better come up with the goods or things will go badly for you.'

Shit he's threatening me, I need to do something precipitate, something that might frighten him off, but what? Bluff, there's nothing to lose, speak to him in language he'll understand'

'Look asshole I don't take kindly to being threatened. The last bastard who tried it on was Marcial Crabaire and things went badly for him, now piss off.'

Myrine looks shocked, my language, but extreme measures are called for. I'm terrified and shaking but I don't think it's showing, hope not. I make a quick decision to hit him again, really convince him to, as I put it, piss off.

'Leonidos Stathos was another fellow who gave me a hard time, he had an unfortunate accident as well. I suggest you back off right now, get on your boat and piss off.'

It works, the fellow goes quiet and gives me a strange look, not sure about what I've said. I'm sure he knows about the murders I've referred to, probably knows about the French thing as well. He's got to be wondering about my involvement, thinking that perhaps he's picked on the wrong person. I glance at Myrine, she's gone very pale, appalled at what's happening, this sort of thing is way outside her comfort zone. Unfortunately it's the sort of thing that's been part of my life, a part I'm desperately trying to rid myself of. I decide to push it while I still have the advantage.

'Did you not hear me, time for you to go. You should have believed me when I told you I do not know anything about Pierre Gorbet's operation, it was the truth. Please do not continue giving me a hard time or things may go badly for you as well, now piss off.'

Our unwanted guest had gone quietly which surprised me, climbed back aboard Yvette and sailed away. I was expecting some retaliation. Just as well he has gone because I don't know what I would have done if he had resorted to strong arm tactics. I'm still shaking, frightened like Myrine.

'Carrie, how did you do it, I was terrified.'

'I guess you know a bit more about me now Myrine, things I've not told you, unpleasant things. I would have got around to it but then would you really want to know. I'm trying to rid myself of my unpleasant past, not easy. There is one positive. My life, before I met you, gave me the wherewithal to be able to speak the same language, give him something to think about, I was not bluffing either.'

What to do, the day, what's left of it, is ruined. We decide to stay where we are for the night and sail back to Piraeus in the morning. I need to talk to Frank and Christos, I'm worried, will I ever be able to shake off my past?

GC Investigations. I'm in their office telling Frank and Christos what's happened. Do I need to be concerned, is this fellow a threat?

'We don't know much about him, just that he owns Yvette and

he's aligned with the Özbirs. The word is he's a bad dude. We'll get Nico on the job, see what he can find out, in the meantime I suggest you get on with your life. Try not to be intimidated. You are not party to anything this fellow would want to know. Perhaps we can come up with some way to get this message across to him, and, as you put it so succinctly Carrie, get him to piss off.'

'There is one thing worrying me Frank. The discussion on our yacht with this fellow would have been overheard by his crew on Yvette and that could be an embarrassment for him. Could it become a problem? an ego thing that he might want to address.'

'The name is Osman Pecker.' Nico's been on the job. 'The word is he's new in Athens and fancies himself as a player in the meth business. That's not going down too well with the resident crims, the Maniot's, and what's left of the Düzgüns and Stathoses, and in the drug business that's dangerous, he will have enemies. He knows he's offside with Carrie as well and after her tongue-lashing he will be wondering what influence she has. Could be her past is now affording her some protection.'

A couple of weeks have passed and I'm back in GC Investigation's office, guess I'm a client now. Frank is bringing me up to date on what they've found out about this new threat, Osman Pecker. Apparently he's throwing his weight around and pissing everyone off. He's got a pack of goons with him but the thinking is he will not be around for too long. Nico has put the word out that Carrie, the girl who was Pierre Gorbet's girlfriend, is a bimbo who knows nothing but has some powerful underworld friends, hopefully this will get to Osman Pecker.

Another couple of weeks go by and life has settled down. I'm back in favour at the fashion house where I work and Myrine and I are now very close, will it last? Should do, the only blemish is Osman Pecker but I think that problem has gone away. Nico's disinformation appears to have been effective. We sail at the weekends and we've been out to dinner with Frank and Ariana a couple of times. The New Zealand thing has come up again. Sailing in Auckland has a lot of appeal, we will do it, soon.

A bright sunny morning, Myrine and I are walking along to the fashion house where we work. I hear the noise of a motor scooter, it's right in close to the footpath, *bang – bang – bang*, gunshots. Myrine spins around and drops to the pavement blood pouring from her head, *bang – whack,* something hits me hard; blackness.

# *Athens*

Will it ever end, the Athens criminal underworld bursting into our lives, how has it come to this? things just get worse.

Carrie and Myrine are in intensive care, victims, it appears, of a contract hit man. It's got to be Osman Pecker, his ego was indeed hurt. It's not looking good. Myrine has brain damage, her survival is marginal. Carrie has been shot in the abdomen and has suffered a bullet wound to her head, both girls are in induced comas.

What can we do? Christos is onto the Athens Police relaying our suspicions about Osman Pecker, they are making inquiries. We call on Nico. He's really pissed the girls have been harmed and declares he will make it his business to find out who's behind it. Poor Carrie, she's been trying so hard but her past keeps catching up.

A couple of days have passed and there's a development, two people have been arrested by the Athens Police. Apparently there were two fellows on the scooter, a driver and a shooter. They had boasted to their mates about the hit and one of the mates had dobbed them in. Who was behind it is not known, it was an anonymous cash contract, however, the prime suspect is Osman Pecker. His crew on Yvette had witnessed his humiliation by Carrie and they had been talking. Perhaps his ego has caused him to make a big mistake. Carrie was known to the criminal underworld. The word is she is not a bad person and harming her was not a very bright thing to do. Myrine has no underworld connections at all, why would she be targeted? Perhaps it was just badly planned by a couple of incompetent hit men?

Carrie is out of her induced coma but Myrine remains comatose on life support. She has significant brain damage. The prognosis is not good.

The police have no evidence incriminating Osman Pecker. The two fellows they have in custody don't know anything, just an anonymous cash deal.

Another visit to Nico's bar, he has news. The Athens crims are not impressed that this interloper, Osman Pecker, has harmed two innocent girls. The underworld is convinced it was him. He had been throwing his weight around since arriving on the scene and has pissed off a lot of people.

There's nothing we can do. The police have put a guard on the two girls in hospital, their thinking is because the hit was not successful there may be another attempt. It's obvious from the girls injuries the intention was to kill them. This Osman Pecker is a real threat, a killer with an inflated ego. We need to do something, but what? The problem is taken out of our hands.

Christos gets an early morning phone call from his contact in the Athens Police. There's been a fire down at the Piraeus Marina. A yacht has been burned to the waterline and sunk, it's Yvette. Witnesses say they heard gunshots before the fire was noticed. Later in the morning the two shooting suspects the police have in custody are found hanged in their cells. It seems the underworld has meted out justice as they see fit.

Is this good or bad? Do we need the local crims fixing our problems? What will be the police take on it? Will they think we are party to these developments? Living in Athens just gets increasingly more difficult.

Carrie is out of her coma and lucid, she's asking about Myrine. The hospital staff are being non-committal. They would appreciate our help in telling her.

We do our best. Myself, Ariana, Christos and Karisa, go along to the hospital and break it to her as gently as we can, no mention of brain damage. Carrie does not buy it, she suspects we are not being up front with her, demands to know the real extent of Myrine's injuries. We give her a sanitised, optimistic, version stressing that it's all we know at this stage, Myrine's still in a coma. Carrie's not buying it.

'She's brain damaged and you're not telling me, right?
It's a direct question, no point in fudging the issue.

'Yes she is Carrie but we've no idea how badly, will not know until she comes out of the coma.'
Carrie cracks up, crying uncontrollably, shit, we have a problem. We decide that one of us needs to be at her bedside continuously, she's distraught and might do something unpredictable.

The girls elect to do bedside duty for the first couple of days. Christos and myself call on Nico.

'Any news Nico? any straws in the wind?'

'Yes, the Yvette crew have been talking. They were not mates of Pecker's, just hired crew, pissed off that suddenly they are unemployed and most of them have lost their things as well. According to them some goons invaded Yvette at gunpoint, bailed up Pecker, and told the crew to piss off. Shortly after that they heard gunshots then the boat exploded in flames. It's a fair bet Osman Pecker is no more.'

'Well if that's true that problem has disappeared, but we've got Carrie, she's in a mess.'

We tell Nico about the girls injuries, how Myrine may not survive, and if she succumbs to her injuries what effect will it have on Carrie, we fear the worst. Nico is upset, he did not really know the girls but he's really pissed that they have been harmed for no reason. The police had better find Peckers body in Yvette, the bastard. So what now, all we can do at this stage is comfort Carrie, keep a close eye on her in case she does something unexpected. We release Ariana from 'bedside watch,' she does have a job that needs her attention, the rest of us can handle bedside duty.

Two weeks on and there's no improvement in Myrine's condition, the brain damage is extensive. Should she survive she'll be a 'vegetable.' We are horrified, Carrie must never hear this.

Another week and the worst happens. We are called in to a meeting with the doctors at the Hospital. There don't appear to be any traceable relatives of Myrine's so we are going to be asked to make a decision about her survivability.

The only thing keeping her alive is the life support system. There is no brain function, it's unlikely she will recover consciousness. Do we wish to continue with life support?

This is confronting, being asked a life or death question about someone who is not related, who we don't even know all that well. We need time, a couple of days perhaps to allow us to come to terms with what is being asked. The only person who's close to Myrine is Carrie and she's in no state to make such a decision. We will have to do it without telling her and that could cause difficulties further down the track, resentment perhaps. It's an untenable position. What are the options? The hospital advise that in a situation like this where there's no one to make a decision they ask the court to authorise them to decide in the best interest of the patient, in this case they would be asking for termination of life support. This is awful, we can't do it, but if we don't the hospital have indicated it will happen anyway. What effect will it have on Carrie?

We can't lay it on the hospital, we need to make the decision but really there is no decision. We can't have Myrine a living unconscious vegetable permanently on life support, Carrie would never cope, she would revert to drugs, an even more untenable situation. We collectively make the only viable decision and advise the hospital. I do not sleep that night.

It's done. Myrine only survives for an hour when her life support is turned off, how do we tell Carrie? is she strong enough yet to handle it? We decide that Ariana and myself will tell her.

Carrie is making a good recovery, the head wound was superficial and the abdominal damage was not as bad as first thought. She's still in hospital but will be discharged soon. Ariana and I bite the bullet.

'Carrie we have to tell you this, it's not nice.'

'She's died hasn't she? That's what you are going to tell me.'

'Yes she has, we're sorry, her wounds were unsurvivable. She never regained consciousness, never suffered.'

Carrie goes very quiet, overcome by the enormity of what we've told her, what she had already guessed.

'Thank you for telling me.'

Will there be a reaction? We both decide to stay with her, how long? depends. The confirmation of what she suspected has left Carrie numb and exhausted, I fear for her, can she handle it?

It must have been around midnight when it happened, Ariana and myself were still by Carrie's bedside. She started screaming and thrashing about violently in the bed. A nurse was quickly on the scene and administered a sedative, what now? We are advised to go home, there is nothing we can do to help. Carrie will be under constant surveillance and sedation, her reactions will be unpredictable, they could be violent, they are worried about possible self-harm.

We are around at Christos and Karisa's place, feeling despondent, recent events have left us all emotionally drained. Carrie is still in hospital, they will be keeping her there sedated until she gets over the shock of Myrine's death. Christos has heard from his police contact. Yvette's hull has been salvaged. There were two bodies, local thugs, no Osman Pecker, shit.

Two weeks on, Carrie has improved. It's been traumatic for her. She had to be physically restrained for a couple of days, quite out of control, however, she's now much better, has come to terms with

Myrine's death. The hospital will be releasing her in another week, can we look after her? Yes we can. Christos and Karisa will take her in. What does the future hold? We'll let that one rest for the time being. Perhaps we should be thinking about getting her back to New Zealand, I doubt she will want to stay in Athens.

It happens, Carrie is released into Christos and Karisa's care. She's perked up noticeably, realised her life has changed dramatically and she must accept her new circumstances. My worry is she will revert to drugs but so far no sign of that. We let her be, don't press her about what she's going to do, she's still pretty fragile. We are around at Christos and Karisa's place almost every evening, moral support for Carrie, let her know she has friends. We frequent the Taverna around the corner a lot. New Zealand comes up in conversation and the suggestion is made that perhaps Carrie might like to go back to Auckland, she does not dismiss the idea.

Life slowly returns to normal. GC Investigations gets back into business, simple stuff only, really picky about what we take on. Ariana and myself are happily cohabitating, marriage? Well we've thought about it, talked about it, should we? why should we? we leave the question unanswered. Perhaps another trip to Auckland, could take Carrie, I think she might warm to the idea. We've got the yacht, we should use it, give Carrie something to look forward to.

Christos and myself are in Nico's bar, 'catching up' with our employee.

'You know that asshole Osman Pecker did not go down with his ship, he shot his way out of it and disappeared. I also hear he's got it in for Carrie.'

'Shit, we don't want to hear that Nico, are you sure?'

'Pretty sure, I've heard it from several sources but don't get too concerned, I doubt he's long for this world. The people who had a go at him are pretty pissed that they failed, I don't fancy his chances. Right now he's an invisible man, vanished.'

'Hmm, not good Nico. We are thinking about getting Carrie back to New Zealand, well away from here, it's not been a good place for her.'

'Good idea.' Nico's opinion.

It's decided, Ariana, myself and Carrie will fly to Auckland. Carrie has warmed to the idea. Athens has lost its appeal, her big OE has been disastrous. She envisions a normal life in New Zealand, well away from drugs. Very worldly-wise now, but it came at a price. A bit of planning and we decide to go in three weeks' time, Carrie will be fit for travel by then and Ariana can exercise the terms of her new contract with her employer. The immediate future looks secure, if only!

It happens on a sunny morning in the street right outside Christos's house. Carrie has gone for a walk. A car drives slowly down the street, a man leans out of the car and accosts her, it's Osman Pecker. He must have had the house staked-out, he's got a gun. It's obvious what he intends, however, his ego demands that he tells Carrie first. Carrie's no slug, wise in the ways of the world now. She's got a shoulder bag and in a flash she swings it furiously at the gun in Pecker's hand that's hanging out the car window. Luck is with her, the gun is knocked out of his hand and spins away on the pavement. She follows up her attack, rips the car door open, grabs a handful of Pecker's clothing and pulls him out of the car. There is a driver, Pecker was in the passenger's seat. The driver panics and attempts to accelerate away, bad luck for Pecker, his legs have gone under the car.

The police have taken Pecker into custody, two badly broken legs. Jail will not be a good place for him, he's offside with the Athens underworld. I don't think we need worry about him any longer. Carrie's ok, her quick thinking saved her life but her abdominal wounds have been stressed and there's some bleeding. It's home care for her and a daily visit from a nurse. Now the future does look secure.

Nico's bar, myself and Christos.

'That Carrie's got status,' Nico tells us. 'Taking down Osman Pecker single handed. His ego's taken a huge hit. Don't fancy his chances inside either, he's got enemies. Then there are the other crims who've given Carrie a hard time, all of them have had bad luck. The word is she's a girl you don't meddle with.'

'Coincidence Nico, Carrie's a girl who's just had bad luck but if that's the perception the criminal world has then perhaps it's a good thing.'

We finalise the planning for our trip to Auckland, Carrie should be fit enough in three weeks' time, however, I'm not sure she's that enthusiastic any more, seems to be losing her spirit. I think the realisation that Myrine's gone is catching up, tipping her into depression, we'll need to be vigilant, don't want her reverting to drugs.

Carrie sinks further into depression. She's not saying much but realisation that her future life without Myrine will be intolerable seems to be taking hold. Going back to New Zealand will not solve anything, there's nothing there for her. What can we do? Then she tells us she's not interested in going to New Zealand, she wants to stay in Athens, the place where she enjoyed her happiest moments. We cancel the planned trip, we need to stay close to Carrie. I fear she's going to do something unpredictable, something desperate, she's very depressed.

It's a Sunday morning, Carrie's gone for a walk. A phone call from the Police. There's been an accident, Carrie's been killed.

## *NZ Herald – August 27th 2021*

Killed In Athens.

A young New Zealand woman died yesterday in a traffic accident in Athens. Miss Carrie Gray was killed instantly when she was run over by a bus on a busy Athens street. Miss Gray had been living in Europe for some time and was involved in the fashion industry. The driver claims Miss Gray was looking straight at him when she stepped out in front of his moving bus.

Miss Gray, who was twenty-five, was well known in Auckland yachting circles.

*Damn, will Athens ever stop inflicting pain, will it ever be a nice place for Ariana and I to live?*

# *About the Author*

Rex Mangin lives with his partner Lynne in a cottage on a beach in Auckland, New Zealand. After a lifetime of flying both military and commercial he has discovered a love of writing and spends a lot of time doing just that, plus, travelling, fishing, chasing marlin off New Zealand's north east coast and all those things you do when you're retired.

# Books By Rex Mangin

These books by Rex Mangin are available as paperbacks and at all e-book outlets worldwide.

---------------------------------

## Infidelity Gun Running & Other Tales

Fourteen short stories drawn from the author's vast treasure trove of experiences. He spent a lifetime in aviation, both military and civilian, became involved in the Cold War in Europe, nuclear testing at Christmas Island, topdressing in New Zealand, and spent many years flying the Pacific. Now retired, he has turned his hand to writing. His aviation background is reflected in many of these stories.

Set in Europe, North Africa, Hong Kong, New Zealand. Sydney, Honolulu, Christmas Island, Tahiti, Mo'orea, Rangiroa, and Bora Bora, it's a diverse and entertaining collection of fact and fiction, all based on the author's real-life experiences.

The dramatic engine failure described in *A Close Call In Tahiti* did occur, July 17th 1980, at Faa'a Airport in Papeete. The *Gun Running* happened back in 1957.

The author flew into Hong Kong's old Kai Tak airport many times. *Remember Kai Tak* describes just what it was like flying into that extraordinary place. The yacht featured in *Andria* is the *Jardilinka*, a well-known vessel in Hong Kong waters. The author was lucky enough to enjoy many cruises on this fine old vessel.

*The Jury* is a true story as are, *A Curious Business, The Bottle*, and *Christmas Island. A Labs Attack* describes some of the things that went on during the Cold War, all true, these things happened.

Aerial topdressing features in *The Greening Of Northland,* an insight into this unique New Zealand industry.

I'm sure you'll enjoy reading these stories just as much as the author enjoyed writing them.

# Flying The Pacific
## *(a memoir)*

After several years in NATO's Second Tactical Air Force on the front line of the Cold War in Germany the author returned to his native New Zealand and joined TEAL, Tasman Empire Airways. During a thirty year career with the airline he was part of the enormous expansion into the present day Air New Zealand. He flew everything from the jet prop Electra to the 747-400. The Pacific, the Orient, America, and during the later part of his career all the way to Europe. It was not a simple process however, there was a lot of angst and heartache.

This book is not just about flying it includes everything else that's involved in an airline pilot's life, the travel, the 'holiday' stopovers, living abroad, interesting experiences, some of them very interesting, the stresses and pressures, the rewards, it's a rather unique lifestyle.

Here's a sample of the first chapter.

# *Joining TEAL*

'Got the checkerboard?'

'Yep, got it,' replies the co-pilot.

'Height ok?' I ask.

'Yep, looking good.'

'Ok when that tall building with the mast over on the right is abeam we'll turn.'

'Yep it's coming up now.'

'That wind's picked up, better turn a fraction earlier,' the co-pilot offers.

'Yep, thanks.'

'Right; go now.'

We are flying a DC8, it's Hong Kong's notorious checkerboard approach at the old Kai Tak airport. I bank the big jet steeply to the right and peer out looking for the runway, there it is, right on cue. It's a murky evening, there's a strong crosswind blowing us right into the checkerboard, it's bumpy and we're in amongst the tall buildings. This approach is one of the more challenging things in aviation, not for the faint hearted. There's a stiff southerly requiring the use of runway 13, the south easterly one and that necessitates the famous checkerboard approach, the one the passengers love, the one that takes you right in amongst the tall buildings. The downside is that when this approach is required there's always a stiff crosswind on the runway. We complete the turn onto finals, assess the crosswind, kick in some rudder and prepare for the actual touchdown still with quite a bit of drift on. Just before the wheels make contact I kick it straight; the touchdown is quite smooth. Hold the wing down, careful with the reverse that wind is strong. We decelerate and turn off the runway; another adrenaline fuelled Hong Kong arrival. How come I'm doing this? I'm 32 years of age and this is one of aviation's more difficult places to be flying and in a big jet full of people. It's quite a story.

# Cold War Warrior
# (a memoir)

A true story about a young lad who grew up in Blenheim, New Zealand, during the 1940s and early 50s. He developed an insatiable passion for flying, travelled to England and became a pilot in the Royal Air Force. He soon found himself involved in the United Kingdom's nuclear testing programme in the Pacific. This took him around the world and in just a few short years he found himself on the front line of the Cold War in Germany.

If things had turned ugly this young Kiwi, along with others, was going to unleash nuclear mayhem on Europe and would no doubt have perished in the process. This is his story.

# Early Days

*'Ok Harry, here we go.' I nosed the big Canberra over and headed for the ground in a steep dive, at about 600 feet with the target firmly in the gun sight I squeezed the trigger. Four 20mm Hispano cannons burst into life and sent a shudder through the aircraft, I could see the shells shredding the canvas target on the ground. When we were ridiculously close I stopped firing, pulled up hard, and climbed away. Harry, my navigator, was jammed up in the nose cone, he must have been terrified. Again! We were at a live firing range in the old West Germany practising air to ground gunnery, I was having a ball, Harry was not! How did I come to be doing this?*

*Well I was a front line jet jock in the Royal Air Force, actually I was in NATO's Second Tactical Air Force in Germany, how did I get to be there? it's a long story.*

In our cottage on a beach in Auckland amongst all the wine glasses there's a copper tankard, it's lined with silver and looks old and tarnished. There are some words engraved on it. *IN HAZY MEMORY OF SALISBURY SOUTHERN RHODESIA JUNE 1962.* On closer inspection the engraving's a bit rough, the Os look like Ds however the quality of the copper, and the silver lining, appears to be surprisingly good. This tankard is a constant reminder to me about the early part of my life, the part that now seems so very far away when I was involved in the Cold War in Europe. On occasions I ask myself, did all that really happen?

*Was that me thundering around Germany in a jet, right down on the deck, eyeballing the East Germans? Was it me out in the Libyan desert amongst the flies, the sand, the heat and the sweat, trying to toss a bomb onto a target from very low level? Did I really shoot up the Larnaca range out in Cyprus with those big 20mm cannons? Did I really fly around those Norwegian Fjords in all that murk, ice and snow? That gun running business in Tunisia, did that actually happen? Was that me flying over the vastness of East Africa, the endless deserts of the Sudan? Did I do that sabre-rattling for Queen and Country in Central Africa? Was I really involved in that nuclear testing in the Pacific in the 1950s? Did I really wander around East Berlin at the height of the Cold War? Yes I did, it was all part of my Big OE, let me explain.*

# Mercenary
## (a novel)

**MERCENARY**
Rex Mangin

Rex Macare, fresh out of the military, a highly qualified pilot, his apprenticeship's finished, now he wants the real money. His quest leads to the mysterious Mr Roberts who makes him an offer too good to refuse. He meets and falls in love with the beautiful Kate, a high end fashion model. He soon finds himself immersed in a whole new world. A heady mix of big money, huge money, dangerous flying, high end fashion, and unbridled sex. It does not last.

The story is set around the world, the South Seas, Vietnam, Paris, Algeria, Australia, and the DDR, the German Democratic Republic, the old East Germany.

It's a fast moving story that I'm sure you will enjoy.

# Mr Roberts

Bzzzz, I press the doorbell, 'Monsieur Robier?' no response, I knock, 'Monsieur Robier?' still no response, have I made a mistake? I'm sure it was two this afternoon, room 202. I push the door, it swings open and I recoil in horror. The place is a charnel house, blood everywhere. There's a body on the floor, throat slashed open, I feel faint, want to throw up, it's worse than a horror movie. I look closer, the body has been mutilated, clothing torn open, blood all over the place, it's Monsieur Robier. There's something on his chest, a note.

*Rentrez chez vous Monsieur Rex, ne plaisante pas avec nous. Go home Mister Rex, don't mess with us.*

French, English, my name, it's meant for me, shit! There's something else, his genitals have been torn off and stuffed into his mouth, the FLN's brutal calling card.

# *Albert McConachie's Bad Day*

A three part tale about the slow decline of Albert McConachie's matrimonial life into total disaster. Albert however, quite unexpectedly, finds love elsewhere. The three parts of this tale are interspersed with a collection of short stories that you will find entertaining and amusing. The trivial, amusing, disastrous, childhood memories that you can probably relate to.

# Travel Bites

'You're under arrest sir.'

'Excuse me?'

'You're under arrest.'

Excuse me indeed; how can this be? I was at the immigration desk at Los Angeles airport, just got off a big jet after flying all the way from Auckland, when I was confronted with this. *I was the Captain!*

A collection of short stories, all travel related. The author spent much of his life travelling the world, and accumulated a mother lode of experiences. Some of these are shared in this book.